SUN SERPENT

GENEVA MONROE

PURPLE PHOENIX PRESS

Sun Serpent by Geneva Monroe

Copyright © 2023 by Geneva Monroe

Hardcover ISBN: 978-1-960352-01-9

First Edition: March 2023

Published by Purple Phoenix Press LLC

Published by Purple Phoenix Press

Book Cover by JV Arts

Illustrations by JV Arts, Natalia Barashkova, k_yu, Igor Vitkovsky, Morphart Creation, T Studio, Canva

Author Portrait Photography by C.D. Redman

Content Warning

Sun Serpent is a work of adult fantasy and not intended for minors. It contains scenes that may be distressing to some people, including strong language, violence, death, themes of grief and loss, attempted assault, and sexual content.

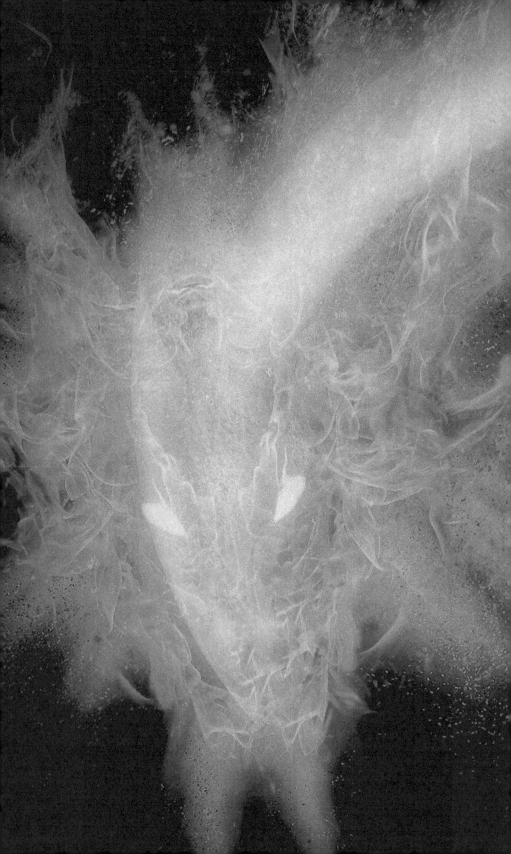

This book is dedicated to everyone who said, "So write it already."
I did it.

PLAYLIST

HERO - MARTIN GARRIX, JVKE

GOLD IN MY HAIR - BLACK MATH

SHE'S AN ACTOR - AUSTIN GIORGIO

...READY FOR IT? - TAYLOR SWIFT

LION- SAINT MESA

WHEN YOU SAY MY NAME - CHANDLER LEIGHTON

PLAYIN' ME BACK - BULOW

UNSTOPPABLE - SIA

THE ONE TO SURVIVE- HIDDEN CITIZENS

CONFIDENT - DEMI LOVATO

INFERNO - SUB URBAN, BELLA POARCH

LIPS OF A WITCH - AUSTIN GIORGIO

WELCOME TO THE JUNGLE- TOMMEE PROFITT, FLEURIE

MARCHING WITH GIANTS - BLACK MATH

SOMEBODY TO LOVE - AUSTIN GIORGIO

RISE - LEAGUE OF LEGENDS, MAKO

LOOK WHAT YOU MADE ME DO - TAYLOR SWIFT

BURN IT ALL DOWN - LEAGUE OF LEGENDS, PVRIS

I DID SOMETHING BAD - TAYLOR SWIFT

AND SO IT BEGINS - KLERGY

Pronunciation Guide

CALLEN - cal-len

ELYRIA - eh-lee-ree-ah

XOC - schock

REIHANEH - ray-haan-ah

ELOAXIA - el-oh-asch-ah

LILANDRA - lie-lawn-dra

TROUPE SOLAIRE - troop sol-air

VENTERRA - ven-terra

SENESTERRA - sen-ess-terra

DESTERRA - des-terra

SUMAN - soo-mahn

SUMENDI - soo-men-dee

OERWOOD - oar-wood

INNESVALE - in-ness-vail

INDEMIRA - in-deh-meer-ah

Ice Fall
Palace Norten

NORTERRA

The Teeth

Mt. Diamenôte

EBIMON

Indemira

BLOOD BIRCHES

DESTERRA

Innesvale

VANFALD

Castle
Shadow Haven   Obsidian Cliffs

Floating Palace

The Deadlands

Floating Lands

Mt. Kriton

Mt. Kraav

SOTERRA

1

CALLEN

Small motes of dust hung suspended in the beams of moonlight that cut through the smothering darkness of my bedchamber. I twirled my index finger, sending out a small spiral of air. The floating bits spun in a delicate, glittering cyclone before disappearing into the ether.

I groaned and rolled onto my back, letting my fingers drum an impatient rhythm against my sternum. Every night was the same, hours laying in the dark waiting for a sleep that never took me. Countless minutes wasted staring at the barely visible painted ceiling and failing to quiet the thoughts rattling in my head.

A prickling feeling of awareness ran down my arm, followed by another at the back of my neck. I knew this feeling.

I was not alone.

With a start, I sat up and trained my eyes on a shadow that slunk along on the far side of the chamber. Quick and soundless, it passed momentarily through a stream of light. Then it was gone, disappearing once more into the darkness of the room.

I sliced my arm out. A powerful blade of hard air rocketed out from my palm. The edges glowed faintly as it flew towards the vanishing assassin. With a loud crack, the mahogany wardrobe burst violently apart, sending an explosion of dust and wood fragments raining down.

Sparks crackled between my fingers in anticipation. I narrowed my eyes and scanned the darkness.

Nothing.

No stranger in the night. No snap of a crossbow. Just scattered bits of silk and tattered velvet strewn across the marble floor. A mannequin wearing my royal parade regalia lay on the ground, broken in two.

I was a paranoid fool. Centuries of training and battle experience, and here I was jumping at shadows. *Pathetic.*

I scrubbed a hand over my face.

This paranoia was nothing but phantom thoughts born from my unconscious need for conflict. Innesvale had been at peace for over a hundred years. There was no logical reason for alarm. There was no looming threat, and no one was coming to assassinate the royal family in the middle of the night.

No, this was boredom.

Sliding out of my bed, I let the satin sheets pool on the marble at my feet and walked to the balcony.

I was bored with this city; bored with all its beautiful distractions and the sycophants.

Waving my hands, a gust of air pushed the balcony doors wide. I stepped into the embrace of the humid summer air. The ocean breeze flowed over me, shifting the hair that hung low over my brow.

Every tedious second in this palace was ticking down to the cold bite of a crown. My father's growing frailty increased daily, and very soon, I would be forced to claim my birthright.

I let out a long and frustrated sigh.

Being stuck in the dark abyss of monotony wasn't living. It was just existing, and I was craving what it felt like to be alive. How long had it been since I'd felt my heart truly race or my blood sing with adrenaline? Too long.

I braced myself against the railing and soaked in the sound of the water rushing beside the balcony, letting the taste of the salt in the air calm my nerves.

And then a scuff echoed in the silence.

That was undeniably a scraping noise, the whisper of a shoe against stone somewhere in the apartment behind me. Reflexively, the muscles in my back tensed.

I spun around just in time to see a green-black blade arcing at me. I threw my arm up to defend myself. A long, wickedly jagged blade carved a trail across my forearm. I hissed at the sharp pain that burned down from my elbow. Dark veins spread out from the cut, mixing with small rivulets of blood. Light reflected off the surface of the dagger. It looked like it was made of a dark, smoky crystal. I had an entire armory at my disposal, and I'd never seen anything like it before.

What that cursed weapon was, was a question for later. I had to focus on my attacker, who was disappearing once more into the darkness of the room. This very foolish assassin needed to be taught a lesson.

I licked my lips as the pump of blood heightened my senses. Each exhalation of air they took vibrated around me, and the steady rhythm of those breaths only made me think of how I would relish ending them. I rolled my shoulders back, readying myself for a fight. The hum of power tingled at the base of my spine, ready to answer my call. I bounced on my toes, and my lips stretched into a mischievous grin. This electric buzz that coursed through me was what I was missing. Even better still, my instincts hadn't let me down after all.

I stepped into the darkness. Whoever this assassin was thought the shadows would conceal them, cloak them in safety. They were wrong.

I summoned a light pulse of air, watching it ripple over the form of a man not far from me. He was crouched in wait behind the large bust of King Edvard III. You could hide from many things, but not the air. I pushed my arms out, forcing a blast towards the pedestal beside the attacker. The bust tipped. I waited to hear the crash of stone.

Instead, I was blown back.

A gust of wind slammed into me, and I toppled backwards over a small dining table. I rolled into the fall and sprang up just in time to avoid the bust careening for me. It smashed into the bedpost. The sound of splintering wood echoed off the walls.

That was *unexpected*. Another Wind Singer—one of my own people?

I reached down, and grabbed hold of the sheet that laid on the floor beside me. Sensing for where to strike, I lashed out into the darkness. The fabric cracked, and I felt the tug of it wrapping around his throat. As I wrenched back, the man stumbled forward. It gave me enough time to close the distance between us. I swung low into his stomach before smashing my elbow into his throat. His head snapped back. White hair flicked before me as he tumbled away.

I moved into the light of the doorway and tracked the shadow that crept around the edges of the room. Surely he must have known by now that staying out of the light would afford him no advantages.

A goading remark was perched on my lips. This pathetic attempt on my life was laughable at best.

In a blink, the man was beside me. His sudden change in location made my head spin. One second, he was near the doorway to the chamber, and in the next breath, he was within striking distance.

The long dagger slashed through the air directly in front of my face. I turned, grabbing his extended arm at the wrist and elbow. Twisting it behind him, I forced the man towards the floor of the balcony. Instead of falling to his knees as he should have, the assailant shifted his momentum, and pushed towards the balustrade. He kicked off the railing, flipping over both of us and breaking my grip on him. With a light, sure-footed step, the man landed firmly on the ground behind me.

I whipped around, ready for his next strike.

Like a veil lifting, moonlight bathed the attacker, finally revealing who he was.

I blinked and failed to comprehend what I was seeing.

Light glistened off the obsidian blade clutched in his boney, too thin hand. Long white hair blew gently in the ocean breeze. His face was stony, and dark shadows were cast into the creases of his ancient face.

"*Father?*"

The word came out as a disbelieving whisper, and disappeared beneath the pounding of my heart. My father, the king of Innesvale, was standing before me.

Showing no recognition, he leapt forward. His speed was *too* fast. His movements were *too* agile. He was almost impossible to track. The evening before last, an attendant had to help him off the dais, and now he was outmaneuvering me. *Me.*

I jumped back, narrowly avoiding another strike. These movements were not the ones of the 800-year-old man who had been leading this kingdom for nearly twice as long as I'd been alive. *None* of this should have been possible, and I didn't have time to wrap my mind around it.

"Father, what are you doing?" I asked, more urgently this time, deflecting another attack away. The fresh wound on my forearm throbbed in anger with each impact.

It was as if he couldn't hear me. He struck again. I dodged, but only just barely. The blade grazed past my ear and strands of auburn hair floated to the ground around me. Once more, he lunged forward. I threw up a hard wall of air and his attack bounced off of it.

I couldn't hit him. The power of landing a single blow would kill him. It would fracture his brittle bones and stop his weak heart. I needed to wake him from whatever spell was controlling him. Or maybe I could knock him unconscious and buy myself time to figure out what the hell was going on.

"Father!" I shouted, feeling the word chafe against my vocal cords.

Nothing. No recognition.

His slippered foot flew out in a kick that hit me squarely in the chest. The breath rushed out of my lungs in one great motion and my body slid, coming within an inch of toppling over the railing. Never, even when I was younger and training with him, had my father's blows had such power behind them.

The old man spun, landing a second kick, and sharp pain bloomed in my side. I heard a crack and felt the pinch of my rib breaking. Beneath the force of his blows my bones were little more than dry twigs.

Stumbling backward, I grabbed hold of the railing to pull myself upright. Before I could fully stand, my father's impossible speed had him on top of me. He swept his leg behind my supporting ankle and my weight fell onto the railing, allowing him to pin my neck against the cold stone.

My skin warmed until it was almost scalding. Father didn't flinch or acknowledge it at all. Instead, his arm pressed harder into my throat. The tendons stretched, and the delicate pipes closed. The hilt of the dagger slammed against my injured side, and my vision streaked with white lightning.

I threw up my arm, trying to summon the wind or anything to shield myself. But my father met my wind with his own, canceling out the gale. The surrounding air fought in an invisible battle. A maelstrom circled around us, whipping my hair and the loose flaps of my father's nightshirt, and still he pressed into me.

I tried to push myself upright. Searching for purchase, my feet scrambled beneath me, but they slid against the polished marble floors. How in the fuck did you fight a man you couldn't hit?

"Father!" I croaked at him through the pressure on my windpipe. "Wake up, you old bastard!"

I punched his chest, praying the hit wasn't hard enough to stop his heart. He looked down, but otherwise didn't move. I threw a backhand at his temple, but Father leaned his head out of my reach.

An uncharacteristically light chuckle came from him, as if fighting for my life was amusing. He brought the knife down at me again. I deflected the blade with my arm as best I could. Icy heat tore into my flesh.

He smiled as he saw me wince in pain.

Twin gashes gleamed bright against the summer tanned skin of my forearms. Tiny black veins spread quickly from the wound and over the back of my hands.

My father's breath drifted over my face. It smelled strongly of the anise tonic he drank every night before bed. I looked into his eyes and saw what I had missed before. The azure blue of his irises was gone. Instead, they were white, and an evil presence swirled in them, like black ink in milk.

I recoiled. *What in the Hells of Kraav was that?*

He stood up, releasing me. Without his weight pinning me, I dropped, slamming my head into the marble as I went down. A burst of stars flooded my vision, followed by the world spinning. He chuckled again.

I fought the oncoming nausea, the blistering pain in my side, and moved to spring up. But he was quicker than me, and he pounced. His knee pinned my arm to the ground. His other leg, firmly jammed into my solar plexus, pushed the air from my lungs and snapped my already cracked ribs. A gasping howl of pain and frustration wheezed out of me.

With a grin stretched by malice, he swung his arms up. Both hands twisted around the hilt of the foreign dagger as he swept it down at me. Moonlight shown clearly through the cloudless sky. It reflected off of the black blade, forming an arc of bright light.

I reached with my free hand, holding his wrist. My arms shook, and the pain in my side screamed.

"*Father, please,*" I gasped with the last of the air from my lungs.

A victorious sneer, entirely unlike my father, pulled at the edges of his lips. He shifted his weight, and the little resistance I had left gave way.

The knife plunged into my chest.

Pain, white and hot, lanced through me as he pushed the blade deeper. A grinding sound vibrated in my bones. The cursed knife, seated to the hilt, scraped the marble beneath me. The darkness clouding my vision closed in on all sides. All I could see in the haze was my father. His white eyes and the cold, wicked smile he cast down on me.

I tried to speak, but was met with more shooting pain. The taste of copper hit my tongue, and a hot, thick liquid filled my mouth and throat. I sputtered and choked on it, droplets of blood splattering my father's blue silk pajamas. My eyes locked on the royal crest sewn to his breast pocket. The same shield of waves and crossed swords that hung over my bedchamber doors and adorned the breastplates of countless infantry, the official royal crest of Innesvale. The white waves were stained red. The knees and waist of the silk were slick and shimmered crimson as they shifted in the breeze. I couldn't bear it—the image of my *father*, drenched in my blood. It made my eyes burn.

Red bubbled from my lips, choking me as I failed to look away. I raised my hand to feel for the hilt of the dagger protruding from my chest. The icy cold of the knife bit into my palm. With a strong yank, I pulled it out, feeling each jagged inch slice free. Thick drops of blood fell from the tip to the ground around me.

But then, the green-black of the blade shifted and disintegrated. It blew away, black wisps on the wind, leaving my hand empty.

Another lance of pain shot outward from my chest, my back arched, and I welcomed the darkness that enveloped me.

One year later...

Suffocating on blood, I clawed my fingers into the threadbare mattress beneath me. My mouth opened with a choked scream that was quickly swallowed by the gloom.

I jolted awake, gasping for air. The echo of that searing pain lanced outward into my fingertips. I struggled against each rasping breath, the memory of that night still fresh in my mind. Blood pounded in my ears, creating a rushing sound that drowned out all rational thought.

Air. I needed air.

I jumped from the bed, fighting with the quilt that was woven around my legs. My head spun, and I stumbled, latching onto the footboard for stability.

Expecting to see sparkling marble, my eyes darted around me. All that was there were the wooden walls of the grubby inn. I grabbed at my chest, feeling for the ridges of the raised scar, anything to give me a tenuous grip on reality.

I swallowed hard, squeezing my eyes shut.

Control.

I needed to regain my composure. I forced myself to take measured steps to the sill and then clung to it like it was a life preserver and I was drowning. That's what this fear felt like, *drowning.* I would not let this memory break me, even if I was forced to relive it every night in my dreams.

Throwing open the shutters, I gulped down sweet air.

It was so fucking real. I was back in that hateful moment, reliving every vile second. I closed my eyes but still saw the blood dripping from his cuffs.

Snap out of it, Callen! I slapped myself in the face, hard, so that a real sting would chase away the phantom ones.

I focused my gaze on the night filled streets of Laluna. Witch light lanterns floated in the alleyway outside my window. They cast a soft, warm glow on the cobblestone streets below.

This wasn't my chambers at Innesvale. The cold and unforgiving white marble of the palace did not surround me. No, I was in the night-soaked city of Laluna, and the smell of moon jasmine lingered heavily in the air.

I slowly inhaled and looked down at where my hands gripped the sill. Scorch marks ringed around where my fingers held on tight. My normally bronzed skin had blanched to a ghostly white. I released my grip, and the blood rushed back into my knuckles.

The moon had already begun rising over the horizon. My eyes focused on the Tower of Night. The monumental crystal at its peak flickered to life and bathed the city in a purple glow. In the absence of the rising sun, the beacon in the tower was as close to a sunrise as one could hope for. Lights in the windows of buildings came to life. The City of Night was waking up.

It was only a dream.

Resolve washed over me, a fiery wrath to make the panic cower away into the shadowy depths of my soul.

I looked out at the lanterns bobbing in the air above the roads and scanned over the gray slate rooftops. The terror of my nightmare slowly ebbed into hope. I had work to do.

I smiled with grim satisfaction.

Somewhere in this city was the girl whose fire could bring an end to the horror that began the night my father tried to kill me, and I was so fucking close to finding her.

2
ELYRIA

I turned my head and scowled towards the open shutters. Cracking just one eye, I took in the dark and dusty wagon. Moonlight streamed through the window. The beauty of that sliver of light seemed like a personal insult, a taunt.

"How is it moonrise already?" I mumbled, my voice rough from sleep.

Macie shifted in the bunk above me and mumbled back something incoherent.

Pushing off the wool sheets, I formed a small fireball between my thumb and forefinger. The dancing spark in my hand made me grin with satisfaction. The reassuring hum of power skating down my fingertips soothed the crackle in my veins. It screamed to be unleashed into the world. It was always worst when I woke. Hours of sleep made the flames fight against the confines of my skin for release.

I flicked the tiny ball into the lamp, and a warm glow filled the crowded space. I sighed with relief. Left unchecked, I knew my power could burn the entire world down and still not be satisfied. It was a beast, hungry, feral, and completely unlike anything I had ever seen before.

I had never met another person with a fire attunement. Wind, water, metal, and ice were fairly common. My travels with the troupe had taken me to all edges of Venterra. I'd seen entire cities of the attuned, but never someone who could command fire as easily as breathing. When I was younger, I would lie in bed and dream that in far distant continents there were cities of fire singers. But no. At best, I was the last of my kind; at worst, I was a singular fluke of nature that never should have existed. It was a silly, childish fantasy, and I didn't have time for daydreams anyway.

Outside, a loud and incessant drilling sound cut through the quiet.

"Gods, those birds!" I muttered, rolling my eyes at the open window as a flash of brightly colored feathers swooped past.

With a grunt, I swiveled my legs and hopped gingerly onto the floor, careful not to shake the bed and wake Macie. Not that it would matter. If the cacophony outside wasn't waking her, nothing would.

Macie's blonde curls were strewn in every direction, her mouth agape, and a long line of drool hanging from her lips. Arms and legs were sprawled like a discarded rag doll. I snorted lightly, making a mental note to tell her the sight she made in the morning. I glanced to the far corner, where a small bed held the neatly tucked figure of Violet. She shifted away from the light and pulled her blanket over her face. For sisters, the two of them couldn't be more different. Even in their sleep, they were opposites.

I walked over to the washbasin sitting on a nearby nightstand and placed my hands on either side of the dish. Gently, I woke the power in my core. Warmth flooded into my palms. A faint pink glow emanated from them and flowed into the bowl. It bubbled, and steam gently rose over the lip. It wafted in curls against my face.

Setting the dish carefully on the table, I pooled the water in my hands and lifted it to my eyes. My awareness brightened, and my distorted reflection floated in the water. Two discontent eyes with flames flickering around golden irises peered back at me. I let out a long, slow breath and then splashed the water, breaking the image.

People had been telling me I was beautiful since I was a child. But I'd never felt beautiful. Not in a heart-skipping, gaze so intense you have to look away, releasing a breath you didn't know you were holding kind of beautiful, that the women in Macie's books were always describing.

I had an attunement, but I didn't have the gracefully pointed ears or the sharp cheekbones I imagined my mother had. No, when I looked into the mirror, all I saw was just how different I was from everyone else. I had the features of a mortal woman but eyes that were an unearthly color. And hair that, while it captivated audiences, only made me realize that I was not like them.

Snatching a ribbon from the stand, I wove it down the ebony strands to where they shifted into spun gold. I twisted and rolled the ends upwards in an attempt to pull my uncooperative hair into an artful coiffure. Small strands fell and framed my face as I lifted my arms. With a light tug, the ribbon pulled tight. One stubborn black and gold-tipped hair popped back up. It stood atop my crown like a candle on a solstice cake, bright and twinkling mockingly back at me.

I huffed, tossing the ribbon back on the table. My hair fell in straight sheets back to my shoulders, and I quickly fashioned it into a long and dependable braid.

I blew out the lamp, snatched my cardigan off the hook, and quietly slipped out of the wagon.

Outside, the moist air was cool, and fog hung low over the glade. I shivered and tightened the cardigan around me. The skin on my arms puckered, making the warm embrace of the sweater a welcome one.

Luminous didn't begin to describe the glade that stretched out before me. Last night, tired from the long ocean crossing, we hurriedly set up camp on the edge of Laluna's dense forest. Consumed by a need to get reacquainted with my pillow, I hadn't stopped to drink in the beauty of our new and temporary home. Like most things found in Laluna, it glowed. The leaves, flowers, and even the ground in places shone brightly with phosphorescence. As if, in the unending darkness, all living things had found an inner light.

"It is wondrous," I sighed.

Cresting the treetops, the moon was large and bright. Beyond that, the glow from Laluna's Tower of Night radiated purple beams of light into the dark sky.

I groaned. If the tower had already been lit, then that meant I'd slept in longer than I'd planned. Gods, this city! It didn't matter how many times we visited; I would never adjust to the ceaseless dark.

I took a deep breath. The rich scent of vanilla and cardamom floated to me on a light breeze. I drank it in. Scanning the field, I spotted the low light of

Gregory's lamp. The thick mist coiled around each plant and stone. In the middle of it all stood a crooked, gray-skinned old man hunched over a portable cookstove.

Wrapping my sweater tighter around me, I stepped down onto the spongy deep blue moss. I pushed my toes into the ground and watched in wonder as it shimmered. The squishy, cold wetness of the moss sent a chill up my leg, forcing out a loud and audible shiver.

Hearing me, Gregory looked up in surprise. He called out in a voice that sounded like a rusty saw on stone. "Good morning, princess. Glad to see you're getting your beauty rest. Now, how's about you get out here and light this campfire for me? That chill in the air is colder than tits on a polar bear."

I laughed, "Good morning to you too, Gregory."

I tiptoed through the moss, trying to avoid the tiny yellow wildflowers speckling the field like glowing freckles, all the while limiting my exposure to the wet ground as much as I could. My feet were already freezing.

He beamed a loving, albeit crooked, smile at me. "Come on now, what's with all the dawdling—and hells, girl, you have no shoes on!"

"Hold on to your knickers, old man. You see me walking over, and what I put or don't put on my feet is no concern of yours."

My gaze followed the trail of luminescent footprints I'd left all the way from the wagon. I'd actually been thinking of throwing on some boots, but I wasn't going to give him the satisfaction of seeing me go back for them now.

An artfully stacked tinder pile sat in the middle of the glade. I waved away the purple moths that hovered in the air around the wood. Each wingbeat momentarily transformed the hazy atmosphere into a tiny glowing orb. I was grateful Duke always made one of the boys set the fire up before bed. Nothing was worse than waking up and having to wait to feel the warmth of a fire seep life into your bones.

"I suppose you couldn't be bothered to just light this yourself?"

"Why? That's what I have you for."

I flicked my wrist, and a small spark of fire flew straight into the center of the pile. With a crack, the kindling ignited. A small, self-satisfied grin crested my lips. The fire bit into the frayed bark and smoldered. I closed my grip, calling the flame higher. It quickly consumed the neatly stacked wood. In seconds the fire had gone from a low smolder to a fiery blaze that beat back the lingering chill.

"This never gets old," I sighed to myself, holding my hands up against the warmth.

"Not like me."

I refused to look at him.

"I was aging with every second you made me wait out in this chill. If you'da dawdled much longer, I'd be a pile of frozen dust."

Gregory laughed, but it came out more akin to a witch's cackle.

I made a grand and sweeping gesture at the fire. "There you go, you old ghost."

Gregory tipped an imaginary hat to me, then gestured for me to come over.

"Mash is ready. Get yourself a bowl. Or did you expect me to cook and serve you? You can get the first ladle since the rest of these lazy freeloaders haven't woken up yet."

Morning mash was an absolute camp staple. Gregory scooped a heaping spoonful of the porridge into my bowl.

"Thank you, Gregory."

I leaned in and pressed a soft kiss to his cheek before plopping myself onto the stump next to him.

Gregory had been the camp cook my entire life. Everyone in the troupe had at least one amazing talent, if not more. Gregory's was cooking fantastic meals from practically nothing. Which was good because, more often than not, we had nothing.

I smiled up at the old man. One time, he'd actually shown me you could take the same blue moss in this field and squeeze it. Out would filter a perfectly sweet water, with an ever so faint blue glow. It was refreshing, once you got past the fact you were drinking moss water. Also dead useful if you should find yourself in a place devoid of fresh drinking water. In fact, I could make out the same pale blue hue in my breakfast.

"Did you sleep well last night?" I asked while stirring my mash in lazy figure eights to let it cool. Steam twisted around my fingers as it wafted up from the bowl.

"As well as these rickety old bones could allow. How anyone here knows when to sleep and when to rise is beyond all reckoning. You're lucky we had anything to eat at all this morning. I couldn't tell up from Aurus's ass, except for those blasted Koolabura birds clattering away."

"Ha, they woke me this morning, too!"

I looked into the branches of the trees around the glade. I gestured crudely at a large male on the branch across from me. He cawed haughtily in response. *Fucker.* That tiny black bastard was one of dozens hopping with their wings outstretched. His oil-like feathers and beak were coated in glowber berry juice. It was a show of dazzling colors, and they'd been doing this charade *all night long*, which annoyingly never ended in this place.

"If only they would just mate and get on with it. Drawing out the entire affair and dancing around obvious attraction seems like a waste of energy to me, and meanwhile, the rest of us could sleep in peace," I grumbled.

I grabbed a stone by my feet and chucked it at the birds. It slammed off a branch. With a raucous clatter, they all took to the sky. Colored juices showered down from the males' wings as they took to the air. I held up my hand to protect myself from the tiny specks of colored light raining down on us. It was absurd, really.

I took a bite of my mash and relished its taste. The sweet and spicy flavor was comforting and felt like home, or what I imagined home would feel like. The troupe never spent more than a week or two in any place. But the one constant was morning mash. It didn't matter if we were in the Oerwood's jungles or at the foothills of the Ice Fall, morning mash. It was as reliable as the sun rising. Well, rising everywhere but here.

"I guess I should wake Macie and Violet up. The boys, too, I suppose. They've already lit the tower and we're burning moonlight. Once we've got the rigging and stage set up, we're heading into town to hang some posters and hand out a few flyers. If we're lucky, maybe we'll even have a semi-decent crowd tonight. Plus, last night, Duke gave me his shopping list. I swear it gets longer at every port."

There was a loud crash, and I turned to see my father, Duke, had flung open his door. He was throwing a white scarf over his shoulder as he descended the steps of his bright red wagon. Years ago, he'd treated himself to buying the stupidly large transport, declaring that he had earned it and that it was payback for his years of generosity. I tried explaining to him that was not how generosity worked, but he had only shooed me away.

"Good morning, beautiful," he exclaimed as he approached. "Good morning to you too, Elyria."

"Meh," said Gregory from over by the stove. "How's about instead of wasting your time on all that buffoonery, you get them kids up? This mash ain't gonna stay fresh forever, and I'd like to sit down at some point this morning. No appreciation, ain't none of y'alls understand what I go through to make sure you get a hot meal."

"It's the dark, Greg, you know that. There's always a period of adjustment when we arrive here." Duke smoothed his coat out before putting a heaping spoonful of mash into a bowl. "Besides, we had a late arrival. No harm in letting them rest extra this morning."

My mind flashed on the dark image of Laluna approaching as our ship came ashore, the glittering lights of a city strung with phosphor flowers and floating lanterns.

"I've got it, Duke," I retorted.

He rolled his eyes at me. While I'd always thought of him as my father, calling him that had never felt right. Duke had adopted me when I was very young, and everyone else called him Duke, so it just felt natural for me to call him that too.

I hopped up and dumped my now empty bowl into the wash bin. Pointing at Gregory with an accusatory finger and tipping my head back to Duke, I added, "You know he'll never let you rest until everyone is awake and as miserable as he is."

I went about rapping on wagon doors and tent poles. Grumpy grunts came from within.

At Della's wagon, I was greeted by a loud crash, followed by the yipping of her puppy. Something was hurtled and smashed on the inside of the door. I looked down and saw a pink liquid dripping from under it and guessed she had thrown her jar of lip tint. She'd be angry about that and probably demand I buy her a new one when I went into town today. Typical.

Quickly, the sound in the glade turned from the hum of the forest to the clatter of the troupe eating breakfast.

I walked to my father. "I'm planning on taking the girls into the city with me this morning to pick up that list of items you gave me and to paper the town. I double-checked our stock. We'll need to make our way to The Bullseye before long and put another order in with the printer. I think we have enough for Laluna, but I'm not sure about any place after here."

He sat his fork down. "Why, my girl, are you always in such a hurry to leave this wondrous place?"

"I don't know." I shifted my weight and looked up at the cresting moon. "I love the feel of the sun on my face. And here, it feels entirely too cold all the time."

Duke gave me a look of pure incredulity.

"Sure, it's beautiful, but not in a real kind of way. I never quite feel like I've woken up, more like I'm wandering around the world only half lucid."

"That's the point," he said, jabbing at me with his spoon. "You need to learn how to just enjoy yourself. There is no place in this realm or any other quite like here. I could die happy in a place like this. You need to learn to live a little."

I rolled my eyes.

"Ellie, it's fine." He took my hand, giving it three quick squeezes. His warm smile reminded me of when I was a child. Reminiscent of all the times he brushed away my tears after a nightmare. Somehow, that single expression could abate all of my anxiety. His eyes closed for a long second, and I could see him lost in a memory too.

"Take the girls, and don't worry about the rigging. I'll get Adolphus and Christian to help set everything up."

"Alright," I breathed, then shook my head, annoyed. I let him distract me with a bit of tenderness. He was too damn good at that.

I walked away, intending to tell Macie to get ready when Duke called back.

"Oh, when you go, stop by that patisserie, you know the one. The place that does those delightful little profiteroles. The ones with the creme and phosphor honey. I've been lusting after them for months now. Grab some money from the kitty and get a few dozen. We can share them with the group as a midday treat." He stammered for a second and waved his hand at the sky. "Midmoon snack, you know what I mean."

"That's rich. Like you'd leave any for the rest of us," I said, patting my belly and emphasizing the bit of weight he'd put on over the past year. I walked away before he could regale me with another story of this place and some love conquest of decades past.

As I moved down the row of tents on my way to grab Violet, I heard a lilting, singsong voice call out to me from the tent at the end of the row.

"Elyria, darling." A red wig of curls, piled high, poked out of the flaps of a tent. "Oh my, you're right here. I had no idea."

Jess, the costumer, stepped out with a bewildered hand placed over his heart. He had on high-waisted bespoke pants with neat rows of brass buttons across the waistband, no doubt nicked from some military uniform. He counterbalanced all of this with a tight-fitting sleeveless top and a heavy plum velvet robe. Jess spent as much time creating his persona for the day as he did the costumes the rest of us wore nightly, treating each day as a new performance and new character.

"The Duchess?" I asked, gesturing to the wig and robe. "I haven't seen her in a while."

"Psh. Never mind that," he dismissed my question with a little wave. "I have something I'm dying to show you," he declared, gesturing wildly with his arms. Each movement was emphasized by the jangle of his many bracelets lining each wrist. Then he spun with a flourish and went back into his tent.

I pulled the flap aside and saw the sewing table, laid out with a glittering gold fabric and one of my fire whips. It looked like he'd been working through the night.

"Okay..." I uttered questioningly. "I'm curious."

"I spent the whole voyage here experimenting with an idea. I bought a bolt of this fabric when we were last in the smithy. It does a slow burn and leaves no ash behind. I was thinking we could incorporate this into your act. Just look at how it flows in the air." He beamed. "Of course, you'd only get one use out of it. But can you just imagine it?"

Jess held up the bolt, pressing it close to his body as if it were his dancing partner. He hummed and spun a bit, beaming jubilance. His eyes crinkled, and the tiny red feathers attached to the ends of his eyelashes fluttered.

"It's beautiful, Jess. Truly." I looked down at my whip, trying to imagine what one had to do with the other. "I'm sure whatever devious prop you make me will awe the crowds."

"Just you wait. It's going to be *glorious*." He clapped his hands in tiny mock applause. "You will slay them, my dear."

Then he pinched my cheek for emphasis. I paused, remembering my plans for the morning. "I'm headed into the city. Do you need anything?"

He bit his lower lip, thinking for a second. "No... unless you happen upon Lumus Glowworm Silk. But I'm sure it's ghastly expensive. Maybe just a few yards of the thread. I could make some appliqués for the triplets' body suits. Ooo, lining the insides of cuffs. Could you imagine an inner glow to a suit?" He shook his head, the red beehive swaying back and forth. Jess reached up to straighten it. "No, it's too expensive. Pretend I didn't say anything."

"I'll see what I can do," I said with a wink and walked out to where Macie and Violet were already waiting for me.

Macie was leaning on a post, twirling one of her blonde locks around her finger. Violet was fingering an imaginary violin, no doubt thinking through a new composition she'd been working on.

"What are you two doing here? I was just about to come and get you," I said.

Macie hopped up and bounced excitedly on her toes. Her golden curls jostled and gleamed in the moonlight. "Duke sent us your way."

"All he had to say was *town,* and Macie went running to the wagon to grab her change purse. She didn't even wait to hear what he wanted us to do."

Violet rolled her eyes at her sister.

"I'm so excited," Macie trilled, ignoring Violet's taunts. "I've been saving for months. Laluna's market has the *best* stuff."

She did a little twirl, taking off down the path. Macie was always so free and happy. Just being around her infectious joy could make your heart feel lighter.

Violet and I slid into step next to her. "I just want fresh strings," she informed me. My current set is one pluck away from whipping me in the face. Honestly, they stay in tune for all of a minute before they go flat."

We walked at a quick pace, eager to see the giant Tower of Night and the purple-lit markets.

"How about you, Elyria? What do you want?" Macie asked brightly.

I readjusted my grip on the flyers and shifted the satchel with the adhesive from my right to left hand.

"I don't know. I guess I'm not sure what I'm looking for. But I usually know what I want when I see it."

CALLEN

I propped a leg up on the edge of the central fountain in Laluna's main square. I'd been sitting here for nearly an hour. Where in the name of Belhameth was Xoc? Seriously, how long did it take to get one little copy of a manifest?

Xoc had insisted on coming with me when I'd told him what I planned to do. We'd tackled every challenge together since we were kids. 500 years later, things were no different. I was pretty sure if I asked, Xoc would follow me straight into the Seven Hells of Mt. Kraav's fires. And, to be honest, there was no one better to have my back.

But none of that changed the fact that I'd been sitting here the entire morning. I'd grown painfully bored of staring out at the people, watching one older woman scrutinize every vegetable in the market before finally placing a single tomato in her basket. It was excruciating.

I flicked tiny pebbles from the rock wall into the water. Waiting never was one of my strengths. Shifting my weight, I let my feet dangle from the edge of the outer fountain wall. Merchant stands of every kind were packed around the base of the tower, and a consistent hum of activity thrummed around the square. The tower rose high overhead, and everything had a vaguely purple hue in the crystalline moonlight that streamed down from it. People hurried about, buying whatever goods they needed. Tourists loitered in doorways and

"Finally!" I shouted a bit louder than necessary, and the old woman at the vegetable stand scowled at me. I scowled right back at her. *Stick to your vegetables, you old crone.*

Maybe it wasn't the boredom making me surly. I hadn't eaten a hearty meal since we left Innesvale, and I refused to acknowledge the toll my nightly dreams had been taking on me. I was probably just hungry.

The crowd parted around the brawny figure of Xoc with each of his long strides. People were always bending and shifting for him, like water around rocks in a riverbed. He threw me what looked like a slightly misshapen pear.

I froze its motion in midair, then created a small spiral that sent it on a slow rotation. "What is this?" I asked.

"I'm pretty sure they call it a pear," replied Xoc, with one eyebrow perfectly raised, crinkling the tattoo above it. "I figured by now you'd be hungry, and I didn't want to have to deal with one of your low blood sugar tantrums."

That asshole knew me too damn well. "Princes do *not* throw tantrums."

Xoc snorted. "But they are delusional. Just shut up and eat the pear."

It looked and smelled like a pear, but in the dim light of the tower it had a slight pink iridescence to it. The skin shimmered as it turned. I released the magic, and it fell from the air into my open palm.

With a shrug, I rubbed the fruit on my shirt. "So, what did you find out?"

"About the pear? Very little. It's pink."

I scowled at him in annoyance.

"A ship docked yesternight with the performing troupe on it. They unloaded and are setting up a camp on the forest's edge. Apparently the outdoor theater is cut into the hillside near there."

"Makes sense," I said, taking a bite of the odd fruit. Sweetness burst across my taste buds. Damn, this was good.

"The dockmaster said that if it's anything like the past, there will be an introductory show tonight, and then they usually have a massive crowd by the end of the week. I guess they come here every few years. The troupe is rather famous in these parts. I wouldn't be surprised if they draw a lot of attention while they're here."

"Excellent. It'll be easier for us to blend into the crowd. Let's head that way. We can do some recon on the camp and find a way to meet this fire dancer before she ever takes the stage. If they really are as popular as you say, I don't want to be playing second fiddle to some suitor."

"Ya know, we could just tell her everything upfront. She might come with us and help for the greater good," Xoc added flatly. "Everything doesn't need to be subterfuge."

"Sure. Maybe she's the selfless kind. Or maybe she's the kind who won't travel to the other side of the world, leave her family, and place herself at risk for a prince she owes no allegiance to. I won't take that chance. There's too much at stake."

"You mean you won't risk your chance at revenge."

Xoc pressed his lips into a disapproving, thin line. But we'd spent too much of our lives together for his stoic faces to sway me. Instead, I doubled down on his intensity. "Abso-fucking-lutely. I will avenge every single soul Malvat damned. And I will wring rivers from him for every drop of Innesvalen blood he's spilt."

The water in the fountain bubbled, and the coins in the base glowed red before being enveloped by a thick plume of steam. The old woman at the vegetable stand stumbled back in shock, dropping the basket with her single tomato. She superstitiously clapped her hands and scurried from the square.

I sighed and brought calm back into my voice. "So yes, I will get my revenge or I'll die trying. And I'm not going to let the whims of some girl jeopardize that. We get exactly one shot at this. I'm not going into it blind. First, we do recon, then we will decide if the truth really is the best way to handle things."

I stood on the wall, about to jump down, when a glimmer caught my eye. In the far corner of the square was a girl with long, shining black hair that looked like it had been dipped in molten gold. It was loosely braided into a long plait that hung over her shoulder. Stray strands had fallen from the braid and framed the delicate features of her face. Her smooth, pale skin almost appeared to glow in the unearthly light of the tower.

Every cell in my body froze. Watching her from my stoop, the rest of the square might have disappeared, leaving only her. The chair she stood upon was tipped onto its corner leg, the remaining three all suspended off the ground. One foot was perched on an arm and the other atop the back. Her balance was so steady you'd think it was easy to stand like that. Gracefully, she reached out, plastering the last corner of a poster high on the wall. Effortlessly, she rocked the chair onto all fours and hopped down.

"Unbelievable," I whispered.

A petite, bored-looking girl took the brush and tucked it neatly away. Quickly, the two of them took off. They wove through the crowd and down an alley. A sign at the entrance read, 'Breton Patisserie'.

"Actually..." I said, jumping down. "I feel like something sweet."

Not waiting to hear Xoc's reply, I took off, weaving between the people until I reached the alley the girls had disappeared down. It was tiny, barely wide enough for two. A single lantern floated in the entranceway, casting a faint red glow onto the flour crates stacked against the side. At the end of the narrow path, an adorable bakery was wedged between two larger brick buildings. The black display windows were overflowing with all kinds of danishes, biscuits, and rolls. Through the window, I could see the girls talking to the baker at the counter. The golden-haired one was smiling and laughing at something the man had just said.

"Are you going to go in?" Xoc asked, having silently walked up behind me.

I jumped, realizing I had been staring. Shaking myself from my stupor, I reached for the handle, then paused and looked over at him. "You should probably hang back. The space is tight. I'll be out in a second."

Xoc nodded, walked back to the corner, and leaned nonchalantly against the wall.

I pulled the door open and was hit in the face with the delectable scent of warm bread, sugared glazes, cinnamon, and honey. My mouth watered, and it brought up memories of the hours I would steal away into the palace kitchens.

"So, you want five dozen profiteroles, then?" said the rich voice of the baker, muffled slightly by his bushy white mustache.

With a voice like silk, she replied, "Please, the honey and creme kind. I can come back later to pick them up if that is more convenient." She smiled sweetly at the man.

The daintier of the two girls was bent over and peering through the display case at rows of cookies. "Do you think Duke would notice if we got a few of these Butter Roses too? They look positively sinful, don't they, Elyria?"

Elyria. My heart clenched. Her name sounded like music.

She walked over and peered in at the tiny cream-colored roses. "Andre, can you give us three of the Butter Roses, too, please?"

The little one squealed with excitement and jumped up. To avoid her flailing arms, Elyria stepped back and tripped over my feet, directly into my arms. She latched onto my bicep and a buzz of energy shocked me. Her eyes met mine, bright with golden amusement.

"Sorry," she laughed. "I'm usually pretty steady on my feet."

Elyria stood, and straightened the sleeve of my shirt. She gave me an abashed smile, and then spun, smacking the girl on the shoulder.

"Violet, you have to be more careful. Look what you made me do." She gestured to me.

Violet leaned in and raised her hand, covering her mouth, and not so quietly whispered, "I'd do that any day. Did you look at him?"

I pretended not to hear her.

"It's no problem, really. Perhaps you can make it up to me by letting me take you to lunch," I said with my most charming affectation and the smile that always had the ladies of the court raising skirts and dropping inhibitions. It whispered of immediate gratification... and Elyria seemed completely unbothered by it.

Violet's mouth dropped open, and she gaped at Elyria, who only squinted her eyes as she scrutinized my face.

"You..." She paused and looked over at Violet, who was grinning like a fool, before flicking her gaze back to me. Elyria tilted her head to the side. "Sorry, I don't think I caught your name."

I shifted my weight and extended a hand. Narrowing her eyes further, she placed hers in mine, and another shock jolted against my palm. It was odd, given how humid the air was here. Ignoring it, I lightly gripped her fingers. Leaning down, I let my lips gently brush against her knuckles. It was an act I had performed countless times, at every ball and with every debutante. And yet, she still didn't seem swayed. In fact, she seemed more suspicious of me.

Keeping her delicate hand clasped in mine, I said, "It's Cal. Calvin Dentross. I'm in town on business." She slipped her hand from mine and flexed her fingers, momentarily distracted, before raising an eyebrow in disbelief.

"Dentross," she said flatly.

"Customarily, this is where you introduce yourself to me."

She glanced over to Violet, who mouthed, "*Go on.*"

"My name is—"

Andre walked back to the counter and sat a bag down. "Come back at ten, and I'll have the rest for you," he said and gave me an expectant look, waiting for an order.

Elyria glanced back at me and, a bit too quickly, said, "No, Calvin. Thank you for the offer, but I couldn't possibly. We've got loads to get done before moonfall."

Violet made a little choking sound of disbelief.

"Elyria," she said, drawing out the word under her breath, dagger eyes pointing from her to me.

Elyria glared at her friend, adding in an overly light tone, "And we've gotta go find Macie. I'm sure she's already bought half the market by now."

"Did you want something too, lad?" asked Andre, bristling at having to ask twice.

I turned my head, looking at him. "I just need a moment."

Elyria moved towards the exit.

"Wait," I said, holding my hand out to catch the door. "Let me get that for you." I stepped over and opened it wide. Violet skipped by me, dragging a long smile as she passed. Elyria walked to me, meeting my gaze. Her eyes were the most striking shade of gold. Warm and sparkling.

"Can I at least know your name?" I said again. Elyria smiled a bit too sweetly, tilting her head to the side in contemplation. She stepped past me, walking through the doorway.

As she reached the cobblestone, she turned around. "It's a small city. Who knows, maybe next time you'll be falling for me." She spun on the spot and laughed to herself as she took Violet's arm.

As they walked away, Violet said, "I can't wait to tell Macie."

"Come on, boy! I've got five dozen profiteroles to stuff now. What's it gonna be?" Andre's gruff voice barked behind me.

"Um..."

I glanced at the counter and then looked back out the window. Elyria was already rounding the corner. She slowed as she approached Xoc, assessing the potential threat he posed, and was certain to give him a wide berth as she passed. Smart girl.

I glanced back to Andre. "Nothing. Turns out I'm not really in the mood for something sweet after all." Quickly, I ran out the door. I slid to a stop just past Xoc and scanned the square. "Where'd she go?"

"I'm guessing you mean the pretty one with the gold hair? She and the tiny one went into the crowd that way, towards the leather stands," he replied, smirking and pointing to the left.

I craned my neck, scanning the crowd, but she had disappeared into the throng. I walked back to the corner wall and looked up. The drying glue shone with purple streaks of reflected light. The poster read, 'Troupe Solaire'. At the center of the title was an ornately designed sun encircled by a dragon eating its tail. I smiled wide. Splashed in the background was the image of a fiery girl, black and gold hair whipping in the wind. The moniker beneath her read, 'Elyria Solaris, The Golden Dragon'.

With an appraising nod, I tilted my head and said, "Xoc, I think I just met our girl."

Xoc examined the poster, turned, and looked back into the crowd, then back to the poster again.

"Yeah, could be. So what's the plan? Do we head to the camp?"

"Actually, I've changed my mind about how we should play this. If we do it right and I can get her to trust me, she might just agree to come with us. They aren't going to be leaving anytime soon, so we can afford to play a bit of the long game here." I gave him a crooked grin. "This might even be fun."

"You're wicked," Xoc replied, shaking his head. He never approved of my devious nature, but then again, he rarely stopped me either.

"Only a little." I winked at him. "We have a couple of hours to kill. What do you want to do?"

"The apothecary. I want to see if he has any roots and seeds from the local plant life that I can use to enhance my stores."

"Seeds? A magical land of night, and you want to shop for seeds?" I said incredulously, raising an eyebrow.

"Well, yeah. I mean, look at the flowers here."

He raised his hand and gently cradled the pink and purple bloom. It hung down from the trellis like a tiny miniature lantern. His entire face was glowing in reverence for the delicate flower.

"You are a complicated man, Xoc. A strange and complicated man."

Xoc only smiled, making the tattoo on the side of his forehead and face crease. The right side of his temple was shaved and exposed the red geometric interlocking shapes tattooed there. It crept over his eyebrow and down to just above his cheekbone. Usually, he wore his long dark brown hair tied back at the top of his head with a leather thong. When he did, it exposed the mark and placed it proudly on display, adding to his already imposing stature. Xoc was born a warrior, and he looked every bit the part. A portrait of intimidation, who also enjoyed a bit of gardening now and then.

"Fine, go and get your seeds. I'm headed to a pub. I could use a proper bite and draft. There's a place called The Crooked Crow on the other side of the square. That's where I'll be if you decide to join me after you finish your seed explorations. At ten, she's returning to pick up the order she placed with the baker," I said, gesturing with my thumb over my shoulder.

Xoc nodded and then continued into the crowd of people.

Before walking away, I stared up at the poster. Elyria was printed there, gazing down with golden fire in her eyes. It felt like fate looking back at me. My stomach groaned loudly. Strangely, fate felt an awful lot like hunger.

4

CALLEN

I pushed my way through the people. It didn't matter which way I went; it was like there was always a hard body standing between me and the direction I wanted to move. I jealously thought of how Xoc effortlessly moved in crowds. People always flowed around him. Of course, this was never an issue in Innesvale. No one ever stood in the way of a prince. And, while the time away from the throne had been a pleasant reprieve from my regular duties, it was at moments like these that I lamented my anonymity.

Finally, I freed myself from the throng and stood before a broken brick building with a heavy wooden door. An ax was lodged deep in the center plank, and a heavy wooden sign swung from a mangled wrought iron holder. It squeaked as it blew in the breeze. The sign looked like it was once in one piece and had the image of a large crow carved on it. Oddly, it appeared to have been sliced in half, and then reassembled slightly askew. The Crooked Crow.

I had heard people during the voyage over talking about the pork pies sold at this pub. One sailor had fantasized for practically an hour about the savory gravy that they were cooked in and the flaky crust that you could only get here. Indeed, love sonnets weren't as long or as detailed as the one that sailor had waxed about a pork pie. But it had sounded delicious, and in that moment, I had decided that if the opportunity presented itself, I would take advantage of sampling one.

I pushed the door open and stepped into the dark interior. My eyes squinted as I struggled to adjust to the darkness. An empty, worn bar lined the far corner of the pub, and the remaining walls all held inset wooden booths. There were several patrons sitting at tables around the room, a row of sailors sat at one end, and I could make out what definitely looked like tourists huddled around a few of the outer booths.

The focus of the room was at the center, where a makeshift boxing ring was posted into the ground. The ropes were old and frayed, and I wondered if it ever saw any actual use. The smell of old wood and earth mingled heavily in the air. I scuffed my foot and looked down, surprised to see that the pub had a dirt floor. I tried to remember the last time I'd been anywhere with a dirt floor.

"Absorbs the blood better," a voice sounded from in the dark behind me. I swiveled to see a weathered old man smoking a pipe, his feet kicked up on a table. The cracks in his face were illuminated briefly as the tobacco in the pipe smoldered.

"Pardon?" I said.

"The dirt. He never put in a wooden one because the dirt absorbs the blood better." The man smiled a crooked and yellow grin, mottled with missing teeth.

"Naturally, although I find sawdust works much more efficiently."

The old man nodded approvingly. "Where are you from, stranger? Ain't these parts."

"Innesvale. I'm in town on business."

"Of course you are. I can smell the marble on you," he croaked back.

"I wasn't aware that marble had a smell."

"Pshaw, you just spent too much time with all them well-to-dos to notice." The old man stood up and started walking toward the center of the tavern. He picked up a forgotten mug from a table as he went, dumping the contents onto the floor. "I suppose you came in here wanting somethin'. I don't mind a bit of pleasantries and banter, but ain't no one comes here to talk to me, strictly speaking, of course. So what do you want?"

He spit into the mug, then took a rag and began wiping out the inside. It made a squeaking sound that raised the hairs on my arm.

I looked down at the mug, and the old man only shrugged. "Trust me, lad, this shine is strong enough to kill anything you'd find in that glass. It'd kill a horse if it drank enough."

I slipped into the seat at the end of the bar. My hands ran over the oiled and well-loved wood. There was something oddly comforting about this place, even with the thick layer of grunge coating it.

"I heard some sailors on my ship talking about your pork pies. One man couldn't shut up about them. I was aiming to try one for myself, if that's on the menu?"

"Course. Pork pies, pork on mash, pork in a biscuit. Sheila is back in the kitchen. She just roasts a pig weekly and then uses that for every dish on the menu until it runs out. You're in luck. Meat's pretty fresh. She only just took it off the spit yesterday. So, it's a pie, then? Do you want a cup of shine too?"

I looked over at the cleanish cup on the counter.

"I... no. I think just the pie should be fine for now. Thank you."

"Gah, you great poodle. I'll get you a *cleaner* mug." He drew out the word with disapproving sarcasm. The old barkeep proceeded to fill a new mug with a clearish liquid, and bellowed, "Sheila, bring me a pie."

"Did you just call me a poodle?" I tried to sound offended, but couldn't keep the smile from my face.

From the back, a woman grunted, "Ya bastard, I'm up to me tits in flour. You come get it yerself."

The old man smiled a crooked grin at me. "Me wife. And I'll tell you what, she's still the rosebud she was at fifteen."

The pub door opened abruptly. A slightly older gentleman stood dramatically in the doorway, silhouetted by the light of the square behind him, a golden cane in his hand.

"Nice to see this place still smells of blood and piss," he heralded with a laugh.

The old man looked over and brightened. "By gods, Duke! Well, ain't you something."

The man walked into the pub and stood at the end of the bar. He was a well-groomed, gray-haired man in an expertly tailored waistcoat with a golden scarf draped artfully over one shoulder. In fact, nothing about this man seemed to fit in a dive like this.

"Nice to see you still got a bit of flash," said the old man as he hobbled from around the bar.

Duke embraced him with a hearty hug.

"And it's nice to see you're just as curmudgeonly as ever. Gods, Amos, would it kill you to take a mop to the place? It's barely fit for animals. Who've you been feeding in here?"

"Ah, the grime gives the meat its flavor. And the tourists like the unsavory nature of the place."

"If only they knew it was because you're too cheap to clean it."

"Sit down, Duke. Tell me of the world. I miss our time on the road. Sometimes I think I can still smell the birches of Indemira on my traveling cloak. I'll get you a drink, and none of this dog's piss I serve the foreigners, neither."

I discreetly dribbled the liquid from my mouth back into the cup.

Amos reached down and pulled an amber jug from under the counter. With his teeth, he pulled the cork from the top and spat it on the bar. He filled two glasses and handed one to Duke. They clinked them, downing the amber liquid in one quick motion. Duke gave a little cough.

"Phoenix Fire. Good, isn' it?" smiled Amos. "Brewed it meself in the still out back."

The kitchen door swung open with a kick. Startled by the sudden entrance, I turned. A stocky woman came walking out with a tray, propping the door open with her back.

Shrilly, she yelled, "Amos! You too important now to come get things yourself?"

Sheila looked up and jumped back with a start. She dropped the tray on the counter beside me and rounded the bar.

"String me up." She looked at the old man, straightening her skirts and knocking the flour dust from her chest. With a glare at her husband, she said, "Amos, why didn't you tell me Duke was here?"

She pushed up on her hair a bit, preening at the newcomer. Duke leaned over and kissed her cheek. "Hello, Sheila. You're beautiful as ever."

Sheila scoffed, but a deep scarlet splashed her cheeks.

"How's your sister?" Duke waggled a brow at her.

"Still heartbroken. But then again, you always leave them wanting more, don't you, Duke?" she giggled. I was surprised to see that a woman of her stature could ever giggle girlishly.

"Precisely, darling. It's the mark of a good showman." Duke gave a little flourish of his hand. Amos began pouring them each another glass.

"Amos, tip me in. If'n you're toasting to our good fortune or Duke's return, then I'll have one too," said Sheila, with a sharp nudge to Amos' arm.

Realizing she wouldn't be back soon, I reached over and pulled the tray with my pie closer. Grabbing a fork from the counter, I took a bite at the same time the trio tipped back their glasses. After seeing the state of this place, I wasn't sure what to expect anymore. To my surprise, it was absolutely delicious. The pork melted in your mouth, and a gravy that felt sinfully rich as it rolled over your tongue. It had me wondering how much of Amos' talk was just an act. I'd never had food of this caliber from a dive before.

The door to the square swung open, and Xoc ducked under the doorway. He squinted as his eyes adjusted to the low light. The moment he spotted me the confusion on his face cleared. In just a few quick strides, Xoc had reached the end of the bar. Each step he took across the room made the people around him go silent, and Sheila's calculating eyes tracked his path to the seat next to me.

Amos said to Duke, "I looked just like him in me youth. Size of an ox I was."

Sheila barked out a laugh. "Sure you was. You cut a closer resemblance to a chicken than you ever did an ox."

She sauntered over to us, putting a little swish in her hips.

"I see you just helped yourself to my pie," she said, pointing down to the half empty pie pan.

"And it was delicious." I smiled back at her.

I hadn't met a woman yet who didn't melt under that smile. Some men, too, for that matter. It was my most dependable and first line of defense in almost all situations. Except for Elyria that was. I could already tell that she was too calculating to be swayed by something as simple as a smile, but I do love a challenge.

Sheila winked at me. "Of course it was. I made it. I'd never serve anything that wasn't delicious. You want one too, big boy?" she asked with an approving look up and down at Xoc.

It was a gaze that I could tell made him uncomfortable.

"Yes, ma'am. That would be nice," he said quietly back to her. Meek. Somehow, this burly woman had made Xoc shrink, and it was positively amusing. There were many things I enjoyed in this world, but nothing was as purely entertaining as seeing Xoc uncomfortable.

"Gah, you're a giant, but you speak like a mouse. Speak up, son." She pointed to her ear. "I ain't been able to hear from this ear since I was a kid. Icicle straight to the head. Shard of ice pierced my drum. Haven't heard so much as a whisper from it since."

He spoke up. "I'm sorry, ma'am. I would very much like a pie. Thank you."

She smiled approvingly and then looked over to me. "I like this one. Never did have a taste for the pretty boys."

"That's true enough," called Duke, throwing a thumb towards Amos. He let out a warm and hearty laugh.

Sheila turned to him and winked, then looked back at us.

"I'll get you a drink too." Her eyes slid to me. "And it looks like you could do with another."

Xoc answered, "Tha—"

I cut him off, placing a hand over my mug, and as nicely as I could, said, "No, that's not necessary. I wouldn't want to trouble you. But, my friend here absolutely needs to try your cooking."

She shifted her dark eyes from my hand to Xoc, and then finally flicked them over to me. "Alrighty then. Let me throw a pie in the oven, and I'll be back in a minute."

As soon as she was out of earshot, I leaned in and whispered, "You can thank me later when you're not spending the night leaning over a privy."

The outer door crashed open, and two girls came bouncing in.

"See! I told you I saw him come in here," said the shorter of them. As they came into the lamplight, I realized it was Violet and another girl with tight, curly blonde hair. They were obviously sisters, maybe even twins. This must have been the missing Macie. Steps behind them, Elyria came bursting through the door. Rage was seething off of her in palpable waves.

My heart quickened. For the second before the door closed, the golden tips of her hair flared purple from the light of the square. I smiled. My luck today. Maybe fate finally decided to give me some slack.

Elyria pushed past the girls and walked directly up to Duke. She slapped him hard upside the head. "If you were planning to come anyway, I didn't need to waste my morning running around the square doing *your* errands."

Seeming not to care in the slightest that she'd just hit him, Duke leaned in and kissed the top of her head. "Aw, Ellie. If I did that, then I wouldn't have had time to visit with dear Amos here."

Elyria, surprised, looked around Duke at the old barman, who was smiling wildly.

"Hello, Amos," she said sweetly to him then resumed scowling at Duke.

The old man began a quick step and shuffle, moving with surprising speed for someone of his age and crookedness. "Aw, Elyria. You're a sight for old, tired eyes. By gods, you're gorgeous." He took Elyria's cheeks in his hands and placed an enthusiastic kiss on each. She looked as if she didn't know what to do. "If I was a younger man." He looked at her again and smiled. "I can't believe how much you've grown. I was just telling your da about my younger strapping years. Though I don't know that I was ever a good enough of a looker for someone as striking as you. Now that lad down there, he's about as beautiful as you are. You shouldn't waste your time on old men like us when you could be talking up the likes of him."

He pointed to the end of the bar. To where I sat, having just shoved a forkful of pie into my mouth. I gave a little wave.

Elyria looked up. Surprise etched its way across her face as she made eye contact with me, and recognition set in.

I swallowed. The lump of pie felt like a stone sliding down my throat.

Amos chortled, "Not that you need to do any talking. Alls you's got to do is bat them big golden eyes of yours, and every man in a mile will be falling at your feet."

From behind Elyria, Violet squealed. She gripped Macie's arm and said, "That's him." Her heels clicked together, and she placed both her hands over her mouth to hide her glee.

Amos went on. "Let me get Sheila. She'll be as pleased as a pig in slop that you're here, too. You know she's always loved you." Then he gently pushed her towards me. She stumbled a step, resisting his nudge. "Go on. Sit down. I'll tell Sheila to throw some extra pies into the oven. You and your girls look like you could stand to have a hearty bite to eat. A strong breeze could blow that one away," he said as he pointed toward Violet.

Elyria seemed to recover from her shock, and I watched as a mask of confidence slid over her face. Never dropping eye contact with me, she half-smiled and sauntered in my direction. She pulled up the seat two stools away from me and sat down. The girls filed in next to her.

"Looks like I get that lunch after all," I said smoothly.

"Looks like." Elyria smiled and lifted her hands in supplication. She threw her golden-tipped braid over her shoulder and tucked a loose hair behind a rounded ear. So, if she was attuned, she wasn't full-blooded.

"Calvin. Wasn't it?" she said, a smile cresting her perfectly full lips. They were a shade of berry that had me instantly wondering if they were as sweet as they looked.

I nodded. "Indeed. And you're Elyria Solaris. You're famous. I've seen you on at least a half-dozen posters this morning." I raised my hand as if reading off a marquis. "The Golden Dragon."

"It's just a stage name. I do a fire dancing act. Duke..." She gestured to the man at the end of the bar. "Thought it had flash."

"Oh, it does. Fire singer, that's a pretty rare attunement," I said, leaning in towards her.

She waved off my comment quickly. "It's an old magician's trick. Nothing really special."

"I doubt there is anything about you that isn't special."

Fire breathers in performing troupes weren't unheard of, and there certainly were street magicians who could manipulate fire. Still, every part of me was screaming that this was the girl I'd traveled half the world to find. It had to be her.

Elyria looked over at Xoc. "Are you his bodyguard? I saw you standing at the end of the alley when we left the patisserie."

Xoc laughed. "Hardly." His green eyes glimmered in the lamplight.

"We're business partners," I interjected. "This is Xoc."

"Xoc? No last name?"

He lowered his eyes. "I wasn't given one. In the Oerwood, bastards aren't legitimized with a family name."

"Oh," she said, a faint blush pinking her cheeks. "I didn't know. I'm sorry, that was terribly rude." She looked at me and then back at him.

"It's fine. I've had my whole life to come to terms with it, and people outside the Oerwood rarely know. A fault of our people never leaving the jungle, except to wage wars."

We sat in an awkward silence for a minute before Elyria decided it was too much. "So, what business is this that you're partners in?"

Xoc flicked his eyes to me. He tightened his mouth into a thin line.

"Cosmetics."

Next to Elyria, Macie trilled. Elyria turned, hitting her with a sharp glare.

"Sorry," she squeaked.

Violet got up, hooking an arm around her sister, and dragged her to the door. "We'll just go find somewhere brighter." Violet gestured around the room. "And cleaner to eat."

Elyria was vehemently shaking her head at her. I smiled, knowing that some part of me must have gotten to her if she was going to protest her friends leaving.

"But *Vie,*" Macie whined, pulling her arm from Violet's grip. "You can't, seriously. When do we ever get to talk to handsome men?"

"Stuff it, Macie, you flirt with guys all the time." snapped Violet. "We're leaving. Besides, you don't want to eat some stinky pork pie from one of Duke's old shady friends. Let's go find somewhere with glowber berry wine instead."

Macie's eyes went wide, and started moving for the door at the mere mention of the glowing dessert wine.

Duke heaved a hearty laugh, watching the girls exit the bar.

Elyria turned back to me. "You expect me to believe that he—" She pointed to Xoc. "-sells rouge and lip tint?" She looked past me to Xoc. "Sorry, but you just don't seem the type."

I looked at Xoc and smiled. "You shouldn't be so quick to judge. There's more to this brute than these muscles," I said with a squeeze of Xoc's bicep.

Xoc pulled his arm from my grip. "Let off. You're embarrassing yourself." Elyria laughed. "I like him."

Xoc smiled triumphantly. As if it were a competition. I just rolled my eyes.

"It's my attunement," said Xoc. "I don't sell anything. I'm a seed singer."

I jumped in. "He helps me to find and select the best raw materials. We make a trip here yearly to restock the unusual components Laluna offers. The elites of Innesvale pay small fortunes for glowing lips, or there are these drops you can put in your eyes that make them glow like a cat's at night."

"See, that makes sense." She twirled her finger at me. "I knew you were a hustler."

Sheila opened the kitchen door, four steaming pies on a tray. She gasped in excitement. "Elyria, my love!"

Elyria brightened. "Hello, Sheila."

Sheila put the tray down and circled the bar. "Let me look at you. It's been too long. Too long." She took Elyria's braid in her hand. "My gods, your hair got long. Actually, all of ya got long. When'd you get so big?" Sheila glared at Duke. "You tell that fool of a father of yours that you lot need to come round more."

Elyria grinned and walked her fingers over to the tray Sheila had discarded. "Are these your pork pies?"

"As a matter, now wait." She scowled over at Amos. "He told me that there were three of you. No matter, I'm sure he could put back some extra," she said, sliding two pies before Xoc and then handing a third to Elyria.

"Now, tip in."

Sheila pulled a spoon from her apron and handed it to her. Xoc extended a hand, but Sheila didn't seem to notice. Picking up the last pie and sliding the tray under her arm, Sheila walked down to where Duke and Amos were downing what, to my count, was their fifth glass of whatever was in that jug. She slid the last pie over to Duke. He made a grand gesture to her, pulling Sheila into him and whispering in her ear. I couldn't hear what he said, but her whole body softened and blushed. Duke definitely knew how to push the right buttons. And, if he was Elyria's father, then she might be even more of a challenge than I'd thought.

Xoc looked down at his pie, frowning. He reached over, snatched the fork from my hand mid-bite, and placed it in his mouth.

Elyria snorted. It was a genuine reaction, and even that seemed beautiful coming from her. "Here," she said, handing me her spoon. She slid off her stool. "I'll just get Amos to give me another one."

Elyria walked down the bar. Her braid glimmered with each step. I couldn't keep my eyes off her. She moved with an ethereal grace that was utterly captivating. It wasn't just me, either. The sailors sitting at the table near the ring were lecherously ogling her ass as she walked. Not that I could blame them for it, but some territorial part of me felt offended.

Elyria leaned over the bar towards Amos, reaching to where the silverware was stored. As she did, the leather of her pants stretched taut, granting every eye in the bar a perfect view.

I took a breath and swallowed hard, but my mouth had gone dry.

A tall sailor rose, tipping back his mug and wiping his mouth with the back of his hand. He grabbed at his belt and hoisted his pants up, not so gently repositioning himself. He said something to his mates at the table, but all I could hear was the word gold. The man started a predatory walk towards Elyria.

Instinctually, I stood. The sailor pulled a dagger from the sheath at his hip. I made a lunging motion for him. Too slow. I'd never make it there in time.

The lech reached out, latching his hand around her braid. With a yank, her head arced back, exposing the long column of her throat. He lifted the knife to cut the golden ends off.

I yelled out, "El-"

Before I could finish the word, there was a bright streak of gold as Elyria turned, the motion like fire in the air. She latched onto the man's wrist, quickly flipping him flat onto his back. Still holding his wrist, she wrenched it. The man let out a pained wail and dropped the knife.

"You bit-"

Elyria twisted harder and placed a foot on his throat, cutting off whatever he was about to say. The man went completely still, a pained expression distorting his face. Behind them at the table, his friends were howling with laughter.

"Oh, go ahead. Say something you'll regret. I'm sure you don't need both of these hands," she cooed at him, tsking at the end like he was no more than an errant child.

Elyria picked up the discarded knife. Then, as naturally as breathing, she flipped it in the air and slid it into the straps at her ankles. I hadn't noticed it before, but her boots most definitely featured lacings to hold all manner and sizes of knives, and that little detail in itself made my blood heat with longing. *Who was this girl?*

She crouched low over the sailor and wreathed her remaining hand with fire.

My heart pounded. Power thrummed to life in recognition of that flame. The fire lit the man's terrified face in a warm glow that playfully flickered. Her once delicate features were now fierce and empowered.

Elyria was, without a doubt, the most beautifully dangerous thing I had ever seen.

She flashed the fire in the man's face, and he whimpered like a toddler about to be spanked. Sliding her hand almost sensuously, Elyria hovered the flames over the man's groin. "Of course, if this does all your thinking for you, then maybe it isn't your hand you could do without."

"No! No, no, I'm sorry," he said hurriedly.

The group at the table laughed harder. One man tipped back with laughter so much that he toppled drunkenly from his chair.

Elyria reached into his pocket and pulled a billfold from it. She threw it over her shoulder to Duke, who snatched it deftly from the air. He handed the bills to Amos, who quickly pocketed them.

She leaned in close to him and hissed, "Get out of here before that little brain of yours gets you into trouble that you can't get yourself out of."

With an impressive display of strength, she pulled him off the ground. Pride utterly shattered, the man whined and cradled his broken wrist.

"Go on, Jack! You heard the girl," yelled one of his mates.

"Run away!" shouted another.

As the man turned to make for the door, she gave him a quick kick to the rear. He stumbled a bit but scrambled to his feet and made quickly for the exit.

"Oi! Thanks for the tip!" yelled Amos with a chuckle.

Beaming with pride, Duke raised his glass to Elyria. "That's my girl."

Elyria snatched a spoon from the counter and strode confidently to me, a definite strut to her step. Now aware she had an audience, she winked and blew a kiss to the table of men.

"Show at moonfall, gents. That's just a taste of what I can do," she cooed.

They all boisterously catcalled her. One man feigning a heart attack shouted, "Boys, I think I'm in love."

He isn't the only one.

In a moment of startled shock, I realized I was still standing like a fool. If anyone needed rescuing, it definitely wasn't her. Quickly, I sat back down before she could acknowledge that I'd stood.

Elyria pulled her stool out and sat down. She ran her fingers over her braid, lovingly stroking the end of it. She looked at me, her golden eyes bright with amusement. That had been *fun* for her.

"What?" she said with a smile and a little shrug. "Some men need to be reminded that all women aren't prey."

Next to me, Xoc choked a little on his food. Elyria smiled around her bite of pie. Absent-mindedly, she turned the spoon over and drew it slowly out of her mouth. Her eyes closed, relishing the savory taste. I couldn't help but stare at her lips as the spoon dragged over them.

"To be that spoon," I said, tracking the way her tongue lapped up the crumbs at the corner of her mouth.

She opened her eyes, realizing the tantalizing display she had just unwittingly put on. Then, with a side-eye to me, she smiled. "Something to dream about." A soft and melodic laugh slipped from her lips. "Of course, not everyone has a fetish for pork pies."

Xoc snorted at the comment, spitting a bit of food.

I smiled and nodded my head in supplication. "Go on, have your laugh."

Despite my attempts to hold it in, I chuckled back. Once unbridled, her joy was light and infectious. I found myself wanting to bathe in it. I tried to speak, something clever to regain composure. But instead, I only managed to choke on my words, and a garbled set of nonsense came out—making everything exponentially worse.

Before I realized it, we had breezily passed the meal with light banter between the three of us. Joking with Elyria was easy, and she fell into rhythm with Xoc and I like we'd known each other all our lives. When we'd finished the last of our pies, and the shortbread that Sheila shoved in front of us, Elyria looked back over to Duke.

"I need to get going. I still have to find someone who sells Lumus fabric, or at the very least Lumus thread," she said. "Plus, I need to drag him back to camp before he can't stand. Last time that happened, they let Macie take center stage, and it was an absolutely absurd show." She laughed at the memory. Pushing her plate to the edge, she leaned over it and yelled down the bar, "Amos, say your goodbyes. We're leaving."

Duke whined, "Aww, Ellie."

"Maybe I could help you find it, the Lumus thread," I said, in a not at all casual kind of way. What was wrong with me? The sentence came out all hurried and breathy. Demons below, I sounded desperate. I *never* sounded desperate.

She smirked at me and then started walking away.

"Elyria," I called to her, voice cracking a bit as unexplainable panic seized in my gut.

I stood and took a step towards her. Elyria sensed the motion and turned. The move was unexpected, and I ended up practically on top of her. She threw out an arm to my chest, halting my motion. Her hand felt too light and delicate to have been wielded with such ferocity earlier. She tapped gingerly, running her fingers over the ridges of my sternum.

"You're sweet, but Cal..." She paused, golden eyes boring into my own. "I know a hustler when I see one."

She stood on her tiptoes and placed a light kiss on my cheek. A spark zinged me, making my heart race erratically. I was still stuck on the way my name had so easily slipped from her lips when I realized what she was saying.

She stepped back, a mischievous grin on her face. "Something to remember me by."

Elyria turned, grabbing Duke by the hand.

"Looks like heartbreaking runs in the family," cackled Amos.

I was completely stunned. I had been dismissed. She didn't even look back at me as she said her goodbyes. Slowly, I settled back into my seat. I looked over at Xoc, who was holding in a laugh.

"So then, are we going to a show tonight? Because if her act this afternoon was any indication, it will be a fantastic performance," Xoc responded, still stifling his laughter.

"No. Best not to seem too desperate," I said thoughtfully.

"Oh, I think we're past that point. Don't think I didn't see you jumping up to go to her rescue, and then chasing after her like that." Mockingly, he said, "*Elyria, don't go. Take me with you. Together we can have fiery babies.*" He laughed. "Gods, I could feel your heart from here, racing all out of control as she touched you."

I rolled my eyes at him.

"Are you finished?"

"Not hardly. This will entertain me for *days*," Xoc replied, a great stupid grin on his face.

I couldn't really blame him. I had acted like a lovesick fool, calling out to her like that.

I stopped for a second. "I think, however, it could be advantageous for us to move our lodgings to ones on the edge of the city, closer to that forest clearing they're set up in," I said, calculating the odds of running into her again.

Xoc simply raised an inquisitive eyebrow at me.

"No. Think about it. They aren't going to eat every meal and have every drink in that camp. They'll want to get out sometimes, and nobody, after performing all night, would want to trek all the way up here."

"You have a point. So, what? We switch to an inn near them, and hope she comes in?"

"It never hurts to play all the odds," I said, looking wistfully towards the door.

I yelled, "Amos? Is there an inn on the edge of town that is decent? Dependable and closer to their camp."

Amos sidled over to us. "That girl is harder to catch than a diamond goldfish, lad. She's more likely to cut your dick off than to give ye the ole one-two. If you catch me drift."

I blinked in astonishment at Amos' unabashed straightforwardness.

"But I can't say I blame ye for trying. If I was half as young and good-looking as you, I'd be doing the same thing. So, hit up Mae at the Drowned Duck. She'll do right by you. Plus, she's a sucker for a pretty face. I imagine a sweet talker like you will have her handing over the keys to the joint by the end of the week."

He poked at me with a knobbly elbow and a bit of a laugh.

I dropped a handful of coins, far more than the meal was worth.

Amos's eyes went wide. "I knew you was the good sort."

"You just like my money," I said.

"That too," Amos replied, the ghost of a smirk on his face.

Xoc got up, and we left in search of Mae and the Drowned Duck. If luck was still on my side, I'd be having morning eggs and Elyria would come walking right to me. But I couldn't possibly be that lucky twice. Could I?

5

CALLEN

Three days had gone by. Every morning and night, I sat in the bar of Mae's tavern, hoping that someone from the troupe would find their way in. Ideally, I wanted to see Elyria again, but at this point, I would settle for anyone from the troupe. Every night, giddy patrons would come in after the show, chittering about the different acts. I would try, and fail, to look calm each time the bell over the door rang. But it would seem that once settled in, the troupe rarely left the camp.

I'd officially given up hope on another chance encounter. So, tonight I was going to the show to see what would come of it, but also because after three nights of hearing people talk, I was genuinely curious.

I walked down the stone-lined path through the grove of trees at the edge of the city. Tiny little mushrooms and lichen pebbled the surface of each stone. They emanated a pale green light that illuminated the road between the town and theater. With each scrape of my boots on the path, the anticipation grew. It rolled itself into a tight energy that clutched at my heart. Xoc and I joined the throng of people. The troupe wasn't just drawing a crowd; they were drawing in all of Laluna.

The theater was a simpler version of the one carved into the black cliffs of Innesvale. The outer edges of the gently sloping hill had rows of stone benches carved from the bedrock, and they wrapped around an ancient stage. It had a sheen that only came from millennia of boots performing on its surface. The troupe had set up an artful rigging over it. The iron curved and twirled in decorative patterns that reached high above us. It was crafted so expertly that it could only have been the work of a Metal Singer. From the center draped large gossamer black and gold curtains. They swung outwards, wrapping the audience in a welcoming embrace of silk. Each web of the tent was lashed to a corresponding rod with a thick golden cord, and from that cord hung a small flickering lantern. The effect was breathtaking.

In the center of the entrance stood Macie. Her tight blonde curls bounced cheerily as she greeted each guest. She had a wide and stiff skirt, completely in contrast to how soft she seemed. Beneath the skirt, her too thin legs showed black-and-white striped tights that extended down to shiny apple-red shoes. There was no aspect to this that hadn't embraced its theatricality. Macie held a wooden box with a slit in the center that patrons dropped coins into as they passed. The rhythmic ching of each donation rang out as she nodded thanks and appreciation to everyone.

Macie's eyes brightened with recognition, and a wide smile crested her ruby-stained lips. "My gods. It's you." She clicked her heels in excitement.

I reached out my hand and dropped three gold coins into the slot.

"Thank you. I hope you enjoy the show." She did a tiny dance of excitement.

I flashed her my best smile and moved to walk past when Macie thrust out her arm and grabbed hold of my sleeve. She leaned into me and whispered conspiratorially, "She's on last."

"I'm sure it will be memorable," I said back with a polite nod and a wink. Macie's red lips spread into a bright grin that could only be described as mischievous.

We continued walking until Xoc and I claimed some seats in the last row.

"Ooo, I'll be right back," Xoc said excitedly.

He pushed his way out from the seat, disappearing into the stream of people entering the grounds before I could so much as question his sudden exaltation.

A heavy smell of butter and caramel lingered in the air from the various treats each patron carried. The seats filled quickly. Within minutes, people had crammed into every space, standing along the back and down the sides. More than once, I had to forcibly remove someone from the seat Xoc had vacated. With this many people, who was left in Laluna to keep the city running?

Next to me, a portly man was jabbering about how he'd already been to see the show twice this week and that maybe The Peacock would finally notice him. Doubtful. The man was about as memorable as the lettuce in a sandwich.

All at once, the band fired up, and the space filled with sound. A thrumming guitar and fiddle played brightly. The drums rolled a steady rhythm that vibrated beneath the soles of my feet. An excited energy and hush rolled through the crowd. I settled back into my seat and looked over my shoulder to see if I could make out where Xoc had disappeared to.

I spotted him shuffling through the crowd, a large fluffy pink stick in his hands. The absurdity of this large warrior with a bit of children's sweets made me laugh. Everything about him right now looked like a contradiction.

"Did you see they have spun sugar?" he asked, a wide smile on his face, emerald eyes bright with amusement.

"Well, I do now," I said, raising my eyebrows and stifling my laughter. "500 years, and you still surprise me. Really? A circus?"

"What? So I like a good show and some sweets. It's not a crime." A too toothy grin smeared his normally stoic face.

"You're a child."

The music slowed, and the fiddle pulled a deep dissonant note. I looked over at the band. The violinist was the small girl, Violet. Beneath her diminutive form laid a true master musician. In this minute, she commanded every single patron's complete and undivided attention. A devious look glimmered across her face as the note held, and she surveyed the audience. She strung along our anticipation like we were all her playthings. When the string finally released, the lights from around the theater shot above us, forming a great shining orb of flickering light. Everything went instantly dark, save for the glow that radiated down from the center.

"*Wooo!*" the crowd sighed. All eyes locked on the sparkling ball. It hovered for a second, and an energy thrummed to life inside me. I could feel the pulse of the fire like it was a second heartbeat. A bright flash lit up the space, and the orb split into thirteen streaks. They flew down to the waiting stage lights. The old stone platform filled with light, and at the center, as though he had just appeared from nothing, stood Duke.

His gray hair was slicked back beneath a black satin hat. He wore a gold brocade jacket and waistcoat that gleamed richly. He was utterly still, both hands atop the cane he had brought with him into Amos' pub. Around me, the anticipation of the crowd was a tangible energy.

Duke looked over the audience and raised one perfectly shaped eyebrow. He kicked out at the bottom of the cane. It flipped a quick rotation into the air. Mid-spin, the gleaming gold rod landed solidly in his hand, emphasized by the band coming back to life and a momentary brightening of the lights.

"Welcome, all. I am Duke Solaris," he bellowed. The crowd clapped enthusiastically. "I will serve you tonight as Master of the Sublime."

He bowed dramatically, throwing out both hands. "And THIS—"

Immediately from behind each curtain stepped a different member of the troupe. Each struck a pose, punctuated by a loud strum from the band. The drums rolled louder, morphing into a thunder that resonated deep in my chest.

"—is the Troupe Solaire!"

The crowd whooped with excitement. I scanned each member. They were all dressed in lavish gold and black costumes. I searched for molten eyes and shining hair, my heart sinking a bit when I realized none of them were Elyria.

Duke held up one hand, commanding a hush to fall over the crowd.

"My first gift to you, The Fates," Duke exclaimed, and three identical girls in black, skin tight bodysuits walked to center stage. The rest of the troupe vanished like ghosts.

The outer lights magically dimmed. A flute began playing a light melody, countered by the violin. In an impressive display of flexibility, the center girl bent her body backwards until her hands and forearms were placed flat behind her feet. She transferred her weight onto her hands and extended her legs over her head. Her sisters grabbed a foot with one hand and simultaneously cartwheeled upward. Each girl suspended upside down, balanced at the end of the first sister's legs, supported only by a single arm.

I clapped my hands in approval. The girls were perfectly in sync and balanced with each other. I'd rarely seen acrobats with such confident grace. The center sister lifted her legs into a full handstand, and the remaining two flipped themselves upright. Astonishingly, they balanced, one foot perched sole to sole with the center sister, and the two atop her joined hands in the center, leaning outwards to form a perfect triangle.

The crowd clapped enthusiastically. The triplets continued this way, flipping and balancing for several rotations, each supporting the other in tandem. They finished their act with an impressive somersault that left them looking like a great black star.

The lights lifted, and Duke introduced the next act: Della, The Peacock. The man next to me bristled in his seat and started waving a handkerchief emphatically. A middle-aged woman with an impressively athletic build for her age began climbing some rigging off to the side. Her long blonde hair had been elegantly braided and pinned up with peacock feathers.

High above us, a trapeze descended, tethered to one side. Layers of blue and green chiffon were bustled at her hips. The tufted skirt trailed behind her. From the ground, she, in fact, looked like a peacock, both beautiful and exotic. I could see why the portly man beside me was enraptured by her.

The crowd held a collective breath. A pure soaring soprano sang out, carrying loudly and sweetly over the crowd. I looked over to see that the voice belonged to Macie, though it was an enormous, ear-splitting sound to be produced by someone so small. Apparently. musical genius was a hereditary trait. Her voice swelled, and the music behind her exploded into a lively descant. The Peacock kicked off, flying and twisting in the air.

Each act was more miraculous than the last. I sat back, surprised to find that I was truly enjoying the experience. During the show, and between each act, I kept my eyes peeled for a glimpse of black and gold hair, any indication that Elyria was here. But it would seem that Duke Solaris planned to keep her a secret, some great reveal to spring on the audience.

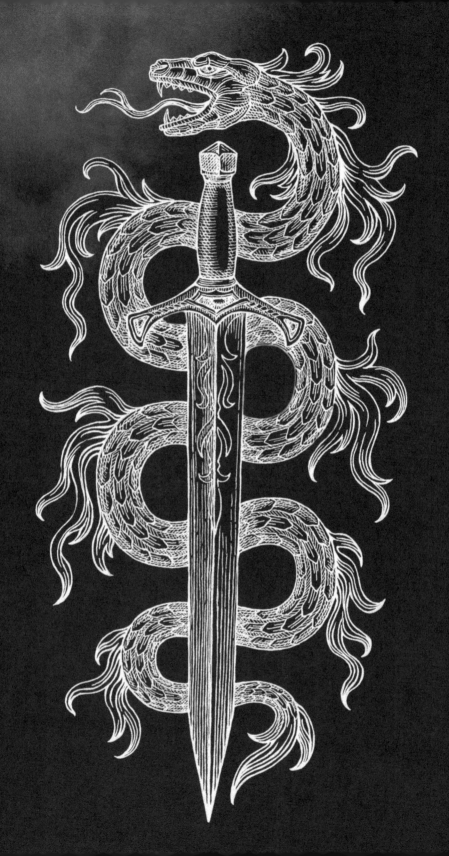

6

ELYRIA

I sat on my perch at the top of the rigging. Three acts were left before I took the stage. When I was fifteen, Duke had reorganized the show to make me the grand finale. Della had screamed and torn apart everything she could at being dethroned. But it was inevitable. The day Duke adopted me, everyone knew that a time would come when he would make me the center of attention.

I looked out over the spiderweb of iron scaffolding. It was an intricate network of beams and ladders, and from it hung the various ropes and swings used by the different acts. Below me, Adolphus' large rolling muscles reached down and grabbed at a rod with two chairs attached at either end. Sitting nervously and smiling like fools were two women from the crowd. With one great muscular hoist, he lifted the two girls high into the air. Even from up here, their excited squealing could be heard as he spun them around.

I reached out my hand and pulled the fire in the lamps higher. With a whoosh, the lanterns at the stage flared. I knew the effect added to the drama of Adolphus' grand finale, juggling not two but four chairs, each holding a different girl. Gingerly, he set the women down. and I lowered the flames, leaving the center one before Adolphus as he took his final bow.

Two acts to go.

The crowd cheered. Adolphus left the stage, and I shifted the light to the band. All five musicians kicked off a bacchanal destra. The deep drums were met hit for hit with the strumming of an upright bass, the accordion and violin each playfully pulled back and forth in a decadent lyrical undulation. Macie and Geoff started singing a loving give and take of counter-melody. While she sang, Macie exuberantly hit a tambourine against her hip.

I loved watching them. Geoff and Jimmy might be annoyingly meddlesome, Violet obsessed with only strings and sweets, and Macie always tittering on about her impossible love stories, but seeing them playing alongside each other and truly commanding their stage was always a sight that stole my breath away, even after all these years. Albert, the oldest of the Crenshaws, smiled down at his younger siblings with pride and joy. Something about the expression made my heart squeeze with longing for family and a connection to something that felt real.

Macie and Geoff finished the last line of their song. Duke took his place at center stage.

I lowered all the lights but one. It highlighted him in the darkness, and the theater went silent. It was so quiet that you could have heard the fluttering of a butterfly's wings. Duke's silver tongue had them hanging on every word, every syllable. He told the story of a prince who'd been lost in the woods. It was my favorite story. When I was little, I would ask him to tell it every night. The story ends with the maiden in the tower saving the prince, which was how I felt all stories ought to end.

While the audience was fully focused on Duke, I lowered my golden hoop into position. Below me, Adolphus held onto the counterweight line. He gave it two good tugs and gave me a thumbs up. I double checked the hooks and gave him a thumbs up in return.

I adjusted my leather bodice, making sure all important bits were firmly in place, and ran my fingers down to the knife holsters, making sure they were all secure. Certain that everything was as it should be, I lowered myself into the hoop. It sagged slightly with my weight but held firm. Hooking my knees around the bar, I leaned my upper body back into the slope of the ring. The metal was cool against my shoulder blades.

I took a deep breath. Relaxing slightly, I released the tie at my waist, and the silk fluttered down from me in a cascade of gold. Jess was right. The gold and the whip were going to be a thing of true beauty, and this was going to blow their minds. I closed my eyes and focused on my heartbeat. The drums sounded, and I exhaled slowly, feeling the bass echo in my chest. With a smooth descent, the ring began to lower.

7
CALLEN

The drums beat a deep and resonating cadence, one I felt in the depth of my very bones. It awakened something primal within me. The hairs on my arms stood on end, and energy pricked at my fingertips.

The men began chanting in a deep mantra, *"Bring the dragon out. Bring the dragon out. Bring the dragon out."* The crowd picked up the incantation and stomped their feet with the drums. The ground trembled in the darkness. *"Bring the dragon out. Bring the dragon out."*

Violet's violin started a feverish rhythm, and Macie's clear voice soared, and still, the chant carried on.

"Bring the dragon out. Bring the dragon out."

Heat rained down upon me. It rolled over my skin and made my blood come alive. My gaze drifted up, and my heart stopped. Shining like she was made of pure sunshine hung Elyria. I sat up, every ounce of my attention locked on her beautiful form.

Directly over the center of the crowd, a shower of brilliant silk clung to every delicious curve of the woman draped artfully inside a giant gold ring. The shape of the Solaire sun and serpent embraced her body as she undulated against the glinting metal. Her ebony hair shifted with the air current and caught the glow from the lanterns. The metallic tips blazed with firelight. Shimmering golden scales had been painted along her neck, running down her shoulders and sliding over her breasts.

I took a shuddering breath. I couldn't tell if my heart was beating or if the thrum of the drums had replaced my own rhythmic pulse.

"*Bring the dragon out. Bring the dragon out.*"

An ache radiated from the center of my chest. It actually hurt to look at her as the ring made its first slow revolution.

Duke's deep voice carried over the intensifying bass and drums. "Ladies and gentlemen, I present to you a legend in this world. The demoness of your nightmares and the goddess of your fantasies. Elyria Solaris, The Golden Dragon."

The crowd roared enthusiastically. Whistles and whoops of excitement filled the theater. Beside me, I felt Xoc's hand on my shoulder. But I could only look at her, the slow way she slid her hand up the ring or the glide of her leg as she splayed it over the edge, dangling in the air before me.

Now I knew how the fish ended up on the hook. She was tantalizing, and every part of me wanted to reach up and touch her. I felt my hand raise as if I could do just that. As if she wasn't feet above me and in the center of a crowd of people. In that moment, the world disappeared, and my vision narrowed so that she was all that remained. Just her, shining in the night.

Suddenly, all the surrounding lights went out and we were immersed in total and complete darkness. Still, the drums beat that unrelenting rhythm.

"*Bring the dragon out. Bring the dragon out.*"

I was blinded, but her power caressed my senses. She could have been draped over me for how keenly I felt her presence. It slithered beneath my skin, locking her into my soul with each passing breath.

A single flame came to life in the palm of Elyria's hand. The warm glow illuminated her face and skated over the curves of her chest. Her golden eyes were lined with darkest kohl, accentuated by the crackle and burn of the fire reflected in them.

I had forgotten how to breathe. The blood in my veins felt like it was sparking and churning. It thrummed and pulsed beneath my skin. Like a siren on the rocks, she called to me, just as the fire in her hands called to my fire.

The hoop began a slow and lazy spin. The flames in her extended palm left a long spiraling streak in the air. She dropped her hand, and the edge of the gold skirt lit on fire, a quick ripple of flame, like a great fiery tail.

The crowd shrieked in excitement. I slid further onto the edge of my seat.

The hoop spun faster and faster. Quickly, Elyria was engulfed in a spiraling torrent of fire. She gracefully hopped from the ring and landed lightly on the ground, the golden silk pooling around her. She reached out, grabbing the ring in one hand and her flaming skirt of molten gold in the other. Artfully, she leaned forward and kissed the mouth of the dragon before tearing down the center aisle. When she reached the end, and the tether was taut, she kicked off the ground and took flight.

Elyria soared over the crowd, trailing that blaze behind her. Forget a dragon; she had become a firebird. The audience on the ground collectively gasped in astonishment. She did two full revolutions of the arena. Her slender body arced, tumbling backwards, and landing gracefully in the center of the stage. As she did, she ripped away the silk draped over her in one long pull, swinging it into a cyclone of streaming gold over her head. With the cover gone, she revealed an entirely different costume. Elyria was clad completely in black leather. The suit was so tight and perfectly molded to her body that it looked as if she had been dipped in oil.

I greedily devoured every detail. Small golden embellishments decorated the edges of her bodice before continuing along the long lines of her legs. Strapped to her middle was a full sheath of glittering knives. There were more on her thighs, and at her back, a dagger with a golden hilt was tucked neatly between her shoulder blades. Elyria shook her head, and her black hair flamed in waves. She had transformed from decadent, ethereal softness to the sharp edge of a guillotine.

Elyria was alluring, and *positively dangerous*.

I leaned forward in my seat and propped my hands on my knees. The muscles of my back and arms pulled, a tingling sensation forming in the middle of my spine. I looked at my hands, amazed by how they were actually moist.

Elyria snapped the fabric. The fire that was smoldering along the edge flamed bright and hot before devouring what was left of the golden silk. When the light died down, Elyria's hand tightened on the grip of a fire whip, a ball of smoldering heat hung off the end. She gave it a loud crack, and the man next to me jumped.

She circled it around her, gaining momentum just as it exploded into roaring flames. A whoosh of hot air cascaded over the audience, making them gasp. With a quick release, Elyria tugged on the rope. With blurring speed, the ball flew backwards. I snapped my head to follow its motion, but just as quickly, the rope twisted around her arm. She spun her body, and the tethered ball swung back in the opposite direction.

My heart quickened with each of her motions. Xoc was saying something low in my ear, but I couldn't hear him. Lines of flame wove in and around Elyria's limbs, snaking along her neck and shoulders. The drumming grew heavy and quick, matching her frenzy as she moved faster and faster. The rope looped over her rotating shoulders, her form lithe under the pressure and speed of the whip.

In the bar, Elyria had said that she did a fire dancing act. This wasn't fire dancing. This was godsdamned fire torture. Watching her was excruciating, and every piece of me needed more. She was mesmerizing, the tone and twist of her muscles, the flicker of her hair, the crack and snap of the whip, the threat of it always looming. She was all at once graceful and fierce.

Elyria thrust out her arms. The fireball extended quickly, hitting a torch which *exploded* in a shower of flames. She turned and repeated the motion in a six-pointed star until she was surrounded by torches. With one last pull, the ball landed expertly in her palm.

The crowd screamed with approval, but she wasn't done.

Elyria tossed the ball behind her, where a boy with thick mittens caught it in midair before disappearing behind the curtains. She pulled three knives from the holster at her waist and splayed them wide between her fingers. With a wave of her hand, fire wreathed each blade. The man next to me shivered. I glanced at him to see that he was chewing on his fingernails. In front of me, a woman twisted a handkerchief into a tight knot. I looked back at the stage. One of the triplets from the beginning of the show was standing on a small platform atop a cylinder. She rolled dramatically, then just as easily steadied herself. She held a red rose aloft, plucking and dropping the petals.

The first scarlet petals floated to the ground.

"*He loves me,*" sang Macie.

Elyria loosed the flaming blades. All at once, they zoomed past the girl, snatching the petals from the air and impaling them on the board behind her.

The girl dropped another handful of petals.

"*He loves me not.*"

A second volley of blades soared into the air. On the board behind her, the hilts of the knives formed a perfect heart, the rose petals making each impact appear like a bloody one. Is this what loving her looked like, drops of blood on the tip of a knife? The idea made me shiver.

Elyria pulled out a gold scarf, and tied it around her head. She did an aerial flip, simultaneously unsheathing the dagger from her back. It had an ornately sculpted hilt that looked like the Solaire sun. Elyria ran her hand over the blade and it lit on fire, just as the previous knives had. The girl on the platform placed a new rose in her mouth. I couldn't believe what I was seeing. A blindfold. This girl was really about to throw a flaming knife *blindfolded*?

The acrobat on the platform was completely still. Elyria held the blade flat against her palm, as if in prayer. Fire snaked its way around the blade. It flickered before her calm face. Then, quick as a viper strike, Elyria spun. A wave of fire trailed behind the loosed dagger.

Around me, the crowd gasped a great collective inhale. My heart slammed in anxious protest against my ribs. The entire theater went silent. I couldn't see where the knife had gone. Elyria removed the scarf from her eyes, blocking the view of the girl and the blade. The tension among the crowd was a tangible force thrumming around me.

With a flick of her wrist, the silk flared bright, momentarily blinding me. The woman in the row ahead of me cried out, shielding her eyes. When the glare died away, Elyria spun low, taking the hand of the girl. Artfully she escorted the young acrobat from the platform. All at once, the crowd saw the dagger. It had flown true, finding its mark. Dead in the middle of the heart was a blood red rose, pierced by the golden dragon blade.

Elyria bowed deep, and the crowd cheered enthusiastically. Mid-bow, the light from the surrounding lanterns snaked through the air. They wove an intricate and deadly path through the audience. People leapt and shrieked as it flew past them. One by one, the beams flew into her hand. She stood with two giant fireballs in her palms before closing them and enveloping us in darkness once again. The theater was utterly silent. That was when I realized the pounding I heard in my ears wasn't the drum but the beating of my heart.

Pressure built in my chest, pressing against my ribs and shooting like lightning down into my fingertips. My vision drained of color, turning everything to cool purple tones. I pressed my hand to my sternum, and sparks crackled. My veins buzzed and sang. Fire surged within me, a building electric pulse rising unbidden. I looked down at my hands and flexed them, trying to resist the urge to set it free. It took all my strength to push it back down.

A giant roar bellowed as a massive plume of fire rolled out from center stage. The stream of flames flowed over Elyria's lips in a fiery breath so hot the edges looked violet. She turned, and it arced over the heads of the audience before transforming. The fire spread into a sheet, unfurling into two large wings. The front of the flame lengthened, opening into a great maw with rows of teeth and two massive glowing eyes.

Elyria stood before us, holding its leash. She had breathed a dragon of flame into life.

The dragon reared back, flapping its wings, and the audience was battered by intense gusts of hot air. People cried out, throwing their arms up in feeble protection. It dropped low over us, circling and prowling above the crowd, before rising high and shattering into millions of sparks that rained down like falling stars.

It took the audience a second to regain themselves and to realize what had just happened. Then they erupted in applause. The man beside me was throwing everything he had into the air. He grabbed on to me, shaking my arm in enthusiasm. I pulled away from him, looking around the room. The surrounding lanterns slowly reignited. Everywhere, people were cheering. I rose and turned to Xoc, who stood, clapping slowly. We looked at each other for a second, then back to Elyria, who was taking a second gracious bow.

She was absolutely, and without a doubt, the Fire Draken I'd been waiting my whole life to find.

8

ELYRIA

I exited the stage, sliding between the silks. On the other side of the curtains, the throngs of people chattered enthusiastically as they made for the exit. My heart was still racing and thumping. A heady mix of power and adrenaline coursed through my veins.

I had finished the act as I always had by pulling the stage lights at the end of my bow. But then, raw power somewhere in the darkness had pulsed and called to me. I reached into that heat and beckoned it to me. This new fire was its own creature, a song in my blood. When I unleashed it, I had *breathed* fire.

I brought my fingertips to my mouth, feeling the warmth on them. It was amazing. I looked at the ends of my hair. The gold had risen another two inches and was nearly to my ears now. It hadn't done that in a very long time.

Purple sparks danced between my fingers. Whatever this was, it felt like I was coming alive.

Duke came around the corner, marching straight to me. I stopped for a second in surprise, but I couldn't stop the proud smile from forming.

"My sweet, amazing girl." He spun me around in his arms, then kissed me on the top of my head. "That was extraordinary. Absolutely extraordinary. The dragon! Why didn't you tell me you could breathe fire? It was sheer brilliance on your part. I think my heart actually stopped."

"I... I didn't know I could," I stammered. "I just sort of did it. The fire came alive inside of me, and I released it."

He turned and started walking towards our camp. "Did you see their faces when you flapped the wings!"

He gave my hand three quick squeezes, then kept chittering about the possibilities for future fire dances. As he walked, his voice seemed distant, my mind already preoccupied as I looked back toward the stage. Already, the sound of the crowd had dissipated.

Was *he* here tonight?

My mind flashed on the warm amber-flecked eyes, those full lips that stretched into an absolutely alluring smile, and the way his laugh had felt entirely too familiar to be comfortable.

What would his reaction to the dragon have been? Would he have shrieked with the rest of them, or just sat back like he'd expected it all along? It had been three days, already week's end. By now, he'd probably moved on to a different mark.

Despite all logic and reason, I felt a curious connection to him. For days I kept catching my mind wandering back to our lunch. I hadn't meant to, but somehow, I had replayed every word and look nearly a hundred times by now.

"Are you coming, my dear?" Duke asked, rousing me from my thoughts and bringing me back to the present. I nodded my head, then looked down at my hands as I began walking back towards camp. Could I even do it again? The idea thrilled me. I started imagining the wondrous fire creatures I would unleash on the world.

I held out my hands, feeling for that distant pulse. It was faint, but I held on to it. I blew out the fire. It was a small and controlled stream, nothing like the torrent I had unleashed in the show. This was just a small ball of flickering light. I molded it into a magnificent bird with long, loping wings that trailed feathers of flame. I let it go, and it fluttered in the air before me. A beautiful firebird, cutting through the night air. It filled my heart with joy. When and how had I earned this new ability?

The firebird dipped and rose, swooping in circles around me. I held out my fingers, letting the sparks kiss them as it flashed by. I laughed and spun with excitement.

Then there was a returning tug on my power. I tripped and stumbled to the ground. A wave of nausea rolled through me. The firebird shifted back to regular flames before drifting away on the breeze.

I swallowed down the pain that burned in my chest. How could there be anything tugging back at me? It was so confusing, but I registered how even now, I could feel that intense power ebb. As if it were walking away from me and becoming a distant memory.

I tried casting the bird into life again, but only a weak flickering flame answered my call. Perhaps I had overexerted myself, using up my stores of magic. It had never happened before, but then again, I'd never done anything like this before. Maybe this was what the bottom of the well felt like.

A sudden small body tackled into me from behind. Two slender, pale arms wrapped around my middle. Followed by a high-pitched squeal.

"So, I'm guessing that means you enjoyed the show," I said, looking over my shoulder at Macie, who still clung to me, her stiff skirt crinkling between us.

"She just about leapt out of those ridiculous shoes of hers," said Violet, walking up to us next, her violin and bow tucked under one arm.

"Oh, shut up. I did not."

"You did so," Violet said, accentuating each word with a poke of her bow. "When that dragon beat its wings. You jumped three feet into the air. For a second, you were as tall as Geoff."

"You talking about me?" said Geoff, towering over us like a slender giant.

I looked up at him, and he smiled broadly back.

Macie gave him a little scowl and then cooed, "Elyria, you were magical."

"Thank you. The crowd definitely seemed to like it," I responded, noticing that the entire Crenshaw family was now walking beside us, having left the bigger instruments set up for tomorrow night's show. Jimmy's accordion hung from its straps against his hip, and it made a little wheezing sound with each step. Albert trailed us, content to follow the group quietly.

"It's true," he added from behind us. I turned over my shoulder to look at him. "I wouldn't be surprised if half of Laluna wrote you love letters tonight."

We entered our camp, and Duke was standing with Gregory, telling him about the night's performance. He flapped his arms, and I knew he was telling him about my dragon.

"We should go celebrate," Jimmy suggested. "How's about it, Duke? We had to have taken in a tidy sum tonight, all those people."

"Yeah, they were even crammed into the aisles," added Geoff conspiratorially. Geoff and Jimmy were another set of twins. The boys were born three years before their sisters. Apparently, the twin gene ran thick among the Crenshaws. Unlike Macie and Violet, these two had an uncanny knack for mischief, stirring it up perfectly in synch without so much as a look at one another.

Duke smiled widely, looking between the two boys. "Well gents, that's a fine idea. In fact, I'll come along. I think I'd quite fancy a drink."

Macie jumped, clapping her hands with excitement. "I'm gonna go change."

Everyone dispersed into their tents, the girls disappearing into our wagon. I watched them walk away. Hoping to avoid being dragged into town, I wandered over to the campfire ring, lighting it as I approached. It felt good to sit down as I started unstrapping my boots, sliding one shoe off and massaging my aching feet. Gregory hobbled over and took the seat next to me. He groaned and his knees creaked as he bent down.

"What's the matter with you, then?" he grumbled, one eyebrow raised.

"I don't need all that attention. I thought I'd stay here and keep you company."

"Girl, you are too young to be wasting your time and attentions on an old man like me."

"It's not that. I just think I'd like to turn in early for a change, get some rest."

"Bah, youth is wasted on the young. If I was you, I'd—"

"You'd have drunk half of Laluna and screwed the other half. I know," I said before he could finish his lecture. I already knew I was going to lose this argument, but that didn't mean I would go down without putting up a fight.

"Go. Have some fun. You're always so worried about how things around here are running. This troupe is not your responsibility."

I cocked my head to the side. Truth was, this troupe had been my responsibility for years now. He knew that. We all did. I had accepted this fate long ago. What I wanted didn't matter. The troupe came first, because it had to.

"Well, it's not supposed to be. It will not be the end of the world if you let loose for once. Everything will still be here in the morn."

I glanced back at our wagon. Macie had lit the lanterns, and I could see the shadows of her and Violet as they shed their costumes. Macie's muffled laughter carried over the stillness of the glade.

"Go on now, wash them scales off you, and go experience something new. Or..."

"Or what?" I challenged, rolling my eyes at him. I was too tired for his moody tricks.

"Or... no mash," he said with a defiant nod of his head.

"You *wouldn't*!"

"I would, and I will. I think I'd quite like being able to sleep in for once."

Gregory smiled, knowing he'd won.

"Fine," I said, standing up. Begrudgingly, I stomped back to the wagon, dragging my boots through the glowing moss behind me. When I opened the door, Macie excitedly jumped up. She had thrown on an indecent slip dress, and it swished as she moved. Violet, on the other hand, was in bed. I quirked an eyebrow at her.

"Why is she allowed to stay behind?"

"I'm not spending all night with her nonsense." Violet threw a lazy hand in Macie's direction. "There are a dozen things I'd rather be doing than watching Macie flirt with everything on two legs. Especially not when I could be finishing this."

She held up a worn brown book, a glowing leaf marking a page about two-thirds into it.

"See, now that sounds like a lovely plan. Did you know that Gregory just threatened me with withholding mash if I didn't go into town with you lot?" I asked.

Violet dropped her book, sternly saying, "You better be going, then."

"This is all her fault, and those two stupid boys. It isn't enough that you three get yourselves in trouble? You've got to drag me along too?" I said bitterly, pointing at Macie.

Violet ignored my tantrum and slammed her book closed. "If I don't get any mash in the morning because you're too stubborn to let that old fool live vicariously through you–"

"No, I'm going. Don't worry, the mash isn't in jeopardy," I said, walking over to the washbasin and dipping a cloth into it. I wiped away the painting that had been done up my neck and over my shoulders. The body paint helped to hide the real scales that would emerge sometimes when I was casting. Duke insisted we keep my fire attunement a secret, and the scale painting helped with that. I went over to the dresser and pulled out sensible trousers and a loose, flowing shirt.

"Don't wear that," Macie said, pointing at what I had just picked.

"Why, what's wrong with these?" I asked as I undid the lacing of my performance leathers. I couldn't wait to wear something that didn't feel like I had been poured into it. The laces pulled apart on my halter and I took a deep, unrestrained breath.

"It's not flirty enough," she said. "Those are so plain, and there's a good chance that *he'll* be at that tavern tonight."

"I don't know what you're talking about," I replied as nonchalantly as I could. The halter came free, allowing a cool rush of air to hit my flushed skin. Silently, I cursed my pale skin's inability to hide my emotions.

"Oh yes, you do. Don't play coy with me, Elyria Solaris," she said, smiling sweetly. "He was here tonight. He came in with that handsome giant."

She paused, watching me keenly to see my reaction.

I opened my mouth to refute any claim that I had been interested in him, but Macie cut off any chance of it.

"And after that unbelievable act you put on tonight, I'd bet everything I own he'll be out looking for you," she said, smiling a know-it-all grin. She reapplied her lip tint and popped her lips. "Hells, Elyria, even I want to jump you after that show."

"She's not wrong," said Violet.

"About the jumping me part?" I asked incredulously.

"No. About the show tonight. You were incredible. So incredible that I stopped playing. And that never happens. If he's interested, he'll be there," she said seriously. "And why wouldn't you be interested? He's charming and handsome."

"And definitely a snake in the grass. He's not telling me everything. I know it," I retorted coolly.

"Or you're just too paranoid to let your guard down and have some fun," Violet argued.

"There it is," Macie said, pointing into the air. I hated when the two of them twinned out and ganged up on me like this. "There's your winner, folks. Elyria could have any person in the city tonight, and she's too paranoid to have fun."

I rolled my eyes at her. "This argument is pointless. I'm going, okay?"

I reached down to grab the tunic I had laid out, and Macie hopped over, snatching it from my hands and dropping it out the window. I groaned in frustration.

Macie gave me a wolfish smile. "Not in this, you don't. Put on that white one with the laces, and leave it undone, mostly. And a pair of leather pants. They make your ass look amazing."

"Fine! If for no other reason than to shut you up," I grumbled, pulling the white shirt from the drawer.

Macie trilled triumphantly.

The leather wasn't as big of a deal. I wore that all the time. Its resistance to fire was a bonus. And she wasn't wrong. They did fit like a second skin, lifting and hugging my form. But girly tops, they were a bit more of an irregularity. At least I could breathe in this, and after wearing my show halter, I welcomed the chance to be unrestrained for a little while.

I took a dagger from the table and slid it into my bootstrap, just in case. Macie just about pushed me out of the wagon to where the boys waited for us.

"There's my star," Duke beamed.

"Yep. Here she is," I muttered, annoyed.

"Well, come on, let's go," Macie said, brushing past me and nearly knocking me from the steps.

Jimmy and Geoff stood beside Christian, one of the newest members of Troupe Solaire.

"Damn, Elyria. You look fine enough to eat." He gave me an approving wink, and I rolled my eyes at him. Christian had been trying to get my attention since the day he'd signed up. Part of me thinks that was his entire reason for joining. When I had firmly shot him down, he'd gone and tangled with one of the triplets. They weren't literal triplets but most of us called them as such given that they appeared nearly identical and often did everything as a unit. Either way, involving myself with Christian promised a whole load of drama I didn't need. Not that I was remotely interested.

I looked past them to where Gregory watched us from the fire. The wave I gave him was dripping with false enthusiasm. He threw back a surly one finger salute. I shook my head, and we started walking down the path.

"The Drowned Duck is only a twenty-minute walk from here. I figure that's our best bet for a pint and a bite to eat," Geoff explained.

"The Drowned Duck it is," Duke announced with a jaunty step forward.

9
ELYRIA

As we approached the inn on the edge of town, the ruckus of a crowd drifted down the streets. It seemed half the town had decided drinks following the show were a good idea. I looked over at Duke, rolling my eyes.

"Maybe we should come on another night when things aren't so crowded," I suggested, turning to head back to the camp. Macie snapped out a hand, latching onto my shoulder and spinning me back towards the door.

Duke waved me off. "Nonsense, that's when it's the most fun."

Macie released me and skipped to the door. She paused for a second to hoist her breasts up in her dress.

Christian said, "Don't know what you're lifting, isn't much there to put on display. Hardly a handful."

"Oi! You get your eyes off my sister's bosoms," Geoff yelled, smacking him in the back of his head. Next to him, Jimmy nodded his head in agreement, smacking Christian once more for good measure.

"It's fine, Geoff. He's only mad because he knows it's a handful he'll never get to feel."

Jimmy howled with laughter, slapping Christian's back. "Ouch."

Macie flicked her ringlets at us, then pushed the wooden door open, spilling warm light into the dark alley.

I followed them in, a tiny silver bell tinkling overhead. My hands flexed at my sides. The sound of the patrons' laughter and revelry was overwhelming. I hesitated, taking a deep breath. I loved the attention when I was on stage, drank it in. The more eyes on me, the bigger the rush, the more intense the feeling of commanding them was. But I'd never quite gotten the hang of the attention my act brought afterwards.

The room was packed with people. I looked warily at Duke.

"There isn't any room for us here," I said.

My stomach twisted in tiny knots. We pushed toward the back. I kept my eyes averted, but it only took a moment before I was recognized.

In the back corner of the tavern, a man called out, "You're the Golden Dragon. Antony, look!"

On the other side of him, his companion was readying to throw a dart. He looked up just as he released it. The projectile flew askew and embedded itself into the wall beside the target. "By gods, she's here. Fuck me, Darren, she's even more beautiful in person!" he proclaimed.

In a minute, the room had hushed. All eyes expectantly focused on me. I froze. What did they want me to do, lay down flames right here? Or maybe I should start throwing knives at drunk assholes.

Macie laced her arm through mine. "Who wants to buy a girl a drink?" she said brightly. Four men with too eager smiles were instantly by our sides.

The room resumed its buzz of activity. The men were already fawning over her curls. "Gentlemen," I said, sliding my arm from hers. "She's all yours."

Macie looked at me with disappointment. The men next to her looked just as dismayed. "Trust me," I said to our newfound admirers. "She's more fun."

Over in the back of the bar, the table by the dartboard had cleared. The two men who had announced our arrival vacated the area so the troupe could sit down. Okay, notoriety had its perks sometimes.

Duke had already settled into the bench on one side, and the boys had taken up positions at the dartboard opposite the two men from earlier. Joke was on them. I had taught Jimmy how to throw myself, and now his aim was damn near perfect. Jimmy was a regular shark. I'm sure all they saw was the pretty boy who could sing. Poor fools. They had no hope of winning.

"Ellie, darling, how's about you see if that luscious barmaid over there can set us up with some refreshments?" said Duke.

I turned toward the bar. Behind the counter sauntered a middle-aged woman of considerable girth. She had a no-nonsense demeanor, and everyone before her seemed to heel to her command. Long blonde and gray hair had been artfully braided to hang low down her back. As she walked away, the swishing of that braid was like an arrow across her rather enormous behind. I turned back to Duke and raised an eyebrow. She was hardly his regular fare.

"Oh, don't be so quick to judge. I have found that a woman with generous curves is usually generous in more ways than one," he said with a wink.

"Ew. I did not need to hear that," I groaned, pushing myself up from the bench.

Duke's laughter followed me all the way to the bar. He always got such a rise out of making me uncomfortable. Although I suppose I had that particular quirk myself.

I moved through the crowd to the bar and leaned over the edge to wave at the barmaid.

"Yech," I muttered as a warm, sticky feeling slid down my arm.

I looked at the random mixture of wet substances on the counter and bristled. I scanned the bar for a rag, and realizing there wasn't one, settled instead for wiping my arm on the back of my pant leg. The barmaid seemed oblivious to my presence. I waved, but no. She was consumed by the trio of young sailors sitting at the other end of the bar. It would probably be ages before I got her attention. Giving up, I rested against the least grimy bit of counter I could find.

Slipping my hand into my pocket, I removed a small gold coin. The cold smoothness and weight of it was reassuring. I didn't know what it was about gold, but I loved the feel of it in my hand. Usually, I kept one tucked away for moments precisely like this. I never could stand being idle. Mindlessly, I rotated it between my fingers, watching it tumble and flip seductively in the dim tavern light.

From behind me, a haughty and overly sarcastic voice drawled, "Ya know, I'd be careful flashing that kind of money in a place like this. You never know what kinds of seedy characters it will draw to you."

I rolled my eyes, and despite all logic, my heart sped up. I knew the bright white smile that would greet me before I turned to see a smirk plastered firmly on Cal's face. His chocolate and amber-flecked eyes were bright with amusement. I tightened my expression, not wanting to give him the satisfaction of seeing me smile.

"Being turned down once wasn't enough? You had to come back for a second helping?"

Cal reached out, allowing a handful of my hair to sift through his fingers. His gaze lingered on the light catching the golden ends as they fell. I looked down at his hand, mere inches from me.

"It seems like when I'm around you, I am a moth to your flame."

He smiled gently and lowered his lashes to gaze through them. The fire in my veins heated, rising unbidden from within me.

No, nope, not here, not him, and not with a line as cheesy as that. Elyria, you just put that spark right back where it came from.

"Was this always so golden?" he said, lightly stroking the ends of my locks and making my mouth go dry.

I reached up, grabbing my hair and tucking it firmly over my other shoulder, just out of his reach. "Does that actually work? Ya know. Wherever it was you said you're from?" I asked a bit too hurriedly.

He smiled at me. "Innesvale, and yes." He chuckled softly, taking a sip from his tankard. "It usually does."

The barmaid walked up to the bar, wiping down the spilled liquid sitting there. Her massive bosom, half held up by the counter, heaved with each swipe.

"What can I do you for?" she asked.

Cal choked on his beer. Looking insidiously at her breasts, he sputtered out, "What's on the menu?"

The woman, to her credit, took the beer-soaked rags and smacked him right upside the head with them. Drops of dirty water clung to Cal's hair and dripped down his cheek. Surprised, he wiped it away with the back of his hand, and I bit down on my lower lip to keep from laughing.

"Now, I'll be having none of that cheek here. This is my place, and I'll have the respect I'm due," she said.

"What if it's some cheek I'm after?" Cal said, leering.

She lifted the rags and smacked him again. The wet fabric cracked and flung amber droplets into the air.

Cal flashed her a grin as pure as white marble. "You're absolutely correct. I'm so sorry, Mae."

Mae smiled and shook her head.

"It's just, I saw you put the come hither on those lads down there and thought maybe I could get a bite too."

He gave an exaggerated wink and laughed. Mae guffawed and went to smack him with the rag again. Cal lifted his arm, letting the rag wrap around his wrist. "One day, Cal, you're going to find yourself in a trouble that smile of yours won't get you out of," she warned.

"Probably, but that's not today."

Mae waved off his sassy charm but still smiled, having obviously been won over.

"So, what can I get you?" She gestured to me. "And your lady friend here?"

"Oh, he's not my friend," I said awkwardly. Cal looked at me a bit crookedly. Nonchalantly, I added, "I mean to say, I barely know him. We're not together."

"Is that so?" Mae looked me up and down slowly, then looked Cal up and down. "Why ever not? You two would make some gorgeous babies, his tan skin and your gold eyes." She whistled.

Cal smirked, looking at me with a side-eye as if to say, *See, why fight it? Obviously, I'm a catch.*

"Mae, I'll take another of your house ale when you get a free moment and whatever The Golden Dragon here wants."

"Oh," Mae said with a long exhale. "You're that fire-breathing girl from the show. It's all anyone around here has been talking about tonight. How'd you do that bit with the dragon, then?"

I smiled deviously and leaned in. People were always asking how it was done. Mae leaned over the bar, and I didn't miss Cal leaning in to try and hear my answer. I whispered in her ear, "Trade secret."

"Aww, you had me going."

But I added, "Mae, come round the show tomorrow, and I'll give you a private demonstration. As thanks for taking care of my folk tonight."

"Oh, that's not necessary. Your show has been great for business. These past couple of nights have been the best I've had all year. I even had to lug the emergency ale up from the cellar."

"Emergency ale?"

"Yeh, wouldn't do for a bar to be caught without ale, now would it? Anyway, I can't keep gossiping with you lot. There's half a dozen people down there wanting served. So, he," she said, throwing a thumb at Cal, "wants another ale. How's about you, pretty?"

I threw my head over my shoulder, eyeing the table where the boys were talking animatedly with each other. Macie had rejoined them, a young man with a possessive arm around her shoulders. It made me happy to see them all unburdened like this. And, to my surprise, I was actually glad I had come tonight. I looked back up at Cal.

Of course, there's always room for regret later.

"I'll take a flagon. No, better make it two flagons. Thank you, Mae."

Mae looked at Cal, who just waved dramatically in submission to me. "Whatever the lady wants."

I let a victorious smile crest my lips.

That single expression seemed to make Cal's eyes sparkle with challenge, and he was fucking loving it. If what he wanted was a fight, then he would lose. He'd be begging on his knees when I was done with him.

"Of course. I'll be right back with that." Mae sauntered down the bar, pulling out two large pitchers as she went.

Cal looked at me with a flat expression. "Thirsty?"

"Hey, you said whatever I want." I leaned in, patting his shoulder. A tiny spark shocked my fingertips. I puzzled at them for a second and then looked up, meeting his gaze. "You never asked if I was up here for myself."

Cal tilted his head to the side. His perfect auburn hair shifted to cover one equally perfect amber eye. Remarkably, in this light, it almost looked as if they were rimmed with gold. Everything about him radiated warmth. He had an allure I couldn't deny, and I knew he was aware of just how handsome he looked when he did that.

"I do believe I was just played," he said.

"I'm sure you'd know exactly what that looks like." I shrugged, and bit down on my lip in a failed attempt to keep my face serious.

"You know, Xoc would probably agree with you," he laughed.

"And where is your giant companion tonight?" I asked, glancing around the room to see if he was here amidst the gathered crowd.

"Oh, around here somewhere. Maybe up in our rooms."

"Your rooms? Wait, as in, you're staying here?"

Cal nodded, and pushed the hair back from his face. I tried not to think of Cal lying in a bed somewhere above us or what those perfect waves would look like sleep mussed after a night of bedroom gymnastics.

I cleared my throat and scrambled to change the topic before I did something truly reckless, like ask for a personalized tour. "So that's how you know Mae? I figured there had to be something. You two seemed... chummy."

"Mae is great," he said, sitting up more and taking another drink. "She set us up, and she's funny too. Not to mention that she knows how to whip up some truly fantastic crepes."

"Crepes?"

"Yes, crepes. Preferably with strawberries."

"Strawberries?" I giggled, raising my eyebrows.

"Yes, I'm particularly fond of them. If you're ever in Innesvale, there's this fantastic little café. The chef grows the strawberries in planters on the windowsill and then uses them to make her own jams and syrups. They're a true masterpiece of culinary skill."

"Culinary skill?"

"Yes. Are you going to keep repeating everything I say?" Cal chuckled.

"Well, no." I laughed. "It's just, everything you say is so unexpected and hard to believe."

He tilted his head and leaned into me. I could smell a light scent of sea salt, rich spices, and something raw, dark, like coals in a fire.

"If it's so unbelievable, let me show you."

"What?" I laughed. "Go to Innesvale? With you?"

"Why not? It's a beautiful city, and nobody knows her like I do."

"Her?"

Cal's eyes warmed to a golden honey color, and I couldn't look away.

"I could show you the grottos along the coast and how the black cliffs glitter pink at sunrise." His face softened, and I saw the first glimmer of something genuine in his eyes. It drew me in, snaring me completely as he continued. "The Guardians Bridge at sunset, when the sunlight reflects off of the polished marble to make the statues look like they are walking on fire."

Cal extended his hand. It brushed mine, sending a jolt of excitement through me. "Or my favorite thing, the river that flows through the palace. It crashes from the downspouts, filling the surrounding air with rainbows. The best view is from the ocean, as you approach from the south, where waterfalls frame the crystal windows of the main ballroom. There is singularly no place more beautiful. Even Laluna, with its magical luminescence, can't beat Innesvale in the spring."

I could imagine strolling through the streets and markets with him. Walking in the shadow of the white marble palace. Forgetting all my responsibilities and living with careless abandon. It was a seductive idea. Especially when his eyes were so inviting, and I could feel myself gravitating towards him with each passing second.

I shook my head, forcing common sense to come back to me. "Oh, I'm sure you'd give me a real royal treatment," I said, patting his chest and putting enough distance between us that I couldn't smell his smoky heat anymore. "I could never leave Duke. He'd be lost without me. But, maybe, if I ever find myself in Desterra again, then I could be persuaded to let you show me around."

Cal leaned against the bar, assessing my reaction. "Maybe it's time for Duke to cut you loose. I mean, if you're going to be tied up, it should be with something better than apron strings."

I blinked. How was I supposed to respond to that?

I went with laughter and tried to forget the fanciful daydreams of a life on my own and away from the responsibilities of the troupe. "How did we end up talking about Innesvale, anyway? Weren't you telling me about the long and sordid history of you and Mae?"

He took a slow sip from his tankard.

I tried, and failed, not to watch the way muscles of his throat flexed as he swallowed or the way he licked the glistening ale from his lips when he finished. Damn it.

The arrogant bastard smiled, knowing that, at the very least, I had entertained the idea of his invitation. "Mae gave us the rooms a couple of days ago."

"Days?"

"You're doing it again."

"No, I mean, you've spent days out here? When you could be in town?" I asked, disbelief tainting every word.

"Yeah, well. I was hoping to have another chance encounter. You know, since you so epically shot me down."

Cal smiled sheepishly. It was almost adorable. How did he go from arrogant to bashful in a single blink?

"I did, didn't I?" I laughed, remembering the light kiss on the cheek I'd given him.

"You did." He took another long drink, eyeing me over the rim of his glass. "I saw your show tonight."

"I heard you and your tall friend were there. Macie was quite excited to see you."

"It was a pretty spectacular performance. You were..." His voice trailed off as he thought. "I've never seen anything like it before." He looked almost reverent.

"You breathe fire, throw knives, juggle coins, scare the life out of lecherous fools. Any other unbelievable skills you're hiding?" Genuine admiration underlined his words.

"Well, the coin thing, that's not really a skill. Anyone can do that," I said, slipping it back out of my pocket and letting it tumble over my fingers.

He was watching me, studying the lines of my face as his eyes trailed from my jaw along my neck. It was such an intent look that I could have sworn I felt it caress against my skin. I swallowed and fought against the impulse to move towards him. Instead, I pointedly looked down at my fingers, and finally he let his gaze trail down to where the coin rotated.

"The real skill is—" I palmed the coin, flipping my hand to show it empty. Cal's eyes opened in wide appraisal. I flipped my hand again, and magically, the coin reappeared. He nodded with approval.

"The real trick is getting the full command of someone's attention so they don't notice even the most obvious of things right in front of them." I lifted my opposite hand. Dangling from my fingers was his leather and silver cuff. The band featured a crest of waves and swords, with tiny glittering sapphires set into the waves. Disbelief and surprise filled his eyes. He looked down, examining his bare wrist. I grinned and gave a little shrug of my shoulder.

"You are spectacularly unique," he breathed.

I held the cuff out to him. He took it from my hand, and the light caress of his fingers on mine lingered a second longer than necessary. Warmth filled my palm where he had touched me.

I looked at him, a slow survey of his chest and then his face. When he smiled, his eyes crinkled and seemed to flash in the tavern light. Damn me. The connection felt so genuine.

Mae thumped the flagons on the counter next to me, breaking the spell. I jumped, and Mae was smirking at us. As if she knew I had just been studying him.

"Oi, Mae," a sailor at the end of the bar called. She winked at me before walking back down the bar. I could feel my cheeks and neck flush. This had gone too far.

Cal leaned one arm down on the bar, a self-satisfied grin plastered all over his face as if my blushing was all the confirmation he needed.

I tilted my head to the side and let a bit of the fire within me reach my eyes. I knew he could sense the shift in me, and his look went from smug satisfaction to something more predatory.

I leaned in. The space between us reduced to mere inches. The air felt charged. I could almost feel the electrical current zapping between us. It made my skin tingle, and a shiver snaked its way down my spine. For a split second, I had to remind myself this was all just a game.

"Cal."

"Yes." His voice sounded like his mouth had gone dry and caught on the word. I smiled. Gods, why was toying with him so much damn fun?

"If you thought what I did tonight was special, you should see me when I'm actually fired up."

His eyes lingered on my lips for several long seconds before finally lifting to meet mine. I lowered my head, looking up at him through the hair that slid over my eyes. Cal brushed the errant strands behind my ear and let his fingers trail along my neck for a too brief moment.

"You have no idea how hot I burn," I whispered in a low and sultry voice that I barely recognized. Leaning forward toward the bar, I moved into his space and brushed my body ever so slightly across his chest. My skin lit up, each nerve ending sparking alive. Cal responded with a quick intake of air.

It was definitely time to go.

Moving quickly, I picked up the pitchers and sprang back. Cal's hand grasped at air and hovered in the space between us.

Hoisting the flagons aloft, I quipped, "Thanks for the drinks."

I spun on my toes, swishing my hair in all its magnificence right at him.

"Played. I was just played, *again*."

I looked back over my shoulder, drinking in his disbelief. "You'll get used to it." I winked while mock blowing him a kiss.

He looked caught somewhere between adoration and heartbreak, and it was glorious.

10
CALLEN

I leaned back on the bar, propping my arms behind me. Elyria walked away, effortlessly lifting the jugs of ale. I took a long draft from my drink, appraising each smooth movement of her body.

Xoc, seeing her leave, slid into the seat next to me.

"I'm pretty sure she's swishing her hips like that on purpose, just so that I'll have to watch the way her perfect ass moves with each step," I said to him, not drawing my eyes from Elyria.

"Probably," Xoc replied. "She's a performer, Cal. Of course she's not going to fall for your regular tricks." He laughed. "You two are strikingly similar. I don't know why you're so surprised at the way she keeps playing you."

I rolled my eyes at him. He continued, "It also makes sense that she'd end up being the one we're looking for."

"Oh, it's definitely her." I gestured with my tankard at Elyria for emphasis. "You saw that fire dragon. That's no second-rate magician slinging tricks in a show. She's the real deal. I was pretty sure before, but after tonight, I know. It's her."

Elyria sat down the jugs, her white blouse fluttering. The laces hung open, revealing smooth pale skin. All I wanted to do was skate my hand along those curves. The boy across from her looked straight down her shirt, and some part of me bristled with jealous anger. Elyria didn't miss any of his leering. Instead, she slapped him in the face, and the rest of the table laughed. It made something warm settle in my gut. This girl was a force all of her own making. One I more than wanted to see if I could handle.

She gestured my way, telling everyone at the table that I had bought them the round. They all cheered, raising their glasses to me. I lifted my tankard in a returning congratulatory salute.

"What's more, I could *feel* her magic tonight. It rose in me as it was rising in her."

"Interesting," Xoc mused, peering over his shoulder to take a glance at her. "You're sure? I mean that it was the magic and not," he looked back to me, "other things."

"You ass. I'm not twelve. I can tell the difference between a hard-on and a magical surge. This was—" How could I explain what this felt like? "It was like lightning coursing down my veins, fire but... different from my fire. This was brighter, stronger somehow. I've never, *never* experienced that before. I think if I could focus on it, I could still feel that power thrumming in me now."

Elyria was pouring ale into the glasses at the table. She was smiling so effortlessly; it was captivating to watch. The way she gently kept sliding her hair behind her ear, only for it to fall forward again the next time she leaned in. The graceful slope of her neck that action exposed, a beautiful line that led straight for the most perfect set of—

"Once Master Rith made my power rise," Xoc said, making me realize how lost in the sight of her I was. "I wasn't sure how he did it. Something about that weird draken connection of his. I was having trouble controlling my attunement, and he placed his hand on my shoulder."

Elyria sat up and glanced over at me, smirking. I smiled back, not at all ashamed that I was watching her. Because I could watch this temptress for hours and not be done drinking in the sight of her.

"Are you listening to me?" he asked, his deep voice full of annoyance.

I nodded. "Your impotent powers. I'm listening."

"You are the absolute worst. You know that, right?" he said and shook his head in frustration. "I'm trying to tell you Rith forced my power to manifest. I could feel my magic pressing inside of me."

I turned to look at him, finally registering what he was saying. The ghost of that pain in my chest panged in recognition.

"Once the pressure was great enough that I thought I might explode with it, he told me to exhale, and the power flowed out of me." I nodded, thinking of the great release I felt every time I used my own abilities. "It worked, of course. Everything the old bastard said was always right."

I chuckled. "Despite the number of times I tried to prove him wrong."

I thought about the discerning look Rith would have after every smart-ass remark I made. I massaged my arms from the memory of the pails of water he would make me carry as punishment.

"He had to be touching me to draw out my power. But maybe it's something like that," he continued. "Her fire reaching out to yours, and the two of you don't even know you're doing it."

"Could be," I said, not letting my eyes stray from her. "I don't know that one of my line and one of hers have ever been in the same room as each other, much less cast before them."

"If all you're going to do is watch her from across the room, you could just go over there." Annoyance tainted his words.

"I don't know. I quite like the view from here." My eyes slid down her slender frame, and I took another slow sip of ale.

A bell rang from the other side of the room. I turned to see two more sailors enter the room. Their crewmates, already entrenched at the end of the bar, let up a loud cheer. Then, sliding in on their heels, entered a waif-like thing, a boy with threadbare and moth-eaten clothes. He must have been freezing wearing so little in the cool, humid night.

The boy scurried across the room, carrying a massive bundle of purple glowing flowers. They were bright, beautiful, and in absolute contrast to the grime of the room. He hustled them over to the table where Elyria was now sitting.

I unintentionally sat straighter. My instincts flamed to life. It didn't sit right with me. These flowers should not be here, in this place.

"Careful, Cal, looks like someone is moving in on your girl," Xoc chided, half into his glass.

Elyria graciously accepted the bouquet, beaming down at the boy. She laid them on the table and bent over to drop a copper coin into his hand. Elyria pointed to the bar, and he smiled ear to ear. She pulled an extra silver coin from the air and gave it to him. His eyes went wide with wonder and excitement. From behind the bar, Mae was watching them. Children were probably a rare sight in a place like this. Elyria motioned for her to get him a bite to eat, and Mae nodded in acknowledgement.

The boy went eerily still.

I expected him to run for the free meal, but he showed no reaction to anything Elyria had just said. A moment ago, he was animated and full of childish energy, and now his tiny body was completely motionless. His bony, too thin arms hung limply by his sides.

In a voice much too deep for a boy of his age, he said, "I have a song. Shall I sing it for you?" He turned his head and looked directly at me.

I stood, my stool crashing into the bar behind me. Why would he look at me?

The boy lowered his head, a dark smile stretching across his face. He looked back up at Elyria, and in a sickeningly sweet, deep lilt, sang only a single line.

"The petals fall, and all is done. See how the little mouse runs."

Elyria stepped back, tilting her head to the side. "The Calico Cat?" she questioned.

Duke spoke up, "It's an old Iron lullaby. I used it to sing to you when you were a tot. You demanded it every night, but I'm surprised anyone in these parts would know it."

"I remember." Her voice drifted off in memory. "I haven't heard it in years."

The boy bowed, having finished his performance. The troupe at the table all clapped at the impromptu show. I was overreacting. Elyria must get flowers all the time, and it probably wasn't unusual for children to perform for them. No one at the table seemed at all surprised by his display.

Relax, Callen; not everything is a threat.

I made myself sit back on the stool, glancing over at Xoc, who was shaking his head and laughing at me. Why did I keep doing that?

"Thank you for the coin, ma'am," the boy said, seemingly back to being a normal urchin and happy to receive a tip from a pretty girl.

Elyria smiled, patting him on his head. He hurriedly skipped to the bar and climbed up onto a too high stool before the bowl of stew that Mae had already laid out for him.

Everyone around Elyria resumed their normal banter. Beside her were Macie and two other members of the band, a curly blond mop of hair on all of them that could only be hereditary.

The tallest one spoke up now, proclaiming, "Elyria, you've got an admirer."

He snatched a black note from inside the flowers and began fanning himself dramatically with it. His brother grabbed the three of them around the shoulders. With an exaggerated swaying motion, they sang,

"My lady, my lady, my lady so true.
So what do I owe for this pleasure with you?"

"Shut up, you three. Don't make me slap your heads together," said an annoyed Elyria.

But her outrage only encouraged them. They began laughing and pounding on the table, and pretty soon, to Elyria's dismay, the entire bar was joining in.

"I met her this morning for a minute or two.
That's all that it took to be smitten with you."

Everyone joined in on the chorus.

"My lady, my lady, my lady so true.
So what do I owe for this pleasure with you?"

Macie took the lead, her voice bright and bubbling.

"Your eyes are so lovely, your smile so fair."

To which a fourth lad at the table stood, interrupting her with a hand over her mouth.

"I wonder if the rug matches the color of her hair."

The entire bar erupted with laughter. Elyria's face was flaming a fantastic shade of crimson. Her eyes flashed up, meeting mine, before quickly regaining her composure.

Elyria picked up the flowers and leaned over to their friend. She placed a soft, chaste kiss on his lips and smirked at him, saying, "I guess that's one question you'll never get to know the answer to."

The entire table erupted in laughter again. The boy sank back down, stunned. Elyria looked directly at me and winked.

I laughed. *Point taken. I don't believe it, but point taken.*

"He's onto something, though," Duke piped up, snatching the flowers from Elyria. The purple glowing blooms cast a light glow on his face.

"About my hair?" shrieked Elyria.

"Maybe. Your act tonight was good, but what are you doing to warrant a bouquet of *Lunar Irises*?"

"Maybe it's not her hair that's the only thing golden around here," the tall one joked to another round of laughter.

"Careful, Geoff, my vengeance always comes with interest," she said back with a devilish smirk.

Duke lifted the bouquet to his nose, drinking in their scent. Even from here, I could smell their sweetness, mingling with the undertones of stale beer. It only highlighted how entirely out of place they were in a dive like this.

Duke went on, his expression lost in a distant memory, "I once dallied with a girl who would wear one of these in her hair. I wouldn't mind seeing her again."

He snapped out of the memory and waggled his brows, elbowing the man next to him.

Duke handed the bouquet back to Elyria and then leaned in to pluck a single bloom from the bundle. There was a flash of reflected light. I squinted and was just able to make out a small, glittering black spider crawling up the stem of the flower in Duke's hand.

A prickling sensation spread over the base of my neck.

The spider dropped on a green-black sparkling web, landing lightly on Duke's thumb. It quickly skittered up his arm, nimbly climbing over the folds of his shirt and jacket. Its bulbous, green-black, crystalline body shimmered as it scuttled.

I slid from my stool and started moving toward them, pushing people out of my way. Faintly, from behind me, I could hear Xoc putting down his glass and asking what was wrong.

The spider had made its way to Duke's neck. Elyria saw it. Her eyes went wide. And then—

"Ow," Duke proclaimed, slapping a quick hand up to his neck.

I stopped. The spider fell to the ground. I tracked its descent as it disintegrated into black wisps.

"No," I breathed.

A disappearing knife flashed in my mind. How could it be here? We were on the other side of Venterra. Innsevale was thousands of miles away. Could it be that *he* had found his way here, to her? I mean, if I could suss out that "The Golden Dragon" was the second line of Gold Draken, then why couldn't Malvat?

"Bastard bit me!" Duke pulled his hand away to check for blood, finding only a faint slimy black smear.

"Where'd it go? Little bugger isn't crawling around here still, is it?" Macie asked, clinging to the arms of the man she'd been flirting with all night.

It happened suddenly. Duke's eyes lolled, and his entire body fell to the ground like someone cutting the strings on a marionette. Elyria threw the bouquet to the table. Everyone immediately moved back from it.

"Duke! Duke, are you okay?" She slapped his face lightly. Duke's eyelids fluttered. "I saw the spider a second before it bit him."

I pushed forward to her side. Elyria looked at me with frantic eyes. "I've got this feeling in the pit of my stomach. I've never seen a spider like that before. It sounds crazy, but I *felt* it the second before I saw it. Cal, I felt its darkness."

Elyria was kneeling on Duke's forgotten bloom, now smashed and scattered beneath her. She tore at the buttons of his collar, fully opening up his shirt to expose the bite. I could just make out the tiny puncture. Black veins branched off from it, like cracks in the glaze of fine aged porcelain.

"No." I elbowed one of the musicians out of my way and knelt beside Duke.

"Let me see." I pulled his collar down. Fuck, this was bad. The black veins grew, spreading poison into his system with every beat of his heart, sealing his death.

Shit. Shit. Shit! I looked over at Elyria, whose panic was matching the feeling rising in me.

"You know what this is, you've seen it before?" Concern was etched into every beautiful inch of her face.

"Only once," I said. Subconsciously, my hand raised to my chest. "But I'm... attuned."

"You've been bit by one of these?"

"Something like that."

She looked at Duke's neck, and her eyes narrowed on the growing web of black veins. "We have to go, now. Back to the camp. Laying him down will help to slow the spread of the poison."

"I can carry him," Xoc said, the members of the troupe shifting out of his way.

Elyria looked to Xoc, and then to me. I nodded. She pointedly said, "Go. Jimmy, Geoff, go with him, take him to Duke's wagon. I'll be right behind you." She looked down at the discarded bouquet.

I looked at Geoff, who still had the note in his hands, absentmindedly bending it. "Can I see that?" I said, pointing to the card.

"My gods, I forgot I was even holding it," he said and handed it over.

Xoc bent down gently, cradling Duke in his arms. "Which wagon is his?" he said, already striding towards the door. "I'm going to run. You won't be able to keep up." The command in Xoc's voice snapped the boys to attention.

"It's the largest and red," interjected Elyria. "Go."

Xoc was already out the door. A second later, I could hear the sound of Xoc's wings as he took flight.

Elyria turned to Macie. Tears were streaming down her face, and it left trails of black kohl on her cheeks. Elyria snapped in front of her eyes. Forcing Macie to jump, but the crying ceased. "Macie, you need to see if you can locate a healer. I know it's late, but even a second-rate healer right now is going to be better than nothing," she said.

"The only healer is on the other side of the city, in the Tower of Night," called Mae from behind the bar. "You'll never make it there and back in time. Not with how fast that poison is spreading."

"She can try," said Elyria flatly. She looked back to Macie. "Go. Hitch a ride from someone if you can. Fuck, steal a cart. Do what you have to. Anything. But be quick. Tell them we'll pay whatever we've got. We have to try. Gods, we have to. Duke would give everything he had before abandoning one of us."

I looked the card over, flipping it front to back.

"This is black cotton rag paper. It's very fine," I said, not actually knowing who was listening. "It's not the kind you would find in any common ink and quill shop. It's the kind you'd have to special order, an import..." My voice trailed off, realizing where I'd seen this kind of paper before. The palace, *my fucking palace*. I looked up at them to see they were watching me intently. I couldn't tell them that.

"Is it sealed?" Elyria said.

"Only with a single dot of brown metallic wax," I hesitated, "like... like iron."

Elyria snatched the note from me, tearing it open. She furrowed her brow in confusion and handed the card to me. The hands that were steady enough to throw flaming daggers were shaking.

Inside, in a metallic ink, it only said one word:

SOON.

"What in the bloody rings of Kraav is that supposed to mean?!" she exclaimed.

I looked at it, then at the flowers. I picked them up and threw them into the hearth, where a smoldering fire was still glowing. Before I could give into the instinct to incinerate them, Elyria raised her hand into a tight fist, and the flames roared. "Go back to the hell you crawled out of."

I felt it again. The pull to her was stronger now, an overwhelming urge to touch her. I reached forward. She turned abruptly and looked at my outstretched hand.

I lowered my arm. Elyria's eyes locked with mine. The fire was still raging in them. Her pupils shifted into dragon like slits, an intensity in them I'd never felt from anyone before. I was about to step to her when she said, "Let's go." and walked by me, brushing my shoulder and making straight for the door, never looking back.

11

ELYRIA

Stepping out of the tavern door, I glanced up and down the street to get my bearings. In the dark, I couldn't tell which way to go.

"Godsdamn this city!" I yelled in frustration.

Cal was right on my heels. "That way," he said, pointing the direction we needed to go. One of the floating lanterns hovered over his head and cast a warm glow onto his features. It highlighted the concern on his brow. Concern and determination.

I started jogging toward our camp. Cal kept pace beside me. The rhythmic beat of our feet against the stone echoed off the surrounding buildings. With each step, a reel flickered the scattered images of the last hour through my mind. Everything had changed so quickly. One second we were having the best night of our lives. The next, there was this worry and anxiety so intense that I felt like I was choking on it.

Soon. It had said, "Soon."

I knew what it meant. That song the boy had sung, the cat that lures and eats all the mice. The message was loud and clear. *I'm coming for you, and if they get in my way, then I'll devour them too.* Well, fuck that, not if I come for you first.

I tried to focus on my footfalls, breathing steadily in and out as I pushed myself faster and lengthened my stride. I wouldn't let anything happen to my family. We'd save Duke, and then I'd track down the person responsible and show them I wasn't a little mouse to be toyed with.

We didn't speak for the ten minutes it took us to reach the camp. Instead, Cal kept up with my punishing cadence and respected my need for silence. I glanced at him as our strides fell in time with each other. Of course, the smug bastard didn't even look like he was breaking a sweat.

I slid into the glade. Blue, glowing moss gathered in a pile at my feet. The entire camp was empty. So, I wasn't surprised when I threw open the door to Duke's wagon and the remaining troupe were all huddled in the tiny caravan. Their nervous eyes turned to me.

"Everyone out!" I yelled. Della rose her chin in defiance. "Out!" I repeated. This time, my voice growled with command.

She huffed, wrapping her shawl around her. Jess gave me a small hug on his way out, but I barely noticed. All I saw was Duke's limp form draped on the bed. Afraid of what I might do if they put up a fight, everyone vacated the wagon, everyone except Xoc and Gregory.

Cal stepped forward. "Did you bring any icebell seeds in your kit?"

"I think so," Xoc said, and produced a pouch from seemingly thin air.

"First, this giant beast of man comes in here," Gregory said, slapping Xoc in the chest with the back of his hand. "And I thought we were being robbed. I figured there's still a fight left in these old bones, and if I was going out of this world, I'd do it with me fists raised. But, then I sees Duke limp like a babe in his arms." Gregory's face was stricken. "He wouldn't tell me anything, Elyria. He just walked in here and put him down, started commanding the camp like he owned the place. What the hells happened in town?"

"He was bitten by a spider. Or something. I can't be sure. Darkness? Is it possible to be bitten by darkness?" A shiver coursed down my spine as I remembered the scuttling crystal body.

Gregory did a sharp inhale and hissed, "Witchcraft." He brushed each of his shoulders twice and clapped, a superstitious gesture left over from an older generation.

Xoc was rifling through tiny paper packets, each labeled in a language I couldn't read.

"I've got it," he proclaimed. He took Gregory by both shoulders and moved him to the side, clearing his path out of the wagon.

I followed him to the door. "What are you doing?" I demanded. Someone was going to have to start giving me some fucking answers real soon, or I was going to start throwing fireballs.

Cal stood behind me and placed a warm hand on my shoulder. His thumb brushed gently against the base of my neck. That one simple gesture grounded me from losing myself to the anxiety. There was a connection in his touch that resonated within me. I looked over my shoulder to him, resting my hand over his in gratitude. Had he known instinctively that was what I needed?

"Just watch," he whispered low, nodding toward where Xoc was tearing up a patch of moss. In the tiny hole in the earth, he placed a couple of seeds from the pouch. He replaced the dirt and squeezed the moss. A stream of blue glowing water soaked into the mound of fresh earth.

Xoc raised his hands to the sky, then placed them over his heart and whispered something in Oerish. After finishing the ritualistic prayer, he hovered his palm over the mound. A sprout sprung from the ground, inching into the air as it continued to grow. He turned his hand over, and it doubled in size.

"That's amazing," I whispered.

With each motion of his hand, the plant grew taller and broader. Tiny, almost clear, belled flower buds formed along the bent stem. They looked like drops of dew clinging to the bright green stalk. The delicate petals peeled back, displaying tiny white seeds. The sweet scent of fresh blossoms filled the air.

I'd heard of Seed Singers but never seen one in action. Cal gave my shoulder a squeeze and continued smoothing his thumb in slow, soothing strokes. He couldn't know how much I needed that point of contact right now. Or maybe he did.

Xoc raked his hand over the stalk, pulling the buds into his palm. He turned to Gregory, who hovered in the doorway, watching the whole thing with equal parts fascination and fear. "Do you have a mortar and pestle?"

"Of course, I keep one in me kit," he spluttered out.

He hurried along as best he could to the cookstove, his slight limp more pronounced as he tried to run. A minute later he returned with one gripped in his gnarled hands. Xoc placed the flowers in the shallow bowl.

"Start grinding," he commanded him and then scanned the glade. For what?

"There." Cal pointed to a green fern growing on the edge of the field. "It should work. Of course, everything here has to be some mutated perversion of itself." The fern stood tall with large fronds tipped in glowing yellow that curled at the ends. Xoc dashed for it with impressive speed. In less than a heartbeat, he returned with several leaves in his hands.

"I'll finish," Xoc said, taking the mortar and pestle from Gregory.

He fisted the fern, dropping the crumpled mass of shining leaves into the bowl. He began a gentle rocking motion with the pestle until the flowers and ferns made a white pulp that glowed gently.

"A year ago, I had a similar affliction," Cal said quietly, looking down at me. I looked back at him, the heart in my throat making it impossible to breathe. "The healers used this to slow the spread of the poison. After that, it was up to my body to fight it off. I weakened quickly and nearly died. Everyone was sure I wouldn't make it to the morning. But, a month later, I awoke in my bed, with only a vague nightmare that still haunts my dreams as an explanation."

I could feel the blood drain from my face, and my legs trembled. In a daze, my body turned on its own and I walked straight for Duke. His shirt had been removed. He lay there, incredibly pale, and a sheen of sweat clinging to his brow. The sun-kissed glow he usually had was replaced with a gray pallor, already looking entirely too corpse-like for my nerves. I swallowed down the nausea that rose when I saw the extent of the poison. The black veins were *everywhere*. Near the bite, the skin between the webs had blackened completely, turning to a dark leathery texture that covered nearly his entire neck and shoulder. I bit back a howl of alarm when I spotted the black creeping around the edges of his chin.

In an hour, would there be anything left of the man who raised me?

I took his hand in mine and knelt next to him. It was limp and clammy in my grasp, cold. A tear crept down my cheek, and I wiped it away with the back of my other hand. This wasn't the time to break. It was the time to fight.

Xoc placed the poultice on the puncture wound. From thin air, he produced a bandage and a vine. I really needed to learn how he did that. Before I could puzzle where he was retrieving these things from, the vine wove itself around his neck and shoulder, holding the bandage in place.

Xoc rested a large hand on my shoulder. It was an amazingly gentle touch for someone of his bulk. His brilliant emerald eyes radiated sympathy. They glimmered brighter for a second, and then a wave of comfort rolled over me. It calmed my nerves, if only for a second.

"All we can do now is wait and see if he wakes," Cal said.

"Thank you," I said, glancing between them and tightening my grip on Duke's hand.

I placed a kiss on his clammy temple, and then growled at him. "You're a stubborn bastard. Don't start giving in now." I used the same tone of authority I used whenever his carefree tendencies got in the way. This wasn't any different. He didn't get to shuck off his mortal responsibilities to galavant around the afterlife. There were too many people here depending on him, needing him. I needed him.

"We'll give you some space," Cal said. "Xoc and I will just be out by the fire if you need us."

Xoc swiftly left the wagon, but Cal stopped by the door and gave me a long look. It was intense and full of empathy. All pretense gone. He'd lost someone. Steadily holding my gaze, that look said it all. He didn't shy from the pain I knew must be etched on my face. There was only strength and the unspoken offer to be my anchor in the storm of emotion roiling around me.

I took a deep inhale and let it out in a slow, deliberate breath.

No matter how much I fought the pull, Cal weakened my meticulously crafted defenses. When I was around him, each of my emotions felt raw and exposed. Even more disconcerting was how badly I wanted to surrender to it.

But, collapsing into his arms and letting him soothe away my fears wasn't going to help anything but my foolish heart.

After what could have been a second or an eternity, I closed my eyes and counted my heartbeats. One... Two... Three...

When I opened them again, Cal was gone, and I was alone—still clinging to Duke's hand.

12

CALLEN

I silently closed the door behind me. Lingering on the step of the wagon, I took in the scene before me. What looked like the entire troupe was gathered outside. I could make out the musicians from the bar. The boy who had made the joke about Elyria's hair had his arm wrapped around little Violet. The levity of that bar felt a lifetime away now.

Sitting on the steps of a wagon off to the side were the set of triplets. One stood up when I emerged. Their fear made them seem small and frail. Next to them was The Peacock. Her hair was perfectly placed as if she hadn't just been woken in the middle of the night. A man I didn't recognize, with a jet black shoulder-length wig, was wringing his hands together. Bangles rattled each time he turned them over, and his feather-lined robe billowed darkly around him. Pacing behind everyone, like a great black shadow, was the strong man Adolphus.

They looked at me expectantly, waiting for me to tell them everything was going to be okay. Truth was, nothing was okay. If Malvat's reach could extend to this far off, and forgotten corner of the world, then things were far graver than we had realized.

I cleared my throat, thanking the gods that I had been raised prepared for moments like this one. I mustered all the strength and dignity that had been drilled into me during my lessons with Cressida, my deportment tutor. She had been a tall, birdlike woman with a spine like a plank of wood. Even her nose had been beak-shaped. She was the only woman to ever make me shake with fear. I could still hear her shrill voice echoing in my ears.

"Callen Magnus Shadow, you are a prince of Innesvale, not some timorous schoolboy. You might be afforded every comfort, but the one luxury you don't get is fear." I could still feel the whack of her cane on my shoulder. *"Stand straight, child, and by the gods, speak up."*

I blinked away the memory, rolled my shoulders back, and stood with more confidence than I felt. A mask of authority slipping with practice over my features.

"We've done everything we can for now. You should get some rest. Come morning, we may need our strength."

The troupe collectively slumped, heads drooping. Violet turned into Jimmy, gripping ahold of his shirt and weeping silently. The Peacock stomped her foot as though her indignation could somehow change Duke's fate. The robed man silently turned, moving between the tents like a ghost. Adolphus' shadow disappeared into the darkness of the woods. The branches of a tree rattled as he slammed his fist into the trunk. Through the wood of the door behind me, I heard the telltale sound of Elyria's composure finally shattering. I hesitated, wanting only to take her up in my arms and kiss away the tears that streamed from her eyes. But, instinctually, I knew she needed this time alone with Duke.

"Go on, then!" Gregory croaked, and waved them all back to their quarters.

I was grateful for the old man. Obviously, everyone listened to him. He wobbled up to us, leaning heavily on his walking stick. The wrinkles lining his eyes furrowed, years of experience telling him everything he needed to know about how this night would end.

"So you're staying, then?" he asked. "I was thinking I might put the kettle on. I think we could all use something warm to drink." He shifted his weight, looking down at his feet and poking at the blue moss with his cane. "I'm not going to bed. That boy is the closest thing I've ever had to a son, and I'm not about to abandon him in his last hours."

He sighed and cast a long look at Duke's wagon. When he turned back to me, it was with eyes that were full of immense pain and exhaustion. "I'll get you a drink. Duke used to say there was no situation a bit of cocoa couldn't solve. I think I'll make some up." Gregory moved to walk away and then turned back. "Thank you, to you... and your... friend." He said the last word while looking at Xoc with distrust before shuffling off toward the stove.

I walked away from the wagons, toward a circle of stones where someone had set up a campfire and some seating. Most of the crowd had retreated into their wagons and tents, leaving just Gregory, Xoc, and I... and the crackle of the beckoning fire.

Walking up to the firepit, I inhaled deeply. The smell of the smoke and the warmth called to me. It always called to me, and it had been too long since I had answered. Usually, I kept my draken abilities on a tight leash, relying on my air attunement to satisfy my need to cast. However, every day since waking from my coma, it was getting harder to keep it contained. The lure of the flame was practically irresistible around... her.

As it had been for days, it was impossible to keep my mind from drifting to Elyria. To the goddess who descended on the golden hoop, a long arc of light trailing behind her. The luxurious way her hair flowed, looking like flames drifting in a black stream. How her beautiful golden eyes shone when she had looked at me in the bar, and then I thought of the heart I saw breaking in them before I exited the wagon.

The keen bite of anger swelled in me. I should have seen this coming. I held my hands out and willed the fire to grow higher. I was responsible for that man's death as surely as I was each condemned soul back in Innesvale. Foolishly, I'd believed we were safe here.

Xoc stepped next to me. "He won't make it to morning. You know that, right?" The deep timbre of his voice resonated in the still air.

I looked up at him, trying my hardest to rein back the rage that was already starting to boil over.

"I know that, and you know that, but they don't need to know that. *She* doesn't need to know that," I said, gesturing back to the wagon. I could still make out the faint sound of her crying, and my heart clenched. "I won't take that from them, from her."

He stared at me, and I knew Xoc was assessing the fire reflected in my eyes. I could feel my control slipping, and the dark part of me wanted to let it slip. It would be as simple as letting go. I went back to watching the steady rhythm of the flames.

"That fucking note," I spat out under my breath. "It wasn't even *for* her. That shiny bastard sent that spider here. I'd bet my kingdom *she* was the target, and that note was for me. So that when my last hope was gone, I knew he was responsible for it. Well, fuck him. Fuck it all." My heart hammered against my ribs, the fire growing brighter.

As simple as letting go, and the torrent of power would do all the work. There would be nothing left, a dark void of ash where once there was so much hurt and pain.

"So, what are we going to do?" Xoc replied evenly, calmly. Which was infuriating. He was always so damn calm. Even when our world was falling apart, and the innocent were dying because of it, he was completely placid.

I stepped closer to him. Lowering my voice, I growled through my teeth, "I'm going to rip that iron spine from his body and show it to him as the light leaves his fucking eyes. I'm going to send him straight to the Hell he's trying to unleash." The flames licked higher, and I felt the sting of my eyes shifting to gold.

"Oookay," Xoc replied. "Do you, by chance, have a plan that is a bit less homicidal? Perhaps something that doesn't involve accidentally burning this camp down on the same night the master dies?" He pointed to the fire, and he was right. The heat coming off of it had at least doubled.

That was what I needed. It was like being doused with an iced bucket of reality, reminding me of what was at stake, and bringing me back to the moment. I locked the wrath I was barely containing back in its cage where it belonged. In response, the fire dimmed to a normal level.

"We can't let her stay here, Xoc. He already knows about her and where she is. What's more, he knows we're here too. Tonight won't be the last of his attempts."

"Here's your cocoa, lads," Gregory croaked from behind me, his eyes like daggers. Somehow, in my fury, I hadn't heard him approach. *Careless.* He handed me the mug. I went to take it from him, but his gnarled hands gripped the tin handle.

"I held that girl in me arms when she wasn't more than a babe. You two are schemin' something, and it better not involve hurting her."

He leveled a stare at me. "What's more, that girl has the strength and power to take you both down should you try anything... untoward."

"We're just here to help." I smiled reassuringly. But Gregory still held on, and only narrowed his eyes further. "Look," I said, turning to meet him face to face. "If we wanted to hurt someone, you've all already given up plenty of opportunities."

"Perhaps. Perhaps not." He threw a glance at Xoc and handed him his mug with a thrust. Cocoa sloshed over the rim and Xoc hissed as it burned the back of his hand.

Gregory picked up the two remaining mugs and sidled into Duke's wagon. Once the door had closed behind him, I continued. "I need to get her to Innesvale yesterday. The second the opportunity presents itself, we're going."

"Depending on what he's telling her right now, you might need to just come clean. Tell her who you are and why we're here," Xoc replied.

"Maybe. When the time comes, I will, but not yet. I would say she's just beginning to trust me, but I think if we tell her the truth, she'll blaze a trail of fire straight into Mt. Kraav, and we'll lose the only advantage we might have." I took a sip of the cocoa and groaned. It was delicious. The old man was right. It did somehow make things seem better. "It's better to wait. Let's just see what happens tonight before we start worrying about tomorrow."

13

ELYRIA

There was an old onion crate discarded in the corner that Duke used to tie his boots up. I dragged it over to the bed and perched atop it, cradling his hand in mine. I caressed the surface with my thumb and watched as the black veins crept their way down his arm. Hearing Cal address the group was my undoing. He was muffled by the door, but with that last comment about strength in the morning, the tether on my composure finally slipped. My fear unraveled, and the tears started pouring, soaking the bed before me.

I kept spiraling into my grief until I heard the grunting and groaning that could only be Gregory climbing the steps. He stumbled his way into the small interior of the wagon and handed me a steaming mug. I closed my eyes and inhaled the rich chocolate wafting up.

I smiled, the smell thrusting me into a memory of a time Duke had given me a cup just like this one. It was the day I had my first bleeding. I was twelve, and he had been a bumbling fool with no idea of what to say or do. I was so scared and confused. So he made me a cup of cocoa, and then we laughed over the awkwardness of the whole thing.

"I was there, you know. The day he found you." The abruptness of Gregory's comment caught me off guard and startled me.

"Duke has always picked up strays and forgotten misfits in his travels, but the night he found you wasn't like any other night. You were different straight from

I nodded, piecing together the snippets Duke had told me. It was the one story he never wanted to tell. It took years before he'd even admitted that he wasn't my true father. The one thing I knew for certain was that I was not like anyone else.

Someday I would find out why.

I took a sip of cocoa, and the nerves coiling tight in my chest eased a bit. "When I was little, he would joke about who my mother was. Every time I'd ask, he'd make up a different story, each more outlandish than the last." I chuckled, swallowing another warm mouthful of chocolate. "Ya know, one time he told me she was an attuned queen, sequestered on the other side of the Entlis Mountains. According to Duke, she had every bachelor in the kingdom brought to her chambers in order to find the most virile man in the land to sire her offspring."

"Sounds like him." Gregory smiled. "Storytelling was his gift, after all."

"Is. Is his gift," I corrected.

He smiled sadly and nodded. "Is... I'm guessing he's never told you all of *this* story."

We looked at each other in silence for an entire minute. It was as if he was waiting for me to stop him.

"It was the middle of the night." He paused, looking up at the ceiling. Gregory swallowed hard before continuing. "We had just set up camp outside of this nothing of a town, between The Straights and The Bullseye. Earlier that night, we'd thrown together a bit of a show. Just a rough and tumble song'n dance. Not ought but ten people even came out for it."

The steam from his mug curled around the white strands of greasy hair that hung in front of his face. Aged, brown eyes blinked away tears.

"That night, we'd packed everything up. Duke had some something or other in The Bullseye that he was all preoccupied with. Never did find out what, since finding you changed everything." He shook his head. "I'm getting ahead of meself."

He set the mug down on the desk and shifted to take the weight off of his hip. "That night the world itself trembled. And not like that shakin' that happened when we did that stretch near the trench. No, this trembling happened every-where and in everything. The very air itself shook. We came out of our tents. It was just Albert, Duke, me, and..." He hesitated, struggling to come up with a name. "Gah... do you remember that lad what did the tricks with the staff?"

"Joseph," I replied, filling in the blank. "He's the one who showed me how to throw a punch." I half-smiled at the memory. "And take one."

"Yes, hmm, well. Joseph was there too. The kids in the troupe were all still sleeping." He pursed his lips. "We came out of our tents. There were three waves of that trembling. The first one woke us and brought us outside. But the third one was strong enough it blew half our tents down. In fact, my tent blew straight into our fire pit. It was months before I could get the smell of smoke outta the canvas."

"What was it?"

Gregory waved at me to be patient. "We had just set everything back up when we saws the smoke drifting up from the town. Duke, he looks at me and says, '*We should go see if someone needs help.*' So, we unhitched the horses from the cart and rode into town, 'cept there weren't no town anymore. Just a couple of charred homes, with some scared as shit people running from them, and the black ash that used to be the village. We'd never seen nuthin' like that before. Still haven't. The smoke was drifting up in thick clouds from the thatch on the remaining homes, and the cinders were swirlin' around in little black tornadoes."

I leaned forward toward him. He was right. Duke had never told me *any* of this.

Gregory continued, "Duke got off his horse and walked straight into the center of it all. Not an ounce of fear in him. An... well, Elle, that's where he found ya. Right there in the middle of that nightmare. You was just a white babe in the middle of a soot-scorched land."

Gregory reached out, placing a hand on my arm. "You see, it was you, darling girl. You'd erupted and burned the lot down. And the people of that town, they just left you there, right where your mum had laid you to sleep. 'cept they weren't there no more, they'd been taken up with the rest of the town in the blast."

I felt the realization slam into me. The horror of it made my mouth taste like ash. I'd killed all those people and *my parents*. Duke had said they'd died in a fire that got out of control but never that it was me that set the fire. Not a fire—an explosion. I'd exploded.

"Duke, though. All he saw was the most beautiful baby girl he'd ever seen. He picked you up, and you smiled at him." Gregory paused and swallowed hard. "And sweet girl, from that moment, you had his heart forever. He loved you from the start, you know."

A tear rolled down my cheek.

"He took off his sweater and wrapped you up in it. We hurried back to our camp before what was left of the locals could get an idea in their heads that you was some kinda infernal creature sent to purge them all. And that was it. We were gone before the sun rose."

Gregory pinched the bridge of his nose.

"He was... experienced in the world. I know he's told you some of the adventures he had as a young man."

"When he traveled with that group of for-hires," I said in confirmation.

"Well, he knew right then what you were." He paused again as if considering whether he should share this information. "A draken."

Gregory tightened his mouth, studying my response.

"A draken?" I puzzled. I'd never heard of it.

He nodded slowly. "He knew you were special. Elle, you *are* very rare, an attuned person born of a line descended from the dragons."

"Dragons!" I thought of all those foolish dreams I had as a child, of finding some lost city of fire-attuned people. The questions that had eaten away at me, never fully understanding who I was and where I fit in the world. "Of course." I muttered to myself, "He went and named me the Golden Dragon. Of course he knew. It wasn't just showmanship, he knew all along. He knew and never told me. Is there more? What else has he been hiding from me, Gregory?"

I looked over at Duke. Hurt, anger, and sadness all warred within me.

Gregory looked over at the lantern, watching the flame inside it flare brighter. "That's all I know, or at least that's all he told me. That he had seen one of your kind before, and that's how he knew. Well, that and all the fires you'd start on occasion." He laughed with a sudden memory. "As soon as you could walk, you used to leave these little trails of scorched grass behind you. And one time, by the gods, you burned off Duke's eyebrows. For two entire weeks, he was painting them on. He finally got them back the way he likes, you know, with that inane curl at the end, and you burned them off *again*. Grabbed it right in your tiny fist and singed them off."

Gregory chuckled, smiling as he looked over to where Duke lay. The smile faded the longer he looked at the blackening skin.

"Gods, I've never laughed more," he said in a low and distant murmur. He picked his mug back up and took another drink.

It felt like a missing cog had just been replaced, and my mind started whirring. I thought of the first time I'd asked Duke about my fire. He'd said I was half of a rare line of fire-attuned people that lived in a remote region of Desterra, past the Entlis Mountains and nearly impossible to reach. I'd never questioned it. There were water-attuned people, why not fire? But he said that people feared them, and they'd been hunted to near extinction until they made a home in the hardest to get to part of this world. He insisted we mask my abilities with parlor tricks and makeup. I was only to use my powers in private or on stage when they could explain them away as part of the show. He had been so strict about it when I was a child. Duke was terrified that someone would attack me or take me for what I was. It was why he and Joseph had been so serious about my training.

I looked down again at Duke, fisting a hand into the mattress.

"You should have told me," I said and beat the cotton batting beneath my hands. Hot tears streamed from my eyes, and around the rims of my lids the night air burned.

Gregory got up, his joints audibly straining. He shambled the couple of steps to me. With a withered hand, he reached out to my chin and turned my face to his. "That night changed our lives forever, none more than him. He'd lost his chance at a family with Lila, but with you he got that chance back. It'd been borne to him in dark and ash, and you were a beacon of light. He named you that night. Elyria Solaris, you are his sun."

Gregory cupped my cheek and bent over to place a light kiss on top of my head, then brushed away my tears. There was a quiet knock on the door. Macie peeked her head in cautiously, and I sighed in relief. Seeing her released a tightness in my chest I hadn't realized was there.

Macie whimpered, seeing us sitting around Duke. "I was so afraid that I'd open the door and we'd be too late," she said, her voice cracking. "I had to borrow a cart and promise the man a king's ransom, but the healer is here."

The healer was a tall, spindly man in a threadbare waistcoat. His dark eyes glanced my way for only a second as he took in the room's state. In two long strides, the man was by Duke's side. By this point, the charcoal coloring had spread over most of his torso and down his arms, and those strings of inky darkness were still spreading.

"It was a spider from a bouquet of Lunar Irises," I said hesitantly.

The man said nothing. He didn't even look at me. Methodically, he went about his business, not wasting time with pleasantries. He knelt before Duke and reached for his pulse. I watched as his lips turned down into a grimace. He lifted the bandage and examined the bite. "Hmm," he said, poking at the poultice.

The healer placed his hands over Duke's chest, and a faint, purplish-white glow came from them. Duke's entire body bowed, his weight rolled to his shoulders, and his waist lifted off the bed.

"By the gods," Macie whispered, saying exactly what I was thinking. She reached down and clenched my hand. I took a sharp intake of air and held it, saying a silent prayer to the gods.

The darkness at Duke's chest abated. It was slight, but the darkness retreated. The glow faded, and then the black shadow crept back in. The man crawled on the bed and straddled him. When the healer leaned forward, a leather cord with an iridescent crystal swung down in front of him. It looked like a smaller version of the crystal in the Tower of Night. A light in the crystal pulsed faintly, like a purple glowing ember.

He held his hands up and made a triangle with his fingers. Inside, a ball of light formed. The healer thrust his hands forward, and the ball shifted into Duke's chest. Briefly, the skin turned translucent, covered in what looked like swirling smoke. Like a lantern, Duke's heart lit from within. The light pulsed with the slow beat of his heart before fading back to the dull black of his tainted skin.

The tall man climbed off the bed and pulled a small glass vial from his satchel. A red flickering spark hovered in the center of the vial, but it wasn't fire. I couldn't feel the normal tingle in my fingers that happened whenever I was near a flame. This seemed like the cold of a dying star, anti-flame. He held it before Duke and snapped the vial in half. There was a small tinkle of glass, and then a puff of red smoke lingered heavily in the air before him. The healer pushed on Duke's chest, and when he let up, the smoke was sucked into Duke's lungs. The darkness around his face lightened slightly.

And then Duke stirred.

My heart stopped. His eyes fluttered for a second. My hand tightened on Macie's. Duke's eyes drifted open for just a second. It was brief, but they looked all white before they closed again. When they opened a second time, the white was gone, replaced now by irises that were entirely black. He closed his eyes a third time, and this time when they reopened, they were back to their normal green. I watched as he tried to focus, looking confused at us standing around and the healer straddled over him.

"Duke!" I half sobbed. I ran to him, falling to my knees and clutching at his hand. "I'm here, Duke. It's gonna be okay. You're gonna be okay."

Duke turned his head to me, sweat beaded on his brow.

I looked up at the man, gratitude spilling from me. The healer climbed off the bed but didn't meet my gaze. My heart hitched in my chest as dread began to creep back in. He did not look pleased. His brows knitted together and his lips thinned into a tight line.

"Right? He... He's going to be okay, right?" I stammered, feeling the tears fill my eyes again. My heart rose in my throat.

The healer reached down and grabbed my arm to lift me upright. He guided me over to the door, as close to being in private as you could get in a small wagon.

Vaguely, I registered Macie being shoved out the door by Gregory.

In a hushed voice he said, "This is a terrible and dark magic, not poison. The girl said it was poison. But it's not. He's been cursed by someone or something."

"Cursed?" I asked, confused. The sound of the boy's dark voice snaked into my mind.

The petals fall, and all is done.

"I did this," I whispered, feeling the burn of guilt and anger sting my eyes.

The healer frowned at me and extended his hand to my arm. He was speaking to me, but it was like trying to listen to someone under water. All I could hear was that boy singing.

See how the little mouse runs.

"Miss?" The healer shook my arm lightly. I blinked at him. He gave me a weak and tired smile. "I've tried to counter it with some light. That should help for the time being, but he probably only has a few more hours before the curse consumes him."

What was he saying? That he was done? The healer's eyes softened, and I could see that beneath his all business demeanor, he pitied me and my hope.

"But you can do it again. Do the light again." The words rushed out of me. With shaking hands, I made the triangle with my fingers that he had made.

"I could, but each time I complete the Emanation it weakens me, and will be less effective. If we had a team of healers, then maybe we could prolong the effects by a few days. But it's just me here, and this is the best I can give you. I'm sorry it's not what you wanted to hear." His gaze dropped to his feet. "In my job, it rarely is."

The healer walked to the door, and with his hand still on the handle said, "Oh, and whoever cooked up that poultice, keep them around. It was smart thinking on their part. I don't know where they found fresh icebells around here, but it's the only reason your father hasn't already perished. These hours you've had with him, and the few hours ahead of you, are a gift. Don't squander them."

I felt my knees weaken. I grabbed wildly for the sideboard behind me to help hold me up.

He tipped his hat to me and moved for the door.

"I haven't paid you," I said, my voice shaking.

"No need, the gentleman outside has covered it. Goodnight, ma'am." He looked at Gregory, nodding to him as well, and walked out of the wagon. I flinched when the door slammed shut.

Hours. The word echoed in my head. *Hours.*

My feet slid out from under me, and my body sunk to the wooden floor. . *Hours.*

"Ellie," Duke said with a rasping breath.

I looked up and his hand was stretched out to me.

My vision was blurred by tears. I couldn't bear a life without him in it. My limbs were like heavy stone.

"Come on, girl," Gregory said. He leaned on his cane and reached his frail hand down to me. "That man was right. I don't trust them lads outside, but they gave you these hours. Don't waste a second of it wallowing in sadness and pity. Not when he still breathes."

I shook my head. He was right. I blinked once, twice. I reached up to the sideboard and pulled myself up. Standing on unsteady feet, I pulled my lacy shirt down, took a deep breath, then grasped the hand Duke had extended to me.

ELYRIA

"Help me sit up," he croaked. Duke propped himself up on his arm, only to slump backwards in his weakened state. I grabbed at his pillow and folded it in half behind him, then slid my arm under his shoulder to leverage him up. His skin was hot and slick with sweat... and black. Nearly everywhere I looked, his skin had turned the black of aged charcoal.

"Are you cold?" I said. "Do you want your robe?"

Gregory handed it to me off the peg. Duke nodded, and I draped the velvet housecoat around his shoulders and onto his arms.

I sat down on my onion crate and took his hand in mine. With my other hand, I wrapped my fingers into the cuff of his sleeve and held on. Duke smiled down at our hands.

"You used to do that when you were little. Every night you would hold onto my sleeve or the hem of my shirt when I was telling you a bedtime story. You'd hold on so tightly, like your little hand could prevent me from slipping away unexpectedly." He looked over my shoulder. "Remember that, Greg, how she used to do that? With her tiny little hands?"

"I do." He walked up behind me. Gregory leaned on my shoulder, placing his aged hand over mine and Duke's blackened one. "I do."

"I've loved you both like you was me own," Gregory said, a slight hitch in his voice. "Fate saw fit to take my wife and daughter from me. And I cursed her life for us. But I know that love is something that never fades. It's the love that connects us, and it's the love that will bring us back together one day."

I glanced at Gregory. His gentle eyes were locked on Duke's. With a grunt, he stood back up, squeezed my shoulder, and walked out the door.

"Shall I tell you one last bedtime story?" Duke breathed. My head turned back from the door where Gregory had vanished. The inky veins were pulling over his cheeks now. My lip quivered. I bit down hard on it to keep from crying. A faint tinge of copper hit my tongue. I nodded my head.

He swallowed and licked his lips.

"Once upon a time."

I shook my head, squeezing my eyes shut. I couldn't do this. I wasn't strong enough.

"Ellie. It's okay," he said, and a thumb ran softly over my own. "Once upon a time."

"All the best stories begin with once upon a time," I whispered back. Hot tears splashed the back of my hand. Dammit. I didn't want to cry. Not now.

Duke smiled, and I knew he was remembering the countless times we'd said those exact same words. Every happy ending he'd ever told me always began that way.

All the best stories begin with once upon a time.

But what about my story? How would it end? With my heart tearing open, it felt like the world could never be good again. Happiness, in all its forms, was ceasing to exist with each creeping inch of shadow in my father's veins.

"Yes, they do." One lone tear slipped from his eyes. It trailed over the darkening hollows of his cheeks before splashing onto the collar of his robe. "Once upon a time, there was a beautiful Wind Singer, Elyria Ascheshadow. Elyria sold flowers in a tiny village built in the shadow of a tremendous waterfall. This same waterfall hid the lair of the ancient Gold Dragon, Aurus. Aurus had long since retreated from the world, as the Age of Dragons was over. But he had grown lonely in his isolation. So, whenever the absence of the world would sink his heart, he would distract himself by walking through the dreams of the villagers below. It was here in the realm of dreams and nightmares that he met Elyria.

There were no dreams like hers. They were beautiful and full of unexpected creatures. Aurus would take different forms and stroll unnoticed through the visions she created. He'd find some quiet corner and watch the way her eyes would alight with joy or the way the graceful curve of her lips tipped up with unburdened smiles. He was spellbound by the way her silken black hair flowed in the breeze, and when it landed on her shoulder, it was like a black sea breaking against the rocks. He was so enraptured by her that finally, when he didn't think his heart could take it anymore, he took the form of a man and ventured into the village. It was there, in the waterfall's mist, that they met. Over many conversations and stolen glances, they built a deep and pure bond. A year later, Elyria bore him a child, the first person ever to be graced by a dragon's magic. The baby girl was born tattooed by dragon fire. The dragon coiling down her spine marked her as unique, and hinted to the immense power lingering in her heart. Once a generation, the fates grace the world with a baby who carries the magic, and bears the mark of the Ancient Gold Dragon."

He stopped talking, and the silence was a chasm between us. I looked up at the ceiling, at the door, anywhere but his black-streaked face. I slipped my hand from his and examined my nails.

"You named me after her because that's me. I'm that baby."

"Yes. I knew... the story. The tattoo on your back and your scales. You had to be descended from Elyria, The First. A Fire Draken." Tears rolled from his eyes. "Forgive me for keeping this from you. I knew you'd leave and seek your kin, seek your family. It was selfish, but my heart couldn't bear you leaving me."

More tears flowed from him. My heart ached. How could he ever think I would leave him? I slipped my hands back into his. The velvet of his robe crushed under my tight grip.

"*You* are my family." I tugged his sleeve for emphasis. "You gave me all the family I'll ever need."

"I love you, Ellie," he said. His eyes glistened in the lamplight. "I'm so proud of the woman you've become. You are powerful and fierce but also so graceful and caring. When Lila died, I thought I'd never feel love again. I thought my heart had broken forever. It felt like an irreparable tear at the very center of me. But then I found you. You patched my heart with every smile and giggle, every tug of my sleeve, or midnight dance to chase away the nightmares. Before I realized it, my heart had healed. It grew in a way I didn't know it could grow. Being your father gave me purpose and made me whole again."

He closed his eyes. I laid my head down on his chest and listened to the slow and irregular beat of his heart.

He placed his hand on my back and gently stroked my back, just as he'd done when I was a child. The comfort seeped into me. I inhaled his pepper and caramel scent. Slower and slower, his hand moved. When it stilled, I tightened my hand in his grip and gave it three tight squeezes. Our code. "*I. Love. You.*" Before I would take the stage, if I was ever nervous, he would hold my hand and give it three squeezes. "*I. Love. You.*"

But... no returning squeeze came.

I lifted my head. Panic seized at my heart, stealing the breath from my lungs. "Duke." I shook him. "Duke!"

I laid my head back down on his chest. His heart was still beating. It was slow, but it was beating. His breaths were shallow and ragged. Duke had drifted back into unconsciousness.

I knew that was the last time I'd ever hear his voice. I latched onto the sound of it, locking it into my memory, refusing to let it go.

Being your father gave me purpose.

I laid my head back down on his chest and sobbed quietly while listening to the slow rhythm of his heart. The gentle beat lulled me until, finally, my emotional exhaustion took over.

15

CALLEN

The camp had been silent for hours. When Macie and the healer emerged from Duke's wagon, I knew Duke's prognosis wasn't good. Macie had stormed off, slamming the door of her own wagon and then screaming loudly in bitter frustration. Geoff checked on her shortly after, but her soprano was the kind that rang out, even when she wailed in sadness.

From the second I saw that spider vanish, I knew this moment was inevitable. When I was stabbed, it sent me into a coma for an entire month, and it was another two months before I regained enough strength to walk. Of course, Innesvale's team of healers were at my bedside the entire time, and I was still young. Well, young in draken terms. The leather-black skin never expanded beyond my chest. It was sheer luck, the knife striking where it did. Or perhaps some part of my father had fought back enough to save me. Even if we couldn't *save him*.

I thought of the pain pooling in Elyria's eyes. It was a hurt that was still raw and familiar to me. I closed my eyes, trying to stuff the memory away and lock it up as I always did. But when I closed them, all I saw was the cold look my father had given me while standing over my body, a knife protruding from my chest.

Once they were sure I could handle the stress, Xoc told me his side of what happened as I laid dying on the cold marble balcony. The commotion had alerted my guards, but the door had been barred. The head of my security detail sent for him, and Xoc literally tore the door apart. He'd broken it down to find my father still in the thrall of whatever dark force controlled him, an affliction we later called The Shade.

Xoc noticed the evil controlling him far before I had. He knew if he could restrain him, then later we could drive out whatever darkness had sunk its claws in him. My father, seeing Xoc approach, took a bracing stance. But Xoc, much like myself, was not prepared for his speed and strength. When he reached for my father, the old man nimbly jumped from his grasp and swiftly drew the dagger that Xoc had strapped to his hip. Father stood there, stolen knife artfully clutched in his grip, a scorpion ready to strike.

Xoc hesitantly stepped forward to disarm him, but rather than lunge as Xoc had expected him to do, my father raised the knife to his own throat. With a quick and unrestrained movement, he dragged that perfectly honed edge across his jugular. Blood sprayed everywhere, soaking the front of Xoc's tunic. My father crumpled to the ground, his black blood mixing with my own. As he lay bleeding out next to me, he looked up at Xoc. In a gurgling last breath said, "This is only the beginning. Soon the end will come for you all. Fools."

My mother burst into the room, screaming as she threw herself onto our bodies. When Xoc pulled her up, she raged against him. She pounded her fists and clawed at his arms, fighting with the ferocity of the warrior she once was. Her beautiful white nightgown was stained crimson by our combined blood. Xoc held her tight, whispered to her that I wasn't dead, and that he could still hear my heart beating.

The faint sound of my heart beating, the drip of blood from the balcony, and my mother's wailing. Those were the sounds that filled the chamber the night my father died.

My father was the first that we knew of. But soon after, reports of white-eyed specters started flooding in. Whispers of possession, demons, ghosts, and banshees started circulating around the kingdom. Sprigs of holly and juniper were placed over thresholds and windows to ward off evil spirits. The crown did everything we could to contain the panic and stop the rumors from gaining momentum, but it was like trying to hold water in a sieve.

The palace kept the information of my father's death highly confidential. If the people learned that not even their king was safe, there would be mass hysteria. As far as Innesvale knew, their elderly king had fallen ill and was now bedridden. My mother, Queen Eloaxia, began ruling as regent. And the lie gave me the freedom to devote every waking hour to tracking down the bastard responsible.

No one knew what caused someone to fall to The Shade, only that they were no longer inhibited by their own fatigue, pain, or restraint, so they exhibited superior strength and speed. The only visible indication that someone was afflicted was their white eyes and the swirling black mist of ink. Victims had no control or free will. All thought and function were turned over to an unknown dark commander. They were completely at his mercy. His to control, his to abuse, and his to kill. They became merely a puppet in some master's macabre game, each act more heinous than the last.

I agonized over who could terrorize a peaceful and prosperous nation. There was nothing to gain from tormenting the innocent, and that made the mystery that much harder to solve. How could you track down an enemy when you had none?

It was five months of suffering without a single lead. We got our first break when an eight-year-old boy, Evander Kirst, tried to kill a prominent Innesvalen merchant. When we questioned his mother, she mentioned seeing a man in a cloak approach her son while he was playing on the docks. It was not unusual for people to throw candies at the children who played there. But, rather than bestow sweets on the boy, this man reached out his hand and grabbed Evander by the wrist. Iron claws pierced his delicate skin, causing the boy to cry out to his mother. She looked up in time to see the man pull him close and breathe a cloud of black mist into his face.

Evander instantly went slack, and Mrs. Kirst screamed. The stranger turned to face her, and all she could see under the hood was a smile of pointed iron teeth. Looking at her, he hissed, "Go, tell your prince." Then the boy ran off down the docks. She said the image chilled her to the bone. Rather than face the attacker, she ran off to find her son. And, when she found him, Evander was launching himself on a merchant with a jagged bit of glass.

He was taken to the holding cells where all victims of The Shade were housed, hoping we could avoid them hurting themselves in the same manner my father had. It was Evander's white eyes that had me desperate enough to cross continents to find an answer, and it was his mother's description that told us all who was to blame. The Iron Draken, Lord Malvat.

Stories of Malvat's unearthly dark power had circulated, and I had dismissed them as nonsense. I had known Mal my entire life, and Iron Draken possessed the power to manipulate light, not darkness. To control the dark was the stuff of nightmares and legend, not truth. No one since the ancients had that ability. But now we had confirmation. Somehow, my oldest friend had found the ability to control shadows and was using it to possess people. Hundreds of people and the only way to free those in his thrall was to kill the subject or to end Malvat.

Knowing that he was the one responsible for my attack, that he was the one who had forced my father to take his own life, had filled my mind with a blinding and singularly focused rage. Wrath fueled every step and had me boarding a ship to take me straight to Mt. Kraav. Straight to Malvat. I wanted the iron world to burn. When I was done with him, there wouldn't even be ashes left. I didn't care that there were innocents between us. I didn't care about anything except my visceral need for vengeance.

In the end, it was my mother who talked me out of that dark place. She strode onto my ship as the crew was readying to embark. The black folds of her mourning gown billowed in the wind. Strength rolled off of her, every inch the warrior she was before she became a queen.

I stared her down, feeling hurricanes of power coursing through my veins. My voice was deep, and so laced with venom that I barely recognized it when I said, "Train those dark eyes on someone else, Mother. This ship is leaving. I don't care if I have to sail with you on it. I will kill Malvat or die trying."

With a calm and calculating tone, she replied, "Then you'll get your wish. You will die trying. Someone with the power to control both the light and the dark is more than a match for you on your own."

I steeled myself against her intense gaze, denying that I knew what she told me was true. Malvat and I had squared off in a fighting ring enough times that I knew he was more than a fair match for my abilities, and that was before whatever darkness had corrupted him. She stepped forward and handed me a flier. It was a pamphlet for a circus, Troupe Solaire.

"The star is a fire dancer. She goes by the moniker Golden Dragon. A young woman, the right age to be the next born with the mark. Callen, with the twin to your power by your side, you would be unstoppable. Find her. Then you can burn the memory of Malvat from the world."

I opened my eyes against the agony of the memory, hearing my mother's powerful voice in my mind.

Unstoppable. Find her.

I looked back at the door of the red wagon. I was so close. She was right there on the other side of the glade. The beauty of the clearing was at such odds with the sorrow that filled it. Delicate purple and pink flowers hung down from the surrounding branches. The moon was just cresting the treetops, and I realized it was already moonrise. Six hours had passed since we'd left the tavern. The surrounding forest was waking up and coming to life around us. The chirp of insects and the not-so-subtle cooing of the Koolaburas.

Xoc had propped himself up against a tree for a quick rest. A yellow and green spotted caterpillar crawled its way across his face. I smiled at the streak of green glowing goo it left behind. Xoc's reflexes kicked in, and his enormous hand flew up, slapping himself straight in the face. I stifled the laugh that escaped from me. Xoc glared back at me, but when he brought his hand down, a giant glowing splat stained his cheek. I tried to contain my laughter and instead found myself in a full-body seizure, shaking uncontrollably as I clamped my hand over my mouth. Waking the camp up with the sound of my laughter was just about the most inappropriate thing I could think of.

"Thank you for that brother. I needed a good laugh," I said, walking up to him.

"Always at your service, my liege," he said with a grumble and wiped away the goo with the back of his sleeve. "Anything happen while you were on watch?"

"No, after the healer left, everyone retired. It's been quiet ever since." I sighed. "Just me and my haunting memories to keep me company."

All on their own, my eyes drifted back to Duke's wagon. All night long, I'd stared at the red walls and wondered how Elyria was coping. All night it took everything I had not to walk back in and pull her into my arms.

"No more crystalline creatures trying to make an attack?" he said with wariness in his voice.

"Not that I saw, but who knows? The man can wield the dark, and we're currently in a land devoid of light. So it's probably just a matter of time. At least it's already moonrise. That should help some. Do you think she's okay in there? Maybe I should check." I couldn't break my gaze from the wagon.

"Her heart rate is slow. I'd say she's sleeping... and Cal," The seriousness in his voice was enough to draw my attention back to him. "Her's is the *only* heartbeat."

I swallowed hard. Something tore open within my chest. Xoc could sense every creature within a mile, but only the living ones.

"People will begin rising soon. It might be better to wake her before they do," he said.

"True," I confirmed, already walking in her direction.

16

CALLEN

I hesitated at the door for a second and braced myself. Taking a deep breath, I gently opened it. Elyria sat on an onion crate, her body draped over Duke. Her head was resting on his chest. She was asleep, her black and gold hair spilling over her face and down the bed in front of her. Duke's fingers were woven into the strands. I walked up behind them, quietly checking Duke's pulse. Xoc was never wrong, still I hoped. But the moment my fingers touched his cold black skin, I knew.

I looked down at his hand again and realized that he'd used his last breath to run his fingers through her hair. It was heartbreaking, and an ache pulsed in my chest. I couldn't do this. I couldn't wake this peaceful angel into the hell that awaited her.

I took a step back, but it seemed my presence was enough to rouse Elyria from her slumber. Slowly she raised her head, acknowledging me and taking in her surroundings. Realization dawned on her face. Her expression crumpled. She looked up at me, her golden eyes searching mine for any kind of relief.

I felt powerless. So, I did the only thing I could think of. I reached out my hand to her.

When she took it, a jolt of energy ran up my arm. Her eyes widened, and I knew she had felt it too. Her pulse quickened under my fingertips, and then she curled into me. Slender arms gripped my waist, and she nestled her head into my chest. Gently, as if I was afraid that moving too quickly might spook her, I mimicked her movements and tucked my arms around Elyria's slight frame.

Warmth filled the room, washing comfort around us. I tightened my arms and lowered my cheek to the top of her head. Her height was perfectly posed against mine to do exactly this. I inhaled. Her hair smelled of sandalwood, laced with the heady combined scents of smoke and something more floral. It was intoxicating, and I didn't think I'd ever smelled anything so completely perfect. Elyria's grip tightened on my shirt. I couldn't help but linger on how every place our bodies touched felt warm and pulsed from the connection.

She nuzzled her head against my chest. With each breath she took, that rigid composure shattered. Her fingers dug into my back, and she clung to me, holding on as wave after wave of tears fell from her. I tightened my arms, letting her know I was here to hold her up and wishing there was a way I could lift this burden from her heart.

We stayed wrapped around each other until Elyria's shuddering breaths grew deeper and more relaxed. I reached up and cradled the back of her head in my hands, sinking my fingers into her hair and letting the silken strands slide against my calluses.

What the hell was I doing? *Wrong*. It was wrong to enjoy this so much. Her heart aching felt like it was splitting me open... But I couldn't deny it. Everything about Elyria felt like she fit. When I was a child, a stained glass window had been shattered, definitely not by any wayward princes trying to see if they could make a wooden eagle they'd carved fly. It took nearly a year for the caning to be replaced and the colored glass to be recast. For weeks, I'd ran to the gallery to see if it had been fixed, and each time I left feeling empty, the guilt over what I'd done gnawing away at me. But one day, the last piece was placed, and the image was made whole. That was what Elyria wrapped in my arms felt like. I had been living a life that was only partially assembled, feeling emptiness gnaw away at my soul and feeling like my life was irrevocably incomplete. I couldn't even say how I knew it, but Elyria was what I had been missing all these lonely years.

Her head tilted up, and golden eyes met mine for a long second. Rimmed in red, they glistened with tears, and caught the firelight of the lanterns. Elyria took another long and shaky breath. Beneath my arms, I felt each muscle tightening as she braced to stand upright. She let go, her hands slipping down my back and falling slack at her sides. She stepped back, and already I missed the feel of her.

Leaning over Duke, Elyria placed a kiss on his forehead. She lingered for a moment and then composed herself, standing up straighter, wiping away tears, and neatly pulling her hair over one shoulder. As if she'd given herself the one moment of weakness she would allow. When she was done, she turned to face me. Firm resolve darkened her eyes and hardened her soft lips into a firm line.

The silence of the wagon was deafening. I felt like I should say something, but we just stood there looking at each other.

"I—"

"I know," she said, cutting me off.

I watched her slender neck take a hard swallow.

The need to tell her I knew exactly how this felt overwhelmed me, caught me by surprise. I had to tell her everything. It filled me, consumed every breath. It suddenly felt like each second that passed was a lie. The guilt became a heavy knot in my throat.

I tried again. "Elyria, I—"

"Don't. You don't have to say anything. I know."

"You don't."

"Whatever you are about to say won't change anything. And, I just." She threw her hands up. "I just can't. Someday, you can tell me. But today, I can't. I don't want to hear it. I don't want to hear your sympathy, or your story, or how you know how this feels. I feel this too deeply to handle feeling anything else."

I'm a complete ass. A selfish ass. Here her father lays literally next to us, and I felt the need to unburden myself to her. She's right. How could I ask her to bear this information now just to assuage my guilt?

I couldn't think of what to say next, so I blurted out, "I'm not leaving."

To be honest with myself, I didn't know how to justify that. But I couldn't leave her here, unprotected, and even if there wasn't an imminent threat, I couldn't bring myself to go.

Her eyes glittered with newly forming tears.

"I don't want you to go," she whispered.

"Okay, then."

"Okay," she replied. A heartbeat of silence. Two heartbeats, then, "I'm not sure how to do this. How do I go out there and tell them."

"I could do it." I gave a halfhearted smile. "Gregory already doesn't like me, so why not just give him some more reasons to hate me?"

"That's just Gregory. He hates everyone."

"Elyria, you don't have to say anything. One look and they'll know. There's nothing more *to* say. You don't need a eulogy you just need to give people the space they need to grieve."

She nodded her head in confirmation but said nothing.

Grieve. I could see her struggling with the word. I took a step forward, reaching out my hand to her. But she took a step back, shaking her head no. She was just barely holding it together. I flexed my fingers, resisting the instinct to pull her back into my arms. The need to soothe her flooded through me. Seeing her in this pain, it felt like that knife slicing my heart back open. But if what she required was space, then I'd give it to her. If what she needed was to feel like she was strong enough to handle this on her own, then I'd give her that, too. I'd give her whatever she asked for, because that was all I could do in this moment.

She heaved a heavy sigh and turned to brace the door.

"You can do this, Elyria" she said to herself.

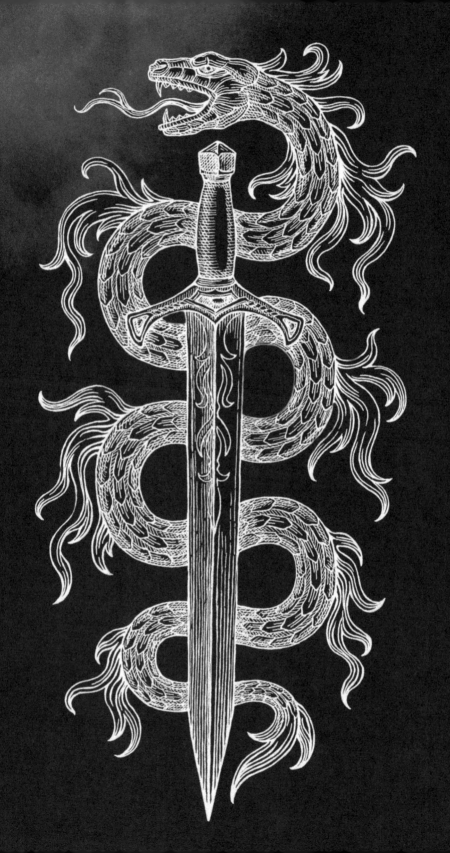

17

ELYRIA

What happened next went by in a blur. I remembered walking out of the wagon, and Cal had been right. I didn't actually have to say anything. Gregory was the only one awake, and he took one look at me and knew. He came up and, leaning on his cane, wrapped an arm around me. I was ushered to the fire. The familiar crackle tried to soothe me, but lost to the oblivion of grief, I never felt its warmth.

Hours passed. It could have been the entire day, two days, maybe three? I disappeared into my spiraling thoughts, processing everything I'd been told the night before. The draken, Duke finding me, the Gold Dragon. It was a lot of information to sift through, and always looming in the back of my mind was that little boy's too deep, velvet voice.

The next thing I knew, a steaming mug of tea was in front of me.

I looked up, and to my surprise, it was Xoc. His great, hulking size cast a shadow on me in the moonlight, but even in shadow, his emerald eyes shone bright with sympathy.

"I brewed it myself," he said, extending the cup to me. "It's my personal blend, from leaves of a couple of different strains of tea that I cross-pollinated. It helps with nerves and fatigue. I thought you might like it. I had to sweeten it with phosphor honey. I hope that's okay."

I took the mug from him. The honey gave the water a faint orange glow. Small tendrils of steam curled up, bringing with it the scent of mint, lavender, nilla, and the mountains in the morning when the dew was still fresh. I puzzled over that last smell, but it was the only way I could think of to describe the underlying earthy scent. I slurped a bit from the mug and smacked my lips in surprise. It was delicious.

I looked down at my hands, and for the first time since this nightmare began, the tremor in them subsided. The penetrating chill abated, and in its place, a feeling of ease lapped over my muscles. I took another sip, and a second wave of peace rolled through me.

Xoc dropped into the seat beside mine, and we sipped our tea in silence, slurping in tandem. By the time I finished my mug, I felt more alert and in control of my emotions. The sadness was still there, but it wasn't in charge of me anymore or making my thoughts scatter at random.

"This stuff actually did the trick," I said, draining the last drops from the cup. "Thank you."

"I don't always break it out. It's pretty powerful stuff. But when the moment presents itself, I have found it to be most useful." He paused, flashing an impertinent grin at me. "One time Cal and I were in an all-night chess match, and this tea gave me the perfect edge."

I raised an eyebrow. "Chess? Sorry, but I have a hard time seeing Cal sit for an all-night chess bender."

"Don't let him fool you. He's a brilliant strategist. Headstrong and impulsive, but also brilliant. He always knows better when he's leaping, he just leaps anyway—and somehow, it always seems to work out for him. It's impossibly frustrating sometimes."

"That sounds exactly right."

"We've played chess ever since we were kids."

"So you've known Cal a long time then."

He nodded his head slowly. When I'd first seen Xoc he'd seemed so out of place, like a warrior without a war. But now his emerald eyes were warm and, with his hair hanging untethered, his features no longer seemed so sharp. It was unexpected, but I was grateful for his company. I flicked my fingers and the fire crackled in time with me. Xoc smiled and leaned back in his chair.

"A *long* time. The things I could tell you."

"Tell me about Cal failing completely. I could use a reason to smile."

He chuckled darkly. "Well, we'd been playing this one game for ten hours straight."

"Gods, that *is* a long match."

"Indeed, but Cal is stubborn and refused to just call it. Somewhere around daybreak, I started noticing his concentration finally fading, so I brewed myself a tea. I'd been saving it for a night precisely like that one." He tapped a nail against the mug for emphasis. "I whipped his ass. He made a fatal mistake and ended up sacrificing his queen for it. After that, he didn't have a chance." Xoc looked over at me with an uncharacteristic smile, devilish and full of pride. "I still bring it up every time that cocky attitude of his gets us into trouble."

I chuckled a little and realized that my heart actually felt a little lighter, like surfacing after a deep dive.

"So, plants?" I asked.

"Mmm. Yes, plants," Xoc replied, back to his more stoic self.

"What was that trick you did with the seeds?" I said, remembering the remarkable— nope. *I would not think about it.*

"I'm a Seed Singer. It's a type of flora attunement. I can manipulate the plants around me, but I can only do it if it's there to begin with."

He reached out, and suddenly, that box with the packets was in his hand.

"That!" I said, feeling myself come to life. "Teach me that! I've done sleight of hand my whole life, but that's not what you're doing. Teach it to me. Where are you hiding all of these things?"

"Oh," he chuckled under his breath. "It's something that Master Rith taught me. The ancient Arapacian Warriors would use the fabric between time and space to store their trove of weapons. That way, no warrior could be disarmed. It was a science that has been forgotten by nearly all of my kin." He sat back, settling into his seat. "The legend is that Belhameth blessed Lord Aexoc with this gift, and others after he reached the top of Mt. Carin. Aexoc was the first leader of the Arapacians and Mt. Carin is believed to be the home of the gods."

He paused, reading me. I nodded in understanding and gestured for him to continue.

"Sorry. I wasn't sure how much you knew. The Oers aren't particularly known for being forthcoming and friendly. Pretty much the only time they leave the wood is to try and kill something."

"You left, and you're not currently trying to kill anything."

He shrugged. "Yet." A small smile tilted the side of his lips.

"Sorry, was that a joke?"

"I don't joke." His face was once more emotionless.

"No, it was. I see you, Xoc No Last Name. You can't fool me." I poked playfully at his chest. "There *is* a heart under all that burly muscle."

He gave me a playful push on the shoulder. It was hard enough I had to use every ounce of acrobatic skill to keep from falling out of my chair.

Giving him a wink, I said, "Don't worry, I won't tell anyone."

He ignored my comment entirely, resuming his story. "Anyway, the story goes, Aexoc climbed the sheer cliff face of the mountain for ten days and nights, never sleeping, eating or drinking."

"Ten days? Impossible," I said in disbelief.

"Ah, but Aexoc had faith," he affirmed with a nod.

"You can't eat faith."

Xoc swallowed down a chuckle, then shushed me. "When he reached the summit and gazed out upon the land, as far as he could see was rock and dirt. He prayed to Belhameth to save the land so that his people could thrive. Belhameth came to him as a great black cat and named Aexoc lord of all he could see. Then he blessed him with extraordinary gifts. The first being the ability to make the world around him grow so that he could breathe life into a barren world and provide sustenance to his people. Aexoc raised his hands and from the ground he sang the forest and the plants of the Oerwood into being. The magic hummed through his veins. The trees grew higher, and their roots ran deep into the ground, connecting the earth to the sky. Then, to give him the clarity and wisdom to lead, Belhameth gave Aexoc his eyes. With them he taught Aexoc how to see the fabric of the world around him and find peace within it."

"That's beautiful," I breathed.

"It's a legend, but I've always liked it," he added, nodding.

"Aexoc, is that who you were named for?"

"It is. Xoc is a fairly common derivative of it. In the Oerwood, a dozen boys of every generation are given the name. I suppose their parents are hoping to channel that ancient wisdom." He stood up before me. "To access the pocket, and to simplify it down, think of the place you want your hand to go before your body can begin the motion. You essentially have to move faster than your brain can process the information. Once you are moving faster than the synapses in your brain can fire, then you can retrieve all manner of things from that realm. Very few can master it. Even Cal could never manage it. You have to be able to slow your mind down and focus, and literally nothing about Cal is slow. He's all full steam ahead, all the time."

"Ha. Yeah, I'm starting to see that." I thought of the warmth of his touch, the comfort it had brought me to feel those strong arms supporting me. I shook the memory away. "Who's Master Rith?" I asked, changing the topic.

"I was sent to study with him as a boy. He was a master of the lost Arapacian arts. He was also a total bastard, a cruel and strict teacher down to his bones. But it was where I met Cal, so something good came from my time with him. We trained together as boys. His mother believed that he needed the guidance only Rith could give. And, to be honest, we both needed a little discipline. Actually, Cal needed the discipline. I was the one who needed guidance. Cal was just plain stubborn, and if there was a rule, he seemed determined to find a way to break it."

I laughed. It was easy to picture Cal as a boy trying to sweet-talk his way out of an unending string of mischief.

"Whereas I was an unwanted bastard who exhibited some unusual talents that led me into doing some ill-advised things. So I was given to Rith. My tribe decided I could be his problem. And honestly, I think it was as much a punishment for him as it was for me." Xoc sat back down, retrieving his mug and taking another sip.

I started nodding my head and then sprang up, facing him.

"So I slow my mind, and then speed my hands up." I clapped my hands together, rubbing them quickly, "And then, bingo-bango, I have my own mystical rucksack?"

"Something like that," he said, grinning and shaking his head.

"Don't laugh. I'm a quick study. I learned how to do a double barrel twist in an afternoon once. Pissed Della off. Apparently, it's hard or something. I wouldn't bring it up when she's around."

I hastily threw a glance over my shoulder to be sure she wasn't lingering anywhere, then refocused. I was about to make this magic rucksack my bitch.

I centered my weight over both feet, standing as still as I could. I closed my eyes and pictured a black hole in the air before me. Slowing my breaths down and marking them, I felt a calm settle into the muscles of my arms. I pictured the void, then sprang my arm forward with all the speed I could muster.

Nothing. My hand gripped only air.

I opened one eye, and looked at Xoc. Wincing, I said, "How'd I do?"

"You're overthinking it. Become the surrounding area. Connect with it. Feel the drops of moisture in the air, hear the blood passing through your veins, sense the fabric of the world around you—then reach. By the time you've thought about reaching, it's too late."

Right. One with the fabric of the world. Whatever the fuck that meant.

"Keep trying. Who knows, double twist, maybe you'll get it."

I opened both eyes and then narrowed them on him, pursing my lips. He only flicked his hand at me to try again.

I could do this.

Centering myself, I struck. Nothing. I reached out again. Nothing.

I kept at it for a quarter of an hour when Cal rejoined us.

"What are you doing?" he laughed. "You look like you're performing some terrible impression of the Koolabura's mating dance."

I kept my eyes closed. I would not let his asinine taunting break my concentra—

"Coo-aww. Brrrrrrk... Caaw."

I opened my eyes and Cal was mocking me, doing an inane dance and squawking like those stupid damn birds that woke me every morning for the past week.

I flicked the tiniest spark at him, lighting the edge of his pocket handkerchief on fire. Seriously, who wears a pocket handkerchief?

"Hey! My mother gave me that," he said, stamping the tiny flame out with his hands.

I laughed. Xoc laughed. Cal was not laughing. Which made me laugh even harder.

Cal's face turned red. Which only incited more laughter.

"Calm down, Dentross," I said between gasping breaths. "It's not like it was a gift from the Queen."

"Well, my mother has queenly taste," Cal said with mock hurt.

"I'm sure she does." I settled back into my concentration stance, then stopped and stood back up. "What have you been up to? I just realized you haven't been here with us. Do I need to be concerned about where you've been?"

"Oh, Gregory put me to work. He had me pulverizing some root. Said it was for the mash, whatever that is. Then I had to fetch some more kindling for the fire. I tried to explain that I was better at starting fires than building them, but he wasn't having any of it."

Cal turned to Xoc. "I told him that you'd round up some meat for dinner, and honestly, I think he was happy with the idea of getting you out of the camp."

I blankly looked at Xoc. I guess I wasn't surprised he was also a huntsman.

"We usually just buy meat at the market of whatever town we're in. Do you hunt? It'd be nice to have some fresh game for dinner. Although in that forest, who knows what you'd find? Some biolumia rabbits, and we'll all be glowing for a week," I said.

"I do a form of hunting," he said. "It's part of those unusual abilities I mentioned. I can communicate with the fauna around me. I can sense them, and then they offer themselves to me. As a way of perpetuating the cycle of life. I give thanks to the animal and honor its sacrifice."

Xoc said it so plainly, it took me a second to process what he was saying.

"Wait, you can talk to animals?" I was sure shock and confusion were plastered all over my face. "And control them? What, like all animals?"

"Yes, I was born with the ability to manipulate flora and fauna."

I blinked. Then blinked again. I'd never heard of such an attunement before.

"So... like, could you get those damn birds to stop squawking every moonrise?" I smiled.

And then we all laughed again.

"I'll see what I can do."

Xoc got up and disappeared into the dark black shadows that surrounded the glade.

Cal slipped into the seat he had vacated, picking up his discarded mug. "I'm going to sit down before Gregory sees fit to put me back to work. As if he doesn't have a half-dozen other lads to command around here. Jimmy and Geoff seem like the sort who get into trouble when they don't have something productive to do. Make *them* smash roots all day."

I sat back down next to him. "Oh, definitely. But Gregory is probably getting a kick out of bossing around someone of your... class." I waved at his fancy, probably too expensive shirt. It looked soft, and I had the strangest urge to run my hands up it. I shook my head. What the hell was wrong with me, thinking about that... now... with him? He tilted his head like he was trying to read my thoughts.

I bit the inside of my cheek hard to clear my mind before he knew exactly where it had strayed.

"Besides, mash is Gregory's specialty." I hesitated for a second, glancing over my shoulder to see who was in earshot. "It's what I'll miss most."

"What's that?" Cal sat forward, and everything about him paused, tensing at what I might say next.

"I've been thinking. Tonight we send off Duke, and then once things are settled here, I'm leaving." I studied his reaction, but he sat attentively listening and gave nothing away. "I just." I sighed, a long and painful groan. "I don't think the troupe has anything for me here without him. I love them, especially Gregory and the twins, but I can't stay here. They don't need me, not really. It was always Duke who needed me, not them. He was right when he said that once I knew the truth, I would want to know more. I need answers and I intend to find them."

He nodded, not wanting to interrupt me.

My soul darkened. I had replayed what happened in the bar a thousand times in my mind over the past few days. The words that boy sang rattled around and around, and the note. I was being warned. Someone wanted me to know that I had been found and they were coming for me. Duke was right to make me hide. I should have tried harder to keep my abilities a secret. He paid for it with his life, and I would have to live with that for the rest of mine. I steeled my heart against the pain, closing myself off against the slice and burn of loss.

"There was something about that spider," I continued. "It wasn't of this world. I could feel the pure malevolence in my bones..." My voice trailed off. I closed my eyes, seeing the tiny crystal body vanishing into wisps of smoke. "The note, the song, it was all a warning. I don't know if it's what I am that drew their attention or something from Duke's past. I'm going to figure it out. All of this, it's all tied together. It's all connected." Cal nodded in understanding.

"I'm not going to stay here pretending nothing happened while some un-known evil picks off the troupe one by one. I will die before I see another person I love cursed." The campfire flared brightly. "I'm going to find what and who was responsible, and they will answer for their crimes."

Sparks shot into the surrounding air.

Cal held my gaze, not so much as flinching from the waves of scalding heat pluming off of me. If anything, it was like the flare of power was drawing him into me.

"And when I do, I'm going to blaze a fire so hot it will scorch any trace of them from this life and the next." I narrowed my eyes, death laced behind every syllable. "Gods help anyone who had a part in this because I will find them."

Cal took a deep breath, and a cool breeze drifted over us. It soothed my heating skin like a loving caress. "And once you've avenged him, then what?"

"Then I'm going to find Aurus."

Cal raised an eyebrow in surprise.

"My whole life, I've wanted to know how I fit into the world. I can't remember a time when being this..." I waved an arc of flames in the air between us. "...didn't make me feel alone. And for the first time, I have somewhere to start. Aurus would know everything. What I am, who I am, maybe even who my parents were."

"Aurus?" he intoned, and then he smiled. "You want to find the Gold Dragon?"

"I mean, it can't be too hard to track down a dragon."

He leaned back in the chair, putting his hands behind his head. "You know where you need to go? Suman. To the library at the Sumendi University. It's the single largest collection of knowledge in the world. If it's ever been written about, it'll be there. You want answers about any of this; that's where they'll be."

"Now that's a great idea. Why didn't I think of that?" I rolled my eyes. "You forget I travel all the time, for my entire life. I've been everywhere, Cal. Senesterra." I glided my hands around us. "Desterra," I said, pointing east towards where I imagined the sea to be, and beyond it the eastern continent. "We go to Suman every year."

"Okay, so you already knew about the library," Cal said, leaning forward again.

"Obviously," I scoffed, ignoring his undeterred enthusiasm.

"So here's the thing." He looked positively thrilled, and I braced myself for the pitch I knew was coming. "Xoc and I are pretty much done here. In fact, before the other night, we had planned to go to the harbor and book a ship to Suman the next day. From there, we were going to sail home over the South Sea to Innesvale. I know some people at the university. Normally, access is restricted to the scholars. But I have a favor I can call in."

Of course he does.

"If you'd like, you can travel to Suman with us. It'd be safer than traveling alone, and..." His hand fell over mine, those amber-flecked eyes drawing me in. "Honestly, I don't want to leave you. I can still book that passage. I'll just get an extra cabin." He looked at me expectantly.

I don't want to leave you.

My ability to think came to a screeching halt, too preoccupied with the thumb brushing the back of my hand to even consider what he was offering.

When I didn't answer, he said, "...Or you can always share mine." When I still didn't say anything, Cal obscenely waggled his eyebrows, forcing a giggle from me at how absurd he looked.

"Don't be perverse." I smiled back at him, but even in that joking moment, I could feel the blood rise to my cheeks. I chucked the rising emotion off with a laugh and hit him with my own flirty eyes. "I'm not going to sail to Suman."

"But you just said you were planning on going to the Sumendi Library," he said, sitting back and sipping from Xoc's mug. I flexed my fingers, the absence of his palm feeling like a cold void.

"And I am. I'm going to take The Steps," I said matter-of-factly.

Cal choked on his tea, spluttering it out.

"Look, I'm not going to waste weeks sailing around The Horn. Not when I can simply cross the continent on foot. I could be in The Bullseye in a week, maybe less. Plus, I've always wanted to climb The Steps. Duke would never let us. He said it was too hard to get the rigging through there."

"Elyria, there's a reason people sail around The Horn." Cal grimaced. "The Steps are—"

"Well, I'm not sailing, and I'm not stupid enough to take the Bone Road," I interjected. "Besides, they're just steps." I ignored Cal's eye roll. "So, you can come with me or go your own way. But I'm not spending weeks trapped on a boat with only you two for company," I said, gesturing between him and the woods where Xoc had disappeared.

"You're serious?"

I nodded, a viscous smile already tugging at the corners of my mouth.

"What about bandits?"

"Don't worry. I'll protect you."

Cal ran a hand through his hair, letting out a long sigh, and I knew I'd won.

"There are dangers worse than bandits," Xoc said, emerging out of the darkness, a magnificent stag over his shoulder.

I scoffed at him. "Yeah, like me."

He gave me a chastising look and thumped the deer onto the table behind me. The beast had a white streak running down its back and two white dots that, in this light, made it look like a menacing muzzle. In the darkness, this would be terrifying to come upon.

"I can take care of myself."

"Sure, until you can't." The look he gave me was entirely too patronizing.

"I could take you down in less than three moves."

"Oh, please do it," Cal bit out, before breaking into laughter.

Winking at him, I hopped up and sank back into a fighting stance. "Come on, big guy."

Xoc shook his head. "I'm not fighting you."

"Fine, don't fight back." I made a quick move at him, slipping my foot behind his and latching onto his elbow and wrist. With my second move, I pulled, tipping my shoulder into his side. At the same time, I swept his foot out from under him.

I spun, prepared to shift his weight and flip him onto the ground. The elation of victory already surged, and I whooped in triumph. There was nothing I loved more than putting a brute on their ass and seeing the shock when they realized a woman was the one handing it to them.

My perfect spin flip was immediately interrupted. Two big hands gripped my waist and lifted me into the air. My feet cycled beneath me, my brain too slow to process that they weren't on the ground any longer. Xoc held me aloft in front of him like I was an errant child.

"That was adorable."

I kicked wildly in the air and scowled at him. *Fuck.*

With a chuckle, he sat me back down on my seat. I straightened out my rumpled shirt and did my best to regain my dignity.

"Well, I'm going, with or without you," I said defiantly.

"We're going," Cal said firmly. "I'm not letting you travel the damn Steps alone. When do you plan on letting them know?"

I shrank a bit and peered over my shoulder to Gregory at the kitchen. A guilty ache burned deep in my chest. But I knew this was the right choice.

They'd be fine without me.

"I'll tell them in the morning, over mash."

18

ELYRIA

Cal spent the day within arms reach at all times. His regular warmth and dark scent seemed to soothe the edge on my nerves. Something about the way he was always assessing the world around us made me feel safer, and the way his eyes were always warm when they met mine brought me comfort. But, despite his best efforts to distract me, my eyes still burned, my hands shook, and I felt like I was constantly trying to decide if I wanted to cry or scream. The one thing that kept me going was the knowledge that, in the morning, I would begin tracking down the son of a bitch responsible for this screaming in my head and the pain on the faces of everyone around me.

That night, the troupe gathered at the farthest edge of the forest where a giant pyre had been set up. We hadn't wanted to make the fire too close to the camp for fear of a spark floating to one of the tents. My emotional state being what it was, there was no telling if I could put such a fire out—or if I would help it spread.

So we found a small clearing at the edge of the forest, and it seemed like as good a place as any to hold the passing. Somehow Amos and Sheila had heard. Maybe Gregory had sent someone out to tell them. Sheila made a cartload of food and set up a sizable feast for after everything was done.

When the time came, Adolphus carried Duke's body out and ceremoniously laid him down atop the mass of branches and sticks. I shuddered when I saw his limp black hand fall to the side. I tried to push all the heartache down, tried to imagine this was any fire on any night. The fire was mine. It bent to my command. It did not control me or how I felt.

I walked up to the pyre and gently placed Duke's hand back over his heart. A tear slipped from my eye, and I didn't bother to wipe it away. It splashed on our still joined hands.

A tiny glint of gold shimmered from near his neck. I reached into his collar and pulled out a thin chain. I slipped it over his head. The two golden rings threaded on it jingled lightly. One was thicker, with an intricate lacing running around it. The second ring was thin and delicate, with a single shallow garnet set into the band. It glowed red in the moonlight. I knew both rings bore the inscription *In this life and the next.* When I was little, I would play with them anytime I sat on his lap. As much as I tried not to get swept up by the memory, I couldn't fend off the images flooding my mind.

"I like your rings," I said, *slipping the smaller one over my tiny finger, admiring it. "Can I have a ring like this someday?"*

Duke smiled down at me. "Ellie, my love, I hope you find someone who matches your spark. Someone worthy of you." He kissed the top of my head and tucked the necklace back under his shirt.

Blinking away the memory, I took the chain and placed it over my head. He had borne the weight of her loss for so long, and now I would have to bear the weight of his. I clutched the rings tightly and whispered, "I hope you're with Lila now."

I kissed the top of his head, just as he had to me countless times. Most of the troupe didn't know about Lilandra, Duke's wife. He rarely spoke of her and when he did it was usually just with me or Gregory.

I faced the group. A knot lodged in my throat and I swallowed it away. Breathing steadily, I forced stability into my voice. "Duke would have either wanted a King's wake—ladies weeping, throwing themselves over him and declaring they would never love another—or he'd tell us not to waste our time in mourning and to just get on with it. So I'm not going to prolong this moment more than is needed. Duke told me once that family aren't the people you choose but the people who choose you. I never really understood that statement, but I do now. I loved him as a father, and that made him my father. He loved me as a daughter, and that made me his daughter."

A tear rolled down my cheek, and I hastily brushed it away. Cal's eyes met mine from the back of the gathered crowd. *You can do this,* they seemed to say.

"Blood has nothing to do with it. In the end, it is the love that connects us." I looked at Gregory. "Duke taught me to master my flame. He taught me not to fear that which can hurt you but to embrace it. Duke left this world not fearing what would come next but celebrating that which he was leaving behind. So I hope that Duke's spirit passes on to whatever lies beyond, and that when he gets there, he is greeted by the adoring masses."

I turned around and bowed my head. Then, to my surprise, a soft, quiet voice began to sing. It was Macie. Her lilting soprano, that was usually full of such life and energy, sang a low and slow elegy. She was singing in Ciqan, the language of her nomadic ancestors, a language she and her family rarely spoke. It was savage and sweet, painful and loving, and it captured every part of how my heart felt in this moment.

I hung my head and summoned a ball of flame into my hand. I should have thrown it, but I couldn't move. My fingers trembled, and I thought my chest might crack open.

Warmth wrapped around my other hand in a tight and loving grip. Gregory's. One by one, the troupe joined hands until we were standing together. I looked at my family, and I couldn't stop the tears from flowing in a steady, silent stream.

Gregory's old eyes flickered in the firelight. He nodded his head and gave my hand a squeeze.

Together, then.

I closed my eyes and threw the fireball onto the pyre. It ignited quickly. My heart raced, and despite the heat of the flames, a chill ran up my spine.

Still, Macie sang that sweet and haunting lament. I reached out my mind and latched hold of the flame. I drove my emotion into it, pouring every ounce of sadness, every flicker of fear, every piece of anger in my heart into that pyre. The blaze roared so high that the flames licked past the tops of the surrounding trees and so bright that momentarily the neverending night shrank away. It burned and burned, devouring everything within it. Heat rolled off the fire, and the troupe pulled back from it. But I remained. I wanted to feel it all. I don't know how long I stood at one with this terrible flame. Eventually, I lowered my hand. The flames lowered with it into a slow and steady roar. In them, I couldn't see Duke anymore. The fire had consumed him.

It was over.

Done.

He was gone.

Gone on to whatever came next.

Gregory squeezed my hand again. He croaked, "You did good, kid."

Whether he was speaking to me or to Duke, I didn't know. I culled the flames back to embers and willed the fire to go out. The group that had gathered walked back to camp, but I couldn't make my feet move.

Breathe.

I had to remember how to breathe. It was like my body wasn't mine anymore, and though I told my feet to move, I couldn't find the will within myself to move them.

The crackle and hiss of the wood was the only sound I could hear. I could still feel the heat on my face. The smoke wafted, thick and twisting in the air. These bits of charcoal were all that was left of the inferno. They were all that was left of the man whose hug I could still feel around me. I closed my eyes and listened to the creak and chip of the wood as it cooled. It was over. My body suddenly felt so cold, and a resonating tremor snaked down my spine.

Cal approached quietly and wrapped a muscular arm around my shoulder. Heat radiated from his touch down into my bones. His solidity and warmth braced me, and I surrendered myself to it.

A light breeze came from behind us, bringing with it the smell of the wild-flowers in the field. It pushed away the suffocating smoke, leaving only a faint lingering memory behind.

"Do you want me to extinguish it completely? I can smother it," he said softly.

"Not yet," I whispered. He tightened his arms around me, and his thumb rocked a soothing stroke over the exposed skin on my arm. We stood there, him holding me up and the wood crackling as it fell apart.

When the embers had finally gone silent, I said, "Okay, I'm ready."

Cal took his hand from my shoulder and began twisting it. The gentle breeze pulled flowers from the field, and a stream of them surrounded the ashes. The glow of the embers died, replaced by luminescent blooms in a rainbow of colors. The air around the coals kicked up and began to spin until a small cyclone of ash took to the air.

My mouth dropped open in surprise as the mix of ash and flowers twirled. It soared near the edge of the forest to where Xoc waited, kneeling before a small hole in the ground. I hadn't even noticed he was there until now.

The ash-flower cyclone sank into the hole and was quickly covered with the freshly dug earth.

Cal pressed his lips to my temple and whispered, "Come with me."

I looked into his warm eyes and at the hand he held extended to me. I fell into that gaze, and the ache at the center of my chest abated. In its place, a sense of safety filled me, and for the first time today, it felt like I could breathe.

Cal laced his fingers through mine and led me to the small earthen mound.

Over the grave, Xoc curled his hand into a fist. A small green bud emerged from the ground.

I held my breath. My grip on Cal's hand grew firmer.

Xoc pulled and pulled. A beautiful Lunar Willow formed before my eyes. Within minutes the tree stretched, reaching out its arms and drooping beautiful boughs. They swayed gently back and forth. It made the tree look like it was breathing.

Tiny buds formed on each slender branch, and when they opened, they glowed a beautiful deep green. Xoc raised his other hand, and brown ropey vines wove their way through the branches. Each responded to him as if he was conducting a great orchestra, and in place of the symphony were vines of rich purple blooms springing open.

A velvety scent filled the air. I instantly thought of Duke pointing them out to me as we walked down the street. Night Blooming Wisteria grew on the trellises that spanned each walkway in Laluna. They were beautiful and one of Duke's favorite parts of the city. He had said that they brought beauty and light to an otherwise dark night. I could have sworn I heard his voice in the whispering of the branches. As if he was saying to me, "Aw, Ellie, I love these flowers." Miraculously, from the sadness of the moment had grown this beautiful and amazing tree.

I walked into the canopy. Purple flowers and swaying branches caressed my cheeks and shoulders as I passed through them. A delicate glow from the tree filled the interior space, beating back the dark. It was quiet, peaceful, and perfect– a refuge from the grief that clawed at my heart.

"Duke would have loved this," I breathed and looked up at Cal. His features were lined with sympathy and something stronger, deeper. Cal gently ran his thumb over the back of my hand. The feeling sent out a warm pulse that rolled up my arm.

I slipped my hand from his, watching as his fingers slid past mine. I wanted to do this next part on my own. I needed to.

Kneeling beside the trunk, I placed my fingertips to my lips, and then transferred them to the tree. One last goodbye. Beneath my hand, the trunk felt solid. I listened to the rustle of the leaves as they swayed in the wind and smiled. I could feel him with us. His spirit was in the glowing light, in the flower perfumed wind, and in the whisper of the leaves.

"Goodnight, Duke," I whispered back.

I walked through the branches, letting them trail through my fingers as I passed in one last, loving embrace.

Xoc was waiting respectfully back in the glade. I gave him a giant hug around the middle. He seemed like he didn't know what to do with his arms, and rather than hug me back, they just hovered over me.

"Thank you," I said, wiping away tears that dropped from the corners of my eyes. "Thank you. It's perfect."

"It was Cal's idea," he said, and I looked back at Cal, who was emerging from under the tree, hands in his pockets. He shrugged, trying to look nonchalant, but I caught something else in the way he looked at me. Like so much of him, there was something he wasn't saying.

We started a slow stroll back to the camp.

I turned for one last look and took in the tree's majesty. It was perfect.

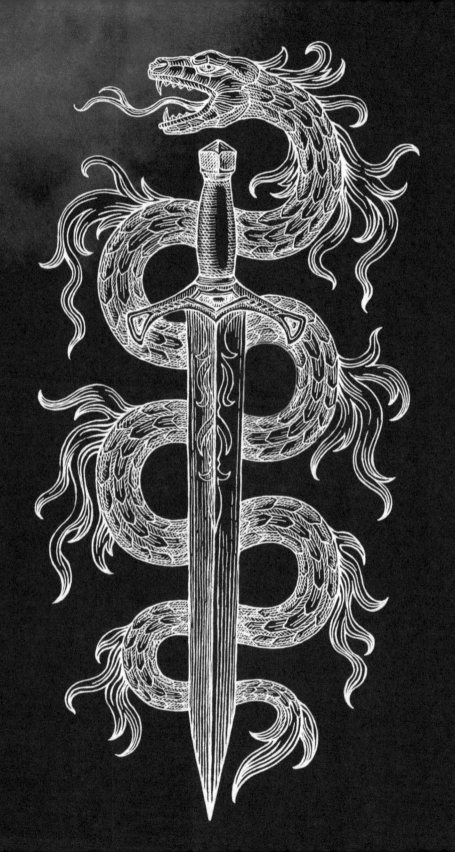

ELYRIA

I sat down across the table from Gregory. He held a flask in his hand, and I tried to remember the last time I saw him with a drink. Unusual circumstances, I supposed.

He scowled at my near empty plate. "I didn't spend all day cooking just for you to sit there with an empty plate," he said, poking at me with a fork.

I poked him back. "You didn't spend all day cooking. Most of this came from Sheila. All you did was put some meat on a spit and tell the boys to keep it turning. Then you sat back on that bony ass and hit them with your cane whenever they stopped."

"Not true. I also seasoned the meat." Gregory slid his full plate in front of me, knocking my empty one to the side. My stomach turned at the thought of so much food.

"Go on, tuck in, girl. You don't honor his memory by starving yourself."

"Fair," I groaned. "That's fair." I sliced my knife into the venison and it slid into the meat with zero resistance. Of course it was roasted to perfection, with a thick crust of herbs lining the edges. Gregory smirked, knowing that I couldn't help but appreciate the mastery on the end of my fork. His eyes twinkled as he watched me take a couple of bites then he sat back, seemingly satisfied.

Around me, the troupe had popped open all that remained of Duke's wine stores. Pink-faced, they laughed and traded stories of the years– First meetings and unexpected moments of hilarity. I listened and took each moment with his long lashes sparkle with the golden gems he'd attached to the ends. How Jimmy would stick his tongue between his teeth in concentration as he tried to discreetly stick things in Macie's curls, and how her cheeks burned bright red with anger when she discovered what he was doing. I loved them, and this was exactly how I wanted to remember my family.

My favorite story of the evening was easily one that Geoff shared. About a year ago, Duke helped get him off the second-story window ledge of a merchant's home in The Bullseye. When the husband of the woman he was bedding came home, Geoff snuck onto the ledge to avoid detection. But Geoff stupidly left all of his clothes in the bedroom. When the husband saw the trousers and shirt on the floor, and didn't find the man they belonged to in the room, he had easily located him on the ledge and locked him out. "How was I supposed to know she was married?" he'd protested defensively. Apparently, Duke's rescue had required a cart of fertilizer. "Don't worry, it will be a soft landing," he had promised.

"Oi, is that why you smelled of shit for a week?" Jimmy asked.

Geoff added with a laugh, "Which time?"

Amid the chatter and laughter, Gregory leaned forward and said to me in a low voice, "When are you leaving?"

I went completely still. How did he know? Feeling a pang of betrayal, I glanced down the table to where Cal and Xoc were refilling their glasses.

He snapped his fingers in front of my face, drawing my attention back to him. "Girl, I have known you your whole life. I don't need some lad to tell me what you're about to do. And you've been watching everyone here like you's painting a picture. I know that look. It's what someone looks like when they won't see this sight again."

"In the morning," I said sheepishly. "There's business that needs to be handled before I can go, but then, I'm leaving."

"Good," he said matter-of-factly.

"Good? You want me to go?" I asked, a bit hurt.

"No, nothing like that. You know I love you. But it's time you found yourself, and you weren't never gonna do that staying here with us. When you're with us, you act how you're expected to act. You're the person you're expected to be. I don't think someone becomes the person they are meant to be until the moment independence is thrust upon them." He held my gaze. "This is your moment, Elyria. Go find out who you are. Become the person *you* want to be and not who *we* need you to be."

I nodded, understanding everything he was saying. I think. I couldn't remember being anything other than The Golden Dragon. Without the troupe, who was I? What would I choose if I could be anything?

An angel of vengeance didn't sound like a bad place to start.

Gregory nodded his head towards Cal and Xoc. "And I still have me reservations about them boys. But they did right by us these past few days. I won't be forgettin' that anytime soon. You just take care while you're travelin' with 'em."

"What about the troupe?"

"This troupe was around before ye, and it ain't going nowhere now that you're leaving."

I looked down the table. Jess was drinking from a tall flute, the rim stained with a bright pink lip tint. His arm was wrapped around Macie, and together they were swaying to some imaginary music.

"I don't know how I'll tell them."

"You don't have to. They'll understand."

I looked over to where Della sat, cradling her puppy. She was feeding him some vanilla mousse from the end of her fork and making little kissy faces at him. She really needed to find herself someone to give all that attention to that didn't have four legs.

"Della will be happy to be the headliner again," I remarked, sadness tinging my words. "I don't think I could ever perform again, anyway."

He nodded in understanding. "Maybe. Pain is an interesting bedfellow. You may find, in time, you've learned to accept it. When that day comes, you may want to take the stage again."

"Maybe," I said, unconvinced.

I pushed my plate away from me, having eaten not nearly enough. Gregory glowered, and I shooed his expression away with a flick of my hand. If I was old enough to find myself, then I was damn well old enough to manage my own eating habits.

Resolve washed over me. Gregory's blessing felt like everything holding me back had just blown away on the cool evening breeze. My mind was made up, and now I was almost eager to go.

I walked straight to where Cal was talking with a few of the boys. I didn't know what they were talking about, or care. He stopped mid-sentence and looked at me, a smile quirking up at the edge of his lips. Could he tell, just by looking at me, what I was about to say?

"Moonrise. If you're really in, then we're leaving at moonrise," I said with newfound determination in my voice.

"Are you sure?" He placed a gentle, caressing hand on my shoulder. His eyes softened with tenderness. "So soon?"

Next to him, Jimmy's jaw dropped.

"You're leaving?" he said a bit too loudly.

A hush instantly fell over the group. Guess I didn't have to worry about how I was going to tell everyone after all.

Macie stood up, her curls bounced, her stricken face full of hurt. I looked from her to Violet, seeing pained betrayal there too.

"You'll be okay," I said. "We're all going to be okay. But I can't stay here. I just can't," I revealed, pleading with my eyes for them to understand.

I turned to Albert, the oldest of the Crenshaws. "Albert, I'm leaving the troupe to you. You started Troupe Solaire with Duke. It only seems right to leave it to you. When I get to The Bullseye, I will transfer the accounts into your name."

He nodded in acceptance and ran a hand through his salt and pepper hair. It was as if he had been expecting this to happen.

Cal slid his hand to my lower back. It was warm and reassuring, giving me the strength to continue. He always seemed to know when I needed encouragement. Was that instinctual, or was my insecurity really that obvious?

"You all are my family. This isn't goodbye forever." I looked at Macie. Kohl tinged tears were now streaming down her cheeks. "There is something I need to do, answers that I need to find. And I won't find them here."

"We understand, Elle," Jess' sweet voice said. "You go find whatever you need. We will always be here for you, sweetie." He wiped a tear from his sapphire-painted eyes. "When you're ready."

Geoff reached past Jimmy and pulled back on Cal's shoulder. "Watch out for her. She's like the little sister I never had."

A roll went flying through the air, smacking Geoff in the head. Violet stood up. "You have two sisters, you brainless string bean!"

Everyone laughed.

Cal grinned and said with a wink, "I'm hoping she'll look after me. Have you met her?"

That was all it took to break the tension. Everyone went back to the feast.

I looked up at Cal. "Moonrise. I'm going to get some rest. Meet me at the trailhead, unless you decide to chicken out."

I patted him on the shoulder and turned before he could have a chance to hit me with some charming comment. I didn't need to know he was coming. He'd be there. And I tilted my head, realizing that I'd be disappointed if he wasn't. I wasn't sure what to make of that.

I stepped away from the feast and suddenly felt drained, as if the tide of exhaustion had been held back this entire time.

Macie ran up behind me and wrapped her arms tight around my middle. I folded my arm around her and we walked like that back to the wagon. When we got in, she flung herself down on my bed. I pulled out my pack and started shoving random articles of clothing into it.

"So you're going with Cal?" she asked inquisitively.

"For a little while, yeah," I answered. "Just until we get to Suman, then he's going back to Innesvale."

She clapped her hands together in a little cheer and fell back onto my pillow. "What do you think he kisses like?" she said dreamily.

"I imagine he does it with his mouth like the rest of us." I threw a shirt at her face.

She pulled it down and cradled it in her arms, then turned to look at me. "He's sweet on you. He has to be with the way he's looked after everyone around here these past couple of days. Why else would he stick around?"

"Why else?" I said in mock agreement. That was the real question, wasn't it?

Pulling out my sheaths, I loaded them with my knives, checking each to be sure they were still sharp. I laid the holsters over the edge of the sack and looked at her.

"You're really going?" she said sadly.

"Yep. But hey." I pointed to my drawers. "You can have anything I leave behind."

She brightened. "Even your frocks?" I nodded, and she jumped up, hugging me. "Gods, I'm really going to miss you, Elle."

"Me too, Mace."

We climbed into our respective beds. Macie started rambling on about day-dreams of all the things Cal would do on our adventure. It was fun to dream along with her but with each passing breath exhaustion filled my bones. Before I knew it, I had let it take me into a deep and fitful sleep.

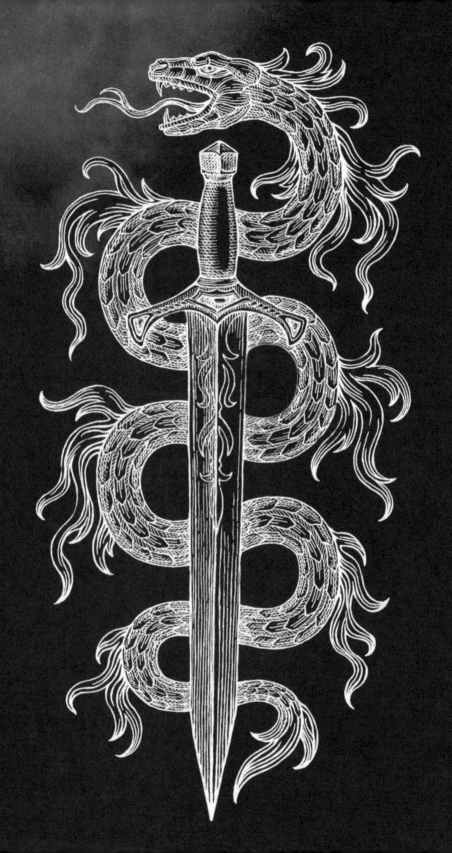

20

ELYRIA

The trailhead seemed extra dark. It was a day's hike to the base of The Steps. I knew I should start walking. It was silly to linger here, just staring at the disappearing path. But the moment I did, my old life would be done. Whatever lay at the end of this path, it wasn't a life like the one I was leaving behind. It was exciting, and I wanted to go. But letting go of that stage of my life was letting go of everything that came with it—letting go of Duke.

My heart rate sped up. A creeping panic seized me, forming a hard lump in my throat.

Breathe, Elyria. Breathe.

Why was breathing suddenly so hard? What was I thinking? My whole life had been that troupe. What would they do without me? How would I manage—

My self-deprecating spiral was interrupted by the goading sound of Cal's voice. "Changing your mind? Rethinking that insane idea to climb The Steps, because I would *not* be disappointed. In fact, I'm sure there's a ship all ready to sail right now. Sailing literally anywhere would be better than climbing those millions of stairs."

Cal stopped beside me, an amused smile plastered on his annoyingly handsome face and a pack slung dashingly over one shoulder. That rakish charm wasn't going to get him a pass to start running his mouth off. I leveled my gaze

"Don't project your fears onto me. Just because *you're* scared of the climb doesn't mean I'm about to take the long way around," I said in a flat, even tone.

Xoc strode past us, an enormous pack strapped over his hulking shoulders. He didn't so much as glance at me. We watched as he was enveloped by the darkness. The shadow of the forest seemed to swallow him whole.

Cal turned and held out his hand. "Coming?"

His smile was gentle and coaxing. The kindness of the past few days lined each of his features, softening them. I fingered the rings hanging from the chain at my neck. I took a long inhale and held it, focusing on each beat of my heart until the whooshing sound in my ears abated. Then I smacked his outstretched hand away.

"I'm not a child. I don't need you to hold my hand." I strode forward, one purposeful step after another.

"I have other more adult things you can hold," Cal said, and even from behind me, I could hear the coy smile beneath his words.

Up ahead, Xoc muttered, "Gods save me."

I didn't bother turning around. I just held up my hand, giving him a perfect view of my favorite finger. Cal laughed and jogged up to my side.

With slow steps, we entered the fold. Slowly, my eyes adjusted to the denser and more complete darkness. Unlike the glade, here the moonlight couldn't penetrate the canopy. But as my eyes grew accustomed, I noticed that the forest was actually teeming with life, all of it glowing. Green mushrooms spiraled their way up the trunks of the soaring trees. Growing in bunches at the base of each towering pine were tall plants. Their black leaves fluoresced yellow, fading into a rich purple color. Thick black veining split each leaf into sections. I had never seen anything like them before. They reminded me of the stained glass windows at the Basilica of Commerce.

The ferns that had lined the glade were even thicker in the forest. They dominated the space between trees in a hostile takeover of ground cover. While we walked, I held my hand out and let it caress the top of each plant. One by one, the tiny leaves of the fern gently curled in, the yellow ball of light at the ends extinguishing with each touch.

Xoc, noticing my curiosity, explained, "We have ferns like these at home, just not the glowing kind. They're very sensitive. It doesn't hurt to touch them, but don't do too many, or we won't be able to see the path anymore."

Above us, millions of Lumus Glow Worms clung to the branches of the trees. They glittered in the canopy like stars in the sky. I paused, marveling at their beauty. It was a shimmering galaxy, each tiny light winking on and off. Hanging down from the worms were several long and sticky threads. Tiny globules clung to each strand and glittered like faint blue diamonds. I thought of Jess and the way he lusted after the Lumus Glow Worm silk. Now I understood why the material was so coveted. It must take ages to gather enough of the thread to form even a single spool.

Up ahead, a bright green strand hung above the path. It stood out amid the sea of blue and draped just low enough that it might have been within arms reach. I stretched onto my tiptoes, extending my hand toward the glowing silk when Xoc snapped out and grabbed my wrist.

"Don't do that. The green ones are predatory." He loosened his grip on my hand. "Their bite can penetrate down to the bone."

"Oh," I said, recoiling and moving over so that I was no longer under it. I squinted into the mass of hanging silk. At the top of the strand, a green worm was eating an unlucky purple moth. "Ghastly."

"Besides, it'd just make your hands sticky, and it's damn near impossible to get that off."

We continued down the path quietly, listening to the symphony of frogs croaking and the hum of insects. We took turns leading on the trail. Usually, it was too narrow to walk side by side, despite Cal's best efforts, so we walked in a line. When Xoc was in the lead, our pace was strong and steady. It didn't take long for me to lose my line-leading privileges. The boys quickly became annoyed by my frequent stopping. I'd never been allowed to venture into the forest before, and every bend proved to show some new wonder.

At one point, a frog leapt onto the path before us. I skidded to a stop, and Cal crashed into the back of me. His hands gripped my hips to keep from knocking us both to the ground.

"A little warning would be nice."

"I didn't think you'd need a warning, what with the way you keep staring at my ass."

"Trust me, in those pants, I'm plenty distracted." He craned his head over my shoulder to see what had caused me to abruptly halt. "Did we really just stop for a frog?"

The frog's skin was thin and nearly clear. Its entire vascular system was on display, even in the dim light of the ferns. The small creature croaked loudly. His neck expanded and its entire body lit up.

"Marvelous," I whispered, bending over at the waist to get a closer look.

Next to me, Cal did a quick inhale. I glanced over my shoulder to shoot him a scathing remark but was caught unprepared for the way he was looking at me.

Cal was biting the knuckle of a tightly balled fist, every ounce of his restraint wrapped up in those fingers. Dark eyes slid along the curves of my body.

"Oh, it is," he replied coolly.

Knowing I was looking at him, he flashed those white teeth and bent down to the frog, as if that was what he was fascinated with the entire time. *And just like that, the spell was broken.* Rather than going with my first instinct, driving my dagger into something soft and fleshy, I chose to ignore him.

I scanned the forest floor for more of the frogs. Their singing was loud, so I knew they had to be hiding in the darkness. Sure enough, now and again, a small area of underbrush glowed in alternating fashion. The frog before us pulsed at regular intervals in response to the call from his kind.

Brought in by the light of the frog, a giant purple dragonfly, nearly half the size of my hand, zoomed in low. Its large wings shimmered as it hovered near Cal's head. He turned to look at the bug, eyes wide as it flew past him. The frog's long pink tongue snapped out and snatched the dragonfly from the air.

A crunching sound came from the frog as it chewed the insect. I scrunched my nose and Cal scrambled backwards to give the frog some space.

I did my best to stifle the laugh that bubbled up. "I can't decide. Was it the dragonfly or the frog that made you jump?"

"I didn't jump."

I snorted and rolled my eyes, "Sure you didn't."

"Shoo," Xoc said, coming up behind us.

At first, I thought he was talking to me and was ready to snap at him. Then I noticed he was gesturing to the frog. He waved his hand, and the surrounding frog song instantly silenced. Shock etched its way across my face. Everything but the plants had gone dark. He moved his hand and the frog followed it off the path. Xoc didn't acknowledge my open mouth and wide eyes, only motioned for us to continue walking.

"Maybe I should lead from now on," Cal said in a gratingly arrogant way.

"Does that neat little trick work on him too?" I said, pointing to Cal.

"I wish, don't think I haven't tried," Xoc said.

"You love it, don't pretend otherwise. If it wasn't for my lovely conversation skills, this hike would be nothing but brooding silence," he said with an infuriating wink.

"I don't brood," I said, gritting my teeth.

Cal chuckled, "Sure you don't."

Blood rose in my veins, and light flames danced across my fingertips.

Xoc looked at the canopy and muttered under his breath, "Did I do something horrific in my last life? Is that why I'm being punished?" He took a quick glance at the map before replacing it in his pocket and pushing past us. "It's only about a half-mile until we reach the stream. If we follow the riverbed, it should lead us right to the cliff's edge. That is if you two can manage to keep it in your pants."

"Funnily enough, that's not actually an issue here."

I could have sworn I heard Cal breathe out, "*Yet.*" But when I glanced at him, it was like he wasn't even paying attention. Instead, he was pushing purple thumbprints into a large leaf he'd picked up, seemingly oblivious to anything that had just been said.

I bent over and plucked a bulbous, blue, glowing orb from a stem growing along the side of the path. Each stalk of the unique plant held half a dozen fruits the size of a small orange. The plants were scattered everywhere, gleaming a chaotic variety of colors. I gave the waxy ball a gentle squeeze. Its membrane flexed, but it felt solid. I gave it a little shake, and juice sloshed around inside. Confident they weren't about to break open, I picked up two more and began juggling them while I walked.

Cal glanced over his shoulder and gave a little laugh. "Don't miss. You'll be covered in glowber berry juice."

"Oh, will I? Who says I ever miss?"

"Okay, but don't blame me when you're covered head to foot in glowing sludge."

He made a quick lunge, trying to knock me off balance.

But I simply maneuvered, my cadence never thrown off. I smiled triumphantly, sticking out my tongue at him. "Careful, Dentross, don't start something you can't win," I chided back, laughing.

He smiled widely at the challenge, his eyes dipping beneath his lashes.

I sped up my rotation, the orbs now a blur of blue and green before me.

Cal picked up his pace and prowled closer. "Who says I'd lose?"

"I do," called Xoc from up ahead.

I cackled out a laugh. "See?"

I did a double throw with the berries, adding in a backhanded catch for emphasis. There was no way he could best me when it came to throwing anything.

"You're lucky. I'm feeling gentlemanly today, so you don't have to learn the bitter taste of defeat," he said with a snide grin and dismissively turned away– actually turned his godsdamn back on me.

"Is that so?" I chucked the first blue ball straight at the back of his head, maintaining the other two in my left hand.

It made a satisfying *thwack*, cracking open and splattering droplets of blue everywhere. Blue ooze spluttered out, painting the back of his head and sliding down his neck. To be honest, the mess was far greater than I expected, and it was glorious.

I couldn't stop the grinning and bit my lip to keep from laughing.

He stopped dead and took a slow turn toward me. Blue streaked in a long splatter across his cheeks. His stare was fierce, and in the low light, his brown eyes seemed to glow amber. He was pissed and shocked. But mostly pissed.

And I lost it. I folded over, laughing, cradling the two remaining berries in my arms. I couldn't stop myself. I croaked out between heaves, "I. Told. You. I. Don't Miss."

A devilish grin crested Cal's lips. In a steady, deep voice, he said, "Oh, Elle, you have no idea of the hell you are in for."

I laughed harder. He was so serious. What was he so angry about? I mean, he'd basically dared me to hit him. Up ahead, I could hear the deep rumble of Xoc's laughter while he moved farther away assuring he'd be out of the crossfire.

Cal quickly bent to grab a fruit. But I was faster. I unleashed the two I had cradled in my arm. In quick succession, a green one landed upside his head, speckling his nose in green spots, and another perfectly aimed blue one hit him squarely in the chest.

He took a step back and unfurled the berry at me. I dove, somersaulting on the ground and snatching three more up as I rolled. These were all pink. He was going to be adorable coated in pink splatter.

I sprang up, but it seemed he had anticipated that. The sting of impact zinged my cheek and orange glowing light filled my vision.

"Yech," I laughed, and sweet juice burst across my taste buds. I wiped the orange goo from my eyes just in time to see blue streaking for me. I turned, but it caught my left boob straight on.

"Ow," I said, laughing and clutching my breast. Cal was doubled over, also laughing. "Now I don't feel even a little sorry doing this."

I heaved the berry in my hand straight for his groin. It broke apart in a dazzling spray of pink and pulp.

"Ugh," he grunted and bent over for a second. "Low, Elyria. That was low."

Behind him, Xoc was barely keeping it together. He stood in the middle of the path with one massive hand covering his mouth. His entire body vibrated with the effort of containing his laughter.

I gave another berry a little toss in the air, catching it deftly. I did it again, putting a little backhanded spin on the rotation.

Cal lifted his head and I could swear flames danced in his eyes. It was a look I was all too familiar with. His mouth quirked into a devious half-smile.

"Oh, shit," I said, knowing exactly where that smile would lead.

Before I could react, a green fruit exploded against my other boob. I looked down to where my nipple was screaming in protest. One breast was blue, the other green.

Cal let out a cackle. "Much better. A matching set."

I brushed the goo from my chest, and long wisps of green pulp flung from my hand. I couldn't even be mad about it. Beating his ass was the most fun I'd had in... it had been a long time.

I snapped upright, unfurling both remaining pink balls at him. They hit his leg and arm. Pink juice dripped down his limbs. Not bothering to acknowledge the hit he had just taken, Cal dove to snatch up more berries.

I eyed the bough of a tree that hung low over the path. Perfect. I charged in a full sprint straight for Cal. Completely surprised, he tried to leap away. As he did, I stepped on top of his back and sprang up, both hands latching solidly around the bough. I threw my momentum forward, swinging my hips and legs over the branch into a flawless kip that would have made even overly critical Della proud. A batch of glow silk clung to my legs as I swept my body through the tangled mess, but I was too caught up in the excitement to care. Nimbly, I placed my foot onto the branch and stood, balancing one foot in front of the other. I held onto the branch above me with one hand and hung out over the ground, gloating at Cal's complete shock.

My springboard action drove Cal straight into the glowber patch he was reaching for, and now he was completely covered. Colors of all kinds streamed down his chest. Not a stitch of his formerly white tunic remained. He stood up, smiling in astonishment. Small crinkles formed at the corners of his eyes. Speckles of tiny glowing dots spattered his face like freckles.

He clapped in mock applause. I strode further down the branch, appraising him from above. Where most people would have looked a mess, Cal actually looked more handsome strewn in juice. It highlighted his sculpted arms, and his thoroughly soaked shirt clung to each chiseled line of his pectorals and abs.

"I'll admit, I did not see that coming," he said. "But, Elyria, I have tricks you haven't seen yet too."

I jumped a little on the branch, scissoring my legs. Dozens of strands of glowing silk rained down on him. He threw up an arm to shield his eyes. Around me, the shimmering strands swayed and glittered. It was then I remembered what Xoc had said about the green ones. I quickly scanned the branches but didn't see any green strands. Sighing in relief, I looked back down at Cal.

Who was gone.

I spun in a tiny circle, looking down in every direction. Where was the bastard hiding? I looked away for one second. Gripping my branch, I hung out wide to see around the trunk of the tree.

Nothing. Cal had vanished.

A tense panic prickled at the back of my neck, flaming at the base of my spine. He was close. I knew it.

Motion flickered in my periphery.

Cal was standing in the branches of the tree beside me, arms full of glowber berries. I made a quick jump forward and swung up to another branch, moving higher and just missing the barrage of orbs that smacked into the trunk. I continued my upward momentum until I was sure that I was well above him and out of his reach. I glanced down at the color-spattered tree and then back to where Cal had been standing.

"What was that about—"

Gone. He was gone *again*! I craned my head. Where in the Hells did he disappear to?

Behind me, lips brushed my ear. "Lose something?"

I screamed, heart leaping into the upper canopy. I tipped forward and scrambled for the branch, but only my fingertips brushed it. My stomach lurched with a second of weightlessness before I began to plummet the several stories down to the ground.

A powerful arm wrapped around my waist. With an electric buzz against my stomach, he pulled me back up. My back pressed against the unforgiving planes of his chest as he held me firm in the cage of his arms. I would have been able to focus more of my attention on the way he felt behind me, if my head wasn't spinning with the dizzy awareness of how close I'd just come to falling.

The stubble on his cheek gently brushed against the soft skin at the base of my jaw.

"I've got you," he said with a voice that had dropped a full octave. The deep rumble of his voice sent a shiver snaking its way down my spine, and goosebumps chased his caressing breath. Cal's arm tightened at my waist, and I could have sworn that I felt his lips tilt into a smile against my neck.

We remained like that for several seconds longer than necessary. I found myself in no hurry to pull away, and I let my libido indulge herself in the feeling of him wrapped around me. Glowing threads pulsed and swayed around us. My heart was racing, thrumming my power to life and charging lava into my veins. Cal laughed, making his chest rise and fall against my back.

I turned in place to face him. He kept his arm folded around my waist but loosened it just enough to allow me to twist. His face was streaked in blue and green, and tiny pink dots flecked the bridge of his nose and peppered his full lips. My gaze lingered on those tiny dots. Knowing they would taste sweet against his skin gave me the darkest desire to lick them off.

I shifted my feet on the branch, sliding them against his to find my footing. The tiny bit of space that separated us closed. Warm fingers pressed into the flesh at my waist, ensuring I remained anchored to him. I reached for a branch or anything to hold on to, but there was only him.

A small amused hum came from within his chest seconds before a gust of wind lifted us into the air.

My eyes opened wide, and I gave a yelp of surprise. I clasped his neck like it was my own personal lifeline. Below us was nothing. There was just air and the path far below. Why did I have to climb so high? Cal chuckled as if he could hear my panicked thoughts, and tightened the arm snaking up my back.

His lips lightly brushed over my ear, overriding my senses. "I'd never let you fall."

Slowly, we lowered to the ground. It all made sense. Cal wasn't climbing into the trees; he was floating with his godsdamn air attunement—and swiftly, from how suddenly he had popped up behind me.

We touched down gracefully, and Cal reluctantly relaxed his grip on me. I took a step back and released a breath that I hadn't realized I was holding.

Cal pulled a silk thread from my hair and then another. "Gods, you're covered," he said, a genuine smile on his face.

The smile I gave him in return came naturally. I reached up to remove some of the blue silk from his hair too. The droplets clung to the auburn strands, making them shine warm and golden in the low light. Even covered in juice and sticky silk, he was handsome. His honeyed eyes flickered at me and my breath hitched. Desire flooded through me, and heat burned deep in my chest. Each of my muscles seized with the same anticipatory tension that I always got before a fight. I almost pounced right at him.

Almost.

I didn't walk up to him, didn't jump into his arms, didn't plaster my mouth onto his. Instead, I stepped back and rebelled against the magnetic pull that was always there. Just as fast as I lost all sense, it came back to me.

I was losing my damn mind. I knew he was keeping things from me, and yet, here I was, panting at him like a street cat in heat.

I walked over to where I had discarded my pack. "A fine mess you started."

"*I started*?" Cal said, incredulity dripping from each word. He leaned over, picking up his own bag.

"Obviously, you're the one who tried to make me slip up while juggling."

"Oh, so I guess I just imagined you throwing one of those at the back of my head," he said, gesturing to the massacre of glowberberries littering the path.

"Technicalities." I waved away his comment. "Important thing is I won."

"*You?*"

"Yes, I won. Gods, Dentross, look at yourself," I called over my shoulder, then spun, walking backwards. "There is no part of you that isn't glowing like a solstice cake."

"That's rich, have you, by chance, seen yourself?" Cal quipped. "Because *you* look like a Koolabura ready to strut and dance for half the forest."

I looked down. He was right. Everywhere our bodies had touched was smudged and blended together into a long tracing of our contact. A clear orange handprint was to the left of my stomach, from when he had caught me around the waist. Another green print was on my shoulder, and I didn't even remember him grasping me there. I stole a glance at him and groaned. Those were my handprints on his arms, his neck... his shoulders.

"Don't worry, you're both losers," Xoc said, standing up. "Lucky for you, the riverbed isn't too far off. You'll be able to wash this nonsense off of you."

"Like you didn't enjoy the show?" I reached up to take his cheek in a pseudo-loving embrace and smiled as his entire body tensed. "Don't pretend. I saw you trying to contain laughter. You loved seeing me hand Cal his ass."

"Lies," Cal said in a fit of fake coughs.

I dropped my hand, leaving a perfect pink handprint on Xoc's cheek. I smiled, pleased with the result. He swiped at the pink goo. "Gods, really?" he said, flinging it to the ground.

I shrugged and moved to hug him. Xoc jumped back. "Get away from me, little demon. You're not coating me in that gook."

I laughed, walking down the path, careful not to let any part of me touch my pack. I tried to run my free hand through my hair to give it a little flick and swish, knowing that the gold always drove the boys crazy. But it was plastered to the side of my face. Hopefully, the goo wasn't as hard to remove as he had said. Then I remembered how glorious that first throw had been. Worth it, totally worth it.

It was another five minutes before the sounds of rushing water filled the forest. Four more minutes and I saw the sparkling stream rush around stones in the riverbed.

"Thank the gods," I muttered. I thumped the pack down on the ground. "I don't know how much longer I could have held this away from me."

And then I really got the chance to look at the water.

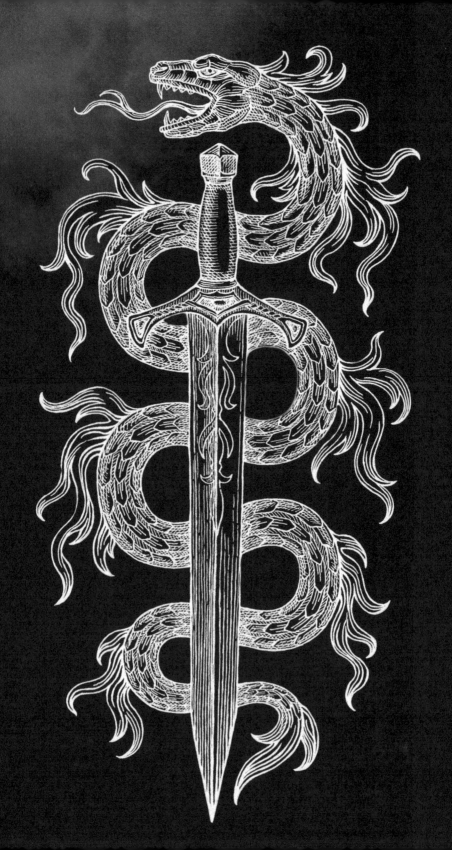

21
ELYRIA

The river was breathtaking. Words could never accurately describe how beautiful it was. I had heard that the waters of Laluna could glow when you moved in them, but I had never ventured inland enough to witness it for myself. Each ripple of water lit up as it flowed and bubbled around the rocks. It looked like living starlight.

I bent down, dipping my hand into the cool water. Where it hit my fingers, it sparkled a light neon blue. Tendrils of glowberberry juice flowed off my palms in streams. I drifted my fingers in the water, and it twinkled brighter with each movement.

Standing up, I didn't know what to say. I looked at Cal and Xoc, who seemed to be as enamored by the water as I had been.

"It's a microplankton," Xoc informed, sitting his pack against a rock. "I can sense them in the water, tiny organisms small enough you could fit three of them on the head of a needle."

"You lie," Cal proclaimed. "Nothing living can be that small."

"Why would I lie about this?"

It was hard to imagine creatures so small that you couldn't actually see them.

"Sometimes you don't have to see something to know it's there. Just look. The agitation is triggering a flight response in the organism. It's a defense mechanism that causes the tiny plankton to glow. To me, the water feels like it has a static charge as it flows around the rocks and other obstacles in the river."

"That's amazing. You can actually feel the water, but you aren't attuned to it?" I asked in disbelief.

"Yes, that's how I know it's not the water I'm feeling. It isn't the first time. There are microorganisms in most bodies of water. They're small, so I don't always notice them unless I'm really focused on their signature. The concentration here must be remarkably high. It feels like the water is churning with them," Xoc replied as he dipped his hand into the bank. "They're harmless, though. You two should be fine to clean off in it."

He splashed a handful of water up at me.

"Hey! I don't want those microthingies getting into my mouth."

Xoc cupped his hands to rinse the handprint from his face. I grinned, having already forgotten that I had put it there to begin with.

"Although that probably makes us even."

My heart felt light. These past few hours had been... *fun*. I felt more like myself again. Had Cal known that a fight was what I needed?

Xoc took another handful of water to his face. Seemingly out of nowhere, Cal came right up behind him and gave him a powerful push. Instead of falling into the water, Xoc spun, and Cal tipped face-first into the river, a blue wave splashing up as he fell in.

Cal righted himself, waist-deep in the stream. He wiped a mixture of glow-berberry juice and water from his face, then spit the water from his mouth.

"You child," Xoc laughed. "I can sense you coming. You have literally never gotten the jump on me." He turned to me. "Did you know he's been trying that exact same attack since we were kids?" He turned back to Cal. "He *never* learns!"

Cal did a two-handed splash, throwing neon blue water straight at Xoc. Xoc quickly waved a hand, and a wall of river reeds grew up to block the onslaught of water. Cal yelled louder, "I think I swallowed some of those plank things. I'll probably be pissing blue in the morning."

"I don't think it works that way," I laughed.

"Okay, but if any of my dangling bits start glowing, you'll know why. They don't normally do that."

"Noted." I pulled a handkerchief from the outer pocket of my pack and dipped it into the water. I rubbed the soft fabric over my face. The water was cool against my flushed cheeks and left it feeling fresh. Next, I unstrapped my knife belts from around my waist and thighs. The dry parts of my blouse hung loose, and the air kissed the exposed skin in a glorious rush of air.

I inspected each of my throwing knives. The dragon etched into the hilt was coated in sticky orange juice. It clung to the dips of the etching, making the dragons glow. If it was on purpose, it would have been rather magical.

I ran the cloth over each edge, polishing the metal to a bright shine. One by one, I lay them on a nearby stone that was covered in a bright purple lichen that contrasted brilliantly against the golden knives.

When I was done, I pulled the dagger Duke gave me for my twentieth birthday from its sheath. It seemed to have been spared by the barrage. The hilt was wrapped with black leather and gold lacing. My favorite part was at the center of the guard, a dragon eating its tail wrapped around an ornate sun, the Solaris sigil. After Duke adopted me, he added the dragon to the symbol. The Sun Serpent, was a tribute to both of us. The ruby in the dragon's eye winked at me, an old friend saying hello.

"Ya know, most people would worry about cleaning themselves off *before* their weapons," Cal said, soaking a washcloth in the river.

"Well," I said, resheathing the dagger, "I'm not most people."

"You most definitely are not."

Cal looked down at his arm and appraised the handprint I had left there. Heat flushed against my neck as he slowly began scrubbing it away.

My cheeks burned, and I twisted away before he could mock me for blushing. I found a good rock to sit on and began unstrapping my boots, dropping them one by one to the ground next to me.

"Not so fast. Go slower," Cal catcalled, followed by a whistle.

I chucked the boot at him, but he stopped it midair and redirected it back to the bank.

"Is there no part of you that isn't despicable?"

"Yes, but it's only the best parts of me that are," he said with a demonic smile and stupid waggle of his brows.

"Ugh!" I yelled in frustration and chucked the other boot at him, which he tossed just as effortlessly as the other one.

"You'll want to watch that. Don't need your boots getting wet."

"You are positively infuriating sometimes."

"Only sometimes? That's progress."

"No, I'm pretty sure it's all the time," said Xoc as he walked up, his face the image of perfect calm. How he could stay so stone-faced while cracking a joke was a genuine talent and something I've never been able to pull off.

"The way I see it," Xoc began, "you two will need to dry everything out after cleaning them, and no one wants to hike in wet boots. So, since we are only about twenty minutes from the base of the steps, I figure we should just make camp here tonight and start fresh in the morning." He sighed. "And then tackle the steps."

He looked pointedly at me. "What?" I said, playing at innocence. "I didn't make you come along."

"No, that would be me." Cal rose from the river and walked over to where I had laid my knives down. Sparkling blue water fell from him in sheets. I did my best to ignore the warmth crawling its way up the back of my neck. He went to reach for my dagger, and then paused, looking back up at me.

"May I?" he said.

My first instinct was to say no, but instead, I nodded. Anxiety shivered through me and plucked at my heart. No one, aside from Duke, had ever handled The Sun Serpent blade before. It was as close to a holy relic as I ever got, especially now. But some stupid part of me wanted to share this with Cal, and the look of genuine reverence he was giving the dagger had me gesturing down at where it laid before I could give into my own insecurity.

Cal gently picked up the dagger, holding it as if it were a dangerous animal that he didn't want to provoke into striking. He gave me a tentative glance before giving it a tiny flip in the air, his fingers wrapping deftly along the hilt.

I raised an eyebrow at him. For a cosmetics salesman, he definitely knew how to handle blades. Someone had trained him—and well, from the way he was flipping and spinning it. If he could do that with a dagger... *What else was he hiding?*

"Like I said, you haven't seen all my tricks."

My heart rate increased, and I tucked the rising attraction back down. Why did he have to look so damn sexy handling my blade?

"It's just a dagger," I said, trying to remain nonchalant but my voice hitched on the word.

Cal's eyes sparkled with understanding, but he played along, redirecting that scorching gaze back to the knife spinning in his hand. "I think we both know that's not true."

I restrained my smile. I knew its craftsmanship was unparalleled, but the fact that he knew that too made my heart flip in ways I wasn't entirely ready to acknowledge.

"A few years ago, Duke struck up an affair with a metal singer in the smithy ring of The Bullseye. Duke would brag, *'She was talented in handling more than metals'.*" I did my best blustering Duke impression, complete with over emphasized waggling of eyebrows. Cal chuckled. I shrugged, still smiling. "For my birthday, he had her design a dagger with The Sun Serpent at its heart."

"It's the second most beautiful thing I've ever seen," Cal admitted as he stared at the dagger, the gold of the dragon reflecting in his eyes.

"The second?"

"Mmhmm."

He looked up at me, not even a bit of sarcasm in his expression. I'd been called beautiful so many times that the word had lost all its meaning, but this... this felt different than any of those times. That one simple word, mentioned so casually, made my heart flutter wildly in my chest. I swallowed hard over the lump forming in my throat. Cal's eyes tracked the motion, one side of his lips lifting slightly in recognition. Did nothing make it past him?

"And heavier than I would have imagined," Cal said, letting the gravity of his previous statement hang between us and weighing the dagger in his hand. He gave it another toss, and it glinted with each rotation.

I snapped out my hand, plucking the Sun Serpent from the air. "That's probably enough show and tell for one evening."

Cal's eyes flared in astonishment. He flexed his empty hand and a flash of pure desire crossed his face.

"Agreed," Xoc interjected, bursting the moment that was building between us. "I'm going to gather some wood for a fire, see if we can dry Cal's boots before tomorrow."

"I wonder how they got wet," Cal deadpanned.

"And you probably want to get that glowberry juice off you," he said, gesturing to all of me. "It looks like you're dressed for war."

I looked down at the streaks and handprints still painting my body. I had forgotten about the juice. *Goddess slay me, I must look—*

"Don't worry about it," Cal said, somehow knowing what I was thinking. "You could be covered in shit, and you'd still be the most stunning thing in Venterra."

"Charming picture," I said sarcastically.

Cal walked over to the rock I had been sitting on and pulled off two very water-logged boots, dumping the contents of each before sitting them aside. They were made of a fine and well-worn leather, ones that someone had lovingly cared for. I skipped over to where he had laid them down and smirked, picking one of them up.

"I could dry them for you," I said confidently.

"You can?"

"I can." I sat the boot before him on the ground. "Watch."

I stood squarely before the boots and held my hands together, forming a small ball of fire between them. It started as a bright white ball and then darkened to a warm glowing red. I guided the ball into the boot. He sat up curiously. Steam began to rise from inside the cuffs.

"I can control the amount of heat I allow the fire to have," I said and coaxed the fire up and down the shaft of the boot. The light it cast on us ebbed as the fireball moved. Dark shadows danced around us.

"If I don't let it get too hot, it makes the water evaporate but leaves the leather unsinged."

I pulled the fire back into my hand, letting it rotate and sparkle in my palm.

"So, not a magician's trick, then?" he said, scanning my eyes.

"No. Not a trick, but you already knew that," I said, looking over to where the ball of light spun in my palm.

"That's a really brilliant way to manipulate the power."

"Thank you," I said proudly and leaned over the other boot, repeating the action. Steam wafted and swirled around us. "I've had patrons of the show hold the fire before. Ya know, as part of my act. Especially if they have something particularly sparkly on that night. No one is paying attention to their pocket chain when they are holding literal fire in their hands."

He looked at me, part taken aback, part in admiration.

"What?" I said innocently, changing my sinful smile into the mockery of an angel. "So I have a thing for shiny gold."

Cal raised one eyebrow. "I've always loved gold, too. I seem to be inexplicably drawn to it."

I glanced down at my braid. It was shining in the firelight, still streaked with lines of blue and green.

"Well..." I grinned sheepishly. "I have a small stash of it I've snatched over the years. I only take it from the rude people—those I've seen mistreating the less fortunate. I'll never understand that. Here are these people, who have more money than they know what to do with, so they buy absurd stones and wear them around their necks like a badge of honor."

Cal nodded his head in understanding. "You're right."

"And that would be fine," I continued, "but then they degrade and steal from the mouths of people who need every copper. Like being born into luxury gives them the right to exploit those beneath them just so they can fill their purses to go buy more stupid jewels. It feels a bit like justice, taking it back."

I flashed my eyes back up to him. His arrogance melted away, leaving something closer to respect, and that made me feel oddly proud. "Anyway, I have a stash pillow that I sleep on."

Then Cal laughed, actually laughed. Not a calculated flirtation, but rather he radiated genuine amusement. Through his chuckling he said, "Like a dragon, sleeping on his hoard."

Then he laughed some more. I liked it. Probably more than I should have.

"No," I said, feigning indignance. "Well..." My composure broke and I joined in his laughter. "Actually, kind of." The fire came back to my hand, bright and shimmering. "And once the stash gets so big that I can't sleep on it anymore, I donate it. To those who actually need the money."

Cal's mirthful expression shifted into one of admiration. "That might be the noblest thing I've ever heard."

"I can't take all the credit. I got the idea from a story Duke used to tell." The shadow of Duke's ghost surrounded me, bringing with it the sourness of loss. I swallowed back the burn in my eyes and extinguished the flame in my hands. "There you go. All dry." My voice cracked as I barely suppressed my emotions.

Sympathy tilted Cal's smile down, but he didn't address it more than the clear change in his expression. He picked up the boot. "That is a very handy trick. We probably could do that with everything."

"It's a bit trickier with fabrics," I said reluctantly. "I *may* have burned a tent down one time trying it."

"May have?"

"So now I stick to only drying leathers that way. And even then, you have to be careful not to do it too fast or the leather cracks. I ruined one of Duke's best pairs of loafers by rushing it."

Sadness slithered free of its tenuous bonds as I remembered the way he had blustered about it for weeks afterwards. Tears pricked at my still stinging eyes. Panic set in and I brushed hastily at the corners before any could spill free. I knew that if I let them free, there would be no containing it. I couldn't allow myself to break that way again.

Cal must have seen the change in my demeanor, because he jumped up from the stone. Kindness came from him in waves, like a pulsing energy.

"You should probably clean up. You've still got juice everywhere. At least Xoc's little dunk in the water got my hair and face clean. All that's left is to wash my clothing," he said, trying to distract me.

Clothing... I tugged at the hem of my shirt to survey the damage. There was no part of me that didn't need to be washed. Effectively removing all of this juice was going to be tricky. I opened my pack, rifling through the belongings for a fresh change of clothes. I pulled out a soft tunic and matching drawstring pants. I had packed them for sleeping in, and I supposed they would do for lounging in while my traveling clothes dried.

I glanced back at Cal, at the damp fabric clinging to his shifting muscles as he walked back towards the river's edge and stood in the glow of the ferns that lined the bank.

Consider me distracted.

He lifted the hem of his shirt and peeled it off in one agonizingly slow motion. Unabashedly, I watched as each inch of his sun-kissed torso became exposed. His abdomen stretched and rolled. A defined V of corded muscle dipped low into the leather pants that hugged tightly to his hips.

The fire in my veins sparked to life, drawing me to him. So much so that I actually took several unintentional steps forward. As his shirt was freed from his head, he looked back over at me, and I quickly glanced away. But not before I saw his wide smile of recognition.

My face burned, but then I looked back defiantly. Cal had already begun unlacing his waistband, obviously more deliberate with his motions now that he knew he had an audience. I continued watching, probably about a half-second too long, before I turned away to repack my bag. I heard a splash of water and glanced back. His pants and shirt were discarded in a pile on the bank. Apparently, washing them was no longer a priority.

"Don't worry. I'll actually look away while you undress."

Cal licked his lips while lifting his chin to me in an obvious invitation to join him in the river. Nothing but his undershorts remained, just a scrap of fabric and too much toned, bronze muscle on display. He never broke eye contact, and even in the flickering light of the river, I could see his stupid grin.

"Good," I said, trying to muster whatever remained of my dignity.

"Unless you want me to watch."

There had to be something nearby I could throw at him. I looked down at my knives. I probably shouldn't. But then again... no.

"There's nothing I want from you," I said with a painfully false bravado.

"Need... want... semantics."

I narrowed my eyes and tightened my lips into a scowl.

Cal titled his head to the side, the wet strands of his auburn hair shifted to veil his eyes. He cupped the water in his hands and dumped it over his head. The water shimmered to life, glowing as it flowed over his shoulders and down his chest. The effect created a blue ethereal halo around his body.

The fire in my veins churned, and sparks danced between my fingers. I clenched my hands into fists. *Fucking showoff. I thought I was the performer here.*

Enough of this. I wasn't playing his games. I looked around for a place where I could undress with at least the illusion of privacy. Not far away, a large tree, surrounded by the stained glass plants, looked like it would give a respectable amount of cover. I glanced back at Cal. His smirk was entirely too damn expectant. The tree would have to do.

Juice was pebbled and splattered everywhere on my pants. They clung to my skin as I peeled them off. Seeing them made me wonder what exactly the rest of me must have looked like. I flipped them over. There was clearly a handprint, centered perfectly over my ass. It must have happened when I turned, and he had drawn me in closer to him. I had been so focused on the way my chest had pressed against his and the feel of his cheek on mine, that I hadn't even noticed his hand was on my ass.

The white cotton of my shirt hung loosely around my waist. I ran my thumb over the hem while trying to decide how much I was actually willing to remove. It was entirely too much fabric to bathe properly. I scowled at the glowing orange handprint. *Fuck him.* He deserved this. I was about to make him swallow his tongue, right along with all that arrogance.

I pulled the shirt off, and it stretched out over the plants. The purple and yellow glow of the leaves shone faintly through the white fabric of the blouse. The cool forest air nipped at my skin through the light underclothes. Grinning wickedly, I pulled the camisole off, too, leaving only the underwear on. There were areas where the juice had soaked through my clothing and left a glowing stain on my skin, which, incidentally, was where I had taken the two shots to my chest. One taut nipple had a faint blue hue to it.

I ran a hand over my face and huffed a silent laugh. What was I doing? Could I really walk out there nearly nude? Maybe I should put the camisole back on. After all, I—

"Did you get lost over there?" Cal's voice carried over the burbling river, interrupting my thoughts. "I could come help if you need my... *assistance.*"

I growled in annoyance. *Assistance.* My fire sparked and rolled beneath my skin with renewed determination. Even as I felt my ire rising, my heart rate picked up in anticipation. That smug bastard had it coming to him. He had a place, and it was about time I put him in it. This was going to be fun. I slid my underwear off, letting them fall to the ground with a little kick. Locking my confidence firmly in place, I stepped out from behind the tree. I knew how to make men beg, and this one had no idea who he was playing with.

"Or I—" Cal's voice abruptly stopped. The arrogant expression he had been wearing was wiped completely clean, replaced by a complete and perfect shock.

A single flame lit beneath my feet, and the surrounding darkness shrank back. Fire snaked and grew with each deliberate step. Deep red flames licked at my knees and thighs. Sparks crackled around me like glitter. I moved in a direct line towards the water, crossing each step to exaggerate the sway of my hips.

Cal's eyes were wide and golden as I approached. They dropped to my feet where the fire wrapped around my ankles, following the line of flames as they coiled up my bare legs. I snapped my hand to the side, and flames sprung to life on my fingertips. Cal's eyes locked on my fingers, exactly where I wanted them. With a long slow caress, I dragged my hand up the inside of my thigh.

From the water I heard him gasp, "Well, fuck me."

I felt his gaze ascending like a physical caress, as if it were his hand and not mine, that slid over my stomach and trailed around the curves of my breasts. He smirked, and I knew it was for the blue glow streaking over my nipple.

Finally, his eyes met mine. I held the contact, confidence etched into my features, never straying or looking away, but he did. His stare dropped to my lips and lingered there. With a coy smile, I wet my lower lip and bit down hard enough to make it swell.

Cal almost imperceptibly sucked in a breath.

He belonged to me now.

I felt unstoppable. Beneath my skin, my power came to life in a torrent of energy that intensified as I moved closer to him. When I reached the water's edge, the coolness of the bank lapped at my feet and hissed. I increased the heat at my soles, forcing steam to rise in thick blankets. The roiling neon water glowed brightly as the space between us diminished.

Cal stood waist-deep in the river, seemingly made of stone from how still he was standing. I wasn't even sure he was breathing. I continued my prowl until I was mere inches from him, and still, he didn't budge. He simply devoured my every movement.

My gaze roamed over him, a cat admiring her prey. Then I puckered my lips and held out my hand as if I were about to blow him a kiss. I blew gently. At first, it was just a hot rush of air. It fluttered the stray locks of hair that hung over his eyes. I focused the heat, the air sparked, and slow dancing flames slipped into my outstretched palm. I turned my head in the other direction, blowing flames into my other hand.

Cal's pupils constricted, making the rich gold of his eyes glow brighter in the firelight. His lips parted with quick, shallow breaths. I moved in, holding my hands flat between us. Another inch and my nipples would brush his chest. From how he tensed, I was sure he was imagining the press of my body against his. His hands fisted in the water. The restraint Cal was showing was impressive. But he knew, just as well as I did, the moment he moved for me, this would be over.

In tandem, I raised my palms. Then slowly traced each curve of taut muscle, letting the flame lick the surface. The water that still clung to his skin steamed off of him in blue wisps. Cal breathed in with a hiss, then loosed a long, slow breath.

I was careful to make sure that the gentle caress of flame was the only thing that touched him, keeping the heat just this side of painful. Despite the naked flesh before him, Cal's eyes never strayed from mine, making it impossible to miss the way they burned right along with me. The intensity should have scared me, but it only made me want to push him further.

Time to beg.

Leaning in so that my mouth barely hovered above his, I smoothly exhaled. Our breaths tangled until light flames were licking at his lips. The caress of heat against flesh was the most deeply erotic thing I'd ever done, and yet we still weren't touching.

The fire in my hands lengthened, snaking along the curves of Cal's strong shoulders and coiling around each arm. After a slow trace back to the slope of his neck, I brought my hands down the center of his chest until they were met by the water with a hiss. The darkness that enveloped us was immediate, leaving only the pulsating glow of the river and the sound of my breathing. Just mine. Cal, it would seem, had forgotten how to breathe.

"Elle..." Cal's voice was deep and husky, then something snapped in his expression and he moved to close the space between us.

With a wink, I disappeared beneath the glowing roil. The cool rush of water against my face extinguished the heat in my veins. I willed my power to calm itself and slowed my pounding heartbeat. I had lost my damn mind, but fuck if I wasn't enjoying every second.

The water was surprisingly clear. Cal's perfect blue silhouette glowed in front of me. The current crashed off the curves of his hips and thighs, and a large hand that decidedly looked like it was covering a raging erection. *Victory was sweet—and large.* Demons below, it wasn't fair that the universe had made this man handsome, charming, and well endowed. It simply was not fair. Cal was playing with a stacked deck, and worse he fucking knew it.

I rose to my feet, making sure to keep my ascent slow and measured. I had learned long ago that the art of performance was not in the finale but the wind-up. The tighter you coiled the spring, the more dramatic the release, and from the looks of Cal, I had wound him good and tight. Too bad for him, there was no release coming.

Neon blue starlight cascaded down my shoulders and ran from the tips of my breasts. Cal stood with his jaw hanging wide open. I gave my hair and shoulders a little shake, letting the water fall off of me like diamonds.

I tilted my head to the side with a little half-smile. Then remembering his offer to *assist* me, I said, "No, that's okay. I can manage just fine by myself."

I reached forward and gently shut his mouth for him.

"I—" He choked on the word.

Ha. Forget begging. I just rendered the silver tongue speechless. To think, all I had to do to shut him up was take off a little clothing.

Cal cleared his throat. "I can see that."

"You could at least have the propriety to look away," I said, bright amusement filling my voice.

"Right," he said dreamily, then snapped out of it. "Right, of course." And held one hand up as a blinder, only to immediately peek through his fingers.

I breathed a laugh and walked deeper, so the waterline was just above my breasts. I leaned back, spread my arms wide, and let the buoyancy support me.

Cal lowered his hand to draw lazy figure eights in the water. "What was I thinking? I mean, an exotically beautiful, naked woman comes walking, on *fire*, out of a dark wood into a glowing river, and naturally, I should look away."

Unexpected laughter bubbled out of me.

"Well, I certainly wasn't about to be upstaged by that *little* performance you put on." I made a twirly motion with my finger.

"There is absolutely nothing little about anything here tonight," he said, throwing up his arms. "I could prove it to you right now if you want me to." He moved a step closer. "Please, let me prove it to you."

Ignoring that, I reached up, and freed my hair from its braid. Running my fingers through the ends, the water ran off in rainbow streams down the backs of my hands.

"You should have seen the shock on your face. That alone was worth it." I smiled victoriously. "Perfectly satisfying."

"If that is your definition of perfectly satisfying, then you've never really been satisfied."

I halted my fingers in my hair and looked up at him through wet lashes.

He grinned darkly back at me. His eyes were a hook that snared into the very center of me, and its tug demanded I move closer. My heart drummed in my ears, and the skin at the back of my neck prickled in awareness. The water itself was charged with the energy coursing between us. He was feet away, and yet, I could feel him on every part of me.

"I..." Unable to fight the pull any longer, I shifted slightly in his direction.

"What in the gods happened here?"

Startled, I whipped my head toward the voice. Xoc was looking at the trail of singed footprints I left on my path to the riverbank. I suppose I had dialed up the heat a bit more than necessary. Then Xoc turned to look at me, and immediately realizing I was naked, looked away.

"See!" I said, gesturing to Xoc. "That's what averting your eyes looks like."

"Oh, I know. Just why would I ever do that? It'd be like looking away from a masterpiece, and Elle, you are most definitely a masterpiece."

"I've been gone for all of five minutes, Cal! Ya know what, never mind. I'm leaving," Xoc said, exasperation and judgment fuming off of him as he turned to walk away.

"*No*, don't start that. This was *not* my doing," Cal said defensively. "This is just Elyria determined to put me in my place by putting on a show."

"He's not wrong," I said matter-of-factly.

"Joke's on her." He turned to look at me. "Proving your point by getting naked will mean I win every time. It's really the perfect scenario, you getting naked as punishment. So feel free to remind me of my place more often."

"Ugh," I growled in frustration, and splashed the water at him.

He only laughed, and so I splashed him again. Which made him choke on the water, since he was too busy laughing to shut his mouth.

"Careful you don't choke on the microwhatevers," I said and then walked determinedly out of the river to where I had laid my change of clothes.

Xoc blushed bright red and turned completely away from me this time.

"You didn't wash your shirt," Cal called. He got out of the water and retrieved his clothing from the bank.

I stomped to where my shirt was still artfully draped on the stained glass plant. I picked up my juice painted blouse and chucked it at him, hitting him right in that perfect smug face of his. "Since you're washing clothes, feel free to do mine as well," I growled.

"It's amazing how fucking sexy a naked, angry woman is," he quipped.

I threw my pants at him too, but unfortunately, this time, he ducked. Shame. The buckle on my waistband would have made a glorious sound connecting with his skull.

He laughed, picking them up and carrying all of the clothing into the river to scrub them clean.

Quickly, I slipped my tunic over my shoulders and pulled my drawstring pants on. I picked up my bedroll and waterskin, then walked over to the fire bundle Xoc had erected. I immediately snapped it to life. Not with a simple spark either. An entire plume of heat shot high into the air. Xoc jumped back, not entirely ready for me to light it. The fire warmed my bones and calmed the growing sense of annoyance setting root there. Then I remembered Cal's face.

"What are you smiling at?" Xoc asked, reading me.

"Just remembering Cal's face when I walked out naked and thinking that it was completely worth it."

I bit down on my lower lip to keep my grin from being too wide and looked at him with a side-eye.

"It's about time someone dished it back and gave him a taste of what he gives out. I don't think he's ever met a woman with his caliber of manipulative skill." He looked pointedly at me. "Of course, you know it will only make him want you more. So bear that in mind the next time you decide to put on a display of—" He paused, carefully choosing his next word. "Power."

I unfurled my bedroll and sat down on it. Then took a long draft from my waterskin.

"I know exactly what I'm doing," I said calmly. "I can take care of myself."

"So I've been told..." he said and lifted his chin towards Cal. "But that one over there. He thinks the whole damn world is his to save, especially you."

I looked at Cal as he scrubbed the clothing.

"Well, he's doing a fantastic job at saving my shirt right now."

22

ELYRIA

That night was a restless night's sleep, mostly because I kept opening my eyes to look over at Cal. Somehow, I had let my guard down, and he had wormed himself into my mind. It didn't help that he seemed like he could sleep anywhere. When we finally settled, he simply laid down and, in what seemed like seconds, was sleeping soundly. My brain, however, saw fit to use this time to replay every look and conversation we'd shared over the past week.

So, instead of falling asleep, I stared at the swaying glow worm threads and watched the moths swoop and dip in the air. Then I'd look over at Cal and watch the subtle rise and fall of his chest as he slept. Motion flitted beneath his lids, and sometimes he would flinch. Seeing him fight some invisible foe made my heart clench. What demons did he have that haunted his nightmares? Where did he go when he closed his eyes? Somewhere in that cycle of thought, exhaustion had taken me.

Too few hours later, I woke to a scraping sound. Xoc was stirring a small pot of rolled oats over a tiny portable cookstove. Cal's bedroll was already rolled up and stowed away. I looked around me but didn't see him anywhere.

"He's not here. Cal told me not to wake you, so I figured I might as well heat something up. I picked oats. I hope that's okay. I thought we could use the energy today for the start of our climb."

"Where is he?" I asked, rubbing sleep from my eyes.

Xoc looked up and ladled the oats into three cups that laid on the ground before him. "He's refilling our water stores and will be back any moment."

Xoc handed me a cup. "Thank you," I said, taking it. "Not from the river? I don't want to drink those photothingies." I shook my hand at the river.

"No, there's a spring not far from here. He took our skins there to refill them."

I looked down at the plain white mush in my cup and frowned. A pang of homesickness fluttered in my stomach.

"Hold on."

A memory sparked to life in my tired mind. I rolled over and pulled my sack to me. Rooting my hand around in the pack, I latched onto a small bottle and held it aloft victoriously.

"Here," I said brightly, displaying a small brown glass bottle in my hand. "It's the seasoning Gregory uses in the morning mash. He gave it to me before I left camp yesterday. A 'taste of home', he called it."

I smiled fondly at the memory, then leaned over and put two drops into his cup and mine. I slowly stirred the oats. Immediately a spicy cardamom scent floated up. The smell wrapped around me like a warm blanket, and I sighed in comfort.

"You're not going to put any in Cal's cup?" he said, one eyebrow raised.

The arrogant ass deserved to eat bland mush. "No."

Xoc gave me a look of disbelief that filled me with guilt.

"Okay, fine," I said in supplication and reached over, putting drops into his cup as well.

Just that moment, Cal came back into our camp.

"The trail looks clear," he said, three water skins slung over his shoulder. "I don't think we have much farther to go."

He tossed the skins down at our packs and then sat between us. He picked up the cup Xoc left for him. "This smells…"

He paused, trying to remember where he recognized the scent from.

I smiled over my spoon at him. "It's Gregory's mash seasoning."

"That's it. Exactly." He stirred his cup a bit. "I didn't realize he gave it to you." He blew on the spoon. I couldn't help but watch his pursing lips. Over a mouthful of oats, he said, "Thank you for sharing."

Xoc gave me a look and I smiled sheepishly at him. "You're welcome."

"What?" Cal looked between me and Xoc. "Did I miss something?"

"Oh, you're missing plenty of things," I laughed and downed the last of my oats.

I strapped my knives on, and cinched my pack down. Quickly, the boys followed suit, and before long we were walking down the path. It followed the river, and I enjoyed watching the bubble and glow of the water as we walked. Heavy mist hung over the ground, catching the light of the forest plant life. As much as I loathed to admit it, I would miss the silent beauty of this place.

Duke would have loved this part of the forest. I couldn't help but wonder if he ever walked this path. There was so much about his past I didn't know. For a moment, sadness gripped at my heart. After a few controlled breaths, it passed.

Progress.

I looked up and up... and up at the emerging gray stone. Cal whistled. It was hard not to be humbled by what loomed before us.

On first look, it appeared to be a sheer cliff, one that extended forever. Small tufts of a glowing reedy grass grew in cracks and crevices sporadically. Carved into the rock were an impossible number of high and narrow stairs. Each flight extended approximately fifty feet straight up, and was met by a narrow landing. This pattern repeated itself, over and over... and over. My legs ached at the mere thought of climbing them. *Too late now.*

Then, high above us, I saw the first traces of sunlight, a speck on the cliff that finally breached the eternal shadow that blanketed the valley floor.

"The sun!" I exclaimed, hitching my pack up higher. The sight of it, however slight, filled me with energy. I couldn't wait to feel its warmth on my face.

"That's what you notice?" Cal said in disbelief. "That tiny sliver of sunlight way up there?"

I looked at him blankly.

"Not the near sheer elevation? The narrow walkways? The never ending stairs?" He threw his hands into the air. "*No*, you see the tiny flash of sun at the end."

"That's how you should go through life, Cal. With your eyes on the sunshine at the end of the night." I smiled sweetly. He shook his head in amusement.

I walked up to the stone and placed my hand against the wall. It was cool and unforgiving. Moisture clung to the surface, and tiny streams of water trickled over the craggy exterior. Along the base, pools of water flowed toward the stream we had followed. I rested my forehead against the rock and breathed in deeply. I stood in quiet meditation for a few minutes thinking of the climb and journey before us, and how glorious the sun would feel. This complete darkness would soon be a thing of my past. Maybe the way it weighed at my heart would ease and, through the journey, I would emerge into the light.

I turned around. They were watching me. Cal had a curious expression on his face, like he was trying to figure me out. I ignored him, flicking my hair into his face as I brushed past his shoulder.

"How long do you think it'll take us to climb it?" I asked, walking over to Xoc.

He pulled the map back out and began counting the rings of elevation. "Well..." He shook his head in disbelief and raised his eyebrows slightly. "That can't be right. Let me count it again."

This time, I could see him mouthing the numbers as he counted. He looked up at Cal, eyes wide. "If this map is correct," he swallowed. "It's an elevation gain of nearly 15,000 feet."

Cal rolled his eyes and looked pointedly at me.

Xoc continued, a deadly seriousness to his deep timber, "15,000 feet in five miles."

"Tell me again why we couldn't sail around?" Cal grumbled, hands on his hips, looking back up at the invisible summit.

"Because I've never been able to go this way before," I said with my best smile. "I mean, five miles isn't far. We walked four times that yesterday."

Xoc turned to me, folding the map back up and sliding it into his pocket. "Yesterday, we had zero elevation gain. We're still below sea level. That..." He pointed up at the cliff. "Is a considerably different five-mile hike."

I waved him off, dismissing his concerns, and looked to see where we would access the beginning of the climb.

"I wouldn't have taken you for the sort of man who balks at a challenge."

My fingers grazed over the crags and divots as I walked along the stone. Up ahead, a structure emerged from the mist. It was an old iron shack bolted into the side of the cliff face.

"I think I found the elevator," I said and walked up to the rust-eaten iron caging. Above it sat two giant wheels attached to tracks that were anchored to the side of the cliff. The doors to the main carriage were crooked and looked as if they had been repaired and reaffixed with rusty wire.

I looked back to Cal. "Yeah, we're not taking this death trap."

He looked at it, turned, and looked up at the zigzagging staircase, then back at the elevator. He gave it a good tug and shake. The scraping of metal on metal echoed up the chamber, forcing my entire body to rebel and every hair to stand on end.

"I mean, it's-"

"*No*," Xoc and I said simultaneously. Beside the housing was a small metal plaque. I walked up to it and began reading aloud.

Elixant Mountain Stepped Trail
est. 1321 D.A.
Peak altitude 13,253 feet.
This trail is named in honor of Arturo Elixant.
He and his team carved and established
the first traversable path over the mountain,
and created a first means for land-based trade on
the continent. The ground-breaking invention of
the cliff elevator was installed in 1440 D.A.
as a way to transport larger quantities of goods.

"1440 D.A., Cal!" Xoc said, pointing at the plaque. "D.A. as in Dragon Age! That means that this contraption." He kicked the post. "Is nearly *five* thousand years old. It's amazing there's any metal left."

"I mean—"

"*No*," we repeated in unison.

"I'm just saying there's no way all the parts are that old. It had to have been repaired at some point in the last..." He paused, looking at the rusted pieces of metal. "Millennium." He turned and looked at us. Conceding, he added, "Okay, point taken."

I walked away from the boys and towards the several narrow steps carved into the rock face. They were smooth from centuries of use and gleamed in the low light. Each step looked barely wide enough to fit my entire foot. I looked over at Xoc's enormous feet. They were nearly twice as large as mine, and I wondered if it would even be physically possible for someone of his size to travel in a space as confined as this.

"So, who wants to go first?" I asked hesitantly.

"Oh, Sunshine," Cal began, a devilish smile on his face. "I think you get that honor. This was your dream, after all."

"Yeah," I sighed, looking up at the long... long climb ahead of us. "I figured you'd say that."

A long iron chain ran along either side of the staircase. It was bolted into the rock face and was polished from the thousands of hands that must have run over them. It followed along the stairs as they snaked their way up to the first platform.

I gave it a gentle tug. It held but it also squeaked when it moved and vibrated so completely that the tremor reverberated down my arm. I looked back at Cal, who mouthed, "Go on," at me. I shook out my apprehension, raised my knee to hip height, and hoisted myself up.

"One," I said and then lifted to the second step. "Two."

"Please do not count every single step out loud."

When I was about ten steps up, I turned slightly to look down at him. "Are you coming? Or did you chicken out already?" I laughed, hauling myself up another step.

"Just admiring this perfect view," he called up to me, and then he began his ascent as well.

Behind him, Xoc grumbled something to himself, and I could just picture the way he was rolling his eyes.

It was fifty steps to the first platform. I knew because, despite Cal telling me not to, I had, in fact counted them all. The platform itself was really more of a ledge, about four feet wide. Fifteen feet down, it connected to another flight of steps. When I climbed onto the second landing, I breathed a sigh of relief and sat down. Waiting for the others to reach me, I pulled a water skin from my pack and took a long drag of water. It was cool, and even just climbing two flights had my skin flushed.

Cal climbed onto the platform and looked down at me. Then he leaned slightly, looking over the edge. "Gods, we're barely up."

"Don't be a baby," I said, getting to my feet. "We've got to be at least 200 feet in the air." I gestured to where the treetops glittered below us. It was like looking down on a sea of stars.

I began climbing the next flight. These stairs moved in more of a diagonal than the others, and I had to cross my feet with each step. At one point, I lost my balance a little, and I felt a hard wall of air push me back to the rock face. I looked down at Cal. Concern tightened his soft features.

"Thanks," I said breathlessly.

He smiled and nodded for me to continue climbing.

By the sixth platform, my thighs were *screaming*. I had done squats and climbed rigging as part of my daily conditioning since I was a child, but these stairs were a new form of torture. Each step was so high that my legs had to stretch nearly their full length to crest them. Xoc handled them with ease, his substantial height actually an advantage. I laughed to think that I had ever wondered if he'd be able to manage the climb because of his size. I had been so naïve.

I sat on the edge of the platform and let my trembling legs dangle over the ledge as I drank more water, my skin nearly half empty now. Cal shuffled over and sat next to me. Beads of sweat glistened on his brow. I smiled. His perfect complexion was finally cracking.

I handed him my skin and he gratefully took it. At this elevation, we were well above the tree canopy. The glittering glow worms that had looked like starlight had long since faded into the black void beneath us. Now that the moon had risen fully I could actually see the Tower of Night off in the distance, and Laluna was a glowing speck on the horizon. The tower shone like a beacon in the distance, one that actually cast light as far as to light up the cliff face. Farther beyond that was the black expanse of the ocean.

"Thank you for the push," I said, glancing at Cal.

"Well, I couldn't very well let you fall," he said, handing my skin back to me. I took another swig.

"It got me wondering. Why can't you just fly us to the top?" I asked.

"Air attunement doesn't really work that way."

"You let us fly out of that tree in the forest."

"That was a controlled descent. It takes much less magic to let something go down than it does to fight gravity and push it up," he explained, mimicking the motion with his hand. "I might be able to lift myself to the top, but that would leave you and Xoc stranded. Plus, my elemental stores would be empty, and if something happened. Well. You know..." He made a falling motion with his hand. "Splat."

"Oh." I scooted myself away from the cliff edge.

"Yeah, so. It's safer for us all this way."

Xoc climbed onto the platform, looking down at the two of us. He made a motion to keep going.

"Take a break," Cal said, leaning back against the wall and placing his arms behind his head. "We need to pace ourselves, or we're never making it to the top."

"We've only done six sets," he said matter-of-factly.

Xoc stepped over both of us, then stopped abruptly before the next flight.

"Yep." I didn't bother looking at him. I knew what he saw. There was a reason I stopped when I did. "Sit down, take a break."

The next flight wasn't steps. Bolted into the cliff face was a ladder wrapping over a hump in the stone. The angle was so steep that you could only see about ten of the individual iron rungs before they disappeared behind the weathered stone, or at least I hoped they continued past where we could see and didn't leave you stranded halfway up the cliff. To make things worse, the chain that usually ran along the edge was now gone. From the bottom post, a single remaining link hung ominously.

Cal had been so focused on me and the view that he hadn't bothered looking up yet.

"What is it?" He glanced over me towards Xoc. His eyes widened, and he scrambled to his feet. "I do not want to climb that."

"Yep," I repeated myself. "So let's all just take a break."

23

ELYRIA

The cliff would never end. It was an endless line of dark stone. Now that the moon had risen, my spot of sunlight was gone. No matter, it just meant that the next day we might be able to finally see it rise.

After a long rest, Cal stood up, scuffing his feet. He walked over to the ladder and began investigating its integrity. He fingered the remaining link, letting it swing. It made a scraping sound that sent shivers running down my spine. Cal pulled hard on the second rung. It held. He put his foot on the bottom bit of twisted metal and gave a little hop on it.

"Well," he said hesitantly, "I think it's fine." He shrugged. "But, let's let Elyria go first since she's the lightest."

"Oh, great," I mumbled, letting my head roll against the rock. "I get to be the test subject."

"I'll go last and hopefully catch anyone if they slip or fall."

"Well, that's reassuring," I grumbled under my breath.

"Let's go, Sunshine," he said, holding his hand down to help me up. I was exhausted enough that I actually let him.

Clambering to my feet, I gave my sore legs a long, lunging stretch. My front leg folded forward while my back leg sank into a near split, dipping deep to the ground so that I felt it in each inch of my overworked muscles. I exhaled a soft moan in relief that probably sounded entirely too sexual. It felt so good that I couldn't bring myself to care.

The pained sound of Cal groaning made me snap my head quickly over my shoulder, a tug of alarm pulling at my heart– until I realized he wasn't groaning in pain at all. Cal's amber flecked eyes were wide, and he was biting onto his fisted hand hard enough to make the knuckles turn white.

My lips thinned into a fine line, my jaw clenching tight. If he wanted something to groan in pain over, then I'd give him something a hell of a lot better to cry about than the curve of my ass.

While his eyes were still too preoccupied to notice, I leapt up. Using the full power of my twisting body, I swung my open palm into his elbow. Cal's hand tore from his mouth with the impact, ramming that tightly strained fist straight into his perfectly sculpted cheekbone.

"Ow," Cal whined with a laugh, cradling his already bright red cheek.

Xoc barked a laugh. "That was your best act yet, Elyria. I'd take Cal punching himself over flaming dragons and acrobatics any day."

I gave a tiny bow. Still brimming with satisfaction, I hitched my pack as tight to my body as I could, then ran a hand over my knives to be sure they were all secure. Taking the rung in my hand and looking sidelong at them, I hoisted myself up.

"Come on, boys. There's no time to ogle."

"You didn't seem to have any problems with ogling last night."

I refused to look at him. If I looked at the blinding grin that I knew in my bones would be waiting for me, then it was entirely possible that the next hit he took from me would pitch him right off the side of the cliff. Instead, I pushed all of my annoyance into scaling the wall.

The angle was steep, so steep it felt like climbing upside down. The slope curved out, and the weight of my pack pulled me backwards. My arms ached from fighting against the gravity that wanted to pull me down.

It made me think of the first time I had climbed the acrobatic rigging. My legs shook the entire time. When I got to the top, Della pushed me. I tumbled head over ass, arms flailing into the practice net. She laughed my entire fall and then yelled down to me, "See, there's nothing to worry about." I was furious with her. But she was right, of course, that's what safety nets were for. After a while, I got used to the height and the climb. Eventually, I was as at home on my perch as I was on the ground. Maybe it would be that way with the cliff too. By the time we got to the top, we'd all be laughing about how foolishly scared we'd been. Although I supposed the difference here was that if the rigging collapsed, then I'd go plummeting to my death.

Probably not best to be imagining epic falls right now.

The path curved, and finally, thank the ever loving gods, the rock became vertical once more. I could see the next platform, and I gave a sigh of relief. Until, I saw that there was not one missing rung but five. In the fifteen feet between me and the platform, there was only one remaining rung, and holes where the ladder had once been bolted into the rock. I paused, not sure what to do. I tried to look down, but the curvature of the rock prevented me from being able to see Xoc or Cal.

I yelled into the void, "Problem."

"What's wrong?" came Cal's worried voice.

"I'm out of rungs."

"Did she just say she's out of rungs?" Xoc questioned with hurried concern.

I hooked my arm into the bar at the top to give myself more stability. Then I leaned out, trying to see if there were any other handholds that I could use to breach the gap. It wasn't far, and I had climbed distances farther than that without a harness before. I lifted my leg and found a decent foothold. Just out of arm's reach was a crook in the stone, just large enough to hold onto. Beyond that was another crack in the stone. I could do this.

"I think I can scale it," I shouted, trying to muster as much confidence as I could.

"*You're what?* Elle, I can't catch you if I can't see you," he said hurriedly.

"It'll be okay," I said back as calmly as I could. "I can see grips. It's not far."

I pulled my body in as tight to the stone as I could. It was rough and cold against my chest. I extended my right arm. The first handhold was just beyond my fingertips. I looked down and put my foot into the crook.

With my feet secure, I pushed up in one quick motion. My body slid along the stone, and with my momentum still pushing upwards, I locked my hand onto the grip I had seen. I let my bottom foot sit on the top ladder rung that I had just been holding and steadied myself. Ahead to my left was a crack that ran diagonally towards where the ladder had once been secured. That would work for my next grip. I pushed up on the leg that was standing on the last ladder rung; my hand latched onto the stone. My grasp was strong and secure. But my dangling foot scrambled along the surface to find purchase.

Nothing.

There was nowhere to prop my next foot on. I tried looking down but couldn't push my torso away for fear of the weight of my pack pulling me back.

"Elyria," Cal yelled up. "Please tell me you are not free scaling the cliff."

"Shut up," I yelled. "I'm trying to concentrate."

My heart was pounding in my ears. Wind rushed around me and buffeted against my body. I pulled myself against the stone and breathed, letting myself relax slightly. Panicking would help nothing. Feeling my heart rate slow, I looked around me again.

There, a tiny shelf. It was high, but if I stretched, I could just get a toe on it. I lifted my leg up, bending it as high as I could.

"Okay, Elyria," I said to myself. "You've got this. You just need two more handholds and then you can reach that top rung. Two more."

A foot above me, a ridge in the stone protruded. "That will work," I said aloud.

"What will work?" Cal said. "Who are you talking to? Damn it, Xoc, start moving."

I pushed up on my tiny foothold, just the very edge of my boot staying on the crevice. But it held, and I was propelled upwards. My fingers curled onto the ridge, and I pulled myself in towards the rock before I could start falling backwards. My other hand gripped a little divot on the surface. *I was doing this.* Adrenaline-fueled elation rocketed through me. One last push and I could reach that last, lonely rung. The crack in the rock beneath me provided a perfect place to sit my left foot. It could be enough. If I pushed hard enough to jump, I would just be able to reach the ladder rung. Then I could pull myself up and over the ledge.

I looked over my shoulder towards the boys. I could just see the top of Xoc's hair beginning to poke over the edge of the hump, then I looked back up and locked my eyes onto the bar. Its rusted surface was pebbled and aged. I swallowed hard, then pulled myself as close to the stone as I could get. My foot shifted on the crack, assuring a solid foundation to leap from.

This was just like the trapeze. I could do this. The trick was not to hesitate. I drew in one slow breath and held it for a second, then let it out slowly. I counted my heartbeats. I took a second breath in, and on the exhale, I launched myself upwards.

Arm outstretched, I sprang up. My fingers solidly wrapped around the rough metal of the rung. An exhilarated feeling of victory rocketed through me. My body weight sank back down with a hard tug against my palm. With a wrenching sound, the iron shifted in the stone, and the metal beneath my hand gave way. Cracks appeared around the anchors, and tiny pebbles showered down onto my face.

My mind failed to make sense of the loose bit of metal still grasped in my hand. I had a second of surreal weightlessness before I hurtled backwards.

A scream ripped from my chest.

"*Cal!*"

I flailed my arms. Gray, craggy rock rushed past me in a blur. My legs and arms scraped against the stone as I plummeted. I was just passing the hump in the cliff when Xoc pushed off from the rock, one hand holding onto his rung. Swinging wide, he reached his long arm out, and a large hand latched around my wrist. Firm and strong, he held tight.

In a grip that was practiced reflex more than panic, I wrapped my fingers around his arm. With a sudden yank, my entire downward motion halted. The aggressive jerk of my body shook one of my throwing knives loose from its sheath and it went tumbling end over end like a flying star. It skimmed past Cal, slicing a thin cut along his arm. His eyes were wide and filled with terror. He looked down, tracing the knife's continued descent. Then he looked back up at me.

Hanging from Xoc's arm, I stared into the black abyss of the forest far below us. Panic took me and I twisted, looking for anything to grab ahold of.

"Stop wriggling," Xoc grunted at me. "My grip is only just holding. You'll take us both down."

He was right. I calmed myself and stopped moving, imagining that we were doing a trapeze act. This was just like any time Christian had helped me practice catches. Anytime he helped me practice catches while being suspended 5,000 feet in the air, above a pitch-black forest, and wearing a fifty-pound pack.

"Xoc," Cal yelled up. "You're going to need to swing her up."

"He needs to what?!" I yelled, and twisted, trying to look down at him.

"Elyria, do you trust me?" he said.

"*No!*" I yelled down at him.

"Yes, you do," he said as calmly as he could.

"Whatever we're doing, we need to do it quick," Xoc said, a grimace on his face.

"Xoc is going to swing and put some momentum behind you. He will fling you straight up, and then I'm going to give you a push. Hopefully, you'll land on that platform."

"Hopefully?!" I yelled. "You're going to have him fling me into the open air on *hopefully*?!"

"Trust me. This will work. It's just like leaping from a swing."

"Oh gods, okay, let's do this," I whimpered.

"Xoc, are you ready?"

Xoc nodded. "I'm good."

Then he swung me. One long drag into the air, then back. Each arc of his arm raising me higher and higher.

"On the count of three," said Cal. "One... two.... three."

Xoc gave a roar of exertion, and I soared upwards. My stomach launched into my throat with the sudden change of inertia. A powerful push of air hit my back, and I began flying even faster. I saw the ledge and turned, contracting my body forwards and attempting to dive. I crashed onto the ledge, rolling several times before slamming into the cliff wall. My head hit the stone with a resounding crack. Black and white alternating spots filled my vision.

I laid there panting, my heart beating wildly. My arms fell limply to my sides. The world spun out of control. I closed my eyes, trying to center myself. Nausea roiled up inside of me.

Then, in a moment of what I was sure was concussed delirium, I heard the beating of wings. I opened my eyes, and a massive beast was hovering above me.

I screamed, throwing up my arms and sending fire wildly in all directions. To my surprise, laughter came from the creature. I squinted my eyes against the dizziness and realized it wasn't a beast.

It was Xoc.

He had two large green leather wings protruding from his back. They flapped slowly, holding him aloft above me. His long hair, usually a warm brown, was now a rich forest green color. Gusts of wind buffeted around us, whipping his hair furiously. Shimmering green scales spread over his shoulders and arms, reflecting the moonlight. They were only slightly less brilliant than his eyes, which blazed an intense shade of emerald. The red of his tattoo contrasted sharply against the green scales along his temples. He was savagely beautiful to look at.

Gracefully, he alighted on the ground next to me. Seconds later, a cyclone of air lifted Cal to the ledge. He stepped onto the stone as easily as stepping off of a ship.

Intense concern had Cal walking swiftly to me. Kneeling down, he leaned over me and brushed strands of sticky hair from my face.

"Are you okay?"

I blinked at him in a foolish attempt to clear my blurred vision. I tried to sit up, but the world spun. My eyes rolled in my head, the world turning a bizarre shade of pink, and a second wave of nausea hit me.

"Whoa." He cradled my head in his hands. "Easy now."

He gently lowered me onto the rock. I closed my eyes and tried with everything I had not to vomit all over him. *Nope, eyes closed was worse.* I opened them again and gripped onto Cal's arm to help stop the feeling of spiraling out of control.

"Gods, Elyria," he said, pulling a rag from his pack.

He held it to my head, where a steady stream of blood flowed over my left eye.

"You're bleeding too," Xoc said, pointing to Cal's arm.

"That's nothing," he said, not bothering to even look at his arm.

"My knife," I mumbled, remembering my blade striking him as it fell. I attempted to lift my hand to his arm, but it felt strangely heavy. I willed it to move, but it was like moving in quicksand. The more I tried, the heavier it got.

"I told you not to climb it," he growled. I looked up at him. Despite the clear anger in his voice, fear entered his eyes. "For one terrifying second, I thought..." His voice hitched with the concern he didn't bother hiding. "That was the longest second of my life."

"Me too," I said with a choke. "I think I can sit up now," I added, a bit too slowly, and my words slurred.

Cal frowned, then helped to prop me up. He slid my pack off and unfastened my sheaths. I attempted to push myself against the wall. I wanted to be as far away from that drop as I could be.

Then I remembered great wings extending over me, silhouetted by moonlight. My head swung around to where Xoc stood. The motion was too quick, and the world spun out of control again. I brought my hand up to my temple while using the other one to anchor into Cal's arm.

"You should avoid making any sudden movements," Xoc said. "You gave yourself quite the hit."

His wings were folded neatly behind him. I squinted at Xoc, my mouth hanging open.

"What? How?" I was having the hardest time forming a sentence. I looked at his scales and then thought of when my own scales emerged. He must be draken, like me. It was the only explanation.

The recognition must have shown on my face, because he quietly said, "Yes, I'm draken too. Remember when I said that I had an extra attunement? Well, this is why."

"But wings? I don't have wings," I said.

"You probably could have wings. You just haven't learned to manifest them. Or didn't know to try. But I rarely use them. The manifestation, it..." He paused. "It's painful. If I'm going to pull them out, then I'll only do it when I can have them around for a while."

"Plus, they get in the way," Cal added. He rolled my knife sheath neatly and slipped it into my bag. I'd have to remember to thank him for that when I could think straight again.

"True, while I have these on, I won't be able to wear my pack, or a shirt, for that matter. You have to have specially modified clothing to accommodate them."

"That makes sense," I said. A pounding headache began to throb beneath my temples. "I think I'm gonna be sick." I pushed the heels of my hands along my forehead, trying to soothe the pressure.

"We don't have to talk about this now," Cal said, a flicker of concern traded between them.

"I'll be fine," I said. "I just need a minute."

"You need more than a minute." His hand brushed back the hair that had fallen in my face, tenderly grazing the wound along my temple. "We're staying here for the night, and then in the morning, we can try to continue. Xoc and I can fly whatever we can't walk."

I tried to protest, but the pounding head and spinning world seemed to win, and all I said was, "Okay."

Xoc pulled a medical kit from his magical rucksack and made quick work of bandaging Cal's arm. When he was done, he examined my head, a needle and thread already prepared to set some stitches.

"Seriously?" I said, looking at what he held.

"The gash is pretty deep," he said back calmly.

I put my hand up to my hairline. A large cut was there, and the surrounding skin was puffy and inflamed. "Okay," I said, lowering my hand. A tremor shook me. I wasn't sure if it was from my mild fear of needles or the shock settling in. Probably both.

Xoc gingerly sewed my head wound. I grimaced at the pain, feeling my nausea return. Just when I thought I was going to collapse again, Cal slid behind me, lacing his fingers through mine. When Xoc finished, I let my head settle onto Cal's shoulder. I felt drained and cold. Cal was warm, so incredibly warm. It drowned out all other sensations. All I could focus on was how comforting that warmth was. Seeming to sense my need, he pulled me into him. Already surrendering to the pull of unconsciousness, I didn't bother resisting, and let Cal fold me into his embrace.

24

ELYRIA

When I opened my eyes again, I was greeted by a warm smile. It took a second for my eyes to focus and recognition to settle in. My head rested in the perfect space between Cal's shoulder and neck. The arm around my waist and back tightened, causing a soothing comfort to ripple through me. Had Cal held me like this the entire night? From the looks of it, he hadn't slept. Exhaustion lined the eyes roaming over my face, lingering on the wound on my brow.

"How's the headache?" he said softly.

An almost imperceptible shimmer arced around us. I marveled at the magic keeping us safe. This was why Cal was so tired. He'd kept a wall of hard air around us the entire night, ensuring no one tumbled in their sleep. Xoc was sprawled on the stone next to us, his wings wrapped around him like a blanket.

"It's fine, mostly." My voice was rough from sleep. The tension in my head had eased considerably after resting. "Did you sleep at all?"

"No. I kept watch." His head dipped so that his cheek barely brushed my temple. My mind was still in the sluggish haze of waking, but it was impossible to miss the way his body tightened around me. "I needed to know you were safe."

A pulse of warmth thrummed in my chest. It felt too good to be watched over, cared for. "You didn't need to do that." I uncurled myself from under his arm and turned to face him. Of course, he'd already been doing that for days. Before Cal, if you had asked me when the last time someone took the time to care for my needs, I don't know that I could have answered. Months, maybe years. I was always taking care of everyone, doing everything. Then there was Cal, who somehow knew what to do before I even recognized that I needed the support. And it felt good, really good. He offered the kind of comfort I'd been running towards my entire life.

"Yes. I did," he replied sincerely. Running his hands through his hair, Cal lifted his eyes to the black sky. "I couldn't let... I couldn't..." His brows pinched together. "Elle, you screamed my name."

I tried to make sense of what he was saying. "I don't understand. When?"

Cal winced. The gaze that hit me when he lowered his eyes again was intense. It brushed against my senses in a wave, and I shivered despite the heat I felt radiating off of him.

"When you fell, you screamed my name. It was the only thing you said. You didn't say help, or arrrgh, or any of the things you'd expect someone to say when plummeting towards their death. You said *Cal*."

"I did?" I couldn't remember. All I could remember was the rock rushing past me.

"I flung out my power, but I *couldn't* see you. By the time I did, you were moving too fast for me to stop you. If Xoc hadn't grabbed your wrist..."

He swallowed hard, and his eyes searched mine. They burned brightly with some undecipherable emotion. Fear, or maybe longing? I'd have almost said love if there wasn't so much genuine pain in them. Whatever it was, I could tell the well ran deep.

Cal pushed the stray locks of my hair behind my ear. "I couldn't stand the idea of anything else happening to you."

He lightly ran his thumb over my stitches. It was a tender gesture, laced with caring and concern. I threaded my fingers into the hand still cradling the side of my face. "I'm fine."

Caught in Cal's gravity, I drifted closer to him. The space between us crackled, filling the air with the faint smell of smoke. While I looked into his blazing eyes, I wondered why I had moved away from his embrace when it felt blindingly obvious that it was the only place I wanted to be.

Cal gave a lingering look at my lips that reflexively made me wet them. His hand, still entangled with mine, trailed lightly over my cheekbone and down to my jaw. With each descending inch, my heart slammed harder against the confines of my ribs.

That dark, delicious scent that was uniquely his pressed against my senses, making my mind grow fuzzy. His thumb extended to caress my bottom lip. My mouth parted with a small exhale that sounded surprisingly like his name.

Cal's eyes rose from my lips to lock with mine before delving his hand into my hair to draw me closer. My fingers tightened on his, the unruly strands of my hair tangling between our fingers. He angled my face up ever so slightly. It was only a fraction but it felt like my soul reaching out to him.

His lips brushed mine as he spoke. "Elle, I... I..."

The anticipation was too much. I felt consumed by it, and the lingering feeling of his hand wrapped in mine was only driving my desire higher. I wasn't sure what he was waiting for, or why he hesitated, but I was done wasting the precious seconds of my life.

Raising my head, I cut off his words. The press of our lips was feather soft, but that was all it took to make my skin spark and my blood sing.

Cal broke away for a second of sublime recognition before his mouth crashed back into mine. The tension that had been building between us uncoiled, cracking with fire whip intensity. The longer we held on, the more that connection ricocheted between us.

I became acutely aware of every inch of my body touching him—and it wasn't enough. I released my fingers from his and fisted my hand into his shirt. I needed the ferocity of the kiss to match the feeling surging within me. This tender embrace wasn't going to do that. With a hard yank, he fell forward and had to brace the stone to keep from crushing me.

With a groan, Cal surrendered to the moment. All pretenses of restraint shattered, and he hauled me onto his lap. The powerful cage of his arms snaked around my body, his palm searing up my thigh, the other beneath the hem of my shirt to explore the long line of my spine. All the while, he trailed kisses along my jaw and down my neck to the dip of my collarbone.

I melted into him, taking and taking as if the connection between us could never be enough. I guided his mouth back to mine. The curve of his full lips locked perfectly into my own. It was like we had been predestined to fit into each other, just like this.

And then he paused. Cal's entire body went still—except for the smile breaking against my lips.

From behind me, a deep voice said, "So this is a thing that's happening now?"

I looked over my shoulder. Xoc's wings flexed wide above us. His hair was untethered, laying in a green pool over his shoulders. Despite his serious expression, there was laughter in his eyes.

Cal placed a single finger against my chin and redirected my gaze back to him. "Jealous?" Cal said, stroking the back of his knuckles down my neck.

I felt my cheeks flush, molten heat trailing in the wake of his still stroking hands.

"Hardly. I could care less what you two do, except for when your panting wakes me from some much needed sleep."

Cal leaned back, resting his head against the stone.

I went to peel myself off of him, but Cal tightened his arms, effectively pinning me in place. The hand at my waist slid beneath the hem of my shirt. His warm fingers traced gentle figure eights against my lower back, causing a chorus of shivers to erupt along my spine. He leaned in, kissed just below my ear, and whispered, "This isn't finished."

I bit down on my lip. Heat pooled in my core, and I smiled.

Smiled... and then had a moment of clarity. How had that just happened? When had I gone from thinking he was an arrogant bastard to smiling at the idea of his lips on mine? Although, his lips hadn't just been on mine, had they? No. They'd lavished kisses against my neck... my collar. A fresh wave of heat thrummed in my chest. If we hadn't been interrupted, then–

I was concussed. That had to explain it. That cliff had knocked all the sense from me.

I pushed against the wall to stand, but again Cal tightened his grip, holding me to him. This was bordering on absurd. He couldn't just keep me here, locked on his lap, his hands questing up my shirt while holding a conversation with Xoc as if nothing was currently happening.

"Did you bother checking Elyria to see if her concussion has subsided, or did you just go straight to devouring her face?"

Cal looked up at him like he didn't have a care in the world. "Her eyes are dilating normally, headache has abated, and she's shown no signs of dizziness." Cal gave him a know-it-all grin and turned back at me. "Anything you'd like to add?"

I glanced back at Xoc, or at least I looked at him as much as Cal's grip would allow.

"I'm fine," I said. He didn't look convinced. "Seriously. We can probably continue the climb once we've had something to eat."

"I don't know that I'd go that far," Xoc replied. "I'd like to assess your mobility once you're standing. Repeating yesterday's feat is not something I'm overly willing to attempt."

"Agreed," Cal said.

I swiveled my head back around to him. The two of them didn't just get to decide what I was going to do. That's not how this worked. But, before I could snap at him, I marked the exhaustion that lined his face, and thought of the genuine concern he'd shown when I woke. Maybe he had a point. Maybe.

"I'm more worried that Cal hasn't rested at all," I added.

"Oh, I'll be okay," Cal reassured me. "I can take a minute nap."

I must have looked confused because Xoc added. "It's a ten–or fifteen–minute power nap. We can both do them when necessary. It keeps you focused when you find yourself unable to rest fully."

"I've done them before, after days longer and harder than this one," Cal replied, placing a tender kiss to my temple.

Xoc added, "And at our next rest, I can take watch, and he can sleep."

He walked over to where I was still nestled in Cal's arms and extended a hand to me. "Let me help you stand. Dizziness can come on unexpectedly, and I can help to steady you if that happens." Xoc kicked at Cal's foot. "You're going to have to let her go now."

"If I must."

I felt a last tight squeeze. Cal's hand shifted to slide down my back, leaving a line of tingles in its wake. Then his grip loosened, and he opened his arms to release me.

I took Xoc's hand and let him pull me up. My head throbbed when I stood, but the world didn't spin. That was a definite improvement over what I could remember from the night before.

Xoc scrutinized my expression and then stepped back. I stood on my own and extended my hand to the wall next to me, my other bracing against the wall of hard air. I looked up the spanning cliff. Images of my climb and subsequent dive flooded my mind. I closed my eyes against the onslaught. I was fine, probably. *No, fuck it, I am fine.* I've never let a fall scare me before, and I wasn't about to start now.

I purposefully released the wall and walked along the ledge, proving that I felt sure on my feet. "See. I'm okay."

I said it to convince myself as much as Xoc.

Cal, satisfied with my steadiness, nodded in approval. Then he stretched out, laying his arm over his eyes. I was all right, and it seemed like he was finally going to allow himself to give in to his exhaustion.

Xoc was still assessing me. Eyes narrowed, he looked completely unconvinced.

"I'm fine," I repeated. "I haven't toppled off a cliff at all today, already an improvement over yesterday." I gave him my best smile, trying to make light of the situation. Panicking over the past wouldn't do anyone any good.

Xoc grunted in affirmation, and I suspected he would not let this go so quickly. He walked over to his pack and pulled out a package wrapped in brown paper. In it were the strips of dried meat Gregory gave us. He handed one to me before tearing off a hunk for himself. The meat was tough and salty, but I was famished.

Together we sat against the cliff and enjoyed our morning snack.

"So, are we going to talk about how you look more dragon than man now?" I said, making a twirly gesture at him with my jerky.

"That's an overstatement," he said. "But I could understand you being surprised by it."

"I'm draken," I said matter-of-factly.

"I know."

I raised my eyebrows at that. "You could have told me."

"I could have. But, to be honest, I wasn't sure if I could trust you. We'd only just met, after all."

I thought about that. It was true, a lot had happened, but we'd only really just met... little more than a week ago... and... and...

Oh, gods, had I really just been wrapped around Cal?

I could still feel the phantom touch of his hands on my skin and the echo of his kiss on my swollen lips. I looked over at him. He was already asleep. Soundly. What in the Hells was I thinking?

"That's fair," I said, feeling my cheeks flush.

"You probably have a lot of questions," he added, pretending not to notice where my thoughts had just obviously drifted to.

I did have questions, many of them. It was hard to think of just one to voice. My thoughts tumbled over each other. Focusing on just one was like trying to grab a single leaf in the middle of a tornado. So I said, "Can I touch your wings?"

He laughed. "Of all the things to ask." Xoc smiled gently at me. "Ya know, normally that wouldn't be something that I would advise. Wings are immeasurably private, but just this once, sure."

He kneeled down on one knee, a deep green wing extended out to me. Thick glittering scales that looked like jewels lined the ridges of each wing and continued arcing over his shoulders. Between each ridge, a thin membrane was stretched taut and semitransparent in the moonlight. I ran my hand over the top, feeling the smooth scales. They were so similar to my own. I swallowed hard around the lump forming in my throat.

I was not alone.

Deciding not to linger on that epiphany and the emotional implosion that would probably follow, I ran my fingers down the membrane. It flexed slightly under my touch. He shivered and then laughed.

Questions began tumbling out of me, one after the other. "When did you know you could do that?" I made a flappy bird motion with my arms. "Manifest wings? No, wait. When did you know you were draken? Wait, are there others? Are there more of us, more like me? *Oh my gods, are there other Fire Draken?*"

Xoc held out his hands, motioning me to slow down. "Easy, baby draken. I'll answer all your questions, and you don't need to ask them all now. We have days ahead of us. You can ask me anything, and I'll answer whatever I'm able to."

I sat up in excited anticipation, drawing my legs in close to me.

"Of course," he continued, "I don't actually know everything. But how about I start at the beginning, and you can ask questions as I go?"

"That sounds good." I took another hunk of jerky and began chewing on it.

"I was born in the Oerwood. My parents were no one of consequence. My mother was poor and sometimes offered herself in exchange for food or shelter."

My jaw hung open with shock, letting the small piece of jerky I was chewing nearly tumble from my mouth.

"My father must have been a member of one of the draken lines, but my mother never knew which. When I was sixteen, she died from a fever that struck down many in the wood."

"Oh," I sighed in compassion, and unbidden images of Duke's blackened skin came to mind. I blinked them away.

"It's why I dedicated so much of my schooling to learning the medicinal properties of plants," he continued. "The first signs of my draken abilities showed themselves when I was a toddler. But my mother knew at my birth. I, like you, have a dragon mark. Mine is here."

Xoc gestured to his hip. He pulled down slightly on his waistband and revealed just the hint of a glowing emerald dragon tail tattooed against warm, tan skin.

I lifted my hand over my shoulder and pointed to my back. "Mine is here."

"Yes," he cleared his throat. "I've seen it." And then *Xoc* blushed.

I tried not to let my disbelief bleed into my voice. "Right. My stunt in the forest. I suppose you got a look at much more than my mark that night."

I didn't know it was possible, but his blush deepened. Xoc cleared his throat, trying to look anywhere but at me.

"When I was a child, I would often call animals to me. Birds would perch atop our tiny hut, lizards would nest around the walls, occasionally, a swarm of bugs."

I scrunched my nose at the idea of being plagued by bugs.

"Yeah, my mother wasn't too fond of that one either. But, the thing was, I didn't know that it was anything special. I thought everyone could talk to animals. It felt normal to me. But there were other, more obvious things, too. When I would get angry, my hair would turn green, or my claws would manifest."

"*Claws!*" I sat up. Could I have claws? Claws *and* wings?

He smiled deviously and let one long claw manifest as he tapped the side of his nose.

"Oh, yes. I clawed a sizable gash in the wall when my mother wouldn't let me have sweets before dinner once."

I laughed, choking a bit on my jerky. "When I was young, maybe three, I burned down a wagon.... and the whiskers off of Gregory's cat." I smiled at the fondness of the memory, then laughed. "That old cat. He was a mess, always getting into scrapes with the local wildlife." Laughing still, I said, "I haven't thought about him in years. By the end of it, he was missing an eye and half an ear, plus he had a broken tail, so singeing his whiskers was the least of his injuries. Duke used to call him Lucky, and Gregory hated it."

I did my best Gregory impersonation. "*Ain'ts nuthin' bout that cat tha's lucky.*" Xoc laughed. "He was an ornery bastard too. The cat, I mean."

Xoc raised his eyebrows.

"Okay, well, Gregory is also an ornery bastard, but that cat wouldn't let anyone but Gregory or me touch him. Gods, one time Della—"

Xoc was laughing at me. His wings shook against the ground making a scratchy sound where scales met stone.

"Sorry. I'm getting off track. Go ahead, continue," I said, realizing I had taken over the conversation.

"It's perfectly fine. It's good to see you smile," he said, but he continued his story anyway. "My mother was always trying to hide that I was draken, but I was too young to understand."

"Hide it? Why would she want to hide it?"

I couldn't help but see the parallel. Duke had insisted we hide my abilities as well. And that turned out to be wise, even if I didn't take that direction wholeheartedly.

"Draken are not looked upon fondly in the wood," he said and then paused. "Draken children rarely live to be adults."

My face went slack. "Children? What, they would kill children?"

"Yes."

"Monsters. Why?" I said in pure disbelief. It was ghastly.

"Many fear that an Emerald Draken at full adult strength could control people as well as animals."

"Can you?" I asked hesitantly.

I had joked about him silencing Cal, but I hadn't actually thought he could do it.

"Not exactly," he said, adding, "Sometimes, with someone weak-minded or in distress, I can persuade them in a certain direction. In extreme moments I can influence mood. But I could never fully control a person. That's not something any draken *should* be able to do."

He closed his eyes, and I wondered why saying that pained him.

"So people are afraid of something that probably isn't even true, and that's enough for them to murder children?" I said in disgust.

"Fear makes people do extreme things."

We sat in silence for several long minutes, staring out at the far off City of Night. Somehow under the heavy weight of that sentiment, the night felt darker, even the sky, as if the stars were shook by the actions of ignorant men and chose to turn away.

Was it this fear that caused Duke's death? Was someone afraid of me, and Duke paid the price? I threaded my hands together, holding them tight enough to cause my nails to cut into my skin, praying for the voice of that young boy to disappear.

Xoc placed a heavy hand over mine, anchoring me in the present. When I finally relaxed, he continued, "There was an old man who lived on the edge of the Oerwood, Master Rith."

I nodded in recognition. "Yours and Cal's teacher."

"When my mother died, I went a bit rogue. My actions were... less than admirable, and I no longer cared who knew what I was. The Oerwood Lords tried to take me out, but that ended badly for them. So, instead, I was banished and told I could live on my own or find Master Rith. I had no money, and no way to earn a living, so really, I had no option other than to trek out to the middle of the jungle and find him."

"Was he draken also?" I asked, hopeful that I was about to hear about another of *our* kind.

"Not exactly. I'm not sure of the particulars. He wasn't necessarily the sharing kind. But, he has some draken-like abilities," he said.

"Has?" I asked. "He's still alive?"

"I assume he is. I don't actually know. I haven't been back to the Oerwood since I left. Rith was well over 1,000 years old when I was sent to live with him, and that was nearly 500 years ago. It probably depends on how much of the draken power he had tapped into. You should know, Elyria, draken don't age."

"They what?"

"The attuned lifespan can be upwards of a thousand years. You know that, right?"

I nodded.

"Well, the draken exceed the attuned. A draken could theoretically live for eons." He said seriously, that hand returning to rest against mine so that I felt every hit of the next sentence, "You could live for eons."

"Except..." I added. "There has to be an exception, or the draken would rule this world."

"Who says they don't?" Xoc said pointedly.

"But we'd know if someone who was part dragon was ruling the kingdoms of Venterra."

"Not if they didn't want you to know it. You can tell an attuned by their slightly pointed ears," he said, pointing to his own ears. "But drakens are only visibly draken," he gestured to all of him, "when they manifest their abilities. A draken could be sleeping next to you, and you'd never know."

"Have you ever met any other draken?"

"I have come across two others." He paused, contemplating his response. "But I'm not really at liberty to discuss them. Their secrets are their own," he said resolutely.

"That's honorable, I suppose," I grumbled, choosing to toss tiny pebbles over the edge rather than pout. Eventually,, my curiosity got the better of my pride and I asked, "How many kinds of draken are there? I mean, I can manipulate fire, and you can talk to animals."

"I believe there is a draken line for each of the Ancient Dragons. Aurus," he pointed to me. "The Gold Dragon."

He pointed to himself. "Smarag, The Emerald Dragon." He ticked off the remaining dragons on his fingers. "Argen, Silver; Ferrus, Iron; Caerule, Sapphire; and Terran, Ruby." He looked at his fingers and recounted. "Yes, that's six. There were six Ancient Dragons, or at least that's what I know of them. It's possible I'm missing one. My knowledge of the dragons is fairly limited."

"Did you ever meet your dragon, Smarag?" I said.

"The sire of my bloodline? No. To my knowledge, most dragons have not made their resting places known. I think the only dragon who didn't fully retreat was Ferrus. The Iron Draken has a fairly close relationship with him. It's under his guidance that he rules the Floating Lands."

"Lord Malvat is The Iron Draken?" I said. Xoc swallowed hard and then nodded. "I've been there. I mean, it's not like I met the guy. But his face is plastered on banners all over the capital city. Do the people know what he is?" I asked.

Rather than answering, he just shook his head, seemingly not wanting to discuss him further. "Elyria, the Oerwood is not the only place where draken are persecuted." I didn't miss his deliberate avoidance of the topic. "There are many lands where the draken are hunted or imprisoned. You need to be careful. This, being draken, it should be your most guarded secret."

Seriousness veiled his emerald eyes.

"I understand," I said and looked into the darkness beyond the cliff, mulling all of this new information over. Other draken, immortal life span, wings, claws. Claws were badass. I looked at him.

"So, how do I grow claws?" I asked, letting my smile spread wide.

25

CALLEN

I smelled something sweet, laced with smoke. I closed my eyes tighter, trying to avoid waking. I was so damn tired, and I ached... *everywhere*. Something sharp dragged over my cheek.

"Wakey, wakey," a light voice whispered into my ear.

I pulled my arm away from my eyes to see Elyria crouching over me. She was dragging... *claws* over my cheeks. I smiled.

"Looks like someone learned a new trick," I said to her, pointedly looking over at her hands.

I sat up and looked out over the dark vista before us. On the horizon, I could just make out where the sea lightened. That meant the sun must have risen. I turned to look up. The sliver of sunlight above us was much closer and brighter now. I definitely slept longer than a minute nap. Although I supposed we were in no specific hurry. The danger of Malvat couldn't reach us here... No, the dangers *here* were far more primitive.

I closed my eyes on the memory of Elyria hurtling past the side of the cliff and flexed my hand, trying to will away the feeling of impotence. When I reopened my eyes, I couldn't help but be stunned by her mischievous smile. *Gods above and demons below, she was—*

"Xoc helped me figure it out while you were sleeping," she replied.

I watched with amusement as she bit down on her lip and furrowed her brow. Her entire concentration was focused on her fingertips. Slowly, the claws pulled back. Triumphant, pure joy sparkled in her eyes. She was spectacularly beautiful, especially like this, unburdened. Memories from the night before flickered through my mind. The feeling of her wrapped around me, the softness of her skin beneath my hand, the small exhalation she had made when I kissed her neck... and the drowning need to keep her safe.

My eyes roved over her. Elyria gave me a distrustful look and moved to stand up. I darted out my hand, pulling her off-balance, and she fell right into my embrace. I smiled wickedly, and she laughed, making a move to get back up. But, rather than release her, I pulled her in tighter to me. Our bodies aligned, and everywhere we touched, a primal energy pulsed.

I tucked my face next to hers, letting my cheek and nose caress the soft shell of her ear before gently kissing her neck. Elyria made a soft humming exhalation.

Fuck, I would bottle that sound if I could. I groaned as I drank down her smoky, floral scent. And I'd top it off with that decadent fragrance. She was my very own personal poison. The first and only thing to ever make me feel weak. I ran my hand up her back, and she reflexively bowed into my touch.

I was in so much trouble.

"Yeah, we don't have time for that," Xoc's resolute voice came calling down to us.

I looked over Elyria's shoulder at him and smirked. I mean, he couldn't blame me, right? She was intoxicating. I couldn't help myself. Xoc only glared back at me. Yeah, no, he did not look amused.

"Fine," I said, releasing my grip.

"He's right," Elyria added, and she peeled herself away from me. "We need to start climbing. If we're lucky, maybe we can make it to the top before the sun sets again."

She looked longingly at the streak of sunlight.

"Slow down there, Sunshine. Are you even okay to climb?" I asked. "Waiting another day might be wiser."

It worried me how thorough of a knock she had taken when she hit the cliff. Obviously, it was better than the alternative, but that night on the ledge I watched her eyes roll in her head, actually roll back so that those deep gold irises disappeared entirely. But she seemed to be sure on her feet now.

"I can handle it." She did a small pirouette, proving how steady she was. "Besides, Xoc assured me he would fly me up to the next ledge if I feel any bouts of dizziness come on."

I looked at him, uneasy by all they'd shared as I slept. Which was inane. This was Xoc. He probably had more interest in the scrub grass growing on the rocks than her. In all the decades we'd been together, I'd never seen him hold a substantial interest in anyone.

With an adorably impetuous stomp, she said, "I want off this cursed cliff. I want to feel the sun. I need sanity to come back to me, and it's not going to happen playing with shadows."

She nudged my pack to me with her foot. With absolute authority, said, "So strap up, Dentross, because we're leaving!"

"Here's how this is going to happen," I said to both of them. They both raised their eyebrows at me as I got to my feet. "We check every flight first. No more ladders. We just fly them. Xoc, you and I will take turns carrying Elyria up." She made an indignant little sound. "If she needs it," I added, placating her. But I'd be damned before I let her place herself in danger again. I didn't care if it drained every last ounce of my power, until we were off this cliff, I was going to wrap her in an airshield so thick she'd probably start floating.

I slid the straps of my pack over my shoulders. Elyria did the same. She tightened her knives, and reflexively I raised my hand to my arm. The bandage seemed to be fine, but another foot to the right, and we'd have been dealing with an entirely different emergency last night. I shivered, remembering all too well what it felt like to have a knife piercing my flesh.

Xoc picked up his pack. Elyria looked at him inquisitively.

"You can't carry your bag in your hands," she said to him, pulling a leg up behind her and stretching her quads.

I shifted the belt on my pants to loosen them. Elyria's display of flexibility was not helping. Not that I'd make the mistake of blatantly ogling her ass again after last time.

Except, I was staring.

The grip on her ankle forced her chest to thrust forward, begging for someone to notice. I really had no other option than to give her tits my full and undivided attention. It was only polite. I wouldn't want them to feel ignored.

"Don't need to. I have a *magical rucksack*, remember." Xoc winked at her.

"Magical rucksack?" I said, confused. Elyria giggled.

Hold the damn reins! Did he share some kind of private joke... with my girl?

He flung the pack out. It disappeared into the space before him.

"I seriously need to figure that one out," she said longingly.

Xoc flexed his fingers in an exaggerated show of strength, causing a faint popping sound to come from his knuckles. He smiled. Xoc never smiled, and I just knew he was taunting me.

We started climbing, taking turns who would lead. Elyria remained in front of me at all times. I refused to take my eyes off of her, leaving a protective wall of air, just in case. Even so, it didn't stop my heart from racing every time her foot shifted on pebbles or her hand slid on the railing.

By midafternoon we were only a couple of levels from where the sun shone. The ambient light increased with every flight we crested. The texture of the stone changed too. It became more porous, and for as far as I could see, the rock face was peppered with holes and divots. They were in varying sizes. Their presence felt bizarre. Just looking at them filled me with a general sense of unease that I couldn't shake; it pricked at my base instincts. When I walked past them, the tiny shadows around the ridge of each hole shifted. It looked like millions of little eyes watching me. With each step, the unnerving vision sent an increasing shiver snaking down my spine.

Quickly, we crested the final two flights that stood between us and the sun level. With a determined step forward, I let the light wash over me. It was warm, bright, and surprisingly painful to see at first. I hadn't realized how accustomed to the dark I had become.

Walking into the sunshine, Elyria spun. Her black hair cascaded in sheets behind her and shone as it caught the light. Her elation was catching, and it made my fatigue fade. She laid down, stretching her arms out wide, stroking the sun-warmed stone and letting the light bathe her.

I swallowed my aversion to the pockmarked stone and was about to sit my supremely tired ass against the wall when I noticed that there was a strange material coating the surface. It was hard and semitransparent, like dirty glass. The substance, whatever it was, ran over the stone, creating a formation that reminded me of roots spreading in the ground. I ran my hand over it and found it to be warm and a bit sticky.

"What is this?" I asked and motioned for Xoc to look at it.

"It seems familiar to me, but I can't quite place it."

He examined the lingering goo between his fingers, gave it a little sniff, and then wiped them clean on his pants.

Elyria sat up, propping herself on her elbows. "What's the matter?"

"I don't know..." I paused, trying to explain. I had a weird feeling about it like it was unnatural and shouldn't exist. "I've just never seen anything like this, and..." I walked down the platform. "It's everywhere."

I slowly ascended the next flight of stairs, watching as the webbing continued to snake and twine itself in and out of the many, many holes.

Above me and to the right of the stairs, I spotted what looked like a cave.

"Did you know The Steps had caves?" I called down.

"No, but it makes sense. This is a porous enough stone," Xoc called back to me from the bottom of the steps. "Maybe there was a diverted water flow that has long since dried up."

I summoned the wind to glide me over the opening. The cave was really more of a tunnel, long and dark, spanning nearly twenty feet across.

"Odd. It's a tunnel," I called down.

It would be interesting to map it, see where it led. It might even run to the top of the cliff in an alternate route to the surface. Maybe it was a shortcut.

"Please don't go exploring," Xoc yelled.

He was climbing the stairs now, catching up to me.

I looked back at him in pure indignation. *Psh. He doesn't know me.*

"I know you," he said, reading my mind. "and I know what you sound like when your curiosity has been piqued."

I gave a last look into the tunnel, squinting my eyes to try and focus on how far down it went. It looked like maybe it turned before vanishing into complete darkness.

I brought myself back over to the stairs and frowned at how little he seemed to care about my discovery. It would seem that Xoc was too preoccupied with the entirely gross webbing along the walls to be interested in a boring tunnel.

"Ooo," he said, "This makes so much sense. I knew I could feel something in the stone. These little guys are fascinating."

"What do you mean, *feel something* in the stone?" I said warily, stepping down to him.

Elyria, also curious, began climbing up to see what he was talking about. Xoc was examining a small worm that was crawling out of one of the holes. It was a dark red color, with tiny white spots freckling its body, and it was fuzzy. It actually looked like it might be soft to touch. Twenty stubby little podlike legs ran the full length of his body. Protruding from its head were two long antennae that wiggled around independently from each other. As it moved, its tubular mouth undulated.

"It's a Velvet Worm, or at least a cousin of them," Xoc said. "These little guys live on Mt. Carin too, but they are exceedingly rare."

He was completely entranced by the little thing. "Watch," he said, pointing to it.

An ant crawled along a blade of grass. The worm began moving, each thick leg pulling it from its hole.

"I'd rather not." I grimaced at the way it moved. It reminded me of a chubbier and less lethal-looking centipede.

"It's actually kinda cute," Elyria cooed, and in a baby voice added, "Wook at its stubby wittle wegs."

"I hate bugs." A shiver ran down my spine and a tingly feeling crept over my body as if millions of little legs were all crawling on me. It wasn't fear. Okay, it was fear-like, but it was manageable. And I'd never clue Xoc into that. He'd never let me live it down. The prince of Innesvale being undone by a worm.

Elyria, on the other hand, didn't seem to care at all. She reached for it.

"Ew. Please don't touch that," I said. Why did she always have to touch everything? Ferns, worms, frogs. This woman was touching everything except the things that mattered, mainly me.

"But it looks so soft."

"Ya know what isn't soft? Its defense mechanism," he said, holding up a hand to her.

From seemingly nowhere, the worm shot out two long white tubes.

I jumped back, not wanting to get too close to the thing. Not if it could spit whatever that was. "Did that just shoot from its mouth?!" I exclaimed.

Elyria leaned in for a closer look. Fucking leaned in. Her perfect damn lips not even an inch from the tiny monster.

The tubes grew, sprouting veins out in every direction. They spread until it looked like branches on a tree. The tendrils continued to reach and scatter on the surface of the stone until it covered the ant, leaving the insect completely encased.

"That's its proboscis," Xoc explained, pointing to the white tubing that had branched over the stone. "That's what the sticky substance below reminded me of. I never thought we'd see them here, though. See, this..." He pointed to the newly formed tubing. "It breaks off and holds the worm's food in place. It dries hard, effectively trapping its prey. Then the worm can eat whenever it gets hungry. The best part is that the worm can regrow the proboscis as many times as it needs to. Also, it looks like the worm actually has two of them. I've never seen that before. Evolution is marvelous."

I scanned around me and tried to keep from touching the stone rising on either side of the staircase. "There's so much of it."

Yep, I was done here. I pushed past them and began climbing.

"Oh, okay. Look!" Xoc said excitedly.

Morbid curiosity had me looking. In the back of my mind, I could hear a voice say, '*just keep walking*', but still, I turned around to see what could make stoic Xoc jump with enthusiasm.

The worm had crawled up onto the ant, and then a long black hook swung from its mouth. It sliced into the abdomen of the ant.

"What in Kraav is that?!" I said, pointing a furious finger at the worm.

"It's like its own cutlery," Elyria laughed, seeing my reaction.

"It's horrific."

"It actually slices open the body," Xoc added analytically.

I'm sure my face must have shown horrified shock because it seemed like Xoc relished in adding, "And then it injects it with an acid that liquifies the prey from the inside."

"Wicked," Elyria said and leaned in for a better look.

"Genius, really. Nature is amazing," Xoc replied reverently.

Just that moment, a bigger Velvet Worm crawled out from another nearby hole. It silently crept over to the smaller worm, rearing back on its hind, stubby legs.

I stopped and looked at the millions of holes in the surrounding stones.

Was there a worm in all of them? Oh, fuck no.

The smaller worm reared up in response. In an instant, the stocky worm shot out its flying web of doom. It whipped into the air and wrapped around the body of the smaller one. The proboscis continued to grow and expand. As it did, the growing tendrils pulled the worm down, locking it to the stone.

"It must have smelled the blood from the ant. Worms can't see very well, but they have an excellent sense of smell," Xoc added.

"I've seen enough." I began hiking up the stairs with renewed vigor, taking many of them two at a time. "Thank you for the lesson on how horrific nature can be. The sooner we get out of here, the better."

From behind me, I heard Elyria say, "It's so much bigger than the other one."

"The longer they live, the bigger they get. They never stop growing." Xoc said.

I would never get that image from my mind. The way the glassy whips had veined out and encased the smaller worm. Another shiver snaked down my spine. I tried not to look at the holes, especially the ones that lingered just below the handrails. Millions of holes. Dark, peppering every inch of stone. The idea made me gag. I picked up my pace and now was actually running up the steps. I didn't care. I needed to get off this cliff.

We weren't far from the summit. Maybe another few hours and we would have scaled The Steps. I could just fly it, might be worth it to get away from these... *things*.

I reached the platform and bent over, trying to catch my breath. I could hear Xoc and Elyria approaching from behind me. Xoc was clearly laughing. I groaned. I'd be hearing about this for the rest of my life.

Not wanting to face his jibing comments, I walked towards the next flight. I looked up at the wall and stopped. I spun back towards the stairs. Xoc was helping Elyria on to the platform now. He glanced at me and said with a laugh, "Wow, you just ran those steps. I've seen people chased by jungle cats run slower than you. You'd almost think you were *afraid* of something."

I looked back at the wall. My stomach sank and bile rose in my throat.

Ahead of us was a veining of smoky, clear-looking glass. But, unlike before, when the webbing never looked bigger than my little finger, this webbing was giant. I took a few hesitant steps, following it along the wall. It looked like it had wrapped around something. I peered into the surface and could just make out the skeleton of a small animal.

"Xoc!"

"They're just worms, Cal," he said, smirking. "And your arm is bleeding."

"What?"

I looked down at my bandage. Blood was seeping through the outer layer. Probably my vigorous running had reopened my wound.

"You didn't change your bandages before we left, did you?" he added.

I shook my head, then looked back at the skeleton. Tiny hairs on the back of my neck tingled. This wasn't right, and a slow panic seized my gut.

"We need to change them before we climb anymore," Xoc said, coming over to me and pulling off the wrapping.

Elyria brushed past me and bent down to investigate the skeleton. If I hadn't been so alarmed by what she was looking at, I might have been able to appreciate how she looked half bent over. But skeletons and worms in holes drowned out any pleasant thoughts, like Elyria bent over the desk in my office. *Okay, maybe not all thoughts.*

"I think this might have been a rat." She scrunched her nose at it. Not breaking her gaze away from the skeleton, she added, "Xoc, how big did you say these things can grow?"

She tapped on the glassy surface.

Xoc sat down a small jar of ointment on the stone and began cleaning my wound. I hissed at the stinging that burned in my cut.

"There's no limit, really," he said back simply. "I think an old one could be large enough to prey on rats."

Elyria kept walking down, and she squinted into another mass of veins. "And what about the really old ones?" she said, retreating with a look of near abject terror.

She backed so far up she almost walked right off the ledge. I raised my hand and threw up a wall of air just in time. She bounced off of it and landed on her knees. My heart instantly started to race. "Sunshine, you need to stop walking off of cliffs. My heart can't take it."

"Cal?" Her face had gone white.

I went to pull away toward her, but Xoc held my arm. "Stay still," he growled.

"Cal," she said more urgently, "there's a person in there."

"What?!" Xoc and I both said in unison.

She walked further down the ledge. "Actually, correction, there are people in there."

I yanked my arm from Xoc and walked directly to her. Beneath the veining were the carcasses of several people. They were withered and desiccated inside their glass cocoons, liquified and sucked dry.

"What the *fuck*!" I said, stumbling backwards into my own wall of hard air.

I looked back at Xoc. A thick and immediate sense of warning rose inside me, the beat of my heart like a war drum. A small trickle of blood dripped down my arm. I brought my hand up to stop the flow.

Xoc shook his head.

"This shouldn't be. There is no way one could grow to be that big. It'd have to be ancient," he said in disbelief. "Cal, we're talking tens of thousands of years old, older than the dragons even."

Elyria pointed to their clothing and the shriveled imprint of a tattoo. "Bandits. I bet they were down here trying to get the jump on travelers."

"I don't give a fuck what they were doing down here. I just don't want us to end up like them." I looked at Xoc. "We're flying out of here."

I moved towards Elyria and gripped her hand tightly before she could protest.

"Your arm," she said, pointing to the blood flowing more freely from my wound. It ran in thick streams down my bicep. "Before we go anywhere, we need to wrap it."

She pulled her hand from mine and walked over to the discarded bandage, brandishing it like a weapon. Her expression was one that couldn't be argued with. I could just grab her and deal with the fiery temper tantrum that followed, but how high would we get before having to contend with drained magic and blood loss? We'd drop right out of the sky. I couldn't put her at risk like that.

"Fine. But let's be quick."

A light rumble came from the ground. Tiny pebbles tumbled down the walls of the cliff. Xoc took a step back and turned to look at the wall. He went perfectly still, wings gently unfurling to their full breadth.

Slowly, he raised an arm to me. We locked eyes, and he mouthed, "*Go!*"

"What is it?"

"Large. Something *very* large is approaching."

"Where?"

I scanned the cliff face. I saw nothing, but the trembling was growing stronger.

"There," he pointed to the wall.

Xoc's eyes blazed to life, turning a bright and iridescent green. Claws extended from his fingers, and his scales spread the full length of his torso and arms. He held out his hands as if to brace whatever was coming. With a whoosh, he lifted off the ground and hovered just off the edge of the platform.

Elyria's hand gripped mine, and I pulled her into me.

"We are leaving. Right. Now."

Her arms wrapped around my shoulders. I summoned the air behind us.

The trembling became more of a grinding, defining roar as whatever was beneath the surface approached. I raised my hands to pull up the gust of air I was calling, and then... it stopped.

The world went completely silent. No grinding. No tumbling pebbles. Just perfect stillness. I looked at Xoc and went to say something, but he held up a finger to his lips and slowly shook his head. He gestured to the wall directly before me. I looked at the withered bodies beneath the veins of glass. Sunlight shone brightly off of the glossy surface of the webbing. Whatever it was must be right below the surface.

I wrapped myself around Elyria and held her tight. When I flexed, a stream of blood flowed freely down my arm and dripped from my elbow. I watched as it dropped onto the gray stone. It made a tiny splashing sound as it spread into a bright red fan.

All at once, the world exploded. The stone directly before us burst apart. Bits of the glass veins and viscera from the carcasses flew out. Xoc took flight upwards. I grabbed Elyria and together we jumped off of the platform, plummeting towards the ground.

Elyria screamed. I squeezed her tighter and summoned gale force winds to buffet us. Our descent slowed. From below, we watched as a gargantuan blood-red worm reared over the edge of the cliff. Elyria clutched at my neck. Above us, Xoc hovered just out of reach. He checked that we were secure on my platform of air, then soared higher.

The worm seemed to sense his movement and tracked him with its antennae. It clambered from its hole. At this great size, the stubby "cute" little legs were each the size of a horse.

"Still think it's cute?" I said to her quietly, and she answered with a tiny whimpering noise.

With amazing speed, the worm turned and began following Xoc up the cliff wall.

Xoc noticed the directional shift and moved to turn. But the worm increased its speed, simultaneously firing its proboscis. Glistening white tubing shot from the worm. Xoc maneuvered the side, but the spray latched onto his wing. The impact hurtled him into the wall with a resounding thud.

Xoc yelled out in frustration, twisting and tearing at the quickly growing mass pinning him to the wall. The tubing spread incredibly quickly over the surface of his wing. Within seconds, it had spread to cover his arms and torso, too.

I heard him yell, "It's too big. I can't control—"

His voice became muffled. When I saw him next, a vein of glass was covering his throat and mouth.

"Fuck," I cursed and increased our speed.

The worm closed in on Xoc.

"Get me up there," Elyria said. "Fuck, Cal! Get me up there. I can hold it off."

We flew. I pushed us faster than I had ever traveled by air before. As the edge came into sight, Elyria leapt from my arms. Graceful as a cat, she soared nearly five feet onto the ledge. Her landing was solid. She rolled, shooting a blast of fire from her hands directly up at the worm. It recoiled from the instant plume of blistering heat.

Fucking hells, she was amazing.

The great worm's mouth undulated, making a sucking sound. In response, Elyria let out a battle cry and fired a second inferno at the beast. It backed up slightly. However, sensing its new foe, the worm recentered on Elyria. Black pincers protruded from its sticky mouth. It made an unearthly clicking noise that made my entire body cringe.

Lightning-fast, it thrust for her. Elyria flipped back. The pincers grazed her chest.

"Cal!"

I flung out a blast of air, slamming it against the cliff face, but it recovered quickly. The worm recoiled, readying for a second strike. I threw out a wall of air. The black blade in its mouth sliced down at her. The worm bucked against the barrier, but it held.

Elyria reached behind her, pulling her serpent dagger from its holster on her back. She spun, slicing the mandible that protruded from its mouth. White fluid sprayed unpredictably into the air. It sizzled on the ground. A thick globule splashed her arm and she howled in pain.

Acid, which it used to liquify its prey.

She backed up against me, cradling her arm to her chest. The worm let out a deafening screech and thrashed wildly. It shot a second proboscis straight for us. Elyria held up her hands. A blast of fire barreled towards the white fluid, incinerating most of it. I went to pull her back from the cliff, but my foot was stuck. To my horror, veining expanded down my leg and over my foot. It thickened and lengthened, pulling me toward the ground.

"Elyria," I said, pulling on her arm and dropping to my knees.

"Fuck," she said, looking down at my foot. "Not you too."

She kneeled down and began swiping at the white webbing with her dagger. Knowing it had us trapped, the worm crawled entirely on the ledge, the wet sucking sound of it's mouth reminding me in too much detail of exactly what our fate would be if we didn't get off of this cliff. It's blade clicked against its remaining mandible. The disgusting sounds of our death closed in on us.

Panicked, I looked up at Xoc. The veins had expanded to cover his entire form. How long before it would be hard as glass and he couldn't breathe?

"Give me that," I said, gesturing for the dagger.

She handed it down to me, simultaneously pulling her two remaining knives from the sheath at her waist. Elyria sent off another warning blast of heat while I cut furiously at the veins, but they continued spreading over my legs faster than I could cut them away. One shot out and extended over to my other foot. By the gods, could this get any worse?

A dark shadow fell over us.

My heart stopped, and Elyria let out a near silent scream. The worm on the platform had slunk back from Elyria's last fiery blast. But, behind it, an enormous dark maroon worm had crept silently over the ridge. It dwarfed the wounded one by nearly double its size. By slicing off that mandible, Elyria had effectively rung the dinner bell for any giant predators in the area.

Terror, complete and all encompassing, paralyzed me.

Elyria's form rose tall, stark against this new foe. She settled into a deep protective stance above me, ready to take on whatever happened next.

"Demons below, we are so fucked. Keep cutting." The new behemoth reared back on its hind legs. The wounded worm recognized its significantly larger competitor and raised up, mimicking the motion. His stubby legs undulated wildly in the air.

Remembering what came next, I sliced at my bonds. "Elle, you need to get out of here."

Elyria bent down and began cutting too. "I'm not fucking leaving you to be sucked dry by a godsdamn worm."

The giant worm shot its proboscis at the injured one. Massive white blasts shot out, coating the worm before us. I flung up a barrier, and blankets of fluid rolled over us. The worm fell just as we freed my feet. I grabbed hold of Elyria, and we rolled off of the ledge just as a massive maroon body crashed onto the platform–– exactly where I had just been pinned. We narrowly missed being crushed but once again we were falling. I slowed our descent and let us hover in what I hoped was relative safety.

Perched midair, we had no choice but to watch the grisly scene play out before us. The behemoth worm crawled the remainder of the way from its tunnel, the exact same tunnel I debated exploring earlier. My skin bristled with the idea of what I might have discovered in the deep of the rock.

The giant worm loomed over the fallen one. A hook, nearly the size of a wagon, speared out from its mouth. With a *thwack*, it snared its prey. I cringed in horror as it dragged its victim back into the darkness of the tunnel. With each tug, the fallen worm made a sickening sloshing sound.

"I will never again suggest we explore forgotten caves and tunnels. Never again," I said.

I flew us up to where Xoc was still pinned against the cliff wall. Elyria and I cut away at the bonds. It had already hardened in many places. Anywhere that couldn't be cut, Elyria deftly burned away. When we freed his face, Xoc's expression was stark.

Laughing, I said, "Was that close enough for you?"

Xoc could barely speak. "Yes. I don't think I'll *ever* need to repeat that."

"You're not allowed to poke fun at me for having an aversion to bugs ever again."

"I think that's fair," he said.

Elyria pulled a chunk away that had been pinning his chest, and he took a deep, unrestrained breath, adding, "Fuck, I think *I'll* be having nightmares of worms for the rest of my life."

A few minutes later, we had freed Xoc. With a last look at the nightmare scene we were leaving behind, I took to the air. Elyria tucked herself safely beneath my arm. Xoc and I hurtled toward the surface. Pausing only when absolutely necessary, within the hour, we were breaking over the clifftop and looking down at the trees that lined the hillside. I had never felt relief like what flooded my senses seeing those trees. Xoc pointed at a lake at the base of a waterfall that tumbled down from the mountains and angled for a small clearing.

The moment we touched down next to the shore, I let my body fall completely flat to the ground. Adrenaline poured from me, taking with it the last semblance of energy I may have been storing. I watched the clouds float above us. They cast patterns into the surrounding grass. I sighed, then rolled over to where Elyria was stretching in the sun like a cat.

She gave me a withering smile.

"Next time," I said to her, "we sail around."

She laughed, "Agreed."

26

CALLEN

The roar of the falls soothed my nerves and calmed my soul. It summoned memories of home and the sound of the water cresting over the castle walls. It was one of my favorite features of Castle Shadowhaven. The waters of the Vanfald ran in channels through the marble castle until it cascaded from spouts to the turquoise waters below. Not only did it provide running water to the interior of the castle, but it made Shadowhaven exactly that– a haven. The streams of water were my sanctuary, my escape from the noise in my head.

A light mist rose from the base of the waterfall and filtered into the air, splitting the light into graceful rainbows. In all, this place was serene and welcoming. It was nothing like the nightmare that lived below the edge of the cliff.

I leaned back in the grass and propped my arm behind my head. My gaze drifted to the sapphire blue lake glittering in the late afternoon sun. Elyria walked to the water's edge and began washing away the grime of our climb. This was nothing like the seduction she had put on in the forest, although her camisole clung to her in ways that evoked the memory of every inch of her glorious ivory skin.

I sighed and pressed a hand against the blooming ache in my chest. For the first time in my long life, I was falling... and hard. When Elyria was done with me, my heart was going to be nothing more than a pulpy and bruised mess on the ground. She was gorgeous and compassionate, all wrapped in the heart of a fearless warrior. The way she'd leapt from my arms, not pausing to consider the cost she was taking, filled me with awe. When the beast roared at her, my girl roared back. Elyria was more than I ever imagined a person could be, and I wanted all of her.

She was wounded badly but didn't let it slow her down. Her pride made her downplay it, but I could tell it hurt by the thin line of her lips and the way she'd kept her arm tucked against me on our flight. Elyria gingerly rinsed the acid wound. The way her features twisted, I knew my conclusion was right; that burn was worse than it looked.

She dove beneath the water, and when she resurfaced, her dark hair was slick down her back, and the droplets shimmered on her skin. Elyria pulled her hair to the side and the nearly transparent camisole put her dragon mark on full display. The tail coiled against her lower spine, the snapping jaws at the base of her neck. It was remarkably similar to my own, not identical, but similar, as if we were two halves of a matching set.

Elyria walked from the water and glanced up to where I lounged. Somehow, she didn't seem surprised to see me watching her. She also didn't appear bothered by it, and that had my limited reserves of energy piqued. She lifted her face to the sun, closed her eyes, and let the dimming rays bathe her in a warm glow. An expression of relief spread across her face. Having given thanks to the sun, she picked up and wrapped a towel around her.

I made a little pouty face, and she laughed the entire way up from the bank to where I was stretched out in my own personal patch of sunlight.

She poked my side with her foot. "You should clean up too." She scrunched her nose. "You reek of worm."

Still laughing, she sat down next to me, tucking her legs beneath her.

Xoc stripped down to his undershorts and ran towards the water. His wings spread wide. They caught the air, causing him to glide into the lake with a graceful splash.

"I don't think he's very comfortable with the idea of bathing alongside me," she laughed.

"No, he wouldn't be. I'm sure some code of conduct told him to give you privacy," I said and stretched back out, running my fingers along the soft grass.

I knew she was right about washing up, but I was so tired. Flying us at speed had nearly drained me, and a deep exhaustion was seeping into my bones by the second.

"The water is so beautiful."

I sighed. "It reminds me of home. I grew up in the shadow of a waterfall similar to this one."

She shifted next to me. "I know. I've seen the Vanfald, or at least I've seen it from afar."

I rolled my head to look over at her.

"You've been to Innesvale? I didn't think you'd ever left Senesterra."

"Oh no, I've been everywhere. Well, everywhere that would welcome the non-tuned."

She twisted her body into a knot, stretching the muscles of her legs and back. She turned, twisting in the other direction. I longed to run my hands over those curves.

"How do you have so much energy? I can barely muster the strength to lie here."

She shrugged. "I suppose not being stuck in that Kraavian Hell has given me a new appreciation for life."

I propped myself up on my elbow. "Of course, I could probably find some reserves if you wanted to pick up where we left off. I can give you plenty of extra reasons to feel alive."

I couldn't help myself. Parting the towel slightly, I traced the lines of her leg as they twisted around her.

"Yeah, that's not gonna happen," she blustered.

I only raised my eyebrows and reached for the edge of her towel. She smiled and slipped it from my fingers, standing up and smacking them.

Placing her hands on her hips, she said, "Firstly, I'm fairly certain all logic had been knocked from me that night, literally. One second, we were sitting there on the cliff talking, and the next, I was wrapped around you. I don't even know how that happened." She shifted her weight anxiously and tucked her hair behind her ear. If only she knew how much I loved when she did that. Of course, if I told her, she'd probably never do it again just to spite me. "Besides that, I'm not even certain that's something I *want* to finish."

"I could show you how it happened if you'd like me to refresh your memory. Then you can decide if you think it's worth finishing."

I reached over and let the back of my hand gently stroke the inside of her ankle. A flush ran up her neck, but she didn't move away. If anything, she leaned into my touch. I smiled. Her breath hitched, and the blush deepened, splashing her chest with a dark red. She pulled her lower lip between her teeth. Was she replaying my lips on hers? Because I certainly was.

"And, *secondly*," she said with exaggeration, stepping into me. I took that for the invitation it was, letting my hand slide further up the inside of her leg, and the heat of her skin only made me want to touch more of her. "I believe I already stated that you reek of worm. I mean, you still have worm veins stuck to your pant legs." I looked down, and there were, in fact, tiny bits of glassy white substance stuck to the cuffs of my pants. The realization made a bit of bile rise in my throat. "And I'm pretty sure that red stuff in your hair is not supposed to be there. Unless..." She leaned down to me. "Unless it's one of the little worms."

She reached out as if to pluck something. I scrambled to my feet and began furiously smacking at my hair. "Fuck that. Is it gone?"

Elyria fell to the ground, howling with laughter.

"It's not funny." I stopped and looked at her. "I don't want one of those fuckers anywhere near me."

Elyria curbed her laughter enough to say, "Relax. Relax. I'm just playing with you. There's nothing in your hair."

I glared at her. "That's not funny."

She waved her hand. "It's a little funny."

"No, it's hilarious. You looked like a plucked chicken," Xoc said, walking up and wringing his long hair out.

Elyria walked towards me and let her towel drop. "But, I mean, if you still wanted to mess around..."

She pouted her lips and walked her fingers along my shoulder. That minx. The whole thing rang with sarcasm.

I snatched her hand, pushing my thumb into her palm, and stroked along the inside of her wrist. I raised her fluttering pulse to my lips and drank in the way her eyes smoldered. Her chest heaved from the labor of breathing against the current elicited by that small embrace. She was so easily affected by my touch. I loved it, craved it, and burned for more.

"You had your chance, Sunshine. I'm going to go clean up." I winked at her, then turned her arm over to inspect the acid burn. "Xoc needs to bandage this before it gets infected."

I released her. She cradled her abandoned wrist to her chest, but the look she gave me was calculating. I wasn't exactly sure what she was evaluating, but I could have her eyes on me every second of the day and never complain.

As I walked away I heard Xoc hiss, "That's one hell of an acid burn. It will need a healer for sure. Otherwise, you stand a good chance of sustaining nerve damage. But I think I have something to put on it to help with the pain. Next time, when you know you're going into a fight, cover your limbs with as much scaling as you can muster. It's saved me more times than I can count."

That night, we let the fire run hot and bright. I knew Elyria wanted to burn away any monsters that might be lurking in the darkness. Xoc procured us some rabbits for dinner. While they roasted over the fire, we traded stories of other near misses and close calls. Somewhere amid the easy camaraderie, we fell asleep.

I wasn't exactly sure what woke me but I jolted awake. The night sky was still black, and our fire had fizzled to embers. Xoc was sound asleep. He'd taken back his wings to curl up in his bedroll. The surrounding forest was quiet. The night air had chilled, and the skin on my arms rose with goosebumps. I flicked my wrist, and the fire sprang back up. It felt good to manifest flames again, even if it was just a small one. It had been days since I watched a fire of mine burn. I summoned a breeze to lift a nearby log from our meager woodpile. The flames eagerly licked at the dried wood. Soon, the crackle and pop of the fire filled the clearing.

At some point in the night, Elyria had moved her bedding to be nestled beside mine. The pride she would have swallowed to do that broke my heart because the only thing that would have driven her past that pride was fear. She twitched restlessly in her sleep, fighting some imaginary foe.

"Shhh..." I whispered to her, lowering my hand and brushing the hair from her beautiful face. She calmed and turned towards me. Her fingers gripped tightly into the fabric of my shirt like she was trying to keep me from running away from her. As if I would ever dream of running from her.

I slid into my bedroll, opening one side. Then I reached out and pulled Elyria into me, letting my arms wrap around her. With a sleepy murmur, she nuzzled her head into my chest. Her lips pouted in the most adorable way before drifting back into a deep sleep. I smiled against her brow.

Natural. Holding her felt completely natural.

I closed my eyes and focused my mind on the sound of the nearby falls, imagining the white spires of Innesvale and The Guardians on the bridge. I thought of walking the length of that promenade with Elyria on my arm, the sun setting and reflecting against the giant statues and the shiny surface of the bridge. I imagined all of the places in Innesvale that I would show her and the smile she would have as I took her to the grottos. Or the way my mother and sister would fawn over her. That was how I fell back to sleep, imagining the future we might one day have. No threats or Shade, just a kingdom of happy moments.

That was, until a scream pierced through my vision.

My eyes flew open. It was Elyria. Another blood-curdling scream ripped from her lungs. Xoc jumped up, his claws fully extended.

She was dreaming.

I gently stroked her face. "Elle. Elyria. Sunshine, you're dreaming. Wake up, Elle."

Her eyes opened wide, and her whole body tightened with the tremor that wracked through her. She looked like a cornered rabbit. I took her face into my hands and let the calm in my eyes communicate that she was safe. I knew what it was to wake up terrified and lost in the clutches of past traumas. Elyria searched my eyes for understanding, and then hers became glossy in the firelight.

"I've got you, Elle," I said. "You're safe. I'm here."

I tightened my grip as waves of tears rolled through her.

"It's okay, Sunshine. It was just a dream. I've got you. I'm not going any-where. You're not alone."

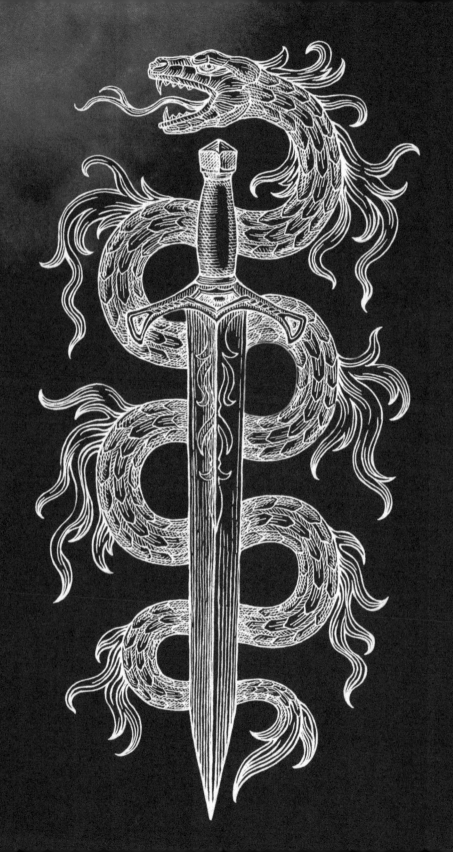

ELYRIA

It was a long night. I had a feeling there would be many long nights ahead of me. As the sun set, a growing sense of anxiety filled me. I didn't want to be back in the dark so soon. We had only just emerged into the light, and being thrust so quickly back into darkness unnerved me. In the dark, it was harder to ignore the images floating in my mind.

Cal was the first to fall asleep. He passed out, sitting upright, cup still in his hand. I took it from him, and then gently laid him down on the ground. He didn't stir at all while I shifted him or when I removed his boots. I pulled the edge of the blanket up over his shoulder, then brushed away the auburn locks that hung low over his eyes.

I sat, for longer than I should have, watching his slow, deep breaths. How did he do that, fall asleep so easily after all we had just endured?

Xoc caught me watching him. "Cal pushed it too far, too close. When you allow your magical stores to bottom out, the magic pulls from other sources of energy in your body. It will continue taking until there is nothing left for you to give over to it. It *will* consume you. This exhaustion is the price he has to pay for pushing past those limits..." Xoc scowled at Cal's sleeping form. "...and he knows better than to rely only on his attunement."

It seemed hard to believe. I'd never come close to running out of magic. The fire in me never seemed to die; it only simmered in wait.

At first, I set my bedding up on the far side of the fire, but I kept staring into the dark surrounding forest. The darkness played tricks on my eyes. It forced me to see all manner of monsters in it. I kept imagining a rotation between crystalline spiders dropping out of the trees and giant worms crawling up from the ground. The barrage was too much. So I slid my bedroll next to Cal's. It was silly, but being near him made me feel safer. I made the fire rise and watched the flames dance. His heat radiated from behind me, matching the heat rolling off of the flames. I focused on it until my eyes couldn't stay open any longer.

I had barely fallen asleep before I was sucked into the most horrific nightmare of my life. I was battling the worm again, stuck back on that cliff. The ledge was narrow, and a wicked wind whipped around me from below. This time it wasn't Xoc plastered halfway up the cliff. It was Duke. I fought the worm, one blaze of fire after the next. Still, he advanced. Then it shot that gross white fluid at me, locking me into position. I tried pulling my feet up, but the webbing held. I reached for my dagger, but the sheath was empty. I reached for my knives, but they were gone too. I tried to burn the webbing away, but each time the fire fizzled in my hands. Helplessly, I watched the veins creep over my body, pulling me to the ground and pinning me there. The glass slowly edged over my neck, covering my face and leaving just enough space for me to see the worm recenter over Duke. It pierced him with that hook. Immobilized, I had to watch as it devoured him, knowing that it would only be a matter of time before it returned for me.

I screamed and screamed. Until the next thing I saw were Cal's warm brown and amber-flecked eyes. Pride be damned, I couldn't help myself. It was terrifying. I was terrified, and all I wanted was for anything to make it feel like I was safe. Cal, and his warmth. He was what I needed. I may have saved him on that cliff, but he saved me in the darkness. He saved me from myself.

I let him hold me for the rest of the night. Every creak of the forest, every sound in the trees startled me. Each time, he soothed me, gently stroking my hair or caressing my back. He held me tight, and I let myself surrender to the comfort he offered. Maybe it was naïve to trust him, but in his arms I felt safe. In that moment, it was all that mattered.

At first light, I awoke. Cal was still sleeping, still holding me tightly to him. His hand was tangled deep in my hair, cradling the back of my head to his chest. His other arm nestled neatly at my waist. I warmed to the feeling of him wrapped around me and nuzzled deeper into his chest. Reflexively, his grip tightened around me, but he didn't wake. I smiled quietly to myself. It felt so right to be in this exact spot, natural even.

After memorizing the feeling, I carefully peeled myself out of his arms. Somehow I managed it without stirring him.

Xoc pulled his wings back in the night. He was just a man again. He sat propped against a tree, flipping through a book on herbs and spinning a sprig of lavender in his fingers. For a second, I wondered where he got lavender from. But then again, this was Xoc. He could grow anything anywhere. He peered at me over the cover and then looked pointedly at Cal. He smirked slightly before disappearing back behind the pages of his book.

I could feel myself blush and glanced back at where Cal slept. He looked content. So what if I had let him hold me all night? It didn't mean anything... probably. *Damn it.*

Lightly, I walked down to the glassy water. I summoned a fireball in my hand, then loosed it over the lake. It hopped over the surface like skipping stones. When the momentum slowed, I fought to keep the ball of light on the surface before it sizzled out. I shot a second and third orb over the water. The light shimmered, sending small ripples to the shore with each bounce. Together the three small streaks of light danced around each other. With a hiss, I let them dissolve into the black depths of the lake.

The lake called to me. I was going to dive into it and wash away the night. The crisp air and cool water would drive the images from my mind and cleanse the memory of that dream. I pulled my clothes off and laid them neatly on the shore. I stepped to the edge and let my toes sink into the sand. A light mist hung over the surface, and the moisture in the air clung to my skin.

Slowly, I walked into the water. It was cold, but not unbearably so. With each step, the water claimed more of me, until finally, I let my entire body sink beneath the surface. I delved my fingers deep into the silt that lined the lake floor. The minerals mixed with the water, making it glitter silver as it swirled around me. I stayed there until the last of my breath screamed for release, then rose up to the surface. The air rushed back into my lungs, and I felt renewed. Alive. Around me, the sky began to pinken, the beginning rays of sunlight heralding a new day.

Glancing back at our camp, it didn't look like there was any movement, so I began swimming out to the waterfall. One long stroke after another, each pulling me toward the rushing water. There was something about being near running water that always made me feel at peace.

The pool grew deeper, and the color of the water sank. I kept swimming until I reached the foam of the falls. Mist curled and wrapped around me.

And then I felt something brush lightly against the small of my back. I turned and saw nothing. The water was black. I could barely see my hand beneath the surface. I turned my head around. Nothing. Then I felt it again. It ran up the length of my thigh. I gasped, yelping at the unexpected contact.

From behind me,, I heard, "Good morning, Sunshine."

Godsdamn him.

I swung my elbow straight back, and was rewarded with a satisfying grunt. "You bastard. You just scared the life out of me."

I turned, and he floated backwards, a slightly pained expression on his face, which quickly turned into a look of pure amusement.

"I didn't mean to scare you," he smirked.

"Yes, you did."

"Yeah, I did," Cal added with a little shrug.

And, despite my anger, I smiled back. "I thought I was alone." I narrowed my eyes at him. "I *wanted* to be alone."

Quicker than I could track, Cal snaked out his hand, latching onto my arm. I gave a little yelp of surprise. One arm dipped around my back and another under my legs, cradling me to him in the water.

Too much skin brushed against his bare chest, causing warmth to spread down my spine and pool in my stomach. The hands at my side and thigh became a brand against me, one whose imprint I felt down to the very core of my power.

"You look so stunning when you blush."

The burning in my cheeks intensified. Damn my pale skin. Cal's smile spread wider, and then we began a slow spin.

The morning light illuminated the tiny drops of water that clung to his lashes, and beneath them, the flecks in his chocolate eyes danced golden in the rising sun. Gods, why did he have to be handsome?

Fuck. Focus, Elyria. You're pissed, remember?

Cal tightened his arms and leaned back, forcing us to drift towards the falls. My hands fell naturally onto his chest. A dark desire within me sparked alive, and I couldn't keep myself from running my fingertips along his perfectly defined muscles.

Into my ear, he said softly, "Did you still want to be alone?"

My heart hammered, and I couldn't tell if the roaring I heard in my ears was from my heart or the falls. I couldn't bring myself to answer him.

Damn him, and his charming... everything.

"Mmm... I thought so," Cal said, and kicked backwards. "Hold your breath."

"What? Wh-"

Suddenly, a cascade of water was crashing over us. Thick, heavy torrents of water filled my vision in every direction, but an instant later, it was calm. I turned my head, brushing the water from my eyes and scanning the small alcove. Light from the rising sun filtered through the waterfall and painted the walls blue. It shimmered and fell in thick, glimmering beams. The mica embedded in the black stone sparkled like starlight.

For the sound of the waterfall outside, this alcove was surprisingly quiet. The surrounding water rippled slightly, but otherwise it gave the illusion of stillness. This ethereal sanctuary was completely blocked off from the outside world, and its seclusion left me feeling safe... and in combination with the cage of Cal's arms, breathless.

How had he known this would be here?

I looked back at Cal, whose eyes never left my face, despite the wonder of the cavern. He was studying my reaction to the falls, and he looked... *enraptured.* I smiled hesitantly, unsure of how to react under such an intense gaze. This wasn't the same as an admiring crowd or a star-struck patron. I didn't think anyone had ever looked at me like this before. I opened my mouth to say something, but I couldn't seem to form words anymore. The intensity of the moment had laid me prone and speechless.

When we reached the back wall, Cal released my legs. They sank down, lacing between his. The pool was just deep enough that the very tips of my toes could touch the ground, but I had to hold onto his shoulders to keep my head above water.

Cal's hand, now free to roam, slid along my outer thigh. It trailed between my waist and side in long, rhythmic strokes. A shiver coursed down my spine with each gentle touch. He lifted his other hand to my face and brushed a stray hair from my eyes.

Why did it feel like every time he did that, I was damning my self-control? Every time. One simple moment of tenderness and my carefully constructed walls disintegrated.

I heaved a shuddering breath, and my chest rocked lightly against him. My very naked chest. If my damnation was in this grotto, then I was about to resign myself over to it.

"Let me kiss you," he said reverently. His fingertips caressed my cheeks. Gliding over my lips, he added, "Let me taste these lips and feel your heart quicken beneath my touch."

The water and the surrounding air suddenly felt very warm and thick. Steam drifted around us in small swirls. My mouth parted and went dry. I looked at his perfect, full lips and remembered how they felt pressed to mine. The way they made everything else seem to disappear. I wanted this, wanted him. But I needed to remember who he was and what I was doing. If I let myself swim too deep, then I'd never reach the surface again, and I'd just be lost in him.

But... *but*...

I swallowed. "One kiss. You can have one kiss."

One kiss couldn't hurt. I could indulge this desire, just a little.

He smiled like I'd just given him permission to harvest the moon from the sky, and discovered it was made of diamonds. His eyes dipped to my mouth, savoring what he saw.

"Cal." He smiled wider, and his eyes flashed at the sound of his name. "That's as far as it goes. That's as far as it can ever go. When we get to Suman, you will board a ship to Innesvale, and I am going to bury myself in the library until I get the answers I'm looking for." Even if what I really wanted was for him to bury himself in me. I bit down on my lip to keep that fantasy from taking root. "That is as far as we go."

He inhaled and his nostrils flared. I wasn't exactly sure how to read his expression. Was he fighting the idea of leaving me behind? Why did that make the thrum in my chest stronger?

Cal's eyes burned, and the hand sliding along my side grew hotter.

"If one kiss is all you will give me, then I will make that single kiss last for days. I will make the flame of that one kiss burn bright enough to light up the night. And, if that one kiss is all I can have, then I will make that kiss be all you ever dream of again."

What had I just gotten myself into? I was going to regret this. But which would I regret more—that I let him kiss me or that I only let him do it once?

He prowled closer, coiling his leg around mine and drawing our hips together. The thin wool of his shorts rubbed against my inner thigh, and brushed the softest, most sensitive parts of my body. I was suddenly aware of the fact that I wore nothing, and what he had on did little to mask how hard he felt against me.

My entire body seemed to go limp and taut all at once. I couldn't move, and yet each sensation had my nerves screaming. Tiny tingles ran along my arms, chasing behind his trailing fingertips. With a fast and deliberate motion, he twisted us. Our bodies spun. The hard edges of him lined up with my soft curves, locking perfectly into place with one another, and pinning the hot skin of my back to the cool stone wall.

The tingling in my limbs increased, and the water clinging to the stones around us steamed. Cal noticed it and smiled. His hands drifted down my sides, settling on my hips, thumbs softly caressing the line of muscle and bone.

He dipped his head low to my collarbone. Breath drifted over my skin, and a warm breeze swirled around us. His nose and mouth traced the curves of my neck. I couldn't stop from gasping at the too brief contact.

"Do that again."

Cal's responding smile grazed against the tender dip of my shoulder.

"Do what?" I said on a breathy exhale that was more a moan than actual words.

That smile rose until he hovered just above my lips. His hand lightly skimmed along the underswell of my breast and I gasped again, trembling against the still too light touch.

"I love that sound. Everything about you is so controlled, but this..." The back of Cal's opposite hand caressed my neck, tracked the curve of my collar, then further south against the rise of my chest. My body bent to his will. When his touch drifted low enough to tease my nipple, a slow exhale floated from my lips in time with his languorous exploration. "This is me slipping beneath that control."

Goddess, slay me. The heat rising within me was threatening to ignite. Each breath I took grew heavy with anticipation, rising and falling into him as he pressed back against me. He'd done this before, hovered until I ached. Waited until I gave in and kissed him.

Not this time.

I slid my hand into his hair. The curled ends wrapped around my fingers. I tugged just enough for him to know that no part of me enjoyed waiting. A sound that was half purr, half growl came from his throat, as if some feral part of him responded to that grip.

I laced my remaining fingers into his. He lifted our joined hands to the wall above my head... just as his lips collided with mine.

Cal's entire body surged into me, pinning our hips to the wall. His mouth parted, coercing mine open, only to push deeper into me.

And just like that, I let go of all doubt and disappeared into the moment.

My leg wrapped around his hip. I rolled my body to pull him in closer. His fingers gripped hard into the soft flesh of my thigh. Cal's tongue ran along mine, flicking against my teeth. Images of that tongue on other parts of me had fire rising to my lips. I pushed forward and bit down, raking his bottom lip. That growl resurfaced, and it called to the primal part of me I never acknowledged.

Fire sprang free of its cage and flared out from where our hands were still twisted into each other. Tiny purple flames skittered along the rock walls, lighting the surrounding cave with alternating firelight and the blue light filtering through the water.

I could barely breathe. Cal didn't seem bothered. He took his time, indulging in each movement and feeling. The grip of his hands and strength of his body against mine made it clear that he wasn't about to relinquish. Instead, he pulled us back, floating into the water. I wrapped both legs around his waist.

The kiss became gentle, and completely at war with the tensing muscles beneath me. His hand slid the length of my spine in one long, smooth motion. I bowed into his touch, breaking away from his mouth and failing to catch my breath. He dropped his head, and my heaving chest rose into his lips. He palmed my breast, his fingertips skating over my nipple, eliciting another breathy moan from me.

His lips. His fingers. All this sensation. Who had I been kidding? One kiss was never going to be enough. I needed more. I needed it right now.

The fabric of his shorts rubbed against me, and I ground my hips against him, greedy for any kind of friction. I reached for the tie at his waist.

Just as my fingers touched the cord, Cal released me.

One kiss.

The words echoed in my lust-hazed mind. Damn me and my need to set up boundaries. Damn him for respecting them.

I drifted backwards until I bumped into the wall. Breathlessly looking at him, I ran my hand over my breasts and up to my swollen lips. The sudden absence of him vibrated through me, and my body ached for his return. I extended my arm in invitation. *Come back to me.* Cal smiled, eyes drifting along the lines of my form.

He took my outstretched hand, spinning me partly into the falls. The cold rush of water cascaded over my chest and down his back. His mouth fell on mine, our bodies melding in the most perfect of ways. The frenzied passion transformed into a deeper emotion. It connected us with each soft motion of our lips. It echoed and resonated within me, binding us together. A blinding heat transferred between us. My vision flared bright purple, and my veins surged from the sheer force of it.

Cal's mouth broke from mine. Thick tendrils of smoke poured from his lips. Our bodies rocked with the movement of the water. He rested his brow against mine. A growling purr vibrated deep in his chest. "You taste like strawberries." He grazed his lips over mine, smiling. "And *violence.*"

My fingers tightened on his shoulders. Cal reached up to brush the damp hair from my eyes. Heat rose from my core, and I slid my leg further over his hip, raising it higher and driving my heel into his lower back to press him to me.

I would have this man right here and now. Boundaries be damned.

"Please, Cal."

I saw the crack in his restraint splinter and grow. His nails raked over my skin, and slipped down to grip my ass. He lifted me higher and fitted my pelvis perfectly against him. I moaned at the feel of him grinding up into me. Arching back, I drove my body down, while his lips once more explored the lines of my chest. A rising wave began to crest within my core, taking my sanity with it. I would give anything to him in this moment, he only need take.

Cal drew a deep, sighing inhale. His fingers dug into my flesh. Nostrils flaring, he almost looked pained. Then, his hands rose to my hips, and he pushed away from me.

I tumbled forward. My hand, which had been reaching for him, splashed into the water.

I pushed forward again, feeling the fire roll under my skin.

Still, he drifted away from me. With a half-smile he said, "I know you said just one kiss. Think of that last one as the encore."

Before I could say anything to persuade him to stay, Cal disappeared through the water of the falls. I watched, stunned, as his shattered silhouette disappeared from view.

My heart was going to leap from my chest, swim around the lake, before doing somersaults and dying on the shore.

I growled in frustration and shot a torrent of flame into the stone ceiling. It crackled, and the water clinging to the stones hissed in protest. I let my whole body sink below the water before I combusted. When I resurfaced, steam and mist lingered in the air.

Yep. I had lost my damn mind.

Now I had to figure out how to go back to the camp and face him. When I did, I wasn't sure if I was going to stab Cal or jump him. Probably both.

By the gods, he was right. I touched my throbbing lips.

How would I ever dream of anything else again?

28

ELYRIA

I waited to exit the cave until my boiling veins had cooled and my fire was firmly back under control. It took a solid ten minutes before I was sure there wouldn't be blood the second I saw Cal again.

The swim back to shore was quick. I walked onto the beach and scanned the camp for signs of either of the boys. I could already feel a flush creeping up my neck and was bristling at the smirk that I knew I'd find waiting for me. He knew he got to me. Fuck, I knew he got to me. Joke was on him. If he so much as twitched in my direction, I was going to smack that smile right off his face. To rub an entire damn bottle of salt into my wounds, the second Xoc saw me, he would know exactly what had transpired between us.

Groaning, I ran a hand over my face and tried to erase the feeling of his lips on mine. It didn't help. It really was like he had branded me. I slipped on my clothing as quickly as I could over my damp skin. Oddly, I still didn't see Cal or Xoc. I half expected Cal to be waiting like a sentinel on the shoreline.

Several yards ahead, Cal's shirt and pants were lying discarded in a messy heap. Curiously, I looked at them. Why, after all this time, was he still wearing only his undershorts?

It felt wrong. My instincts started clawing at my consciousness.

Cal was too calculating to just throw something like this to the ground. And why here? Surely he wouldn't have stripped all the way back here. I spun in a slow circle, waiting to see if Cal was about to spring out at me. I would be just like him, but it would seem that I hadn't just walked into a trap.

Xoc's book was strewn on the ground next to the campfire, the pages half-folded beneath its weight. Tiny drops of blood peppered the pages. Alarm ricocheted through me. *Blood.* Nothing about this was right. Our packs littered the floor like someone had dumped the contents and rifled through them.

My dagger. *Oh, gods.* Please tell me they didn't take my dagger. I ran to my pack, pulling an empty sheath from inside. The leather tumbled from my fingers to the ground.

Those fuckers! I scanned the ground for signs of tracks while trying to puzzle out how anyone could have gotten the jump on Xoc. He should have felt them coming. And Cal, what had happened to him? Had he been too distracted by what we'd shared to see an attack coming?

I felt myself spinning in circles.

A faint clash of metal rang out, the definite clang and scrape of a fight. It came from the northern woods. I narrowed my eyes, but couldn't see anything. As quickly as I could, I slipped on my boots. I prowled through the trees, following the sound of the fighting. A man howled in pain. *Cal.* A flood of panic filled me. I went to run, but then realized in the fallen brush that would be as good as announcing my arrival, so I forced myself to maneuver with caution.

Movement flickered ahead of me and I crouched behind a fallen log to assess. There were five men, rogue bandits. They wore similar clothing and had tattoos that resembled the shriveled corpses on the cliff, most likely hailing from the same clan. A shiver prickled the burn on my arm at the memory. They must have spotted our fire and made straight for us. I made a mental note to keep the excessive burning to a minimum.

At the center of the band stood Xoc. Claws extended, he slashed and ducked. With one powerful strike, he sank his fist deep into one attacker's chest. When he withdrew his hand, it was slick with black blood, and the man crumpled to the ground. Claws were most definitely badass.

The second attacker came at Xoc from behind. Xoc sensed the man's approach, and without turning, grabbed the man's arm, flipping him over his shoulder. With a loud thud, the attacker landed directly atop the previously fallen man. In a single fluid movement, Xoc wrenched the rogue's dagger from his hands and sunk it deep into his chest. The dying man grappled at the hilt for a second, before going limp.

It happened so fast. These men weren't even a little bit of a challenge for him. Xoc might as well be swatting at flies. But, where was Cal? I crept around further, trying to spot him, but it would seem that Xoc was fighting the men on his own.

The three remaining rogues came at him all at once. A vicious smile spread from the challenge, and his eyes glowed brightest emerald. He genuinely seemed to be enjoying himself. Xoc moved nimbly, despite his lumbering size. With a quick, low spin, he swept the legs out from the first man. As the attacker fell, Xoc latched onto his ankle and lifted. He threw him, sidelong, into the two remaining men. They all toppled over, landing hard in a heap on the ground.

Xoc raised his hands, and the surrounding ivy snaked out from the trees. It wrapped around the men, tying them like cordwood to each other. Xoc gave the closest man a swift kick to the side.

Seeing the threat was gone, I emerged from my hiding spot. Xoc glanced up at me.

"Nice of you to decide to join the fight," he laughed. "I thought you might stay behind the log all day."

"Well, it looked like you were doing just fine on your own."

I gestured at the vine-wrapped men. The closest man's eyes were wide and furious. He spat at the ground where Xoc was standing.

Xoc tightened his hand into a fist. A sickening crack came from the ground. The vines tightened, cinching the noose. The sound of the men's spines popping made the hairs on my neck rise.

I swallowed.

"Trust me." Xoc registered my expression. "These men have preyed on countless innocents, and I guarantee whatever they had planned, it wasn't anything as quick as the death I just gifted them. Left unchecked, they'd have kept terrorizing unsuspecting travelers."

I nodded. Of course everything he'd said was true. I'd heard horrific stories of the bandits that filled these hills. We were less than a day's walk from the beginning of the Strait Road. It connected The Bullseye to The Straits, and travelers would often camp in these woods on their journey from the eastern continent to the Center of Commerce. It made easy hunting for those who would prey on the unsuspecting.

There were times when the troupe had been assumed to be easy pickings. Rogue bandits often ambushed traveling groups, leaving none to identify the attackers. More often than not, it was kill or be killed. It was why Duke insisted I learn how to defend myself. Although now I wondered if he always knew there would come a day when being draken would make me a target.

"I was fifteen when I learned that harsh lesson," I said, looking into his green eyes. "I killed a man, or, well, men. There were two of them, brothers. They thought that since I was a young girl, that gave them permission to take advantage of me, and I'm sure to them, I looked like a stray kitten."

The memory still brought the sour taste of bile to my mouth.

"The brigands shoved me down into a pile of discarded fabrics. I watched in terror as the first man undid the buckle on his pants. Joseph's training kicked in and pushed my fear down. Instead of cowering, I assessed them and the distance to the door. The second man sat back, stroking himself and licking his lips."

I flashed my eyes up at Xoc. His head was tilted to the side, reassessing what he knew about me. I was never going to play the victim, even when I was victimized. If he hadn't learned that about me by now, then he hadn't been paying attention.

"Unfortunately for them, this stray kitten has claws. I waited for the first man to pull his pants down. I knew that with his trousers around his knees, he wouldn't be able to move as freely."

"Smart." A warm rush of pride followed his praise.

"So when I sprang up with all of my force, and punched him straight in the cock, the man fell to his knees– too doubled over in pain to do anything but whimper. The second man was startled for a second, and I took full advantage of it. While his filthy hand was still stuck down his pants, I spun and slammed my fist into his solar plexus. The hit momentarily drove the air from him. But it wasn't enough of a strike to gain me the clearance I needed to get to the door, something Duke and Joseph had been sure to fix during my drills the next day."

Xoc shifted his weight, but didn't comment. He just let me finish telling my story, knowing that it was a memory I needed to share with him.

"He advanced on me, wheezing angry obscenities and brandishing a knife. By this time, the first man had recovered and grabbed me from behind. He yanked on a fistful of my hair so hard that stars flashed at the edges of my vision. Then he pressed himself against me and roughly pawed at my breasts. I wasn't prepared for him to recover so soon, and the sudden violation of my body addled my mind. So I used the only weapon I had left to me."

Xoc's face tilted down as if the idea of seeing some man take advantage of a woman genuinely sickened him. His reaction made a bit of respect swell within me. Xoc was a good man.

"I lit up. My entire body burned white hot. A scorching fire radiated from me, instantly scalding the attacker in every place he had shoved his body against mine. He screamed, a sound so raw that I don't think I will ever forget it. Whenever I think of that night, the sickening smell of his burnt flesh still comes back to me."

I looked up into the tree cover and thought I saw movement, but there was nothing there, and my vision drifted to the bright blue sky. I really had missed the sun.

"Seeing his brother writhing in pain only enraged the other man. He lunged with the knife, screaming 'Bitch!' as if I was at fault, and should have just let them do whatever depravity they felt they were entitled to. Instead, I struck at the man's elbow and slammed my heel down into the arch of his foot."

"Duke taught you well," Xoc said approvingly.

"When the knife fell from his hand, I plucked it up in midair. With a quick release, the blade sank into his chest, fully to the hilt. He dropped instantly to the ground. From behind me, the burned man got to his feet and said, *You fiery little cunt.*" I did my best gruff impression. *"That's my brother you just killed. There ain't no part of you that's not gonna regret what you've done here. I'm going to make you scream, over and over, until you can't scream no more. And then when*

I'm done with ya, I'm gonna let me—' I never heard the end of his monologue. I suppose it was hard to talk with his brother's knife lodged in his heart."

I met Xoc's eyes head-on, a wicked smile tugging at my lips. "My knives always find their mark, always. The burned man fell to the ground. I said, 'Sorry, didn't quite catch that last part?' and kicked his body one last time for good measure. That was the first time I'd killed a man, and it wasn't the last either. But that doesn't make it any easier to watch death take a man."

Xoc laughed and nodded his head in agreement. "Well, you have actual claws now. So gods help any man who tries to take advantage of you."

I shrugged and flashed him an innocent smile. "What happened while I was... swimming?" I asked, gesturing at the men on the ground and then back towards the camp.

"Swimming?" He rose a knowing eyebrow at me.

My cheeks were beet red. I knew it. "Among other things."

"Ten of these fools thought they could get the jump on us," Xoc said calmly. He picked up the discarded knife and slid it into his bootstraps.

"And..." I said, searching the men to see if any of them had my dagger stashed.

"And I sensed them approaching just before a rock flew out and landed against my head. It knocked me out for a minute or two. When I woke, our bags had been dumped and Cal was gone. He's up ahead in the woods now. I can sense him. He's fighting another five attackers." He pointed deeper into the forest. "I'm sure he tracked them down the second he saw what had happened."

"You're lucky they didn't slit your throat while you were unconscious," I said, dropping a second man to the ground. "Damn. It's not here."

"What isn't?" he asked.

"My dagger. One of those bastards stole it," I said, gesturing to where he said Cal was at.

We began a quick run through the woods to catch up to Cal. By the time we arrived, he stood in the middle of a small forest clearing, having disarmed nearly all the attackers. His still wet undershorts clung to his firm thighs, and his bare chest shone in the sunlight that filtered down through the trees.

Two attackers laid dead on the ground, their throats slashed open. He fought off two more rogues. His body was lithe as he artfully struck. A third attacker approached Cal from behind. His arm was raised high above him, brandishing a dagger. *My dagger.* The metal shone as it began a golden arc. If that knife met its mark, it would sink deep into Cal's back.

Almost without thinking, I bent down, pulling the dagger from Xoc's boot. In a streak of light, the knife flew past Cal and embedded itself deep into the eye of the rogue. He fell to the ground. Shocked, Cal looked down at the dead man at his feet, then looked up and spotted me.

I blew a little kiss into the air and waved my fingers lazily at him.

He laughed, but pure lust saturated his gaze. Eyes still on me, he landed two more blows against the men that stood between us. It was like he didn't even have to try. Two more men fell to the ground, and I hungrily drank down the fluidity of each of his movements. This display shouldn't be arousing me as much as it was. It shouldn't... probably.

Cal's fighting stance was the kind that only came from years of practice. I thought of what Xoc had said about their master and the level of discipline exacted on them. It showed. It showed in every inch of toned golden muscle. Muscle that alternated between strength, flexibility, and athletic prowess as he spun and flipped in the air. I licked my lips. Strength, flexibility, and athletic prowess that had been tensed beneath my naked body only minutes ago. *Damn.* I was pretty sure he was flexing on purpose now. He knew I was watching him, and this entire fight had turned into an excuse for him to show off.

Cal slammed the closest man to the ground and then, deciding he was done playing, summoned the wind to lift the remaining men into the air. They hung suspended, kicking their feet and flailing their arms wildly. From the way he was looking at me, I guessed he had more interesting things he wanted to play with now.

"Showoff," I yelled, smiling. My heart rate picked up.

He looked down at the dead man. With the side of his foot, he tapped the dagger lodged in his eye and looked back at me approvingly.

"I knew he was there," Cal said nonchalantly. "But it's nice to know you care."

"I don't know what you're talking about. I just wanted my dagger back."

He dipped down and retrieved the Sun Serpent from the grip of the now very dead thief. Giving the knife a little flip, it rotated perfectly before landing solidly in the palm of his hand. His lips quirked up.

That was the only warning I got before he tossed the dagger.

It flipped end over end at me. It didn't move with any true speed or force, so I easily tracked its revolutions. I spun, deftly snatching the knife from the air. Looking back at him, I flashed my heated eyes over my shoulder and pursed my lips into a mock kiss.

Cal looked ravenous, and I thought he might just cross the clearing and take me right here and now. Crazy thing was, I was pretty sure I would let him. The lust in his eyes made my heart skip. I bit down on my lip to try and slow the aching need that was quickly rising in me.

From behind him, one of the suspended men yelled down, breaking the spell. "Get me down from here, you attuned pig!"

The man spat. With a quick flick of Cal's hand, the wad flew back, hitting the rogue squarely in the face. Cal chidingly added, "Wait your turn."

Smile full of amusement, he walked up to me and ran a hand through my damp hair. The strands slid between his fingers. Dropping his hand, he caressed the lines of my neck, dipping down along the curve of my waist and finally settling on my hips.

Gods. It was only supposed to be one harmless kiss. But now, seeing him fight, standing here, all bronze skin and wet shorts, feeling his fingers against my flesh and the weight of his hand on my hip... all I wanted was to dive into him and lose myself in ecstasy.

"I was on my way back to camp, thinking that leaving you was the stupidest thing I've ever done, when I saw that dumb idiot." He thumbed back to the dead man. "Running away with a particularly beautiful bit of craftsmanship clutched in his dirty mitts."

I looked down at my dagger, and then over at the dead man.

"So I went after it. I know how much that dagger means to you." Cal's eyes beamed. "I mean, you've kissed that blade more than you've kissed me, so it must be important."

I rolled my eyes at him. "It is." The Sun Serpent glinted in the sunlight. "Thank you."

Cal went after *my* dagger. I looked at his hands. The tips of his fingers were crimson, and his chest was sprayed with blood.

"Are you hurt?" I asked, concerned.

"Nah, this isn't my blood," he said, twiddling his fingers playfully in the air.

"What are you going to do with them?" I asked, pointing to the two twisting men in the air.

"What would you like me to do with them? Lady's choice."

I thought about it for a second. Cal's calculating eyes sized me up.

"Just knock them out. We've killed enough today. I doubt they'd be foolish enough to come after us again."

I glanced over Cal's shoulder. In the air, the two men nodded enthusiastically. "That's right, miss. You won'ts sees us again," said the man, who until now had been silent. If you could call him that. He couldn't be over sixteen.

Then Cal did something truly terrifying. He stuck out his hand and pulled back. A whoosh of air blew by us. The men in the air grabbed at their throats, gasping like fish on dry land. He had pulled the air from their lungs. Their eyes were wide and bulged from the pressure. Cal brought them in low and whispered something too quiet for me to hear. They nodded, and then the air rushed back at them again. He dropped them to the ground, and they laid there gulping down great swallows of air.

"Yeah, I don't think they'll be going after anyone again," Cal remarked confidently.

"What did you say to them?" I asked as we began walking towards camp.

Xoc was checking the men to see if they had any other pilfered items on them.

"Oh, just the things of nightmares. No one threatens my girl."

He winked at me.

"Your girl?"

Before I could slap him for that, a shuffling sound caught my attention. Behind us, the young rogue was standing in the middle of the clearing. He was frozen still, face completely blank and looking straight at us. His eyes were milky white, and my mind flashed on Duke regaining consciousness after the healer woke him. I couldn't breathe. How could this be?

I looked at Cal, needing his steadiness, but where there should be surprise, his brows were raised and his eyes wide with concern and recognition. No, instead of surprise, there was only steely rage darkening his features. He knew *exactly* what was happening.

My feet edged slowly away from him. Even without meaning to, I was putting space between us. Hurt panged in my chest. He knew, and he hadn't told me. There was only one reason he would keep that information from me. That pain in my chest thrummed stronger and slammed against my ribs. I refused to even acknowledge the possibility. Cal couldn't have had anything to do with Duke's curse. He just couldn't. But even as I tried to sew my heart up with that resolve, a tiny thread of doubt wound its way in.

"Don't do something stupid, lad," Xoc said, sliding into position to strike if necessary. "You're lucky to be leaving this glade with your life."

The man didn't acknowledge him. He simply turned towards me and sang.

> *The calico cat*
> *lost taste for the rat.*
> *He followed the mice,*
> *they might taste nice.*
> *He dangled a treat*
> *to summon new meat.*

The man's voice was like velvet, deep and sweet, and eerily similar to the boy's at the bar. A shiver tingled across the back of my neck. I knew the next verse, and I didn't want to hear it.

The little mice run.
One by one,
They come, they come.
The petals fall
And all is done.
See how the little mouse runs—

The man stopped abruptly, his expression blank. A small trickle of black blood seeped from the corner of his mouth before he slumped to the ground. Gold shone off the hilt of my dagger, now lodged firmly in his heart.

I hadn't even realized I threw it, but there it was. Cal pulled the knife from his chest, wiping the thick black blood on the man's shirt before handing it back to me.

"So much for mercy." His words were full of sarcasm, but his eyes radiated empathy. For some reason, that look, coupled with the horror of the past few minutes, twisted my heart even more.

I took the dagger, dismayed.

"We need to go... now," said Xoc, placing a hand on my shoulder and knocking me out of my stupor.

"What?"

I looked at the remaining man, who was lying on the ground. He looked as alarmed as I felt. He held out his hands to me in supplication. "Please, miss."

"I don't care what you do with him."

I flashed distrustful eyes at Cal. He took a step back and almost looked hurt. *Good.* That bastard was keeping secrets, the deadly kind. I turned, marching back through the woods towards our camp. Behind me, the man was crying, "Thank you. Thank you."

A flash of white hair caught the corner of my vision.

"What in the Hells?" I whispered and scanned the treetops. There was nothing there. "I could have sworn..."

"Elyria. Elyria, wait," Cal called after me.

I dismissed the vision. It was only my own paranoia catching up to me and making me see ghosts, and there was a very real Cal hounding after me. I kept walking before that sweet, lying mouth of his could spin something else to snare me. I refused to give him the satisfaction of seeing how rattled I was.

"Let's just go. Who knows what other dangers are in these woods." Even those in plain sight.

29

ELYRIA

With so many dead in the vicinity, we figured it would be better to leave. I had posited that we didn't want whoever they answered to coming to look for them, only to find us. But, Xoc added that the smell of death would bring in other darker creatures that we didn't want to face. I didn't know what he was talking about, but I had enough nightmare fuel for the time being.

Before leaving, we laid the map out on a nearby rock. Xoc quickly identified the falls and the lake. "It isn't far until we hit the Strait Road," Xoc said, pointing to the road that lay to the east of our location. "Maybe a few hours, half a day at the most."

"We could probably reach one of the outlier towns within a couple of days." Cal made a light, dreamy sound. "Sleeping at an inn, in a proper bed, is not something that I am going to turn down anytime soon." Then he looked down at me. "Plus, maybe one of those towns has a healer. Someone needs to tend to your acid burn."

"I'm fine." I waved off his concern. "It barely even hurts."

Cal whipped out his hand and flicked my arm lightly. Heat lanced out from where he had struck. My features twisted in pain.

"Uh-huh. Tell me again about how fine you are."

How did he manage to make caring about someone so damn infuriating? His face softened as he soothed my hurt arm with a gentle touch.

"I'll tell you what, you let me take you to a healer, and I'll let you have first pick of what bed to sleep in tonight."

He smiled, knowing that would be enough to get me.

"Fine," I said.

"I wonder whose bed you'll choose?" Cal said.

There it was again, that stupid-ass grin that I was going to have to smack off his face.

"Oh, I'm pretty sure I'll choose to sleep in *my* bed," I replied coolly.

"And I'm pretty sure I'm going to ask to sleep with the horses, if it means that I won't have to listen to the two of you all night long," added Xoc.

"Can we just get out of here?" I said, hitching up my knives, trying my best to ignore the face Cal was making. I frowned at the missing knife in the holster.

"We can get you a new one," Cal said, reading my expression. "I know a blacksmith in the Smithy Ring of The Bullseye."

I shifted my weight, cocking my head to the side in contemplation. "Tell me, every time I throw a knife at you, will you replace it? Because I could throw knives at you All. Day. Long."

His eyes flashed. "Oh, and I'd let you too."

"Gods," groaned Xoc.

We began walking at a relatively brisk pace. The idea of a warm bath and a soft bed fueled us forward. The Strait Road had a relatively steady stream of travelers on it. Wagons and people traveling by horseback passed us several times. It seemed like every party that went by made Cal nervous. I asked him why, but he shrugged it off as caution.

I suppose after the encounter in the woods, that was wise, but it still felt odd to me. These were regular people, families, and small merchants hauling their wares. How could a mother and her babe pose a risk? It didn't seem to stop him from assessing each person we passed, and that nagging feeling came back. Cal was keeping things from me, and it made every one of his indifferent shrugs feel like a lie.

After two very awkward nights of nightmares, which inevitably led to snuggling that felt too damn good, we were finally approaching the first of the Outliers, Cambertine. I generally preferred the small villages to the larger towns and cities. The people in places like this were always welcoming, and they took care of their own. You never saw starving orphans begging on the streets. Whenever Solaire passed through these towns, I would imagine this was where I might have lived as a child if I hadn't been orphaned. I would see a small girl playing in front of her home and pretend it was my sister, and the mother who called to her from the window was my own. It was a pleasant fantasy. Not that I was unhappy in my lot. Duke was a great parent. I had a happy childhood, and life on the road had its perks. But the fantasy for me would always be the cozy cottage.

When we got to the town proper, if you could call it that, Cambertine was really only a few streets and a central square. The lamps were already lit, and they glowed warmly in the twilight. The square's highlight was tiers of lovingly tended flowers that spilled over the sides of the flower beds like tiny colorful waterfalls. At the center of the flower cascade stood a tall flagpole, where a flag with the trademark bullseye flapped in the wind.

Technically, the Outliers were the Farming Ring, but they weren't so much of a ring as everything beyond the rings. This part of The Bullseye was represented on the flag by the outer brown ring of color, larger than all the others. You could always determine which district you were in by the dominant color of the bullseye's rings.

"Ah, civilization," I said happily.

No more dark forests, man-eating worms, or nights spent sleeping next to a campfire.

The heavy scent of the summer blooms filled the square. I turned to look at the boys. "So do we stop here or keep going?"

Just then, a girl with chestnut skin and red hair came bounding over to me, her curls bouncing with each joyful skip.

"Are you Elyria, The Dragon?" She beamed brightly at me, two teeth missing from her grin. "You came to town for my birthday last year. You lit my cake for me."

"Oh," I cooed. A vague memory felt just out of reach. I squatted down to her. She was a sweet thing. "Yes, that's me. I remember you, darling girl. Your name is..."

"Maddilyn," she blurted out exuberantly.

"That's right, and you were turning thirty."

Maddilyn's face brightened, and laughter bubbled up from her. "No. I'm eight."

"Are you sure?" I smiled. "I distinctly remember you turning thirty."

She laughed again. It was a spritely tinkling sound. I looked up at Cal, who watched the entire exchange with warm amusement.

"Maddie," I said sweetly, "do you know of an inn in town, one that has some beds we can rent?"

"It's Maddilyn. Maddie was my baby name. I'm all grown now, so you can call me Maddilyn," she said, with an adorable level of authority to her voice.

An older woman called from across the square, "Maddilyn! Blast it all, girl! Where have you run off to?"

"Nannie, I'm over here!" she shouted back. She looked up at me, an idea dawning on her little face. "You should stay at our house."

Before I could say anything, she scampered away.

"You don't actually remember that girl, do you?" asked Cal quietly.

"Noo... but I've gotten very good at faking it. Duke brought our troupe through nearly every town and city in Venterra. You meet a lot of people. If someone would tell me it was a special day, I'd do a little trick and say it was for them. I guess I must have lit some birthday candles for her," I said, gesturing to where she ran off.

I scanned the square but didn't see any signs that looked like an inn.

"Nannie! Nannie, see, I told you. It's her! See, Nannie?"

Maddilyn was hurriedly dragging an older woman across the square. Nannie looked me up and down. Then she looked over at Xoc, who loomed behind me, and then to Cal, who looked terribly amused by everything that was happening. She narrowed her eyes, squinting at me. She looked like maybe she recognized me, then looked down at Maddilyn and said, "Who is this again?"

I blurted out a little laugh. "Good evening, ma'am. I'm Elyria Solaris. I—" It suddenly dawned on me I had never *not* been The Golden Dragon, or part of Troupe Solaire. "I used to perform with Troupe Solaire. Maddilyn here recognized me from when the troupe performed here last year."

The old woman nodded her head, but said, "If you say so. I'm sorry, dear, my memory is for the cats."

"That's perfectly fine," I said, trying to be gracious. "I was never in it for fame. I just like to spread joy."

"Well, ain't nothin' wrong with that," she said and reached up to pinch my cheek. Actually pinched my cheek and gave it a little slap.

Cal finally spoke up. "Ma'am, if it wouldn't be a bother, could you help us?" She turned and looked at him. "We're looking for a place to procure lodgings for the night. Is there an inn in town?"

"Well now, you speak as pretty as you look," she said, and a crooked smile emerged from between the deep creases of her face.

"You have no idea," I muttered to myself.

Cal smiled, and I knew he must have heard me.

She nodded her head in contemplation.

"Nannie!!!" Maddilyn said, urgently tugging on her sleeve.

The old woman shooed her off and scowled down at the girl. "What child! *What?*"

Maddilyn pulled her low and whispered in that version of whispering children do when they think no one can hear them, but really they haven't changed their volume at all. Maddilyn once again asked for us to stay at their home. The old woman looked at us again, then back down at the girl.

"How about you all come to our house for some supper? I've had lamb stew in the kettle all day."

Behind me, I felt Xoc stand taller. I turned, and he looked positively delighted at the idea of lamb stew.

The old woman must have noticed too, because she added, "Like the sound of that, do you? I'm sure a large lad like yourself could put back a whole pot. Not to worry, I made plenty. My Joey is just like you. He could eat a week's worth of rations for a single meal. Still, come and share a bite with us. Then we can see about finding you three someplace to sleep tonight."

Once again, she smiled warmly at me, and then up at the boys. Maddilyn next to her trilled excitement, and began doing a victory lap around the flower fountain.

Maddilyn excitedly took my hand and led me along the cobblestone street. At the top of the hill, just outside of town, sat an adorable thatched cottage behind a stone fence. Smoke from the chimney curled, filling the air with the savory smell of a cookfire. Linens hung from the wash lines and flapped in a breeze that smelled faintly of hay. The sun was setting along the hill, the sky behind it filled with streaks of pink and purple. Fireflies rose out of the grass in the surrounding fields, and the air was filled with a concert of chirping bugs. It was as warm and inviting as a home could appear.

Warmth and elation filled my heart. I turned and looked at Cal. His eyes scanned my expression, and it seemed like some part of him softened. In what felt like a completely natural move, he reached out and took my hand in his. I couldn't keep the joy from bubbling out of me. "This is exactly the type of home I always pictured as a child, right down to the sheets hanging on the line. If we weren't living on the road, this was where I wanted to be. It's as if my childhood fantasy came to life."

The wooden gate squeaked when Maddilyn pushed it open. Along the slate walkway that led to the door, there were little stick figure drawings of a family.

"Maddilyn, did you draw these?" I asked.

She nodded and pointed. "Me, Pappa, and Nannie... and Trixie. She's my pet goat. I make my own goat cheese, wanna try some?"

She was so happy. I looked back at Cal, who held his hands up. "That's all you," he whispered over to me.

I scrunched my nose at him and defiantly said, "Maddilyn, nothing would make me happier."

Xoc snorted behind me.

We walked into the house, and Maddilyn pushed past me. "Pappa! Pappa! Guess who's here!"

A man walked from the back of the house, a pitcher in his hand. When he saw me, the carafe slipped from his fingers and crashed to the ground. White milk sprayed across the tile floor.

"Joseph?" I said.

Surprise flooded me. Not just me. It seemed like the entire room was suddenly soaked in it. I looked around as if an explanation would present itself.

He spoke first. "Of all the people that I thought I'd see walking through my door tonight."

He stepped over the milk and pulled me into a tight embrace. Tears instantly flowed from my eyes. I wasn't even sure why I was crying, but I couldn't stop them. I squeezed him back. It had been too long.

"So..." Cal said, "someone going to tell me what's going on?"

I laughed, wiping tears from my eyes.

"Cal, Xoc, this—" I said, slapping Joseph on the chest, "is Joseph Pendlecost. You know how I keep kicking your ass? This is the man who taught me how."

"Lies, all lies," Cal said, extending a hand to Joseph. "Calvin Dentross."

"Dentross, was it?" Joseph said, slowly shaking his hand.

"That's right, sir. And this is my business partner, Xoc."

"Maddilyn, oh my gods." Recognition and memory clicked into place. "I remember now. Joseph, why are you here, in Senesterra? You and Penny were living in the Isles. The troupe came by, and we all had a party for Maddilyn. Gods, that was nearly four years ago." I looked back towards Maddilyn. "I can't believe she remembers me."

"Remember you?" Joseph said incredulously. "She's pretended to be you nearly every day since then."

"Where's...." I scanned the house and leaned into the kitchen, looking for Penny.

"She's not in there, Elyria," Joseph said solemnly. "She..."

His voice trailed off as he looked down at Maddilyn. "Momma's a mermaid now," Maddilyn said brightly. "She got sick, but we put her on a boat, and she went out to become a mermaid."

"No," I breathed. The glassy burn of tears pricked my eyes.

"So we came to live with my ma," Joseph added, "This is where I grew up. Remember when you were little, I would tell you stories about this place?"

I sighed. No wonder this matched my ideal vision of home. It clicked. So much clicked into place in my mind.

Joseph left the troupe when I was seventeen to start a life with Penny and her family in the Isles. On rare occasions, we would stop to see them, but space on the islands was at a premium, and they didn't really have anywhere to set up our rigging. Then, four years ago, Joseph and Duke didn't part on the best of terms. Not Joseph's fault. Duke was a drunk asshole who was angry that Joseph got to have the family he was denied. Joseph had thrown him out, and that was the last we saw of him. The irony was that these past few years, Joseph probably could have used Duke's support.... and now.

"Ellie, are these lads here new acts? Is the rest of the troupe in town too? Is Duke...?"

"No," I said, and I couldn't stop the tears from spilling out of my eyes. I took a deep breath and tried to push the rising emotion back into the iron cage I kept it locked in.

Had I actually said those words out loud yet? No. I hadn't. I opened my mouth to say them, but nothing came out. I tried a second time, still nothing. So instead, I said, "I left the troupe."

Joseph's face went pale.

Nannie said, "Maddie, baby, how's about you go set the table for supper? I'll help you."

Cal put a hand on the small of my back, a ghost of the hand he had placed there during the funeral. I looked up at him and shook my head.

I couldn't do this.

Instead, I pulled the necklace with the rings out from under the collar of my blouse. They tingled as they shook against one another, catching the light and flashing like a beacon in the darkened room.

Joseph took a sharp intake of air.

I turned my face away from him, leaning unconsciously towards Cal's warmth. I knew that if I met Joseph's empathetic gaze, the tenuous grip I had on my composure would crumble.

"So, lamb stew. It smells absolutely delicious," Cal said. He gave my side a little squeeze and then slid his hand away from me.

Joseph cleared his throat. "Yes, Ma's been cooking it all day. The meat is so tender, you'd mistake it for butter."

The two of them walked from the room. I looked up at Xoc. He stood calmly, looking down at me.

"I'm just not ready," I said to him.

He nodded. "No one says you have to be." He placed a hand on my shoulder. A wave of calm flowed over me. "In your own time." A second wave of calm. The cage of spikes spearing my heart loosened, allowing me to breathe.

He removed his palm and began walking toward the kitchen. I touched where his hand had just been. It tingled slightly.

"Xoc?" I questioned, my hand still on my shoulder. "Did you just do that calming feeling? Just now, when you touched me?"

He didn't say anything, simply smiled, and walked into the kitchen.

30

CALLEN

Dinner was delicious. Thick-cut potatoes, savory gravy, and the lamb did indeed fall apart like butter. Nannie could probably teach the palace chef a thing or two about comfort cooking. Over and over, she kept refilling everyone's bowls until we were all half sedated from full bellies. She went to put another spoonful into my bowl, and the thought of eating anything else turned my stomach.

I put my hand over my bowl and smiled at her. "Nannie, if you make me eat anything else, you'll have to mop me off the ground."

"This is how it should be. Full tables and full bellies. It's nice to have company. I think in the morning, I'll make fresh biscuits and gravy or maybe scones."

She pulled a sack of flour down from a pantry shelf.

I wiped the corner of my mouth with my napkin. Elyria spent the entire meal chatting with Joseph about various changes in the troupe, stories about the antics the boys did. With each story of pranks and misdeeds, Joseph's hearty laugh shook the table. I was happy to just sit back and listen. For the first time, I was getting a picture of what her life had been like before all the drama. I was lost deep in thought, picturing Elyria in her element, when Joseph spoke up.

"Cal, do you fancy an after-dinner brandy?"

I leaned back in my seat and folded my hands behind my head.

"I've been known to partake," I replied, glancing at Elyria.

She was biting her lip as if she knew the punch line to a joke I was unwittingly a part of.

Joseph clapped his hands together. "Excellent. I've been aging this particular batch of honey brandy for the past year." He stood up from the table, stretching out his back in a chorus of pops. From a lower cupboard, he pulled out an amber bottle. The glass was dusty, and he wiped it away with his sleeve. "It's made with honey from our apiary out back."

"Why am I not surprised you keep bees?" Elyria joked.

"Pappa, can I have some brandy, too?" said Maddilyn brightly.

"Nice try, nugget. I think it's probably time for you to be heading to bed. Don't you?"

"Pappa!" she whined. "Nooo, Elyria is here. I want to stay up with you all."

Elyria leaned over. "I'm really not that interesting." Then she added, in a conspiratorial whisper, "But Nannie showed me earlier that she has some lovely-looking cookies over there. Maybe you can get her to slip you one on your way to bed. If you're quick, your father might not see." She winked at the girl and gave her a soft kiss atop her head. "I'll see you in the morning."

Maddilyn glanced at her father, and before he could say no, she went running off.

Elyria looked up at me, and she looked surprised. I must have been staring at her again.

"What?" she said, tucking a hair behind her ear.

I hummed. "You're a natural with children."

She smiled. "Why do you think I'm so good at handling you?"

I was about to tell her all the ways she was free to handle me, but then I noticed Joseph studying our exchange. Elyria noticed it, too, and gestured toward the den. "Let's move over by the fire."

"That is a banner idea," said Joseph. He handed me a misshapen glass. It was half full of a thick brown liquid. It rolled smoothly in the glass, and a sharp, flowery scent wafted up to me.

"Elyria, can I tempt you with a glass?" he asked.

"Oh no, Joseph. I learned my lesson last time."

"I'll take one, if you're offering," said Xoc.

"Good man," added Joseph, handing him another oddly shaped cup.

By the fire, a shaggy wool rug sat on the floor. Elyria curled onto it and leaned back on the arm of a cozy tufted armchair. I moved over to it and sat down beside her. Twisting, she draped an arm over my leg. A laugh perched on her lips.

"Try it yet?" she said, resting her chin on the hand that laid at my knee.

I looked down at the brandy and gave it a sniff. It smelled sweet, and also *very* strong. Shrugging, I tipped the rim to my lips. The fiery burn of the alcohol swished in my mouth, followed by the thick sweetness of honey. It was both spicy and sweet. If I wasn't careful, I might be the one who started breathing fire. My face puckered and I smacked my lips.

"That is..." I paused, trying to think of the appropriate word to describe it. "*Different.*"

Elyria grinned, dipping her head. Silken black waves of her hair cascaded over my leg. I leaned down, letting it fall against the back of my hand and brushing her fingers with mine. She flashed her golden eyes up at me. Was the warmth blooming in my chest from her smile or the brandy?

I held the glass up to the firelight. The amber liquid swirled. I took another swig. It burned down my throat, warming my stomach. I gave a tiny cough and smacked a fist into my chest. Elyria laughed. I tried to smile through my grimace. Stomaching this obscenely strong drink will have been worth it if I could keep hearing her laughter.

She turned her head against the arm of the chair and pulled her hair over her shoulder. The firelight glinted off the golden ends of each strand and gilded the smooth curves of her throat and chest. I clenched my hand into a fist, trying to resist the urge to keep touching her.

Fuck it.

I reached down and pet the top of her crown. She hummed and tilted into the touch. Her temple moved to my knee. I let the soft strands sift through my fingers, occasionally drifting the back of them down the slender line of her neck. I didn't miss how, with each stroke of my hand, she pressed closer to me.

Xoc and Joseph came into the room. Joseph was laughing at something he had just said, and Xoc's almost empty glass dangled from his fingers. He walked over to an old, worn rocking chair in the corner.

"There is no way you can fit in that chair," I said, Elyria's hair still laced through my fingers.

"Watch me," he said and squeezed his massive frame between the arms. The wood creaked, but then it seemed to settle. Xoc rocked gently back and forth, pleased.

"So if you two aren't with the troupe, then where are you all headed that you're coming through here?" asked Joseph.

"Suman," I said. "We were in Laluna when we met Elyria, and since we were headed the same way, we traveled together. Also, she makes infinitely prettier companionship than that brute."

I gestured toward Xoc, who still rocked lazily in the chair. He raised his glass to me and knocked back the remaining cup in one long shot.

Elyria watched him, wide-eyed. Xoc choked a bit, then smiled, licking his lips. He held out the glass to Joseph, who happily refilled it.

"Actually, I'm headed to Suman. These two are going to book passage back to Innesvale."

I swallowed down the guilt and the pang it created in my chest. Elyria edged away from me, exposing the back of her neck. She probably thought she was punishing me by pulling her hair from my hand, but she had to know I was greedy for any part of her.

She added, "And I let them tag along. They were too afraid to travel without me."

Joseph barked out a laugh.

"I'm headed to the library. This one says he can get me access." She tapped the back of her arm against my leg. "Before he..." her voice trailed off. "Duke told me some information about why I can do the things I can."

Joseph leaned forward. "So, he finally told you about the draken, did he?"

"You knew!"

She sat straight up, slamming her hands against the ground, shock twisting her expression into one of anger.

"Elyria, I was there the day he brought you back."

He glanced between Xoc and me, then back to her.

"It's fine," she said, waving her hand in the air. "They know."

"I've seen what you could do from the start." He shifted toward her, smiling at a memory. "Ellie, one time I was watching you while Duke went off with some mistress. You wanted to go into town for sugar ices, and I wouldn't take you. You threw a fireball the size of dinner plate right at my sandwich, burned it to ash in my hands just to spite me. It was a glorious sandwich too, fresh bread and sausage."

He held his hands out, imagining holding it still.

"You said in this little shrill voice, '*If I can't have what I want, why should you get what you want?*' Actually, Maddie is just like you. Not actual fire, but full of fire nonetheless."

Elyria looked bashfully over.

"So basically, you've always been like this," I said to her.

She whipped her hand up with impressive force, and I only just managed to block her fist before it slammed into my balls.

Xoc laughed a bit too boisterously as he sipped his brandy, his russet cheeks pinking slightly. I rose an eyebrow at him. Was he actually drunk? He continued rocking in the chair, looking downright jolly.

Elyria looked back at Joseph. "Well, for the first time in my life, I'm going to get some genuine answers about who I am. That, and..."

A tear fell from her eye, and she wiped it away with the back of her hand. I ran the back of my fingers over her exposed skin, just so she knew I was here, something to tether her to the present.

Joseph studied her, reading her sudden fury, and then his assessing eyes flicked to my hand as it slid comfortably along the back of her neck. "You know, I met another draken once."

Elyria sat forward. "Really?"

"Yes, she lives on the islands. Beautiful, just like you. She doesn't really hide the fact that she's draken, and the people of the island love her for it. She can control the storm fronts, letting ships pass without incident. Of course, if any of the pirates tried to sail up The Mouth into their waters, she could just as easily sink them. As long as she's around, the islands are more or less left alone."

"Fascinating. She could control the weather?" She looked over at Xoc. "Have you ever heard of such a thing?"

He shook his head, still sipping his drink.

"What was she like?"

Elyria pulled her knees into her, wrapping her arms around them. Next to her, the fire brightened with her joy. I smiled at the growing flames and the cord they thrummed within me. Joseph had expertly changed the topic, and none of her previous agitation lingered. Instead, she was elated, and it made her that much more alluring.

"Well, I only got to meet her the one time," he continued. "She has similar coloring to Penny, dark skin and red hair. Her eyes are a brilliant shade of blue. But she's kind, and fiercely protective of her home. Gods help anyone who threatens any of her kin."

"Seems to be a common trait among draken," said Xoc. "Fiercely loving and needing to protect those they care about."

I glared back at him, but he was too busy draining the last drops from his glass to notice. He held the cup out to Joseph, who nodded in approval, refilling it a third time.

Elyria didn't seem to notice at all, and said, "She sounds like someone I would like to meet one day."

An exasperated Nannie came walking in, a bundle of blankets in her arms. "I swear, you tell that girl to go left, and she will go right every time."

Joseph laughed. "Another thing she has in common with you," he said, pointing to Elyria. "You too, Ma. Where do you think she inherited that spirit from?"

Nannie smacked the back of his head. "I'm not so old I can't whoop your ass. You keep being cheeky like that and there's a wooden spoon that will be tanning your hide."

She looked over to where we were sitting. "Now, we don't have much space to spare here. But I have an extra bed upstairs. I wasn't sure if..."

Her voice trailed off as she gestured between Elyria and me.

Xoc spoke up. "You two take the bed. I'll be fine here by the fire."

I eyed the empty glass in his hands. Had he drained the third glass already? Xoc tried to crawl out of the rocking chair, but his wide hips stuck to the arms. He stood and the chair went with him. It swung behind him. He wiggled his ass a bit, trying to free himself, and then actually stumbled.

I looked at Joseph. "What did you make this stuff from? It's probably been a century since I've seen him drunk."

"I'm not drunk. I'm stuck," he protested with a slight slur.

He pushed down on the arms of the chair again. Elyria was laughing hard enough to shake the entire armchair. Xoc did a little waddle and jump step to free himself. With a thud, the chair slipped from his hips and fell to the ground. Xoc turned and scowled at the chair, like it had personally offended him, then took a step back, tripping over his feet. He crawled onto the ground beside Elyria.

Digging his fingers into the pile of the carpet, he slurred, "This is soooft." He rested his head on his hands and promptly fell to sleep. Almost immediately, faint snoring drifted up from the ground.

Elyria gulped down air, trying to breathe over her hysterics. She craned her neck to look up at me. "I knew when he asked for a third glass. I just knew that, however this ended, it would be entertaining."

She wiped the tears that had formed from her laughter. It was refreshing to see her shed tears of happiness for a change.

"Just so long as he didn't crack my rocker," said Nannie, and Elyria roared with laughter again.

I looked at my glass, now very wary of whatever was in it. Sitting it down on a side table, I looked up at Nannie. "What were you saying about sleeping arrangements?"

"There's a bed you can make up in the loft."

She pointed above us to where a railing looked over the room.

"Thank you, Nannie. I'll take those for you."

Elyria hopped to her feet, taking the bundle of blankets that the old woman was holding.

"You're a sweet girl."

She smiled warmly at Elyria before walking back down the hall into what I assumed was her own room.

Elyria took a quilt and draped it over Xoc. Lowering her hand, the flames died down to cinders. A tingle buzzed along my spine as the fire extinguished.

"Last thing we need is him drunkenly rolling into the flames."

Everyone nodded in agreement.

Joseph walked us to the stairs. "In the morning, we can get you a rig and I'll take you down. I've been running the rings for the past two years. It won't take long. We'll get you to the Basilica and you can handle whatever business you need in town tomorrow."

"How do you know we have business to do downtown?" I said, suspicion flooding into me.

Elyria held a hand up.

Joseph shrugged, "Everyone always has business."

"Thank you, Joseph." She gave him a light kiss on the cheek. "You have no idea how much lighter my heart feels seeing you, being here."

"I know the feeling."

He gave me a long look, then turned back down the hall.

31
CALLEN

Chapter Thirty-One

We ascended the stairs to the loft that overlooked the den. Elyria lit a small lamp beside the bed before turning to me and looking uncomfortable.

"Listen, you take the bed. Just give me a blanket and I can sleep on the floor."

I held out a hand to her. Instead, she squeezed the blankets tighter, and I lowered my hand. "Okay...I'll sleep on the floor without a blanket?"

She relented, returning the smile. The frosty unease slipped away from her, instead replaced with her usual playfulness. "That's not necessary." She bit down on her lip. "You can sleep in the bed."

"Oh... *oh*," I said, a bit too enthusiastically.

"Not *ooohhh*. Just, you can stay in the bed. It wouldn't be the first time you've slept next to me. I don't see why it being in a bed matters. And you deserve a comfortable night's sleep as much as I do."

"Oh, well, yeah. That's what I mean by *oh*."

"No, it wasn't."

"Yeah, no. It wasn't."

I smiled wolfishly at her. She handed me the side of a blanket and we laid it over the mattress neatly. The entire time I kept my eyes on her, watching the lamplight shift in her hair.

I perched on the edge and began unlacing my boots. Elyria sat on the opposite side and did the same. Hearing them thump to the ground, I looked over my shoulder. Her delicate fingers were deftly working the lacing on her blouse. She pulled it off, gingerly avoiding the bandage on her arm. I was about to ask about the wound, but the second the blouse pulled free all other thoughts left my mind. I was transfixed.

She wore a pale cream-colored camisole nearly the same shade as her smooth milky-white skin. Beneath the camisole, I could just make out the edges of her dragon mark. The golden dragon snaked and curled down her spine. When she bent to slide her leather pants off, the tail of the dragon peaked out beneath the hem of her underwear.

She turned and locked vulnerable eyes with me, and for the first time, it felt shameful to be watching her. This, whatever was happening here, felt oddly so much more intimate than any of the other times I had seen her barely dressed. She seemed to register a similar feeling, because as she looked at me, a flush creeped up her neck. Blushing? The girl who had walked naked through a glowing forest, putting on the single most tantalizing display of my life, was now blushing beneath the weight of my gaze. And that... that was the sexiest thing I had ever seen. I made a promise to myself to make her blush as often as I could.

Elyria laid her clothing in a neat stack beside the bed before she slipped quickly under the covers. She pulled the quilt up to her chin, the tips of her fingers clutching the satin border. Suddenly, I realized I was still just sitting on the bed, having only removed my boots. I faced her and pulled my shirt up over my shoulders. Cool air kissed the skin of my chest. I shook my hair free of the collar and tossed the shirt aside, giving her my best rakish smile.

Elyria pulled the quilt up to her nose, covering her face and peeking out. A tiny crinkle formed at the corners of her golden eyes, and I knew she was smiling fully beneath the blanket.

Adorable. She was completely adorable. Her eyes dipped, and I felt a rush of heat beneath that look. She was utterly beguiling. Especially in this moment. I exhaled. I was in so much trouble. I was supposed to lie beside her and somehow keep my hands to myself.

I unlaced the leather bands of my pants and swiftly slid one leg out. I tried to coyly remove the second. Instead, the only thing I did was tangle my foot up in my pant leg. I was too busy looking at her to pay attention to what I was actually doing. My foot caught in the ankle lacing, and as I pulled on it, my weight threw me off balance. I hopped twice before toppling to the side with a loud *thunk*.

I laid on the ground with my pride shattered around me.

Elyria leaned over the edge, blinking down at me. Restrained laughter pursed her lips. "First time? It's normal to be nervous."

"Maybe I *should* just stay here," I laughed, raising my hands to my face and peeking through my fingers at her. "The universe obviously does not want me in that bed."

"Suit yourself," she said. "But it's a lot warmer in here than anything you'll find down there."

She pulled the blankets back and slid over to make space for me.

I hopped up with as much grace as I could muster. I tried to read her expression, and completely failed to determine exactly how close she wanted me to be. Her eyes roved over me, studying my body and biting down on that lip again. Did she know that when she did that, all I could think of was what her lips tasted like? Elyria reached over and stroked the bed next to her invitingly.

Yep. I was in trouble.

I climbed into bed beside her. The sheets were warm from where she was just lying, and I slid onto my side facing her. Propping my head up with one arm, I reached out with the other. Then, realizing what I was doing, immediately pulled my hand back. Gods, the urge to touch her was practically instinctual.

Elyria lifted her hand, artfully splaying her fingers. The fire from the lamp flew to her in a tiny streak of light. Images of her spinning on a golden hoop flashed before me, and I marveled. How was it *that* goddess was lying *here* beside me now? She fluttered the flames, and they danced in and out of her fingers. I was mesmerized, feeling every movement of the flame deep in my chest.

The light around us flickered, ebbing as it snaked around her hand. It was not unlike the way she had toyed with the golden coin that night in the bar. A soft smile spread across her face as she watched it pulse. Each beat of the flame pulled me to her. Calling my own flame. My power buzzed in my fingers, demanding release. I wanted to cast my fire into hers. I wanted to watch as they merged and danced as one, and I wanted to feel her flames caress my own. I was going to have to tell her the truth, and soon. Before my own terrible self-control did it for me.

She turned onto her side, facing me, the tiny flame still in her hand. Her eyes glowed a brilliant gold. In them, I could see the reflection of my own.

Dangerous. This flirtation was dangerous, and sweet. And gods save me. It was all I wanted.

She smiled, biting down on her lip again.

I scanned her beautiful face and couldn't help myself. I reached out, gently stroking the side of her cheek with the back of my hand. The flames in her eyes flickered, and she nuzzled into the feel of my fingers.

Elyria closed her hand, and the flame winked out, leaving only darkness and the sound of my heart beating.

She shifted on the mattress beside me. The soft kiss of her hair brushed against me a second before her body settled against my chest. Electricity ran over my skin, and heat flooded into me over every connecting inch. I lifted my arm and gradually ran my hand down her back. The thin silk of her camisole shifted beneath my fingers as I dragged them back up. With each long stroke of my hand, her petite body shuddered against me.

I tightened my hold and breathed in her smoky, flowery scent. I thought about the gardens on the palace grounds. If I lingered long enough, I bet I could name the exact bloom she smelled like. Nothing in my entire life had ever been so intoxicating, not like the feel of her in my arms and her scent wrapping around me.

Elyria's hand slid against my chest. Her fingers toyed with the raised slash over my heart. She grazed her fingers along the scar, exploring its edges. I tensed. That particular wound was still very sensitive, and until now, hadn't been touched by hands other than my own.

There was a light brush of her lips against the mark, then she turned her face to rest her cheek against me. Our breathing rose and fell in tandem. Her legs slipped between mine, tangling her body even closer. That cord connecting us went taut and thrummed with energy. Minutes, maybe seconds, or perhaps my entire damn life passed between each breath. Until the soft sound of her voice floated up to me.

"Cal?"

Hearing my name made my heart leap into my throat. I swallowed around it. "Yes, Sunshine?"

Against me, I felt her entire body smile. I didn't know you could smile with your whole body, but she was doing it. Her nails raked in figure eights across my chest.

I resumed my languorous strokes of her spine.

"Tell me something no one else knows," she whispered.

She shifted. In the darkness, I could just make out her head tilting up to me. Her eyes glowed slightly, like a cat's. No, like a dragon's. I had never considered it before, but it made me wonder how much of my own eyes must be glowing in this moment. I made a mental check to be sure that part of me was firmly locked away.

I leaned down to her and smiled against her forehead. "What? Like a secret?"

My face in her silken hair, I inhaled that heady scent of hers again. Gardenia, or maybe jasmine... and the smoke that swirled around burning embers. Beauty and danger, all coiled into one delicious package.

"Exactly. Tell me something that even Xoc doesn't know."

Lying to you is killing me. Every second I'm with you, I wish I could tell you the truth. I'm terrified you'll leave me when I do, and then I will never feel complete again.

I sighed. "That would be tough. Because that bastard has a way of knowing things, even the ones I don't tell him. He is uncannily perceptive."

"Okay."

There was a tinge of disappointment in her voice, and her body shrank away ever so slightly.

"Why does that matter to you?"

"I don't know. I wanted a piece of you that no one else has."

I stilled my hand. "Trust me, you have plenty already," I said, placing a light kiss on the top of her head.

Her skin warmed against me before she leaned up, softly kissing my lips. I tightened my arms around her. Careful not to brush the arm that was wounded, I slid my outer hand to her lower back. Her hips rotated against mine. She melted into me and the leash on my self-control started slipping.

Whatever she said, the two of us together felt right in every way.

Her lips slowly pulled back from mine. I chased that feeling, continuing to kiss her until she rotated out of my reach. As she turned, her fingers laced in mine and she wrapped me around her. The full length of her slender body cradled perfectly in the curve of my own.

She dragged our joined hands between her breasts and rested them there. I focused on the feel of her racing heart against my flattened palm. Of course, we were close enough that the thundering in my chest was something she could feel slamming against her back.

A potent feeling of contentment washed over me. *This.* I could be content to feel this forever.

I slid my leg between hers, claiming the space there. She lazily moved her warm fingers against mine. I nuzzled into her neck, letting my lips drift over the soft curve of her ear. A tiny sigh came from her.

Then, in a most unexpected movement, she ground back against me. The image of her perfect ass flickered into my mind, popping the bubble of contentment. Raw heat replaced that contentment. I felt myself stiffen and moved to put space between us, but she held my arm in place as she rocked her hips into me again. I took a deep breath, trying not to focus on the feel of my cock pressed into her ass as she writhed.

Into her ear, I said, "If your intent is to actually sleep tonight, then I would not do that again. Or I won't be responsible for what happens next."

She giggled and in mock innocence said, "Do what?"

She released my hand, reached up behind her, and wrapped her fingers around my neck. At the same time, she rolled her entire glorious body, leveraging against me in one long, languid motion.

I'd seen her perform this exact undulation while draped in a golden hoop. A fantasy that had reeled in my mind a hundred times played out before me. It drew a growl from low in my chest. She laughed and did it again, pressing harder against me this time.

I knew what she was doing. She would wind me tight and then abruptly end things, saying something coy like '*goodnight.*' Just for spite and to tease me, or payback for having left her in the waterfall so obviously wanting. Thing was, I could play back. If teasing was what she wanted, I could give her that... and more. I could take her right to the edge and leave her there. She had released my hand, and literally all of her was at my fingertips.

I lowered my hand, letting my thumb graze the underswell of her breast before lightly tracing tightening circles around her perfect rosebud nipple. She bowed backwards against me with a sweet, exhaling sigh of pleasure. Gods, she was so wonderfully responsive. I could spend days drawing out each exquisite sound from those strawberry lips.

Pressing a kiss to her neck, I said, "That. You most certainly should not do that again."

I pulled her hips to me and slid my leg over hers, letting it wrap tight and parting her thighs with the promise of more. It would take nothing to spread her wide. I closed my eyes, imagining the decadent wetness that I would find waiting for me. The way her body would tighten and bend around me as I stroked her. Her breathing quickened. Instinctually, I knew she was picturing the same exact thing.

I placed another light kiss against her neck while sliding my hand up her side. Elyria shivered. She pushed her fingers into my hair and pulled me onto her, twisting so that my mouth was barely an inch from hers. I slid my hand across her stomach, letting it move beneath her shirt. Splaying my fingers wide, the tip of my pinky settling under her waistband.

I leaned into the embrace and murmured against her lips, "There is no part of you I don't want to touch, no part I don't want to kiss..." I stroked my hand against her stomach, pushing it lower "...and taste."

A tiny whimper came from her, and I smiled, drawing her lower lip between my teeth.

"But..." I pulled my hand back to her hip, putting the slightest bit of space between us. The air there felt cold. "You said that the waterfall was the end of things between us, and I respect that."

She groaned and, with the practiced precision of an acrobat, flipped to straddle me. With a hard push, I fell backwards, taking her with me. Her hair fell forward, pooling coolly against my heating skin. Elyria slid her hand down, brazenly cupping my erection. Moving her mouth back to mine, she said, "And if that isn't what I want anymore?"

Well, there was no misreading those intentions. Her grip tightened with each rock of her hips, and warmth seeped from the fingers wrapped firmly around my shaft.

I moved without thinking, pulling on the straps of her camisole, baring her shoulder to my seeking mouth. The light scrap of silk slid to her waist. No longer that barrier between us, the touch of her soft skin against mine sent waves of fire coursing to the surface. I could feel her power rising and my own keeping pace, ramping up into what could be a catastrophic release. The surrounding air had already warmed and charged. Heavy panting rocked her breasts against my chest. I wanted to rip off what little clothing remained between us and devour her. But I knew that if I kissed her in this moment, it would be incendiary. Flames would roll between us, and I wasn't sure that I could contain it, or that I would want to contain it.

The press of her lengthening claws dragged from base to tip, providing a salacious friction through the rough cloth of my undershorts. Slowly, with unrelenting pressure, she stroked me. I couldn't keep from moaning. Admittedly, I may have pushed this a bit too far.

Closing my eyes, I attempted to regain control... but there was the slow drag of her tongue along the column of my neck, and the breathy moan in my ear that was fraying away whatever was left of my sanity.

"Cal..." The sultry way my name rolled from her lips, their velvet surface raking the shell of my ear—I was damned before this night even began. This woman was impossible to resist.

"Touch me..."

A growl rumbled low in my throat.

"Please."

Fuck control.

I slid my hand beneath her waistband. My palm skated over the curve of her ass; slippery temptation only a breath away from the tips of my fingers. Sitting up to meet her, I pulled her onto me and possessively kissed her lips. She turned liquid in my hands, mine to mold and bend as I wished. I leaned down, kissing the swell where her breasts pushed up against my chest.

Indulging every desire I had been denying myself, I dragged a single finger through her folds. The slick heat crying for me to sink into her. I wanted to dive in, drown in it, disappear until there was nothing left of me but her.

Hips tilting into my palm, Elyria arched back, moonlight cresting over her breasts. Gods, she was sexy. Her hair draped behind her. It swayed against my legs. I'd never wanted anything the way I wanted this woman, and now I had her. She was here, literally in the palm of my hands, writhing against my fingertips. Guilt clawed at the back of my conscience, forcing it's way past the blinding desire. We couldn't, not here, and not until I'd told her the truth. My moral compass hardly pointed north. I had done much worse than lie my way into a girl's bed before, but Elyria wasn't one of those girls. She was different. I needed to do better by her. She deserved better. I owed her that much, and strangely, I wanted to give that to her.

Fuck. Fuck. Fuck me and my poor life choices.

I pulled back, saying, "Then..."

I licked her lips lightly before pressing a kiss to the side of her mouth.

Fuuuck, the way she tasted. I'd never get that taste off my lips. I bet she tasted this good everywhere. *Focus, Callen! The day you take this goddess over the edge, it will be somewhere infinitely more suited for the experience than a tiny loft.*

"This isn't where I plan to take you," I murmured, placing another kiss on her jaw and picturing her spread wide against a marble balcony, fingers gripping the balustrade as I made her climax over and over.

"Take *me?*" Her hand, which had never stopped taunting me, pumped hard. "Who says *you're* taking anything? Maybe I'm the one taking you." She pumped again, making me draw in air through my teeth with a hiss. The temptation to rise to that challenge was damn near irresistible.

"Because, Elyria..."

She tilted her head to me, giving me access to her neck. I took full advantage, pulling her hips into me again and biting down on the soft flesh. She gasped as I rocked hard against her with the promise of all I had to give her.

I moved my mouth to her ear. "When I do..."

I kissed that small spot below her ear that always seemed to make her shiver. Her lips parted, her eyes glowed, and her hands on me burned.

"When I do, I will make you light up like the Solstice sun."

I nipped at her ear. "And I'm not about to burn this lovely house down when I make you forget everything, including your control."

"Fuck, Cal," she said breathlessly, her body rolling against mine.

I hesitated for just a minute, letting myself enjoy the feel of her straddling me. Then I reached between us and peeled away the hand that was still stroking my cock. I wrapped my fingers between hers and laid us gently back on the bed.

"Next time," I said into her hair, inhaling the seductive smoky scent of her arousal.

Fuck me. When did I learn this level of self-control?

I felt her growl of frustration rumble against my chest, and then I laughed. I was going to sleep with a raging hard-on, but this had been the right thing to do. And one day soon, I would show her exactly what was worth waiting for.

"You are absolutely wicked," she said, smacking my chest.

I tucked her into my arms and placed a kiss on the top of her head.

"Sweet dreams, Elyria."

"I should have made you sleep on the floor," she hissed.

I laughed again and resumed stroking her back. Her bare skin glided so easily against my palm. I wondered if I could convince her to always sleep topless. I slowed my breathing to match each stroke of my hand. Despite her frustration, I felt her ease. Her heart rate, and mine, slowed. One breath at a time, that bubble of contentment slowly reformed.

I closed my eyes, letting the image of her body in pure ecstasy fill my dreams.

ELYRIA

Sunlight streamed through a small circular window perched on the apex of the wall overlooking the den. I ran my hand over the empty bed. Cal must already be up and gone. The sheets there were cold, telling me he'd been up for a while.

The air of the loft was icy against my exposed breasts. My camisole was still bunched around my waist. I slipped the straps back over my shoulders, trying to ignore the flush to my skin. Flashes of the night before flickered through my mind in a tangled mess of fevered lips and hands. I ran my palm over my neck and down my chest. *Fuck*. I'd have done anything last night to feel his weight above me, moving in me.

I pulled the pillow on top of my face and screamed into it.

How did he do that to me? One moment I would feel completely in control, and the next, I'd be losing myself to him. And last night, I swear he'd done it on purpose. Worked me up, and then that bastard told me to go to sleep. Of course, I'd been doing the exact same thing, or at least that had been the plan. Drive Cal crazy with lust. Pay him back for how he'd left me aching in the waterfall. Somehow, he'd flipped it back on me.

Had he just not been turned on enough? Not possible. I'd felt his erection. Felt how hard he had been in my hand, the way he'd breathed when I stroked him. The pounding of his heart matched mine. The connection between us that couldn't be faked. No, he must have used every ounce of restraint to pull my hand from him. It was actually impressive to have that level of control. Gods knew I hadn't last night. He was right, though. If we had continued, there wouldn't have been anything left of this loft but charcoal.

I stepped out of bed and leaned over the railing to look down into the den. A small fire was crackling in the hearth, and Xoc was no longer sprawled on the floor. The quiet chatter of people talking in the kitchen drifted through the still house. I slipped on my pants and rummaged through my pack until I found a sweater to throw on.

I descended the stairs as quietly as I could, but the wood creaked with every step. I was about halfway down when Cal leaned out of the kitchen doorway. He smiled warmly at me and his eyes dropped lazily over my body. Just that made sparks of heat rise from within me. It streamed up my neck and spilled onto my cheeks. He studied my blush and smiled wider. I narrowed my eyes and breezed by, careful not to touch him as I stepped into the kitchen.

Hearing me enter, Nannie turned from the stove. "Good morning, dear. I just put on a fresh kettle for some tea."

"That would be lovely. Thank you, Nannie."

I looked around the room. Xoc was sitting at the far end of the table and his skin looked green. A light sheen of sweat sat on his brow, and his hands were in his stringy brown hair, just barely holding his head up. Before him sat a fluffy scone, with only one bite taken from it.

"You've looked better," I said.

"Three glasses of the brandy and he's completely bog-eyed. It's fantastic."

Cal laughed and sat down at the table next to him, purposely slamming his hand down to make a loud bang.

Xoc growled, looking over at him through the limp hair that draped over his eyes.

"I tried telling him he'd feel better if he'd just put something in his stomach, but he won't listen," said Nannie, pointing a whisk at him and flinging small bits of batter around the room.

Maddilyn bounced over to me with a spritely step. "Good morning, Elyria."

She spun, and a cloud of white powder billowed up from her. A paste of some sort was plastered on the ends of her hair. I looked up at the room in surprise. Cal barely held back a laugh.

"Your hair is very... shiny... today, Maddilyn," I said, reaching down to figure out what she had colored it with.

"I'm the Golden Dragon. Just like you," she said, twirling in an awkward cartwheel across the kitchen floor.

She came skipping back and gave a little bow. I laughed. "Just wait until you're ten before you start juggling knives, okay?"

Maddilyn smiled exuberantly and looked over at Nannie.

"*No*," she commanded and then scowled at me.

I sheepishly mouthed back, "*Sorry.*"

"Nannie made raspberry scones and cheesy biscuits. Plus, there's this jam here." She pointed to a jar with a pink fabric topper. "I helped to make it last spring. It's strawberry."

Cal's head popped up and he looked straight at me. "Strawberries are my favorite."

The flush in my cheeks grew brighter. *I was going to kill him.* We were in a kitchen, there had to be a knife I could throw at him somewhere. Or Hells, maybe I'd let Maddie try target practice after all.

"I think I'll pass on strawberries." I deadpanned at Cal. "For a very long time."

He simply laughed. "Oh, I don't know about that. You seem to change your mind pretty quickly with just a little encouragement."

Yep. I was going to hurt him.

Xoc gave a pained groan.

Nannie placed a giant plate of baked goods on the table before us with a thunk. Xoc looked at the plate and his eyes rolled. He quickly raised a hand to his mouth before swallowing hard, and two pitiful green eyes looked up at me.

"Don't you have some magic plant to cure hangovers?" I asked him.

He shook his head. "I already tried that. It made my headache fade... a bit. But it's done nothing to help the nausea. I think Joseph poisoned me. It's the only explanation."

"Aye, that swill he brews is definitely poison," agreed Nannie.

I smiled in commiseration with him. "Four years ago, we visited the islands to see him and Penny. He had a whole jug of that swill. Poured me two tall glasses. Shit was as thick as molasses. Of course, I was blown out of my mind. Geoff told me I got on the table and started dancing. I'm not exactly sure if I believe that story or not. Anyway, once I passed out, I didn't wake up for two whole days. When I came to, I was missing a shoe and half my pant leg. Never did find out where they went." I gave him a half smile. "So, been there."

"That is information that might have been useful to know before you let him pour me a third glass," Xoc muttered.

"But you're so big. I didn't think there was any way it would have had nearly the same effect on you." I shrugged, reaching for a scone. "It's impressive, actually."

"Thank you."

I turned around and saw Joseph buttoning a white shirtsleeve. He walked into the room, dressed head to toe in matching white linen. It offset his salt and pepper hair, making him look rather dignified.

"And you did dance on the table. Your shoe you lost because you threw it into the sea in an attempt to take down Jimmy for singing a song about your bosoms."

Cal snorted a sip of milk. White liquid sprayed from his nose. I barked out a laugh. Cal reached for a napkin and wiped at his face.

"Those boys. I do miss them some days," Joseph continued, not even taking notice of Cal's milk fountain. "Did you sleep well?" he asked, looking at me.

Putting down his napkin, Cal added, "Did you dream of me?" He winked obnoxiously. "Because I dreamed of you... all night. Over and over."

I scowled at him. "You have no idea the things I do to you in my dreams."

"That's hot," Cal said, lowering his eyes on me.

"I don't think she means that the way you're thinking, brother," mumbled Xoc.

Cal shrugged. "Still hot."

I threw what was left of my scone at him. Cal ducked and the pastry thudded straight into Nannie's back. She turned slowly as she reached for the wooden spoon on the counter. I sat straight up, then pointed to Cal. Nannie looked to him and thudded the spoon into the palm of her hand. I giggled.

"I'd never. They're too delicious to waste like that," Cal said, white teeth flashing in his classic love me or leave me smile.

Nannie's scowl turned up. "I'm just joking. I knew it was her. She was throwing the biscuit to nail you for the sassy nonsense coming out of your mouth. I remember what it was like to be young and in love. One moment you're falling over yourself to touch them, the next, you're wringing the life from their throat."

My mouth went dry. I wasn't in love with Cal. He was infuriating and sexy. That was all. This wasn't love. It was lust.

Wasn't it?

Cal cleared his throat and took another drink, looking back at Nannie and then over at me.

Joseph clapped Xoc on the back. He groaned, placing his face into his hands.

"Oh, my boy. Feeling that third drink, are you?" He handed him a brown bit of dried, twisted bark. "Chew on this. It does the trick. You'll be feeling right within the hour."

Xoc lifted his head, and with a tilt, inspected what Joseph held out to him. He took the twisted bit of brown and sniffed it. "Licorice?"

"Not exactly. It's bark from the Entlis Tree. But I suppose it smells and tastes a bit like licorice. We harvest it and lay it in the sun. When it twists like that, you know it's ready."

"What's it do?" I asked.

"It's a stimulant. If you chew on it, you'll be feeling like you could conquer the world. The boys and I chew on it when we have a long day of riding ahead of us. It helps to get you back up the mountain. Just so happens it gets rid of the spins, too," Joseph said, nodding for Xoc to try it. "Go on, son. Take it."

He looked over at me as if I might know if what Joseph had just handed him was actually safe to consume or not.

I shrugged. "Can't make you feel any worse, right?" I said with my best encouraging smile.

Joseph shook his hand at him. "Go ahead."

"Says the man who fed you the demon whiskey," laughed Cal.

"It was bourbon, thank you. And that was only half-aged. Fully aged, it knocks you on your ass before you finish the first glass," retorted Joseph, smiling.

Xoc shrugged and popped the bark into his mouth. He chewed it a couple of times, and then his eyes went wide.

"Yeah, mate, I wouldn't chew on the whole thing at once," Joseph said then, with a shrug, added, "Nah, it'll be alright. Go ahead, you're huge."

I laughed. This was going to be some day.

By mid-morning, everyone was packed up and ready to leave. After last night, I hadn't had the guts to be alone with Cal again. So I purposefully waited to go upstairs until after he had come down. He seemed to notice how I was avoiding him. Truthfully, if I were to be alone with him, I wasn't sure if I would kiss or beat the life from him. Then Nannie's words would come back to me, and a hot rush of anxiety would flood through me. I didn't know what to make of that either.

All packed, we said our goodbyes to Maddilyn and Nannie. Maddie's dramatic tears were heartbreaking, and it made me feel awful to be leaving her so soon.

"Don't worry about her. She's like this whenever anyone leaves." Nannie looked down at her granddaughter. "Go on, now. Back inside the house." She shooed Maddilyn up the path before extending an armful of little brown paper packages. "Lunch, for you and the boys. You take care, dear."

She reached up and placed a light peck on my cheek.

The four of us exited the cottage and began walking down the cobblestone street.

"We keep the rigs just on the edge of town. From there, we will take the Chute. With the right level of speed, and hopefully minimal traffic, we should make it to the Basilica within fifteen minutes, give or take."

Cal stopped, holding out a hand to Joseph. "I'm sorry. The chute?"

On his other side, Xoc also held out a hand. "Fifteen minutes?"

"Of course. It's like a big slide to the bottom of the mountain. You breeze past the outer rings, straight into the center of the city. Then, you can hire a cycle-rig to bring you down the rest of the rings all the way to Suman. If you don't take too long in the city, then it's entirely possible to be in Suman by nightfall."

"Good," I grumbled, and didn't miss the sharp way Cal's head snapped to look at me.

"And it's safe? This chute?" asked Xoc, now permanently wary of anything Joseph offered.

I stopped for a second and looked at Xoc. A twisted bit of the Entlis bark was sticking out from the side of his mouth. He was speaking too quickly. His pupils had dilated so wide that very little of their brilliant green shone through. He was wired. I could see it in the way his veins bulged along his neck, and his fingers ticked lightly at his sides. Cal seemed to have noticed too, and pure amusement danced across his face.

"Oh yeah! Used to be we only transported fruit and other produce this way. But, then we got the brilliant idea to move people too. There's a small fortune in transportation, if you just know how to tap the right market."

We stood there blinking at him.

"Look, I've done it millions of times. I drive the rigs about a dozen times daily. We almost never crash."

"Almost?"

Joseph shrugged off our concerns, pointing south. "It's just another block over to the ramp."

We turned the corner and stopped. At the top of the hill was a wooden ramp and several men, all wearing the same white pants and shirt Joseph wore.

"Oh, I see. You're not the only one stylishly in white," Cal joked.

"Yeah, the white helps the drivers in carts spot us as we come down the hill."

I reached out and grabbed hold of Cal's sleeve and tugged on it. This was a terrible idea.

"Makes sense," he chuckled with a side-eye at me and pulled his sleeve from my nervous grip.

It wasn't the ramp, or the men in white, or the casual way Joseph threw around the word almost, that made me freeze. It was the half a dozen rigs sitting perched atop the ramp. They were little more than baskets. *Baskets!* Seats made of wicker on top of wooden runners. Two of the men had one tipped up, and they were running wax over each of the rungs. They spotted us and flipped the rig upright.

I looked over to Xoc. "Hope you're not still nauseous."

"You three coming or what?" yelled Joseph as he waved us over.

"Nah. Joseph was right. I feel like I could take on a bull right now. This is nothing," Xoc said, pointing to the stack of wicker cars.

I stepped up the stairs to the ramp. The other drivers all seemed delighted to meet me.

"Boys, this is Elyria. She's just about as close as I have to a niece. I helped raise her when she was a babe, back when I was traveling along with that performing troupe," Joseph said, gesturing to me.

I waved hello.

"Hey, is you that girl what throws fire?" said a young man, whose face was peppered with light brown freckles.

I held out my hand, and a tiny fireball formed in my palm. The man's eyes went wide. I closed my hand, and the fire fizzled out.

"Whoa, Ellie, fire and wicker don't mix," Joseph said, looking wide-eyed at me.

I only rolled my eyes at him.

"I take it back, Joe. All of it. That is something, that is."

The young man looked at me, full of wonder, and I smiled back.

"So, tell me how this works," I said to the new man, gesturing toward the rig.

"Wells, dearie. You and your..." He looked over to Cal, who placed a posses-sive arm around my shoulders. "...boyfriend sit in here. Joe and I will take either side of the rig behind yins. We push off, and if the rig starts to slow, then we step down and give it a little push back up to speed. Plus, we steer it to help keep the rig from crashing into any of the walls when we turn."

He added that last bit on as a mere afterthought, as though crashing into a wall wasn't really something that needed to be considered.

I could feel the blood draining from my face at the idea of hurtling down these streets in what was basically a giant fruit basket.

"Don't worry, miss. It's made from the finest wicker. She's solid, she is."

The man gave the rig a pat on the side with his hand.

I looked over to Cal. "We could just walk."

He grinned that perfect white smile. "Nonsense. That would take at least a day. Where's that thirst for adventure I love about you?"

There was that word, and Nannie's face popped into my mind.

"I think she's still on that cliff with the worm," I groaned.

Cal hopped onto the platform and shook the man's hand.

"Calvin Dentross," he said.

"Pleasure. I'm Kit. Now, if you and the lovely Elyria could take a seat, we can get started." He looked over to Xoc. "Sorry, mate. You'll have to come down the Chute separately. You're too big for us to take all three of you together."

"That's perfectly fine. They can go first," Xoc said, gesturing to us.

Cal extended a hand to me to help me up onto the platform. I refused it, extending my leg high into the air, and rotating my body onto the ledge. His eyes roved over me, and he shook his head. "Remind me about that trick later."

"You're a pig," I said to him.

He smiled and gave a mock bow. "But I'm your pig."

"Does that mean I can shove an apple in your mouth? Maybe then you'll actually shut up."

Cal flashed a look over his shoulder to see who was paying attention, then leaned in low to whisper in my ear, "It wasn't really *my* mouth that I was thinking about shoving things in."

Heat rippled over my skin, chasing my wave of shock and settling on this side of outrage. Before I could raise my hand to slap him, he took it and guided me to the cart. "After you, Sunshine."

Promising to make him pay for that comment later, I clambered into the compartment. The wicker creaked with my weight as I sat. I ran my hands over the edges and gave them a tug. It flexed slightly. My palms started to sweat. They didn't even sweat when I was tight walking the rigging. But stick me in a giant basket and throw me down a hill, then they're slicker than fish in a rainstorm.

"Oh, Ellie," said Joseph. "Don't put your hands up there. I wouldn't want you to smash them on any of the walls."

"What?!" I asked.

"Hold onto the leather strap inside if you feel like you need some stability," he added.

I reached down and pulled a worn leather strap from the inside of my seat. Cal slipped in next to me. That bastard was smiling from ear to ear. He was thoroughly enjoying how uncomfortable this entire experience was making me.

"This is going to be fun," he mused.

He reached down and slipped my hand in his. I was about to pull it away when the rig lurched forward, and I dug into his grip.

"Here we go!" yelled Joseph.

The rig slid forward. There was a tipping sensation and my stomach leapt up into my throat. I gripped Cal's arm, practically climbing on top of him. He laughed and looked over at me.

We began hurtling at an unprecedented speed. I felt Joseph and Kit jumping off alternately to make us go faster and faster. A scream ripped from me.

"Oh my gods! Joseph! The wall!"

Up ahead, a large stone wall crested around a bend in the road. I could hear Joseph laughing. I turned my head and saw him jump down. We were going to die. This was how I died, in a wicker basket going breakneck speeds down a mountain.

A loud scuffing sound scraped next to us and the entire rig careened to the side. We swung wide, and the back end of the rig kicked out. I felt Kit jump off, and he mimicked the motion Joseph had just done. It was shorter and in smaller force, but the rig righted itself. The two began running before jumping back up. Hitting a second straight away, we picked up speed. The flags zoomed overhead as we flew by, street after street.

"Joseph, what happens when someone in a cart decides it's a good time to cross the street?" I yelled back to him.

Kit laughed. "That would be very bad for the cart."

Another turn in the other direction loomed before us. Kit jumped down, and the rig swung hard to the side. The two ran for another push. The flags hanging from the streets shifted colors as we soared through the rings.

The surrounding buildings went from gray stone and tile to larger brick multistoried buildings. They were all chalk-white, and it was a stark contrast to the deep red of the terracotta tiles on the roofs.

"We're almost to the center," I said, beginning to recognize some of the architecture.

Ahead of us, I could just make out the spires of the Basilica.

The road opened into a small square. Kit jumped down, and we began spinning madly, around and around, until we slowed to a stop. The world around me spun. I held onto Cal to try and keep from vomiting. He was laughing—*laughing,* the bastard had been the entire ride. I was screaming so much that I hadn't even noticed until now.

He looked down at my blanched expression and then laughed harder.

"Aww, come on, Sunshine. That was fun."

He leaned down and kissed the top of my head.

A loud, thundering bellow came from behind us. We turned and saw the fear-stricken face of Xoc just before his rig began spinning. His yelling vibrated as he spun around. When he finally slowed to a stop, he jumped out, tripped over his legs, and slammed straight to the ground. He turned and finally vomited.

"Yeah. I thought that might happen," Joseph said to Cal.

And then they both began laughing.

Xoc looked up at Cal. "Remind me to kill you later. I didn't have to come along. I could have been at home, in Innesvale, having a perfectly lovely time. Instead, this is the second time in a week I've nearly died."

"Psh. This *is* your idea of a lovely time," Cal retorted.

Xoc jumped up, lunging for him. But, still dizzy from the descent, he only fell over. Which made everyone laugh more.

"Later," growled Xoc. "I will beat your fancy ass to a pulp later."

"I think whatever that bark stuff was made you grumpy," Cal said, patronizingly patting Xoc on top of his head.

"No, Cal. I'm pretty sure you bring that out in everyone," I added with a sweet smile.

Joseph walked over to me. "Listen, Ellie. I just want you to know you always have a place with me. I mean, if you don't find what you're looking for. The cottage is as good as your home for as long as I'm living."

Tears pricked the corners of my eyes. He reached over and pulled me into a great hug.

"Thank you, Joseph," I said, wiping tears from my eyes.

"Also," he looked down at my bandaged arm. "When you get to Suman, look up this girl." He handed me a slip of paper. I opened it and saw a name scribbled on it. *Reihaneh Almont.* "She's a friend and a damn good healer. She is..." He paused for a second. "She's your kind of people. I can see you two being thick as thieves. She'll be hanging around one of the gambling dens along the harbor. You should be able to spot her pretty quickly. She has a way of finding herself plenty of attention. Tell her I sent you, and she'll fix you up. She owes me a favor. I got her out of a spot of trouble a few years back."

I nodded, placing the slip into my pocket. "I will."

He leaned in and kissed me on top of my head. After releasing me, he walked over to Cal and gave him a friendly clap on the shoulder, then he pulled Cal in and said something too low to hear. Cal's eyes went wide, and then he nodded. "I give you my word."

Joseph helped Xoc to his feet. "You three be careful out there. The world is a crazy place. You wouldn't believe half the stories we hear from travelers these days. Just yesterday, a woman was ranting about white-eyed phantoms stalking the streets."

Cal whirled around. "What did you just say?"

But Joseph didn't hear him. Instead, he gave a quick wave, and then he and Kit began pushing the rig up the hill. My heart pounded in my ears, and I narrowed my eyes on Cal and the concern he'd just shown. *White eyed phantoms.* White eyes, like the bandit. Like Duke.

"Do you think they have to push that rig all the way back to the top of the mountain?" Cal asked.

"What did he say to you?" I asked, ignoring his previous question. "What did you give your word about?"

Cal looked at me, a pained sincerity filling his gaze. He opened his mouth and then closed it. He took a deep breath, as if he were about to disclose some dark secret.

"We going?" Xoc asked, walking up to us.

Cal turned away from me and began walking.

I jogged up behind him, pulling back on his shoulder. "Cal?"

"Just that I would watch over you. He's worried about you. That's all," he said with a sigh. But something wasn't right. I knew he was leaving something out. "You already know I'm going to do that anyway. I could never let anything hurt you. So it's not really a big commitment to give him my word."

I leveled my gaze. "What aren't you telling me?"

Xoc was bouncing back and forth between his feet. "We gonna do this or what?"

Cal looked away. It was clear he wasn't going to tell me anything, at least not now. I sighed and turned to Xoc.

"I need a few minutes in the Basilica to transfer the troupe's accounts into Albert's name. But after that,, we can keep heading south. Joseph said we could be there by nightfall if we hired a cycle-rig to take us. Do you think you could track one down?"

"That's a good idea. Xoc can get us the rigs. I'm coming with you to the Basilica," said Cal.

"I don't need a babysitter," I added, looking pointedly at him. "Especially one who can't seem to answer a simple question when he's asked. You go with him. I'll meet you both in the square."

Cal traded an uneasy look with Xoc.

"It's not like that. I have business in the Basilica too," He gave me an unconvincing smile. "Joseph was right. Everyone always does. We meet back here in an hour."

Xoc had already bounded off down a side street.

Cal pulled the hood of his tunic over his head. "Let's make this quick."

We began walking towards the dome poking over the rooftops beyond.

"What's the matter, Dentross? Afraid of being recognized?" I asked suspiciously.

"Well..." He drew out the word. "Trust me when I say it's probably better that I keep a low profile while we're here."

"Whatever," I said, waving him off angrily. "Keep your secrets."

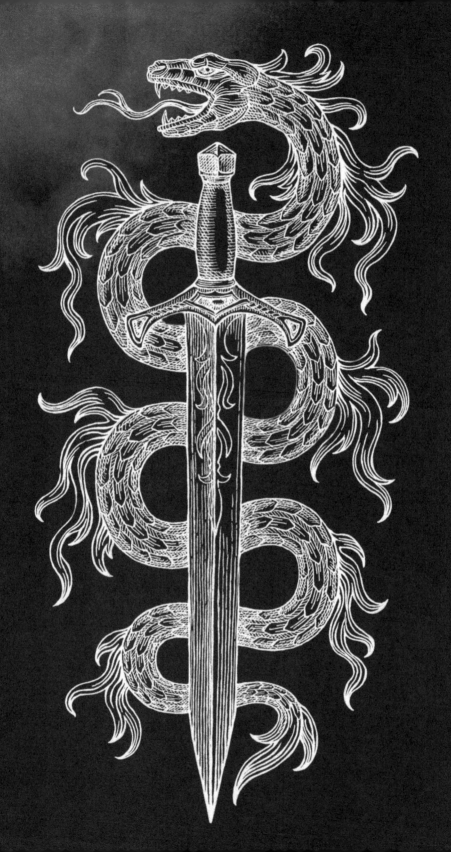

33

ELYRIA

Basilican Square was a large courtyard. Each road in the city ended here, forming a many-sided star of converging streets. At the end of each stood a large gilded statue representing one of the thirteen guilds. We entered the square, passing the statue of a man pushing a plow representing the Agriculture Guild that we had just come from. The smell of coffee wafted over to us from the several cafés that lined the square.

A young woman approached, a basket of roses draped over her arm. Her eyes trailed over Cal, lingering on his shoulders before dropping lower. She licked her lips and waved suggestively at him. It sparked something entirely unwanted in me. Reflexively my hand drifted to the hilt at my hip. He was unfairly handsome, of course, other women would notice.

Cal beamed down at me, scrutinizing my reaction with amusement. He wrapped an arm around my shoulder, caressing the exposed skin at the back of my neck in a clearly intimate way, claiming me and making it clear to the girl where his intentions lay. That one soft stroke rocketed a flush of heat down my spine. Before I realized what I was doing, I leaned into the touch. It felt too damn good.

"A gift for your wife, sir?" the woman said, holding a red bloom before us.

Blood rushed to my cheeks. I hated that I could never feign disinterest. My pale skin was always betraying me. Of course, Cal's keen eyes never missed it. Not once. Not ever, and definitely not at this moment.

He pulled a silver coin from his purse, far more than the blossom was worth, and tossed it to the girl. She gave a small curtsy of gratitude and handed me the flower with a wide smile.

I took a deep inhale of the decadent perfume. It smelled glorious. The petals felt like velvet against my lips. I lifted my eyes to him, to the way he was studying my reaction. There he was, the assessing and calculating man who knew how to bend and twist a woman's heart. It was enough to slap sense back into my head. I scowled at him, rather than the weak kneed swooning I was just about to do.

"What am I supposed to do with this?" I asked, gesturing with the flower for emphasis.

He took the rose from my hand, breaking off the end of the stem and deftly removing the thorns. Pushing the hair back from my face, he slipped the rose behind my ear.

"Lovely," he said in a deep voice that made me arch closer.

Cal's amber eyes warmed and his hand trailed from my ear along the curve of my neck, making my heart rate speed up. *Dammit.* Why did I have to love when he did that? I turned from him before he could get the satisfaction of seeing me smile and walked with a clipped step in the Basilica's direction.

Looming over the square stood an extensive building with a huge terra-cotta brick dome. The bricks laced up the roof in an alternating pattern that created the illusion of the dome having been woven, rather than built. It spanned an impressive width that made everything around us feel diminutive. The facade featured hexagonal tile work carved in alternating black and white marble. Each panel was intricately designed, depicting various trades. The doors of the facade were ornately carved oaken panels, heavy and solid, with exquisitely crafted iron finials. The Basilica itself showed the beauty of when multiple guilds came together, a complete representation of power and cooperation.

The entire city was run out of the Basilica of Commerce. It held the bank, the law courts, and the offices of the Guild Council that ran each independent ring of The Bullseye. It even featured an indoor market, eliminating the loss in wages for merchants when the seasons or weather may have otherwise forced them to close shop. What's more, much of the business from the entire continent was run from here, or at the very least, traded from here. Entire kingdoms trusted the Basilican Bank to run their coffers and manage their loans, not to mention everyone else. So, inevitably, if you needed work, or if you had a job you needed done, information to be had, or something purchased, this was where you came.

The stained glass windows glittered like treasure in the sunlight. With each step towards the building, a deep seated panic rose, until finally, I was choking on it. It was enough to root me to the bottom of the stairs. I was certain that if I took one more step, I might never breathe again. I gazed at the sunlight cresting over the dome.

Cal placed his hand at the small of my back.

"Are you okay?" he said gently.

"No."

I wanted to look over at him, but if I looked at him, the raw emotion in me would be impossible to keep stuffed in the cage. The moment I walked through those doors, I would officially register Duke's death and close his accounts, effectively making it real. It had to be done. Before long, Albert would run out of money to support the troupe, and he needed every coin.

But in this moment it felt like standing before that pyre all over again. For all my bravado, I could not make myself ascend the stairs. The pain was fresh and raw. It was too much to bear, and I could feel myself cracking beneath the weight of it. So, instead, I shielded my eyes to the sun and studied the circular glass window above the central door. The stained glass glittered, showing winding golden flowers wrapped around a crossed hammer and pen.

Cal slipped his fingers into mine, warm and strong. He rubbed his thumb over the back of my hand in a slow caress.

"We can come back later," he said, trying to comfort me. "This doesn't have to be done now. I can take you for lunch, or a stiff drink. Hells, you don't even need to do it today. We'll just walk back up the mountain and try again tomorrow... and if not then, the next day."

I rolled my head towards him. "I'm not doing the Chute again," I said flatly, then looked back at the twisted flowers. I knew they represented life and beauty, but from right here, they felt more like chains strangling the tools of creation.

"Elle, it's okay, really."

Then he squeezed my hand. My heart leapt into my throat. Seeing my reaction, he did it again. A gentle squeeze to remind me he was there. I looked at him, fat tears falling to the cobblestone. He couldn't know. He couldn't know that was how Duke always calmed my nerves. How my father soundlessly told me *I Love You.*

Cal's eyes were warm like honey, and full of empathy. I reached up and grabbed his face, pulling him into a deep and claiming kiss. His eyes opened wide in surprise. Just as quickly as I had pulled him in, I released him. He smiled smugly as if he had just won every argument we had ever had.

So I slapped him. Right in his perfect damned face.

"What was that for?" he said, flustered and leveled by confusion.

I pushed him out of the way and dashed up the stairs.

"Confidence."

"So you slapped me?"

I could hear him walking up behind me. I swiveled to face him. "Something like that."

Then I turned back and continued climbing the steps.

"I mean, I'm not opposed to public displays of affection."

"Gah," I growled out in frustration.

Every damn good thing, he twisted. Every one. He couldn't just let me have this.

When I got to the top landing, I stopped at the heavy doors, bracing both hands on them. My heart was thumping, and it was hard to catch my breath. I couldn't tell if it was my nerves, my climb up the steps, or Cal's proximity, but I needed a second to compose myself before pulling them open. I leaned forward, resting my head against my hands.

Thwack!

Sharp, resounding pain radiated across my ass. I immediately stood up, spinning to see Cal's stupid grin. His cheek was still red from where I slapped him.

Fire boiled to the surface, it wreathed my hands.

He held up his hands in supplication. "Public displays of affection," he said, laughing.

My hands rolled into fists. Every ounce of muscle and power I had coiled tight, then released into swift punch. Apparently, Cal was waiting for me to strike. He easily ducked out of the way, side-stepping me.

"I mean, you slapped me—" Another right hook. Cal dodged, barely missing my fist. "It was a slap for a slap. And your ass was hanging out there so—"

I feinted with my next swing and instead kicked him, then immediately knocked his legs out. He fell hard onto the ground.

"—*perfectly*," he groaned, getting to his knees.

I debated on kicking him again so that he'd fall down the stairs. I even cocked back my leg, coiled to release it straight into his ass. But I hesitated.

He was laughing. The sound took the burn out of my anger, and the flames around my hands winked out.

"You're an ass, you know that?" I said to him.

But, even now, a smile was forming at the corners of my mouth.

"You're not crying. That's all I care about," Cal said back with complete sincerity as he got to his feet.

My mouth opened and closed, like a fish gasping for air. *All he cares about.* I didn't know what to say. So I turned and pulled the door open.

For a second, I was disoriented by the darkness. It was such a stark contrast to the light of the square. Sunlight filtered through the stained glass, washing the surrounding marble in colored tones. The ground was a very expensive-looking, highly polished black marble with tiny blue veins flecked in gold. Our steps echoed as we walked into the nave of the building. Small rooms lined either side of the entryway. Offices for various types of official business. I scanned the doors, looking for the registrar.

I looked at Cal. "You said you had business to do. You don't need to stay with me. I can handle this on my own," I said matter-of-factly, trying to prove to myself that I was capable of facing this alone.

"Do you really want me to go?" he asked, scanning my eyes for answers I didn't have.

"No." I shook my head. "Yes." I sighed. "I don't know."

"Then I'm staying." He gestured to my right. "It's that door over there."

A light wooden door held a brass plaque reading, "*Registrar.*" And from the doorknob hung another smaller sign saying "*out to lunch.*"

I lifted it. The lamp lights from the corridor glinted off the metal. I loosed a long, slow breath.

"So, the bank, then," he said, gesturing towards the end of the building.

Just that moment, the door pulled open, startling me. The sign slid from my hands.

A short, stout man with large glasses peered out at me before jumping in alarm. He had on a waistcoat and hat, obviously ready to head out. The bowler cap and everything else he'd been carrying tumbled from his hands.

"My goodness! You gave me a fright," he said in a surprisingly high-pitched tone, bending down to pick up his things.

I paused a second too long, but Cal seemed to sense my hesitation and stepped right up.

"Good afternoon, sir. We have a bit of business. Is there any way I can bother you to postpone your luncheon?"

He smiled, that classic marble-white smile he always used when trying to persuade someone.

The man squinted, narrowing his eyes at Cal. He pointed at him. "You're—"

Cal cut him off, taking his hand and shaking it.

"Hello, Celnius. It's good to see you again."

The man looked dazed. "You don't have your usual retinue. I didn't even recognize you."

"Do me this favor, please." Cal looked at him pleadingly, then slid his eyes pointedly in my direction. Celnius, confused, looked over at me, then back at him. "I'll buy your lunch," he added.

Celnius nodded. "Alright, then. Alright. Come in."

We followed him into the cramped office. Folders of papers were laid in neat little piles throughout the room.

"Touch nothing. I have a perfect filing system," Celnius said, gesturing to a chair. "Now, what business did you say you had? I can't imagine you're about to tell me about a birth. That news would have been everywhere."

"It's my news," I said, speaking up for the first time, although it sounded more like a timid whisper than a proper statement.

Celnius turned his large bespectacled eyes on me expectantly. "And you are?"

"Elyria Solaris. It's a—" I swallowed hard, "death announcement. I need to file an official record of death... for my father."

There. I'd said it.

He pulled a piece of paper from a long stack. A second set of lenses lowered over his current large ones, magnifying his already enormous eyes. I felt Cal's hand reach over and rest along my thigh. He squeezed gently. My heart raised into my throat.

"Name?"

"Dukant Bartholomew Solaris," I said, willing my voice to remain steady.

"Age?"

"62."

"Place of birth?"

"Bullseye, Artist's Ring."

"Last known place of residence?"

"Laluna, Senesterra."

"Cause of death?"

Shadows. Unknown. I swallowed again.

"My dear. Cause of death? It's the last question."

Cal leaned forward, hand still on my leg. "Spider bite."

Celnius looked at him. "Well, I don't get that one every day." He nodded his head and scribbled the answer on the paper. "Very well. I'll have this information added to the record."

He stood and shook Cal's hand. Cal reached over and wrote something on a slip of paper, then handed it to Celnius. "Just show that to the owner of La Bella Donna. They'll set you up with a meal on my tab," Cal said.

"B... b... but, this is a parlor house," stammered Celnius incredulously.

"And who better to handle the sausage?" Cal winked, reaching for the door and ushering me into the hall.

We walked out of the office and started down the corridor.

I raised an eyebrow at Cal. "You have a running tab at a parlor house in The Bullseye?"

That flare of jealousy returned, burning hotter beneath my skin than before. An inexplicable rage for some other woman running her hands over his bronzed skin. Knowing him it was probably many, many other lovers. I wasn't exactly a shy virgin, but for some reason that didn't help to soften my need to claw the eyes out of some otherwise innocent women.

Cal's eyes flicked over me. "And what if I do?"

Amusement sparked in his expression, and his calculating gaze scanned my face, reading all the emotions that I was failing to hide.

"You are the most..." I trailed off, at a loss for words.

"Handsome? Generous? Charming?" suggested Cal, smiling.

I tried to slap him, but he caught my hand midair. Before I could react his lips were on mine. Coasting his hands along my curves, he drew my body flush to his. I gave myself over to it, until sparks traveled over my fingertips and the buzz brought me back to the moment.

Breaking away from the kiss, I said, "...Impossible."

"Well, you didn't call me an ass that time. So I'll take that as progress."

"You—"

My words were lost on his lips as Cal kissed me, again. He was gentler this time and in a heartbeat I forgot everything but the feel of my body molding against his. The world fell away. My entire sense of being narrowed. Everything but Cal ceased to exist. That impossible connection flamed brighter in my chest, binding us tighter. His hand gently brushed my cheek as he released my lips. The fight in me faded away, like shadows beneath the power of the sun's rays. The sadness and pain were banished, pushed back by the sanctuary of this embrace.

With a lingering kiss against my temple, he threaded his fingers between mine, smoothing his thumb over the back of my hand. He gestured towards the propped open brass gates that separated the bank stalls from the rest of the building. "Ready?"

I nodded and let him guide me into the bank.

The far wall held three windows with bank tellers sitting at them. A woman sat behind the opening of the third stall, her hair coiled tightly in a bun atop her head.

She looked up at us pleasantly. "What can I do for you this afternoon?"

"I need to change the name over on my father's accounts. He's recently deceased," I said, a bit proud that I'd managed the words without my voice cracking.

The woman looked up gravely at me. "I'm so sorry."

Her empathy made my stomach turn. Saying the truth was one thing, but accepting pity from strangers for it was something else entirely. I handed her a card with the account numbers on them.

"I'll be right back."

I slipped the coin from my pocket and began nervously flipping it between my fingers. Cal gently grabbed my hand. The golden coin tumbled to the ground. With amazing speed, Cal reached down with his other hand, deftly catching it. Fingers twining together, his thumb resumed smoothing back and forth over the top of mine. It was a sweet, almost loving reminder that I wasn't alone.

I was too drained to keep fighting, and surrendered to the strength he offered. Resting my head against his shoulder, I closed my eyes and slowed my breathing to match his. Several long minutes passed before the clicking sound of the woman's heels returned.

"Alrighty, I just need to know what names to put on these accounts."
She slid two ledgers over the counter to me.

"This can't be correct," I said pointing to the second one. "That number is…"
Cal leaned over my shoulder and whistled.

"Dukant Solaris. That's the name you provided to me. These are his accounts, a business one and a personal account."

An impossibly high number stared back at me. Duke couldn't have been worth this much money. This was the fortune of a small kingdom, not a storyteller.

Under my breath I hissed, "What did Duke do to amass this kind of wealth?"
"What did he do before the troupe?"

"I don't know. He was a for-hire. He did odd jobs." I grimaced. More secrets. "Amos and Sheila owe me some answers. But I'm not about to turn around for Laluna either." I shoved down my frustration, locking it away alongside the ache in my heart.

"Maybe there's a reason they decided to settle on the farthest, hardest to reach place in Venterra."

I nodded. I just had no idea what that reason could be.

Over the next ten minutes, I laid out which accounts went to which people. Duke didn't have a will, but I knew who he wanted to ensure was taken care of, mainly the troupe. A tidy sum went to Amos and Sheila. The rest, I knew, was supposed to go to me. I kept enough to cover expenses while I tracked down the monster responsible for breaking my world apart. The remainder I had put into the accounts of the individual members of the troupe. I didn't want Duke's secret fortune. I didn't need it. Let Macie buy a new absurdly beautiful dress or Jess can have all the Lumos silk he wanted.

We were walking back to the doors, still hand in hand, when I realized Cal hadn't done any business.

"Didn't you have something you needed to attend to while we were here?" I asked him.

"I attended to it," he said, gesturing to me. "You're the only thing that I want to give attention to."

My heart squeezed. All of the teasing, the kisses, it was to make sure I held it together today, and that he would be there to help me pick up the pieces if I shattered.

"Thank you," I said.

"For what?" he asked.

"For coming with me, and for being so aggravating that I forgot to be sad." I smiled meagerly at him.

"Ah, well. I'm so damn good at it," he said, flashing one of his trademark smiles and pushing open the heavy door to the outside.

34

CALLEN

When we found him, Xoc was shadow-boxing a gilded statue of a blacksmith. He was bouncing back and forth on his toes, throwing fist after fist into the air. One imaginary blow after another.

"Hey there," I said tentatively but full of amusement. "How ya doing?"

Xoc turned to me. His pupils were dilated to the point that his eyes looked black. In his mouth, he was chewing more bark.

"You daft bastard, are you actually eating more of that crazy shit Joseph gave you?"

Xoc smiled wickedly and swung at me mid-bounce. A powerful right hook flew straight for my jaw. I deflected his fist away from my face and into the wall behind me. Bits of brick and cracked plaster crumbled to the ground.

"I owe you for the basket ride of death," he said, laughing maniacally and throwing a returning blow. "I told you I'd kick your ass."

"*You*—" I said, blocking.

"*Are*—" I side-stepped away from a centrally placed kick.

"*Out-*—" I swung back, a strong punch straight at his sternum. He blocked it, and I immediately countered with my other fist.

"*Of*—" My counter hit and grazed the side of his cheek. Xoc's dilated eyes opened wide, renewing his intensity. I chuckled, which only fanned the flames of his fury.

"*Your*—" Block.

"*Damn*—" I spun to avoid his next strike, using the momentum to whip my leg around.

"*Mind.*" The roundhouse landed and Xoc flew backwards into the wall. He blinked at me, throwing his hands down to his sides, and loosed a feral growl.

"I win," I said, dusting off my hands.

Xoc's eyes narrowed on me, and he lunged forward. I threw up a wall of hard air, boxing him in. He bounced off it, striking it repeatedly before roaring in anger.

"I. Win," I repeated more sternly this time.

He beat his fist one last time before finally conceding through clenched teeth, "Fine, you win. This time."

I released the wall and he stumbled forward. Blown out, black eyes flashed with fiery anger.

"Now, now, boys. You're both pretty." Elyria sidled up to us, shaking her head. The rose I got her was still behind her ear, and the deep red of the petals were intense against the shining mass of her black hair. Her lips parted into a stunning smile.

I could look at her forever.

"You are quite literally the prettiest thing in this entire city."

She didn't acknowledge my compliment. But that didn't make it any less true. Pain squeezed at my heart. I wouldn't get forever though, would I? These stolen moments would end the second I told her the truth.

Elyria slapped the bark hanging between Xoc's lips from his mouth. It fell silently to the ground. However, the sound of her hand cracking against his cheek echoed off the plastered walls around us.

He growled at her, and instinctively I raised my fists. There was no way I was going to let him go all strung out draken on her.

Elyria growled back at him, flames sparking in her eyes, and waves of power rippling off of her strong enough to drive the air from my lungs. "Fucking try it."

Xoc took a step back. With that look, Elyria could have tamed a wild jungle cat with only a single glance. Which, at this point, Xoc basically was.

"Did you find the cycles I asked for?" Her words were hard and clipped, demanding.

Xoc straightened, instantly heeling to her command. I practically expected him to kneel. I had a vision of Elyria with a crown, standing atop a marble dais. The clarity of that realization made me stagger back a complete step. This woman was born to be a queen. *My queen.*

"Yes, three rigs will be waiting for us at the edge of the city," Xoc responded in a gruff voice.

Elyria looked at me expectantly, but I was still reeling with new understanding. I ran my hand through my hair. I was in so much deeper than I ever expected to be. She was it. There was never going to be anyone after her. There just couldn't be.

Which meant I was well and truly fucked. With no one to blame but myself.

"Well then, let's get going," I said, gesturing in the direction Xoc had mentioned. Suman suddenly felt too close.

From the corner of my eye, I saw a flicker of white. I looked up just in time to see long white hair duck over the edge of a nearby rooftop. At first glance it looked like one of the Fasmas, a pair of Innesvale's best spies. But that couldn't be right. They shouldn't even be on this side of Venterra. Before we left the capital, I gave them orders to shadow Malvat.

Unless he was here too.

Fuck.

I swiveled my head around, scanning for any cloaked figures or someone out of place. But there was no one like that in the square. Just regular people going about regular business.

How long had they been trailing us? They were basically invisible, more ghost than man. If Andros and Andromeda didn't want to be seen, then you wouldn't know they were there until you felt the burn of a knife slicing your throat open. Either one of them could have been following us the entire time, and we never would have known.

Questions sprinted through my mind. Did my mother send them to find us? Worry sank into my gut. What would be bad enough that she would send them after me? I needed to discuss this with Xoc, get his take on what it meant.

"Are you coming?" Elyria said from down the street. I looked back at the rooftop where I saw the trailing ghost hair. Nothing was there. "Cal? What's wrong?" she asked, walking back towards me and glancing up at the rooftops.

"Nothing. It's nothing," I said, trying my best at nonchalance. I wrapped a hand on her shoulder and twisted her back towards the alley. "Let's get going before our rigs decide to find themselves another fare."

She squinted at me, not entirely convinced. Hurt and anger flashed in her. Gods damn me. This was just another lie coming from my lips that she knows isn't true.

Panic at seeing the Fasmas edged my senses, but it was eclipsed by the guilt I felt seeing that hurt in her eyes and knowing I put it there. It fucking gutted me but I'd come this far, there was no point in stopping now. A few days from now we'd be on a ship to Innesvale, and I would make it up to her then. That is—if she ever spoke to me again after I told her the truth. Icy guilt twisted that knife in my heart just a little deeper.

Taxis sat in a line against the city wall, all waiting for fares. Each bicycle sat inside of a large rounded shell. It was highly lacquered, with a green finish and white stripes along the edges. They looked more like beetles than bicycles. The imagery of riding in a beetle made me shiver.

Xoc walked over to one of the drivers and the man hopped up. He motioned to the guy next to him, and they both got into their taxis. The vehicles pulled out from the line and slowly rolled into place before us.

"You know what this reminds me of?" I said, gesturing to Xoc.

Xoc shifted his gaze sideways at me. "That time you cheated in Ebimon?"

"You mean that time I won in Ebimon," I corrected him, with as serious an expression as I could muster.

I mean, I did cheat, but only a bit.

"*No*, I'm pretty sure I mean that time you *cheated* in Ebimon."

"I merely exploited a loophole. We never determined that shortcuts were illegal."

"Shortcut! *Cal, you flew over a building.*"

Xoc's exasperation was palpable, and it was delicious. I never got to have the thrill of winding him up. He was always so composed.

Behind me, Elyria snorted. "Imagine that, Cal *cheating* with magic."

I smiled, knowing it grated them both to see me gloat.

"Fine!" He said, "Let's bet."

"Bet what?" I said, genuinely curious.

"I bet my cab makes it to Suman before yours."

Xoc turned to face me squarely. His immense size loomed over me. As if he could ever intimidate me. He forgets that I remember the first time he tried to fly and fell on his face, or that time he shat himself from eating too many of those berries he made by cross-pollinating flax with prunes in an attempt to make a digestive aperitif. So, no, his window of intimidation has long since passed.

"Stakes?"

Xoc thought for a while, then looked over at Elyria.

"No, she stays out of it," I said, putting my foot down.

"I think I get to decide what I am and am not a part of," she interjected.

"And..." I added.

"And you two can leave me out of whatever display of testosterone you are planning," she replied.

"Exactly." I turned back to him. "So, Xoc, stakes?"

"I get your bedroom when we get..." he paused, "...home. And you have to stay in my..." another pause, "...quarters."

He might be raging on that root Joseph gave him, but at least he was smart enough to keep our cover.

"Your rooms have nothing in them," I said, rolling my eyes.

"Exactly, and your bed is so damn comfortable. After a long trip, it will be nice to have such a... palatial sleeping arrangement."

Xoc's mouth spread into an uncharacteristically wolfish smile.

"No deal, there's nothing in it for me," I said, walking towards the nearest cab.

"Fine, if I win I get your rooms," Xoc said.

Elyria looked up at the word rooms.

"And if you win..." Xoc's voice trailed off as he thought.

"If I win, you have to spend a week working in the Suite," I laughed, already picturing it.

"Not with Larissa. You know I can't stand her. All she does is drool over me and grab my ass the entire time," he said, shifting his weight, just the idea of it already making him uncomfortable.

I laughed. "Nothing would make me happier than seeing the way she makes you squirm. That's what I want. I win, you have to do a week in the Suite. You win, you can have my rooms for a week." I walked over to the cycle, shooing the driver from the seat. "But we drive. Not them."

"Oi," said the driver in a heavy Sumendi accent. "That's my cab you're talking about."

I looked at him. "Let me drive and I'll pay you double."

The man stepped back, gesturing that the cab was all mine. I smiled deviously and climbed onto the seat.

I looked up at Xoc. "Come on, pussy! Let's do this."

"As a woman with a pussy, I take offense to that comment," Elyria said, settling seductively into the seat behind me. "Pussies are stronger and scarier than any man I've ever met. You should respect the pussy."

I twisted around and looked up the long lines of her legs. It would be so easy to reach out and drag my hands up those thighs. "My apologies, Sunshine, you just let me know what I can do to make it up to you."

Elyria almost imperceptibly squeezed her thighs together.

I raised my eyes to hers and added, "I could get on my knees, and..." I licked my lips. "...make sure your pussy feels properly *respected*."

She slid forward, putting her boot heel against my throat. "You can start by turning around and getting us the fuck out of here."

I tossed my head, getting the hair that fell into my eyes out of my face. I wanted her to see them clearly so she didn't miss an ounce of my intent. I tilted my head down and kissed her ankle, running my hand along her calf to stroke her inner thigh. She sucked in a breath and that blush I love so much spread over her chest.

"Are you done making lame advances? I want to get to shoving your defeat in your humiliated face," Xoc said, walking over to the other cycle.

Elyria sat back, swallowing. I didn't drop the heat from my eyes as I let them trail over her body. The driver slipped into the seat beside her, breaking the spell.

"Why is it so hot in this cab?" the driver said, shifting uncomfortably.

I smiled to myself. *I wonder.*

"Do you have any idea where you're going?" Elyria asked.

"No," I replied. "But that's what he's for."

I turned to look at the owner of the cab. "If we win, I'll give you triple your normal fee."

His eyes glittered. "Done. You go south. All streets south pretty much get you there. Try to stay as close to the water as you can. Just keep the water on your left, and listen when I call to you."

I looked over to Xoc. His long legs poked over the handlebars, and I cackled with my impending victory. I probably should have waited for him to figure out how to shift the seat, but I didn't.

"I'll be waiting for you in Suman," I yelled, and kicked off.

The Cycle Cab clattered and clanked for a second, and then we were moving. Xoc yelled something that ended with, "...*Fuckhead.*"

We started moving down the street, a slight decline ahead of us, and the cab picked up speed. Buildings flew by in a blur of white and red. A missing stone in the road hit the wheel, and we careened off-kilter for a second before righting ourselves. The man behind me started yelling obscenities in Sumendi.

A second later, a roar came from behind us. Xoc barreled down on us, a great battle cry echoing from him. He was pedaling while standing, bending over to grip the handlebars, each leg pumping furiously after the next. I couldn't believe what I was seeing. Veins bulged from the sides of his neck and the very tendons in his legs pressed into the leather seams of his pants.

He was gaining on me.

Oh, fuck no! There was no way I was going to let him pass me. I peddled faster, moving the cycle to the center of the road.

"What's the matter? Losing your edge?" Elyria shouted, leaning forward to look around the walls of the cab at where Xoc was approaching. "What in Kraav?!"

The strung out draken pushed up next to us. Elyria leaned against my back, trying to get a better view of him.

"Sit back. Stop moving around, you're creating too much drag," I yelled back to her.

"I can see the cording of his muscles," she shouted up to me. "I shouldn't be able to see his muscles like that."

I couldn't turn and look, though, I couldn't risk slowing. I pushed myself, pedaling faster.

"Take the turn up ahead." The driver sitting behind me tapped my shoulder. "Just do it, take the next turn."

A narrow street opened to our left. I twisted the handlebars hard. The entire cab tilted on one side, nearly tipping over. I shifted the gears and we picked up speed. I could hear the rattle of Xoc's rig ride past the road.

"Now, up ahead, take the bridge," the man added, pointing to where a narrow walking bridge crossed over the canal and connected to the harbor road. "Trust me."

"That's a walking bridge," yelled Elyria.

"It'll be fine. I take this shortcut when I'm in a hurry all the time," he said.

"Okay." I aimed the cycle for the narrow bridge.

368

"Oh, and go faster, you'll want to take the end at speed."

"Why?" I called back to him while pushing the pedals as fast as I could.

With a bump we leapt onto the metal bridge. We crested the top and now I knew why he said to take it at speed. Ahead of us, the bridge didn't cross the canal. It ended with a viewing platform. A platform that had the end barrier removed. There were rubber track marks from where past cabs had done this same trick.

"Go faster, or you'll never make it to the other side. Go! Go! Go!"

"Cal!" Elyria shouted. I could sense her body tensing behind me.

We broke over the edge, sailing into the air. I could see the far wall of the canal approaching. We were just going to make it. My heart lifted and the sheer thrill of the moment broke over me.

Until we weren't anymore.

The cab tipped forward. *Shit. Shit.* The dirty brown canal water rose quickly before us.

"*Cal!*" she screamed.

"I've got this," I said, and from below an intense wind pushed us up. I intensified the gale. Like a kite, the air caught the curve of the taxi's roof. We rocketed forward, landing on the road.

"*Waahoo!*" I yelled. A victory cheer as much as a cry of exhalation.

I went back to pedaling, relishing the burn in my legs because I knew that ache equalled victory. From a road above us, I heard Xoc yell, "You cheating fucker!"

Gods damn it.

"You've got him for sure now," the driver said. "He's going to have to double around to get to this level." The man was laughing and rambling on in Sumendi.

I leaned forward. The surrounding buildings changed from being all white to a more natural red brick. We were getting close. Masts from distant moored ships peppered the horizon.

Almost there.

The driver tapped me on my shoulder. "You're going to want to take the inner road here when it splits up ahead. It winds less."

"Okay."

The road forked when a large triangular building split the lane before us. I leaned right, and the cab shifted into the narrow straight road. A taller square building was near it as if the road itself had sliced away a chunk of the building. We rode down the corridor, the dark shadow of the buildings looming over us. Light at the end of the road grew closer, and I could just see what looked like docks.

I gave a victorious whoop. We were going to win and I would shove it in his bitter face for days.

The light at the end of the corridor started to blink out. The ivy once growing along the buildings' walls shot across the road to form a giant net.

Oh, that cheating bastard! Off somewhere I could hear demonic cackling.

I sped up. It was only ivy. If we went fast enough, we would blow right through it. The cab drove at full speed into the tangled web of vines. The ivy stretched around us, then snaking tendrils whipped out. Vines ringed around the handlebars, into the wheel well gripping the axle. They latched over the pedals and gears. The cab lurched to a full stop. I pedaled and pedaled, my feet straining against the vines.

"*Xoc!*" I roared in anger, slamming my hands in frustration against the handlebars.

Slowly rolling in front of the wall of ivy came the tall, proud figure of Xoc. Both he and his driver were laughing. My skin heated and I felt my blood rise.

"You plant-loving fuckhead! How is this not cheating?"

I tore at the vines, feeling them slice my hands when tiny, unnatural thorns formed.

"I'll be waiting for you at the docs," Xoc yelled back.

"I'm gonna kill him," I growled.

The musical sound of Elyria's laughter shook the cab. I twisted, and she had slid down in her seat, apparently so overcome with hysterics that she couldn't even sit up straight. It was hard to stay angry when I could see how happy my defeat was making her.

"I guess we're walking the last couple blocks." She wiped at tears spilling from her eyes.

"My cab!" The driver was looking in dismay at the green vines that had punctured the metal in places.

"Oh. I'll buy you a new one," I said, hopping down from the seat.

I kicked at the ivy net. Through the leaves and vines, I watched Xoc flick his middle finger at us.

A vine wrapped around my ankle. My feet were ripped out from under me and the next thing I knew, I was hanging upside down. Deep, booming laughter echoed over the narrow alley. I swung and kicked my free foot at the vine and pulled uselessly at the knot around my ankle.

Elyria climbed down from the Cycle Cab, which was half lifted into the air by the ivy. She stood for a moment, admiring my squirming.

"A little help would be nice. Or were you just going to stand there ogling me?"

She chuckled and pulled a throwing knife from her hip belt.

"Just admiring the perfect view," she said, throwing my own damn words from The Steps back at me. "Hold still."

"At least you're not blindfolded," I said, groaning and knowing what was coming next.

"I don't know, I quite like my blindfolds," she winked and released the knife.

It slipped past the vine, cleanly severing its connection, and I tumbled to the ground with a painful thunk.

"Thank you," I said, dusting myself off and straightening my shirt.

I walked around to the back, where our packs were strapped into a compartment. I reached into my bag, pulled a card from a pocket, and handed it to the driver.

"Give that to the teller at the Basilica. Ask for whatever you need," I said.

Elyria's eyes went wide. "Do you have any idea how much one of those must cost?"

"My gods. I had no idea. No, sir. That won't be necessary." The driver said, trying to push the card back into my hands. This sudden humbling wasn't unusual. Whenever someone figured out that I was the crown prince, they often fell over themselves to be accommodating.

"That's not necessary. Please fix your cab, or buy a new one, whatever you need. Thank you for letting me use it," I said.

"Abuse it more like," said Elyria as she slipped her knife back into its sheath.

"Thank you, sir," the man said, bowing low. I sighed and rolled my eyes.

"After you, Sunshine." I gestured onward and slung my bag over one shoulder. Elyria hit the wall of ivy with a ball of fire and it quickly fizzled away.

"*Waah*. She's amazing," said the driver.

I stood back, admiring her as she walked through the tangled mass of burning vines.

"Tell me about it."

35

CALLEN

By the time we made it to the edge of the Sumendi Harbor the cheating bastard, that I called brother, was leaning against his cab. He and his driver were sipping on bottles of something fizzy and cold.

"I'm not giving you my rooms," I said as I walked up to him.

Xoc laughed. "You cheated first. Don't think I didn't see that little flying over the canal stunt you pulled."

"To be fair, the driver told me it's a perfectly acceptable shortcut."

Xoc rolled his eyes. "Sure he did."

The driver of his cab spoke up. "Actually, we do jump the canal there sometimes. But, if you ask me, it's a stupid risk."

Xoc glared at the driver and the man shrank back.

Elyria grabbed Xoc's face, roughly turning it from side to side, inspecting him. "Well, at least that run on the cycles helped burn some of whatever that bark is out of you. Your eyes don't look nearly as crazed anymore."

She was right. His pupils were much more normal now, and his entire demeanor was less frenetic.

"Where now?" I said, looking at her, an ache already rising in my chest. The time for subterfuge and playful flirting was coming to an end. Whatever this building connection between us was, it would shatter the moment I told her the truth. I had promised my morals that I would not allow her to board a ship without knowing everything. If Elyria left the continent, she would do so fully understanding the consequences. She deserved a hell of a lot better than this, but my own selfishness had brought us here, and there was no undoing it.

"We're here." I pointed to the enormous tower at the far end of town. A plateau rose high above the city, and sitting at the top of it was what looked like an ornate fortress. An audacious building with a large, spiraling tower sprawled in red brick across the expanse of the cliff. "There's your library."

She looked up at the large hill and grimaced. "I didn't remember the plateau being so high."

"How else were they going to look down on everyone?"

She walked up to the wall that lined the harbor. Neat lines of blue boats knocked against each other with the shifting of the sea.

"Water taxis, they used to be a symbol of luxury," she said. "I used to beg Duke to take one instead of walking the canals when we came here. I wanted so badly to be one of those girls settled into the plush velvet seats, buzzing by the pedestrians. Now they just look like empty boats."

Elyria turned her back to the water and closed her eyes. She ran her fingers lightly over the bandage on her forearm. "Since we're here, maybe we should find this friend of Joseph's." She slipped a paper from her pocket, and handed it to me. "Reihaneh Almont. He said she's a fine healer."

She'd been favoring her other arm for days, cradling the damaged flesh when she thought no one was looking. "Yes, let's start there. The sooner we fix that arm, the better. Everything else can wait." It was pathetic. I was scrambling for seconds now. "Does she study at the University or is she already at a House of Healing?"

"Actually..." Elyria looked almost sheepish. "He said she'd be in one of the gambling dens. Here in the harbor."

She sighed and looked over at me. "So, where's the best gambling den?"

"Why do you assume I know this?" I said, crooking one side of my lips into a smile.

She merely kicked a hip out and tilted her head at me.

"Okay, well, I do know *one*," I replied, my smile spreading wider.

"Well, lead the way," she said, gesturing towards the lower wharf.

The entire city was built on the solid foundation of science and mathematics. Originally, it was the Academic Ring of The Bullseye. In time, it grew its own system, and became something wholly separate from its neighbor to the North. Suman's architecture was based on science and mathematics. It was clear in every detail, from the proportions and dimension of each structure, to the tessellating blue tiles around the doorways. It was decadent and exotic, even down here in the poorest part of Suman.

We walked down a series of side streets until we reached a staircase that descended into a basement establishment. Double metal doors were propped open, and from inside, the warm smell of spiced oranges and whiskey wafted up on colored puffs of smoke. Sweet and hazy memories of evenings spent here came to mind. Nights sprawled on plush pillows and smoking various forms of intoxicants while beautiful women served me emerald liquors in tiny ornate glasses.

Suman had hit a point of learning where the normal barriers of social constraint were no longer considered necessary. Instead, the Sumendi government had dissolved most normal social structures in favor of a more communal sense of living. The open-mindedness of this city was always refreshing, especially if I'd traveled recently to the more archaic parts of Venterra. Here, all people were welcome, attuned or not.

There were some places where the attuned believed their powers and longer lives placed them above the unattuned. That kind of prejudice corrupted every part of their society. Innesvale had been the first kingdom to abolish racial prejudice in all its forms, so such places were ones that I never was able to stomach being in for long.

At the Ice Fall, the unattuned were enslaved. If a baby was born powerless, they would be given to one of the houses of servitude until they were old enough to be put in a permanent placement. It's a barbaric act that Innesvale has vocally stood against for millennia, despite the rough edges that formed politically between the two Desterran nations. I absolutely loathed having to treat with them.

We stepped down the stairs into the den. The air was thick with colored smoke. Along the exterior walls, booths filled with large silk pillows sat in circles on the ground around small fire pits. Colored bricks of the local leaf sat atop coals, and a blue glass dome covered each pit to catch most of the smoke. A pipe affixed to the top of the dome funneled the smoke down to the glassy-eyed patrons, who blissfully sprawled on the pillows, puffing away.

I glanced over the room, catching the men and women at the back in various stages of repose. I smiled and looked over at Elyria. Fantasies danced in my mind of laying in one of those shadowy corners blowing rings of colored smoke at her heated and bare body. She, on the other hand, either hadn't seen what was going on or didn't seem to care. Instead, she was standing on the bottom step, eyeing the card tables in the center of the room. People crowded around them, cheering as different patrons took their turn.

"So do we know what this girl looks like?" I said, leaning into her and inhaling her flowery, smoke-laced scent.

"No, he just said that she tends to draw attention, and we'd know her when we saw her." Elyria shook her head, annoyed. "Maybe we should just go. This is pointless."

She started walking back up the stairs. Clear defeat, turning down her expression.

At that moment, the bartender at the far end of the den yelled out, "Rei! I need a clean up over here."

Elyria swiveled on her heels, craning her head to see who had called, and more importantly, who answered.

Two tables over, a woman sat up, pulling back from the man she was straddling. She looked up at the bar, obviously annoyed. Kicking back her head, she flipped back the shaggy, chin length hair that hung low in front of her face. Mixed among the brown were strands of pure white that glowed.

She yelled back to the bar, "Fuck off, Brend, I'm occupied."

The man she sat on ran his hands up her nearly bare back. Her loose, cropped shirt exposed her entire midsection, and hung scandalously low off of one shoulder.

"Rei. I ain't paying your ass to get fondled. I've got other girls for that," the bartender yelled back.

She sighed and swung her arm from around the man. Truly stunning inkwork ran intricately down her arms. They pulsed a brilliant, light purple and were in complete contrast to the tawny skin tone.

Rei licked up the column of the man's throat, moaning loud enough to hear from our location near the door. She said something in his ear before taking the lobe sensuously into her mouth. The man roughly pawed at her ass as she slid off of him. When she stepped away, his hand lingered in the folds of her wrap skirt, pulling the slit open to expose her upper thighs.

"Well. I think we found our girl," Elyria said, just as taken aback as I was.

"She certainly does make an impression."

I let my eyes trail over Rei as she sauntered to the bar, golden chains clanging off her hips as she walked. She was definitely beautiful, the kind of girl that was impossible to ignore.

Elyria flashed me a scowl. I flicked my eyes to the side to catch the deep red staining her cheeks. "You are absolutely gorgeous when flushed with jealousy, you know that?" I said, smirking.

She pursed her lips, and I braced for a backhand that I knew was coming. But, instead, she simply dismissed my comment by walking straight for Rei.

We took up a spot at the bar, not far from where Rei had stopped. A heavily intoxicated man swayed on a stool. Rei roughly grabbed his cheeks, and turned his head from side to side. She snapped in front of his eyes, checking for his reflexes. But he didn't track her hand, only drooled onto her breasts.

"This the one, Brend?" she asked, already sounding bored.

"Yeah, he paid double, so make it good."

Rei leaned into the drunkard. "Aww, honey, did you have a bit too much fun?"

The man smiled, but never looked up from her cleavage.

"My eyes are up here, baby."

He reached out to her exposed stomach, but Rei smacked the man's hands. Before he could react to being struck, she braced his head on either side. The tattoos that swirled up her arms glowed radiantly. It looked like she had been tattooed by a shooting star. Cool purple light splashed across the man's face. His slackened facial muscles righted themselves and his swaying body centered.

"Now that's a trick," I murmured.

The man was now completely sober. He rubbed his hands across his face.

"That tingling will go away in a minute," she said, holding out her hand for a tip.

The man gave her a gold coin. "Thanks, Rei."

"Go on, get out of here before your wives figure out where you've been," replied Rei with a wink.

She began walking back to her card table, sticking the coin into her cleavage. As she walked by us Elyria grabbed Rei's arm. A blast of purple light exploded from her. Momentarily, my senses were completely stunned. My mind spun and my vision blurred.

Amid the clamor in the bar, the bartender muttered, "I've had enough of her shit."

White spots danced across my vision. I rubbed my eyes, trying to make my sight come back. When it did, Rei was nowhere to be seen. Elyria was cursing and rubbing furiously at her eyes. I walked up to the bartender, about to ask him what he knew about this girl, when Elyria smacked my shoulder and pointed.

"Xoc has her!"

I looked over to where Xoc barred the door, the massive hulk of his frame filling the space. Rei seemed to be trying to sweet-talk her way past him. *Fat chance of that happening.*

Elyria approached with a uniquely serious and friendly expression that only she could pull off. "Are you Reihaneh Almont?"

"That depends," she replied, cautiously eyeing her.

Elyria raised an eyebrow in question.

"Depends on what you want," Rei quipped back, and looked up at Xoc.

"We have a mutual friend," I said. "Joseph Pendlecost."

"Joey!" She laughed. "I don't know that I'd call him a friend. More like the guy who almost got me killed."

"We have that in common too," Xoc said.

Rei flicked her eyes up to him. "Yeah, you and half of The Bullseye."

Elyria gestured to the bandage wrapped around her arm. "I was burned by acid. He said that you owe him one, and that you're a damn fine healer."

"He said that, did he?" She snorted. "I owe him something, alright, just not what you're thinking. Joey is the right kinda wrong sorta man. He's got all the right intentions and the worst ways of getting them done."

"Yeah, that's actually a perfect way to describe him," Elyria agreed.

"Let me see that arm." Rei swiveled her head, looking at a vacant alcove. "Over there. There's an empty booth. You all want something to drink, or anything?"

"Sure," I answered. "The emerald liquor here is damn near as perfect as a drink can get."

"Brend, send over a round of the green shit. I'm helping some friends," she yelled over to the bartender. She looked at me and winked a kohl-rimmed eye. "Come on, sugar. Move that sweet ass of yours."

Rei whipped out a hand, smacking my butt and giving it a little squeeze. Beside me, an actual rainbow of rippled heat radiated from Elyria. I smiled.

The four of us settled into a booth amidst pillows in varying shades of green. I leaned back into one of them. The exhaustion from our ride settled into my bones or it could have been the heavy smoke that hung in the air. Probably both.

Xoc floundered over the cushions, turning and twisting to figure out how to sit comfortably. His gigantic figure dwarfed the spray of pillows. With each shift of his body, they slid away and his ass landed awkwardly on the tile floor.

I chuckled at him. "Need some help?"

"I hate these places," he grumbled, while awkwardly wrangling a pillow under one arm. "We couldn't have done this in a nice cafe? Suman has great coffee."

Rei sat cross-legged before Elyria, not caring in the least how the position made her skirt rise, or what indecent places were on full display to Xoc–if he ever managed to settle down long enough to actually notice.

"Let's see what we're dealing with here," she said, cradling the wounded arm in her slight hands.

She tenderly undid the binding. Elyria's delicate features wrinkled in pain with each twist of the bandage. There was a sweet smell that came from the wound, and the skin around the edges looked almost green. *Fuck*. We shouldn't have waited so long. Elyria was too damn good at hiding her pain.

Rei took a sharp inhale. "That is one wicked wound. How did you say you got this?"

"Saving their asses from a Giant Ribbo-Velvet Worm," said Elyria coolly.

Rei smiled. "Oh, I like you already."

"I sliced off a mandible that housed an acid sac."

I leaned into the girls, smoothing the ends of Elyria's hair between my fingers. "I feel like somewhere in there it should be mentioned that taking The Steps in the first place was her idea."

"You all came over *The Steps*? No wonder Joey likes you, that's just plain reckless."

Rei seemed genuinely shocked. She raised a hand to Elyria's forehead, inspecting the stitches there. The stitching from her fall had almost healed.

"These stitches are very well done. I bet she doesn't even have any scarring." She turned to look at me. "Is this your handiwork?"

"That'd be me, actually," said Xoc, raising a hand and awkwardly slipping to the ground again.

Rei gingerly picked Elyria's arm back up, hovering one hand over the wound. From here, I could see that the swirls of her tattoo were actually tiny lines tracing out star charts. They wrapped all the way up Rei's arms, and over one shoulder, before disappearing behind her ear. The tattoos pulsated softly, brightening as she tightened her grip on Elyria's forearm.

Elyria's eyes tightened, wincing against whatever Rei was doing.

Rei noticed it too. The light from her arms flashed brighter. At the same time Rei leaned in, and kissed Elyria with an aggressive and well placed kiss. Everyone sat up, completely taken by surprise. Rei deepened the kiss, while the light intensified beneath her hand. A second later, Elyria broke away from Rei and howled in pain.

The entire room went silent. For a second the only sound was Elyria's pained panting.

My heart leapt into my throat. I hopped up and slid behind Elyria, catching her as she collapsed into my arms. A tremor wracked her body with every breath. Whatever the hell Rei had just done hadn't been good.

"Sorry about that," Rei said, wiping at her lips. "There's no way to deal with that level of nerve damage without it being quite painful, and tensing only makes it worse. So, I've found that distraction usually works best. I figured you'd never expect me to kiss you." Rei looked up at me. "Don't worry, big guy. I'm not making moves on your woman. That was purely clinical."

Elyria's voice cracked. "It's okay. I just wasn't prepared for that."

I looked down at her arm. It barely looked like Rei had done anything. The wound was still open, inflamed, and raw.

"You didn't heal her," I said.

"Yeah, I know. She pulled her arm from me before I could finish knitting it back together." Rei grimaced slightly, shadows passing over her dark eyes. "We'll need to try again."

"No," said Elyria, cradling her arm to her chest. "I'm fine."

"Actually, you're not," replied Rei.

"I will just let it heal naturally."

Rei's face softened, and she reached out, placing a gentle hand on Elyria's knee.

"If we don't take care of that now, you'll lose your arm. Do you see how the edges of the wound are turning black? That's necrotic tissue, and if it isn't dealt with, then it will only spread."

I could feel Elyria's heart rate quicken, and I tightened my arms around her.

Rei continued. "Also... you have an attunement I've never felt before. Healing you actually hurts. It was like trying to pour a bucket of water on a forest fire, only I'm the bucket."

Elyria looked over to Xoc, then back to Rei. "I'm draken."

"Well, then that makes sense. I've never actually treated anyone who was draken before. I don't even think I've met a draken before. But it's going to take five times more power to even approach your cellular level than the average attuned person. We need to do this now, or your wound will become too hard to heal, and I won't have the strength to try."

"Distraction?" I said.

Rei nodded in confirmation. "Yeah, distraction."

"I can do that."

Elyria shook her head. "I'm not having sex with you in this parlor, if that's what you're thinking."

I looked over at Rei. She laughed. "Well, I mean that could work."

"Go ahead and start," I said, all joking and playfulness gone from my voice. "Just don't let what I tell her distract *you* to the point of not being able to finish."

Elyria tensed and her breaths quickened, but she said, "Do it."

"Okay. Hold onto your tits, everyone."

Rei lit up again, and Elyria's face twisted.

I took her face in my hands, directing her gaze to me and only me. "Elle, I need to tell you something, but first, kiss me."

Elyria flinched. Panic rose in me as I saw the pain intensifying on her face. "Because I'm afraid that after I tell you this, then I may never get to kiss you again."

Before she could deny me, I pulled her face to mine, claiming what I hoped wasn't the last kiss we would ever share. That connection between us flared to life. Heat rose from her, but she still whimpered against my lips. This wasn't enough. *I had to tell her.* I was always going to tell her in Suman. Maybe this way something good would come from my confession.

I broke away, taking a deep, bracing breath.

"Elle, I'm not who I say I am. I've been lying to you. This whole time. Gods. I'm so sorry. But you have to know I only did it to help keep you safe."

"I know," she said, grimacing. "I know you don't sell cosmetics. I've known this whole time."

"You do?" I said, sitting back on my heels.

Shock flowed over me like ice water.

"Yes, *Callen*. I do."

I blinked at the sound of my name, my real name.

"Shit, you do," I said resolutely. She'd known, and she still came with me. Still let me kiss her...let me...

Fire flashed in her eyes, and from the corner of my vision, Rei flinched. "You're a freaking *prince*. You think I wouldn't recognize you? I've been *everywhere*. For fuck's sake, Solaire performed at your father's 700th jubilee. I was there, five feet from you, the whole godsdamned night. You probably don't remember me because I was ten. But I remember you. You were just as arrogant then as you are now."

My mind traveled over the memory of that night. I remembered the party and performers, but nothing particularly remarkable.

A cry of pain slipped from her, snapping me back to the moment. Elyria gritted her teeth, and her breathing became labored. Tears slid from the corners of her eyes, then she continued. "I've known this whole time. From that first moment in the patisserie. I knew you were lying right then. The question was always *why*?"

"Fuck. This whole time," I whispered, sitting back. "Why didn't you call me out on it then?"

"Well... *ahhhhhh*..." Another wail of pain choked off her words.

I leaned in to take her free hand, but she pulled it out of my reach. "I was waiting to see why you would hide your identity from me, what you were playing at. Then everything happened. When we were sitting at that fire, and you said that you could take me to Suman, I realized, who better to get me access to the library than a prince. Plus, I'm not an idiot. I know I look like a target and I'd attract less attention traveling with the two of you than I ever would alone. Who would ever try attacking us with him in our group?" She looked over to Xoc. "So I *let* you come with me."

"Fuck," I whispered again. She'd been playing me this whole time. Gods, I was a fool thinking that I ever had any kind of control.

"Of course it didn't matter. We were still attacked," she gritted out, taking deep and measured breaths against the pain.

"Almost done," said Rei. "Keep talking."

"Elle, I'm sorry." That's all I could think to say. Every other thought had been whisked away, along with the air from my lungs.

"So why, *Callen*?" She spat my name like venom, and laughed. "Or should I say, Your Highness. Why? Why did you come all the way to Laluna looking for me? How far were you going to take that lie to get me to leave with you? Why?"

"Because you're a Gold Draken. Because Innesvale needs you. Because, Elle, *I need you.*"

My heart clenched. Her golden eyes, usually so warm, had a biting cold beneath them. I couldn't tell if it was anger, hatred, or pain in her eyes. And it scared the shit out of me.

Another tear rolled down her cheek, and I moved to brush it away but she leaned back.

The glow coming from Rei's hands died, and the den suddenly felt too dark. Elyria leapt to her feet. I reached out for her again, forcefully taking her hand and pulling her to me. She was not about to walk away from me.

I needed to make this right.

"Elle, I had to. I needed you to come to Innesvale with me. You would never have just come with me outright. I couldn't risk simply asking you."

Desperation coated my words. I didn't care. I *was* desperate.

"Why? Why do I have to go with you? What is it you need from me so damn badly?" she asked coolly, slipping her hand from my grip.

"I need your fire." I paused, looking around the room. There were too many ears. "For reasons I can't discuss here. You've just gotta trust me."

"*Ha!* Now you want my trust. The only place I'm going is to that library," Elyria said matter-of-factly, pointing up the plateau. "And then I'm going to find Aurus, and the fucking bastard responsible for killing Duke. Those are the *only* things that I am going to do."

"Elle," I whispered.

My hands were shaking. It was breaking me to see the damage those lies were causing.

"You can come with me. I'm sure a prince can still come in handy along the way," she added sourly, each word stinging like a knife. "and you *were* fun to play with."

She got to her feet and began walking away from me. If she left this room, I would lose her for good. I would lose everything.

Thick desperation wrapped its icy claws around my throat, choking rationality from me.

"The Gold Dragon," I blurted out, and then I looked back at Xoc. He only shrugged. "Is in Innesvale."

She stopped mid step and spun around.

"You're lying. You're still fucking lying to me."

I shook my head. "I know where," I continued. "The Shadow Crown has always been his guardian."

Shock and then betrayal ricocheted across her face.

"I'll take you to him," I said, and then, seeing her expression, I added, "I was always going to take you to him. I just didn't know how to tell you."

Elyria walked straight to me. A small ember of hope growing brighter with each of her steps. Maybe I hadn't lost her after all.

"Elyria," I whispered, reaching for her face. "I'm going to fix this."

A flash of light filled my vision as a fiery fist connected with the side of my face. The force of her blow knocked me back and I fell into a pile of cushions. I should have seen that coming. A second fist flew at me, and I didn't bother blocking it. I let her hit me, deserving each strike of her wrath.

Xoc took hold of Elyria's arms. She whirled, stomping down hard on his foot. He released her. "Damn, Elyria, that was not necessary."

"Not necessary! Don't fucking lecture me about necessary."

"Well. I gotta hand it to you, princey. You are fantastic at this distraction stuff," said Rei, standing up.

The man from the bar handed her a tray of drinks. He scowled at Rei as she took it from him. He leaned over to her, saying something too low to hear. Rei shrugged, then set the tray on the ground.

I could already feel my lip swelling.

Elyria glared at Xoc. "I suppose you've known all along, too."

Xoc simply nodded his head. "I've been head of the royal guard for the past 400 years. I know everything. To be completely honest, I probably know more than him."

Anger steamed off of her like boiling water. Elyria leaned forward, picking up a glass of liquor. She threw it back in a single shot. Her hands, still glowing with heat, shattered the glass in her palms. Elyria didn't even notice the shards as she paced back and forth, prowling like a cat ready to take down its next kill.

"Fine. I'll go to Innesvale with you," she said, reaching down and grabbing my shirt collar. "But before we board any boat, you *will* tell me everything."

I bowed my head. "I always was. I was never going to put you on a boat to Innesvale without you knowing the full truth."

My words slurred on my swollen and bleeding lip. Elyria let me go and I slumped back down to the ground, feeling completely broken.

A too long silence hung between us.

"Elyria," said Rei softly. "If you still want to go to the library, then I can get you in."

Elyria looked at her. "Really? So I don't need my knight over here to wave a magic prince card to get me in?"

The ache in my heart was truly a tangible thing. It felt like my chest was tearing open. As if I put my hand to my chest, then it would come away bloody.

"Yeah. I'm a student at the University, or rather I was. But my parents are big benefactors. I can pretty much have the run of the place whenever I want."

Elyria glowered at me. Her eyes were darker than they'd ever seemed before.

"Tonight. You are going to get us passage on a ship, *with my own room*. I'm going with her to the library. We can meet in the morning at the docks."

I opened my mouth to protest.

"And before you say anything about it not being safe, and that you need to come with me, I want to remind you it was me that saved your ass, not the other way around. I can handle myself."

Rei sat back and sipped on her liquor.

"You guys are not boring, I'll give you that."

36

ELYRIA

My blood was still boiling as Rei and I hiked up the plateau to the University. I didn't even know why I was so angry. Hadn't I known this entire time who he was? I'd been waiting for him to come clean to me. I'd told myself that it wouldn't matter. He'd tell me the truth, and I would laugh it off, put the fucker in his place by beating him to the punchline. I'd play him at his own game, and win. That was the plan. But, when he'd told me, all I had wanted was to leave. The pain of my arm paled compared to the feeling of heartache that came from finally admitting that everything we shared was a lie. Or, at least, founded on them.

Flames pulsed in my hand. "This whole damned time he knew about the dragon. *This whole damned time!*" I yelled it to the sky, not caring who could hear me.

"Elyria," Rei said, a bit out of breath. "Can you just slow down?"

I turned around. Damn, I was practically sprinting. That cut me. He had made me so angry that I was literally running away from him.

"Sorry," I said. "It's just..."

I growled in frustration.

"Oh, I get it. I've had plenty of *tada* reveals in my life."

I looked at her, feeling the need to voice the torrent of thoughts swirling around in my head.

"He's an idiot," I said, pointing back down the hill. Not that she needed clarification on who I was talking about. "If what he had wanted all along was for me to go with him to Innesvale, then he should have just led with that. If he had just come clean about who he was and that he guarded Aurus, then I would have just walked right onto a ship. Fuck, I would have helped to raise the damn mast."

"I'm pretty sure you don't raise masts," Rei laughed.

"You know what I mean. This nonsense of protecting me. I don't *need* protecting."

"Obviously."

"His entire story reeks of bullshit."

A huge stone retaining wall loomed before us. I summoned a ball of flames that looked remarkably like Cal's head and chucked it at the wall. It burst on impact. The flames skittered harmlessly across the stone. The evening dew that already clung to it hissed. I roared another yell and threw a brighter, hotter ball.

Rei held up a hand to shield herself. "That's hot," she laughed.

I turned, looked at her, and then started laughing. Uncontrollable laughter. I wasn't even sure why I was laughing.

"I wish I could do that," she said. "Just yell and throw fiery punches, take down a wall or two."

I caught my breath, and somehow, I felt better. The release had cleared my head and calmed my nerves.

"Sooo..." Rei said, pointing back up the road.

We started walking again, this time at a reasonable pace. Behind us, the sun was setting, and the sky was streaked in hues of orange and pink. If I wasn't so angry, then I might have been able to appreciate just how beautiful the view was.

"I don't think I told you thank you," I said, realizing that this kind woman just dropped everything to do this.

"Nah. It's nothing. You were... distracted," she said, a carefree smile replacing the serious one she had just a second before.

We walked another block in silence before Rei said, "You managed to string along a prince. That's pretty badass. I've had plenty of conquests in my day, but never any so... lofty."

"Eh. He isn't everything he seems to be," I said, trying to dismiss the idea.

"Yeah, he's probably a whole lot more," she added, and of course, she was right.

There was so much to Cal that he hadn't told me. So much I had glimpsed beneath the surface in those moments of raw honesty. My mind flashed on the way he kissed me in the Basilica, how my blood had hummed at the rightness of his embrace, and a longing for that uncomplicated moment squeezed at my heart.

I shoved it away.

"It doesn't matter. Whatever was there between us before is done now," I said, trying to convince myself it was true.

"You know, in every smutty book I've ever read, that's usually when they run right into each other's arms," Rei laughed.

"Yeah, well, this isn't like any storybook I've ever read, and he sure as hell isn't Prince Charming," I said.

"I wouldn't be so sure about that. He seems pretty charming to me." Rei glanced over at me, smiling. "I mean, he doesn't make my toes tingle or anything, but that doesn't mean I wouldn't give him a spin on the merry-go-round."

I scoffed, but images of Cal kissing my chest and the hard feeling of him as I straddled his hips flickered in my mind. Godsdamn me... no, fuck that, godsdamn him. I tightened my hands into hot fists by my sides. I needed to throw a knife and cut something. Maybe carving something into tiny bits would make this insanity go away.

The gates to the University were made from alternating brass and stone carvings, and a tremendous scalloped arch looped over the main entryway. Beyond that was a lush green courtyard, at the center of which a large fountain fed streams of water that ran along the walkways.

I bent to look at the tiny running rivers. The water burbled as it flowed over ridges in the ornately carved channel.

"They cool the air," said Rei. "The moving water keeps the air around us cooler. The scholars figured it out centuries ago and put these everywhere. It really helps when we're at the peak of a brutal Sumendi summer, and you have to run around campus in full scholar's robes."

I laughed. "Solaire did a long residence here one summer. It was so hot that it felt like my face was melting, and made so much worse by a full-body leather suit. After four very long weeks, Duke vowed to only visit Suman again in the winter. So, I can empathize."

"You know, I think I might remember that."

The fountain in the central courtyard was a giant mass of moving parts. Large rotating spheres shifted in alternating arcs along huge rounded circles of brass. The water splashed and pooled over each of the surfaces before falling into the basin at the bottom.

I stopped, admiring the artistry. "This is amazing."

"That's an orrery," said Rei. "It shows the movements of the sun, the planets, and other distant stars."

I read the large brass plaque aloud, "The Almonteri Orrey."

Rei waved off my questioning eyes. "The library is this way."

We navigated our way through the maze of walkways that wound between large brick buildings. The university was so intricately detailed that it was hard to decide where to look. Every stone was carved with tessellating patterns. The negative space was painted in a rich blue lacquer that contrasted vibrantly against the red stone.

"So, why did you say you *used* to be a student?" I asked as we walked.

Rei sighed. "The lead administrator, Master Talensi, seems to think that I'm too *mercurial* for the refined study of the healing arts."

She flourished her hands in a grand gesture. Joseph was right, I did like her.

"Yeah, I don't get a very scholarly vibe off of you."

"I think he just couldn't handle the fact that I showed more strength and power than him. That, or he had a problem with me sleeping with half his staff." She winked at me. "Probably both."

I wasn't exactly sure how to respond to that. She reminded me a bit of Macie, only sharper and less prone to distraction. If I ever got them together, it would probably be a riot.

"After Master Talensi made it clear that I needed to realign my priorities, I left. Technically, I'm probably still registered as a scholar." She laughed. "But I'm not going back. The entire system is too pedantic. I tried showing them that we were capable of more. I took my enhancer—we call it a Diamendti. The apothecary ground it down into a powder for me. Then he mixed in some oils and ink to help with absorption. I spent months studying the alchemic properties of different elements until I found the perfect blend to amplify the Diamendti. When it was done, I brought the entire mixture to a tattooist. I had them impress the most important star charts into me with it." She wiggled her fingers. "Because the entire universe is quite literally at my fingertips."

"That's a bit insane... and genius."

"Thank you." Rei tipped an imaginary hat to me. "After the tattoos healed, I went to the Adminstrati. I showed them all how much more efficient the ability to tap the well of magic is this way. I can harness double the energy they can. But they didn't want to hear it. They just went on about *perverting an ancient and noble study.*' So, I figured, fuck them. I need them less than they need me. They just don't know it yet. One day someone will realize that *mercurial* is just what they need. They'll come looking for me, and on that day I'm going to tell them to fuck off."

I snorted. Yeah. I definitely liked this girl. I'd never had an actual friend before. Macie and Violet had been more like sisters, family. I usually tuned Macie out after five minutes of her mindless chatter. But I imagined this girl could be the sort of friend you traded secrets with and stayed up all night talking to.

We walked up the steps to the tall tower, stopping before a pair of iron doors. Cast into the facade were two large seated figures, nearly double my size. One held an open book in his hand, pointing towards the ground and the other pointed to the heavens with an orb in his palm. An inscription at the bottom read, *The Marshals of Knowledge*.

Rei pressed a random brick beside the door. It sank into the wall, but nothing happened. She held up a finger, motioning for me to wait. Then a loud grinding of gears came from inside the doors. Rei gave a dramatic gesture towards them and, slowly, the figures swung out. She did a little kick of her heels and walked into the building.

The dark interior was filled with rows and rows of books. A woman sat at a massive central desk, hidden behind a tall stack of papers. I could just make out her brown hair twisted and held aloft by a pencil. I began walking towards her, but Rei reached out, grabbing my arm. Silently, she shook her head. Instead of approaching the woman, she walked up to the podium that sat next to the desk, and signed her name in a very old-looking register.

We walked further into the depths of the building until we reached the back of the tower, where a tall staircase disappeared in the enveloping darkness high above us.

"Here," I said, a small fire bloomed in the palm of my hand.

"Oooh." Rei quickly closed my hand around the flame. "Libraries and fire don't really mix."

"Right. I hadn't even considered that," I said, embarrassment making my cheeks flame red.

"It's fine. Here."

She turned a knob anchored to the wall. It clicked for a second, producing a small spark that I felt more than saw. A beat later, a small glowing light filled the lamp above it, illuminating the space around us. The wide double staircase spiraled endlessly above us in a zig-zag formation. One flight overlapped the next just like the tesselations I'd seen carved into the brickwork. It seemed to go on forever.

"That is clever," I said, tapping on the glass of the lamp. "Where does the light come from?" I asked. I could feel a source of power for the fire, but couldn't see it. "Is it an oil?"

"It's a flammable gas. It's fed into the lamps from pipes that run through the walls."

She said it so matter-of-factly, as if this sort of thing was completely common.

"Wondrous."

We ascended the stairs, lighting the lamps as we went. Flight after flight, we climbed higher until we reached a level labeled *Historica*.

"Here we are," she said, walking into the stacks. "Now we just need to find the volumes about the Dragon Age. I assume that's what you're looking for. Information on the Seven Ancient Dragons?"

"Seven?" I said questioningly. "I thought there were six: Gold, Silver, Iron, Emerald, Sapphire, and Ruby." I ticked them off on my fingers one at a time.

"And Diamond," she added.

"Diamond?" I asked, genuinely curious.

This was the first I'd ever heard of a Diamond Dragon.

She began pulling large leather-bound tomes off of the shelves and stacking them in my arms.

"Some people would tell you it's a myth. Or, well, most people would. But I've read some pretty compelling stuff that really makes me believe Adamis is out there. When I was younger I was obsessed with the different legends about the dragons, but Adamis was always my favorite. She's a prism. The Diamond Dragon possesses the powers of all of the others."

Rei's eyes sparkled with excitement.

"Yeah, that doesn't sound real," I said. "That level of power would be god-like... even a dragon wouldn't be able to contain it."

Rei shrugged and added another even heavier book to my stack. "Let's go find a table."

"Wait." I worried my lower lip. "I need information on something else... shadow curses."

I sat the heavy stack of books down on a weathered oak table overlooking the stairwell.

"That's some dark shit, literally." She snorted with amusement. "What could you possibly want to know about shadow curses for?"

"My father," I gulped. "He was cursed. I was hoping to get some information that might point me toward the person that will soon be ash beneath my boot."

"Curses and poisons are on the second floor." She looked over the edge of the railing at the many flights below us. I groaned. Rei pulled some sheets of parchment and some pencils from a holder against the wall. "Let's skim these first, then we can search for curses on our way back down."

"That's fair," I said, pulling a volume from the pile. "Look for any mention of the Gold Dragon, or anything about the draken," I added, turning pages.

I looked out the window nearest us. The sky was now fully dark and peppered with tiny pinpricks of light. My mind drifted to Cal, and to the tortured look of regret that twisted his handsome features. Maybe I overreacted... a bit. I sighed, thinking of his gentle and calming eyes, the reassuring touch of his hand against the small of my back whenever he knew I needed his strength, the kiss on the cliff... in the falls, by all the gods that man knew how to kiss.

No! I mentally slapped that doe-eyed, lovesick girl. Cal lied and manipulated me. Held the truth from me—was still withholding information. I could probably fill a wing of this library with everything he wasn't telling me. Xoc too.

Rei had one thing right. They can all just *fuck off*.

37

CALLEN

"*Ass.*"

"*Ass.*"

"*Ass.*"

Each scrape of my boots on the ground seemed to keep echoing it. Xoc and I strolled along the harbor. It was a slow pace, with guilt weighing down each of my steps. The entire right side of my face throbbed with a pulse of its own. I ran my hand over my jaw. I'd give her this—the girl could throw a punch. The flaming hands probably didn't help any, but I deserved it. Every blow. It's why I let them land. I could have blocked or stopped her. Fuck, I could have restrained her. I sighed. Even fantasizing had lost its luster. No, Elyria could have driven a knife into my heart, and I wouldn't have stopped her. And with the daggers she threw at me with her eyes, she might as well have.

My heart felt torn open, bits of viscera trailing along beneath my feet.

Xoc stopped at an extensive building built into the end of the pier. The harbor master.

"You go in. I don't care what we sail on, so long as it sails by midday. I'm just going to sit over here and wallow in my own self-pity."

I leaned back against the railing and slid to the ground. My fingers gripped my hair in tight fists, resting my head on my knees. Behind me, the blue water taxis rattled against each other with the sway of the bay, reminding me of Elyria's off-handed comment about them and my heart seized with guilt all over again.

"You knew this would happen. Whatever made you think she would be okay with being lied to this whole time?" Xoc said, not an ounce of pity in his voice. "I was against lying to her from the beginning but that wasn't my call to make. We deserve some wrath, and since you two are uncannily alike, I'm sure it's going to get worse before it gets better."

"Gods, I know. Fuck." I ran my hands through my hair. "I have to tell her the truth about Duke."

I looked up at him. Physical pain tightened my chest at the idea of telling her the truth of his death.

The stern look Xoc gave me was one I had seen him give his regiments many times, ever the commander. It was the face that ordered men into a fight that would most likely kill them, the kind that only the lucky survived. And here I was, no better than an insubordinate rookie.

"And that you're draken. Cal, she didn't care about you lying about your name or your past. She only got truly pissed when you told her you know where the Gold Dragon is. She isn't angry about what you've told her, only what you haven't."

I let my head thunk back against the wooden beam and closed my eyes, shutting out the world around me. He was right about everything. He was always right. *The bastard.*

"I love her, Xoc."

I said it before I had even thought it. The feeling had been growing stronger by the day, by the second. And now, I didn't even need to consider it. Loving her had just become a part of me. The same part that now laid shredded on the dirty ground.

"I know."

I opened my eyes and stared up at the sky. The last bits of light were fading over the horizon. Pink clouds drifted over the rooftops—clouds and a *shadow*. I sat up with a jolt. But, just as soon as I saw it, it was gone. Under normal circumstances, I might have written it off as an alley cat or a trick of the failing light. But nothing had been even close to normal in a long time.

"Xoc. There's something I didn't tell you earlier."

He swiveled around to see what I was looking at. "I think I saw—"

"One of the Fasmas," he said, finishing my sentence.

I jumped to my feet. "How did you know that?"

"Because I can sense one of them. Andros, I think."

He pointed towards the building, the same one I had seen the shadow float across.

"Any idea why he'd be tracking us this entire time?"

He knew the twins better than anyone. They'd been working under his command for years.

"Not at all. I gave both of them orders to trail Malvat, and to send back regular reports on his movements. Neither one of them should be here. But, if Andros is here—"

"Then Andromeda is, too," I finished.

I gave a quick scan of the rooftops and alleyways. A pale figure emerged from the shadows cloaking the side of the building. He was clad head to toe in black leather. A heavy hood concealed most of his long white hair. Strands caught by the wind came loose and floated in the air.

Instinctually, I kept my guard up as I walked towards him. The phantom assassin being here triggered every internal warning I had.

Andros lowered onto one knee, his hand curling into a fanned fist above his heart, the traditional Innesvalen salute.

"My liege," he drawled.

He kept his head lowered. Over the edge of the hood, I could just make out the smile stretching across his face. Andros never smiled.

I didn't wait. Everything about this encounter was wrong. I twisted around him, just as a hidden blade struck out of his sleeve, narrowly missing my center.

I threw my hands up, and a gust of air blasted Andros off the ground. He flew backwards into the wall of the building. He kicked his feet and swung his fists, beating against the invisible force holding him back. I strengthened the air restraints. The carved brick and tile scraped against the tooled leather of his assassin's garb as I stretched his limbs wide and anchored them into place.

Andros began laughing.

I looked at Xoc. In the decades the Fasmas had been sworn to me, I had never once heard Andros laugh. The sound drove icy daggers down my senses. We approached wearily. Even pinned, we knew he was still deadly. Andros once killed a man by spitting a needle through his eye. He didn't need to have access to his hands to be lethal, and we both knew it.

Andros's eyes, usually a uniquely pale blue, gleamed white—white dripped with a swirling midnight malevolence.

"The Shade," Xoc said, confirming what I saw.

"Oh, *poor little Calico*. Still a bored kitten? Where'd your little mouse go?"

Andros' voice was smooth like velvet. Nothing like the soft-spoken ghost he usually was, and it drove chills down my spine. I knew that voice.

"Calico?" I whispered, realization hitting me.

Only one person had ever called me that. A joke, held over from a drunken night out. Somehow that dark power of his was letting Malvat talk through Andros. He hadn't just turned him into a mindless attacker, he could see and speak through him, too. Controlling someone, taking their will away, was terrible enough. But, this? It made me sick.

"So, Malvat." I forced calm indifference into my voice. I wouldn't give him the satisfaction of knowing how much this display was rattling me or of the pure rage that was being contained beneath the surface. "You've learned a new trick, I see. Not man enough to come after me yourself? Instead you have to send ghosts and spiders to do your work."

Fire roiled beneath my skin, made worse by the realization that I couldn't even take my anger out on the man in front of me.

Andros hissed, "Oh, but it's so much more *fun* this way."

"What do we do with him? We can't just let the best assassin in Venterra run around fully possessed by a madman," I said to Xoc.

"The only thing we can do," he said in a resigned tone, and brandished a long, curved dagger from the pocket of air beside him.

"I know another trick, too. Shall I show you?" Andros cackled.

Xoc walked determinedly up to the man. Andros was still laughing. "I have a mouse to catch, anyway. Thank you for fetching her for me. Laluna was such a long way to go. I will say, I didn't see that worm coming."

Xoc raised the blade high in an arc. "I'm sorry, my friend," he said.

The knife swung down...

A clang echoed off the buildings as the dagger slammed into stone.

I couldn't believe my eyes. All that remained of Andros were fading wisps of black-green smoke.

Images of the vanishing knife in my chest, and the spider on the ground, flashed before me. My brain couldn't make sense of what I was seeing. Andros was gone.

I turned, looking everywhere for a sign of him. The black vapor dissipated, not a trace of him left. I threw out waves of air, hoping to connect with an invisible foe. But there was nothing. I looked at Xoc with bewildered desperation.

"He's gone," he said. "Cal, I can't sense him. It's as if he doesn't exist anymore."

Panic clawed at my chest, Malvat's words registering too slowly. "Mouse... Fuck! He's going for Elyria!"

I looked up to the tower sitting so far away atop the plateau.

"Andromeda," said Xoc.

"Andros was just a diversion. *And I fucking fell for it*," I roared in frustration and took off full speed up the hill.

38

ELYRIA

The light flickered in the lamp on the wall next to me. I pushed a pile of books to the side so that I could look at Rei. "Is it always so quiet in here?"

"It's a library, fire girl. They're supposed to be quiet." She was spinning a pencil between her fingers absentmindedly, too absorbed in the history before her to bother looking up.

"Well, the quiet doesn't help the creep factor of this place." I eyed down the line of books to where the cases disappeared into the dark.

"This is interesting," she said. "Did you know dragons can dream walk?"

"In the story Duke told me about how my line was started, Aurus met Elyria The First while dream walking."

"Yeah, but they can do more than just walk. They can actually manipulate the dream. They could make you be anywhere. There's this fascinating account about Lord Gregor and his dream encounters with Ferrus, the Iron Dragon. Apparently, Ferrus uses dream walking as a regular contact with his progeny. The Iron Draken rule the land under his command, more as a regent than a king." Rei turned the page, still twirling her pencil. "Fascinating."

"Rei."

"Hmmm?" she mused, running the end of her pencil along her bottom lip, eyes locked fast to the page.

"Thank you. For bringing me here, for helping, my arm, the company. All of it," I said, genuinely grateful.

"Oh, it's nothing. I love to read. Books should be like lovers, a different one every night."

She raised her eyes to me with a playful wink.

"Didn't you have somewhere to be?" I said, suppressing a laugh. "I mean, weren't you working tonight? We just left," I dropped the book from my hands onto the table.

Rei nonchalantly shrugged a single shoulder. "I got fired tonight. So that kind of freed up my schedule a bit."

My mouth dropped open. "You did?"

"You probably didn't notice. You were sort of beating the shit out of princey," she said, full of amusement. "Again, not that I blame you. That prick had a beatdown coming, and you had more important things on your mind than my job."

"Gods, Rei. I'm sorry." And I really was. It was probably my screaming that had pushed her boss over the edge.

"It's not a big deal. I never hold jobs for very long. I just go wherever the road takes me. And..." She gestured between me and the window. "I have a feeling this road is going to be one hell of a ride." With an exaggerate wink, she added, "And there's nothing I like more than a good ride."

I turned the pages of a slightly newer volume, *Historica Dracoania vol. 9*. All of the *Dracoania* volumes were a collection of personal accounts from all over Venterra. They were decidedly more interesting to read than the typical scholarly texts. Most of the books featured stories of chance encounters, nothing of serious note. Until this one, it focused mostly on the Ruby Dragon, Terran.

"If what I am reading is accurate, and my Sumendi is admittedly not the best, then Terran is no longer living. It would seem that this account from

Elric Everheart describes the death of Terran during an event that he calls The Primativus," I said, reading the transcribed journal page.

"Let me see."

I handed her the tome. She leaned over the page, running her finger along the line and mouthing the words as she read. Her chaotic waves rocked as she nodded her head, the few shining strands shimmering like starlight in the night sky.

"Have you ever heard of The Primativus before?" I said, taking the book back from her. "What could kill a dragon?"

She shook her head. "I don't know. Nothing good."

"According to this, there might not be any surviving Ruby Draken either. The Order of the Silvertine Shard hunted them down. That's who Elric Everheart was a knight of. They eradicated the entire family line for..."

I looked up suddenly, the book falling with a thunk. I couldn't believe what I just read. I must have translated it wrong.

"For what? Don't leave a girl hanging." She leaned forward in anticipation, looking thirsty for the information. It made me think of how people would hang onto Duke as he spoke. A twinge of sadness pricked at me just beneath the surface. "Elyria, tell me."

I flipped back to the page I'd been on. Maybe I'd read it wrong. I carefully skimmed each of the glyphs. "Shapeshifting. Ruby Draken can *shapeshift*."

"You're lying. Like actually make themselves appear... as what, anything?" she asked, lunging over the table for the book.

I pushed her back, flipping through the pages for any kind of description. "I don't know. That's all it says. That and they made it their 'mission to eradicate the devils from the plains'." What in the Hells of Kraav kind of company was The Order of the Silvertine Shard? Why would anyone want to hunt draken, much less kill off an entire family line of them?

I hurriedly read ahead, stopping on a long passage written in Everheart's own hand. "Here. It says the Order's divine mission was to prevent Revanescence at all costs."

"Revanescence?"

"He goes on stating that the draken will bring Death to Venterra when the Primitus once again walk."

"Revanescence? Primitus? How have I never heard of these, and why the draken?"

Xoc was right. I needed to guard my draken abilities more closely. Although at this point my secret was out. But, if there were draken hunters... "You don't think this order is still out there hunting draken, do you? I mean, this account is dated from nearly six hundred years ago. They can't still be around."

A hissing sound came from below us, reminding me of air slowly leaking from a balloon. I leaned over the railing, half expecting to see Cal walking up the stairs to beg for my forgiveness. The only thing he would be getting from me tonight was my fist in his face.

One by one, in succession, the lamps on the levels below us each made a popping sound as they puffed out.

"That's odd," I said. "Do the lamps usually do that?"

Rei leaned over the railing next to me. "No, they're all on a central line. I suppose if something cut off the gas, then maybe it would make them all go out."

The lamps on the floor below us went out. I looked to my left, at the lamp mounted on the wall. I heard a fizzling pop, and then finally the tall tower of books was swallowed by shadows. I was truly beginning to loathe the dark.

"Fortunately, I always travel with a light." I let a small flame sit in my hand. Rei's eyes went wide. "I promise not to light the stacks on fire, probably."

A scrape scuffed against the floor behind me. I was still trying to make sense of what I heard when Rei screamed. My heart jumped in alarm. The palest woman I'd ever seen held a knife to Rei's throat. She was clad head to toe in black, but her skin and her hair were as white as a ghost. It gave her an ethereal beauty, except for her eyes. Her eyes were all white, and a black mist swirled around in them.

"What are you?" I said, letting the fire expand to wreath my entire hand.

Books be damned when this specter held a knife to my friend's throat. The haunting account of The Order of the Silvertine Shard was still fresh in my mind. Was this who Cal was trying to protect me from? Suddenly his motivations didn't feel so selfish.

Slowly, I brought my other hand to the remaining knives at my waist.

"Hello, *little mouse*. I've been looking for you."

Her voice was slick like oil. It filled the air and suffocated everything around it. I felt coated in it. Filthy.

She pulled Rei close to her, the screeching of her chair against the tile floors echoing as it was pushed aside. Our new friend, tilted her menacing smile to draw a deep inhale, then placed a kiss on her cheek. "Delicious."

Rei grimaced, and the knife cut a small slice into her throat. A rivulet of blood dripped down her neck and splashed on to the back of the pale woman's hand. The red seemed to glow bright against the dark leather of her bracer. It pooled into a design that was stamped into the leather, a shield of waves covered by crossed swords. The image panged with familiarity at the back of my mind. I'd seen it somewhere, but it was like trying to remember a dream.

Rei's tattoos glowed and the cut fused together, instantly healing itself. The phantom flashed her yellowed teeth at me and then she lapped up the streak of blood with a long, slow lick. She hummed in satisfaction when Rei recoiled from the intrusion.

Rei's terrified eyes screamed at me. I had to do something.

"I don't think we've met before," I said, taking a slight step to my side and away from the railing. The distance between us wasn't too great, but there was a table blocking me from being able to make a direct attack.

"Oh, but we will. I plan to get to know you... *intimately.*"

She hissed the last word at me, and the sound creeped over my skin like tiny insects. The shadows around her fluttered, and the surrounding darkness deepened.

I tried to keep my voice light and unconcerned. "Sorry to disappoint you, but I don't think that's going to happen."

I pulled a knife from my waist and released it straight at the woman's face. I had never been so glad for Duke's endless hours of weapons training. My aim was perfect, and Rei's eyes went wide as the knife whistled past her cheek.

Instead of sinking into her flesh, there was the dull thud of the blade striking wood. The woman vanished. One second she was there, spectral and terrifying, and the next she had dissolved into black-green smoke.

Wisps floated in the air. *Just. Like. The. Spider.*

"Elyria, Elyria!"

Panic seized me, clutching at my heart and turning my limbs to stone. I tried to breathe, but the world only spun.

"We don't have time for this." Rei slapped me hard in the face. "I'm sorry. You were frozen."

I looked at her, nodding and feeling my senses come back to me. I scanned the room and saw no sign of the phantom.

"She's gone," Rei said breathlessly. A slight tremor shook her hands.

I grabbed Rei's arm. "We have to get out of here. How good on your feet are you?"

She blinked at me.

"Rei?"

"I mean, I have two of them."

"That will have to do."

We ran for the staircase. My feet were moving so quickly, I wasn't sure if they were touching the steps anymore, but it wasn't fast enough. "Can you jump?" I asked, cursing the near dozen floors between us and the ground.

"Not a ten-flight drop!" she exclaimed, already out of breath.

The pounding of feet descended behind us, picking up speed. I swung my arm wide, shooting a blast of flames at the phantom. They rolled off of a black wall of shadow, leaving her completely unscathed, except for the ends of her hair that smoldered a deep red. The hit didn't slow her down at all.

"You just have to drop to the next flight. The staircases overlap."

Like so much of Suman, the staircases tessellated in an alternating fashion. When looking up from below, they formed a many-sided star. I had admired the formation on the way up, and now I was praying it would save us.

I hurled a second fireball at the woman. She ducked and the flames went soaring past her, landing amid the stacks of books. I cringed. Rei could hate me later. I kicked up and leapt over the side of the railing. Ten feet below, I landed firmly on the next flight of stairs. "See, it's easy. Now jump!"

A loud whoosh sounded from above, and the dark stairwell was suddenly awash with light.

"Did you just set that shelf of books on fire?" she exclaimed.

"Priorities, Rei. *Jump!*"

My eyes flicked back to the woman, who was moving faster now. Rei wasn't as agile as I was, but she still managed to throw herself off of the steps and land beside me with a thud. Unfortunately, she wasn't the only one. Like a spider descending on its thread, a dark shadow dropped on us from above and was silhouetted by the quickly spreading flames above her.

"Again," I yelled, urging Rei forward and pulling my remaining knife from my side. "Don't stop, just keep going."

I brought the knife up just in time to deflect the woman's blade. The vibration of her intense strike shook into my core and it threw me back into the stone filigree atop the railing. Her strength was unbelievable. If she landed one of these blows, it might very well be the end of me.

Her maniacal laughter filled the tower, setting my teeth on edge. She skipped down another couple of steps to where I had fallen. Taking up my stance, I let my hands ignite. There was no point in holding back now. I couldn't do any more damage—the tower was already burning. The staircase was full of red dancing light. From the corner of my vision, I saw Rei jumping over the railing. *Good*.

The phantom attacker smiled. There was a puff of black smoke, and then she reappeared nearly on top of me. I spun away from the attack and her dagger carved into my shoulder. She had tricks, but so did I.

"I've played with knives my entire life. You think that little cut will stop me?" I quipped and shoved my flaming hand into her throat.

It was a hard jab straight at the softest part of her jugular. The fragile tubes in her throat buckled under the force of my fingers. Her white ghostly skin crumpled, and a wet choking sound gurgled up from the woman.

The specter took a step back, and I used the opportunity to jump flights again, but she held on. Thin white fingers dug their way into my shirt and pulled me back. How was she completely unbothered by her collapsed windpipe?

With a hard backhand, she slammed into the side of my head. I knocked against the stone railing, the nearly healed gash on my forehead reopened, and a stream of blood flowed into my eyes. She followed the hit with a quick knee to my side, and I groaned. The surrounding staircase shifted, and it was suddenly hard to breathe. A gurgling sound that might have been her laughter cut through the crackling sounds of the fire above us.

I swallowed down the panic rising in me and thought of every lesson Joseph ever taught me. I twisted my body. Her grip broke, but she kept her momentum advancing forward and shoved me back into the railing. I brought my foot up and, with all of my force, kicked her back. At the same time, I let my weight shift backwards and tipped over the edge of the railing into a backflip. My foot landed on the railing below, but my head spun and I wobbled for a second, barely maintaining my balance.

I glanced up at the enraged ghostly face glaring over the railing at me. With a quick wave goodbye, I launched myself into the black expanse of the stairwell. Below me, the flights of stairs were cloaked in shadows. But I knew that if I extended fully, two floors down, I could grip the railing on the other side. It was risky to do in the dark, but it would give me the space I needed. There was no way this woman had my trapeze experience, or could maneuver in the air the same way I could.

I reached out. My hand locked onto the railing. There was a twinge of pain, and I was roughly reminded of the gaping wound that had been on my arm only hours earlier, not to mention the gash throbbing in my shoulder.

"Elyria, I'm down," Rei yelled from below.

"Get out of here. Don't stop running."

Repeating the trick, I flipped down another two floors. When I landed, I spotted a shadow scuttling along the railings behind me. It was the mirror image of the spider crawling along Duke's neck, forcing a shiver to course down my spine. This woman was fearless, and nearly as comfortable as I was flying between bars. It wouldn't be long before she caught up to me again.

With a final thud, I landed on the ground floor. I looked up at the silhouetted star of staircases and bookshelves. Fury seethed beneath my skin as I watched the assassin descend.

I was done.

Done with lies.

Done with fights.

And done with phantoms who won't fucking die.

High in the tower, the flames roared. I reached out to them, felt their power, and wrapped my mind around them. The sheer force of this inferno was more than I had ever handled before. But it was nothing compared to the fire I'd kept on a leash my entire life.

The woman was only three floors above me now and readying to make another leap.

"This is for Duke, you demon bitch!"

The phantom leapt into the air, arms extended to grab onto the next level. I ripped my hand down, and with it, the full might of the blaze soared down the cavity. It enveloped her body, slamming into the ground and roiling around me. Wrath, strong and fierce, churned within me, and I poured it into those flames. In that moment, I could have let it devour all of Venterra. The fire bit into the books and old wooden furniture. Power rose in me the more the flames raged, or maybe my rage was making the flames rise.

The woman disappeared amid the blaze. I coiled the fire around me and lashed out, waiting to feel it wrap around the phantom's flesh. But it didn't come. Again and again, I whipped out, and with each crack I met only air. She had instantly burned to ash in the initial blaze, maybe. Unless she had disappeared again.

I looked over my shoulder towards the exit and thought of Rei. It snapped me back into the moment. I couldn't stay here. I had to be sure she made it out okay. Releasing my connection to the tower inferno, I exploded from the stairwell and took off at a full sprint for the entry doors, flame lapping at my heels as I went.

My steps thundered through the quiet halls. Smoke poured out of the tower and flowed between the shelves. At the central desk, the woman with the high bun was slumped over. A pool of red dripped off the desk and soaked the stack of papers blanketing the floor.

Locking my eyes on the door, I picked up my speed. Hopefully, Rei got out ahead of me, or was smart enough to be hiding somewhere. Whoever—no, fuck that—whatever this was, they weren't natural, and they weren't here for her.

Moonlight filtered in through the open door. The large molded Marshal of Knowledge was propped open by something on the ground. Wind fluttered white robes and an icy fear clawed at me. *Dear gods, it was a body.*

I was still reeling from the realization of the corpse before me when the light winked out. A sudden, hard mass materialized before me. I slammed into the phantom woman. She was still smiling that wicked grin. How in the fuck did she survive that blast? She should have been incinerated the second the flames hit her.

"*Well, little mouse,* that was *fun,* but I'm done playing," she hissed at me. "It's time we were going."

Her hand reached out to grip my wrist. I struck low, driving my elbow into her stomach. Grabbing a fistful of white hair, I drove my knee into her head. Her face made a loud and satisfying crunch. Errant strands that I'd pulled loose floated to the ground. I kicked hard at the side of her knee, and her legs buckled out from under her. She collapsed to the ground. I didn't wait to see the effect my blows made on her. I leapt over her fallen body and ran for that door.

As I reached the doorway, the man on the ground came into full view, red blood haloing him. His long white robes were dyed a deep mahogany from the gash across his throat. He was most likely a scholar, or an unlucky patron here at the wrong time?

I slipped through the door and followed the trail of bloody footprints down the staircase, heading straight for the winding streets. If that last strike didn't take her down, then maybe I could lose her in the maze of alleyways and corridors.

Rei peeked out from behind a nearby doorway, waiting for me. Damn it. Why wasn't she hiding? I slid around the corner and skidded into her petite frame.

"You made it out," she said, almost sobbing. "What in the layers of Kraav is going on?"

"Shh. You have zero sense of self-preservation, don't you?" I whispered to her and turned to see if the woman's ghostly form had followed me out of the tower.

She stood at the top of the stairs, her left leg bent at an unnatural angle. Above her, pillars of fire poured out of the windows of the tower and plumes of smoke blotted out the sky.

The assassin walked down the stairs as if her knee wasn't bending in the wrong direction with every step. It was like she didn't register any pain at all. Demons below. Collapsed windpipe, swallowed by flames, broken nose and leg. What did it take to stop this woman?

A thundering boom echoed from above us. At the top of the tower, an explosion rocketed out. Chunks of brick and tile slammed into the ground and the surrounding buildings. A massive block of masonry plummeted into the Orrery. The iron rings clattered loose, and a planet went rolling across the ground.

Boom. A second explosion lower in the tower sounded, followed by three more in quick succession. The final detonation shook the ground. The buildings rocked, and the concussive blast knocked us back into the shifting wall.

"That would be the gas tanks," Rei mouthed, or maybe she had said it aloud.

My ears were ringing, and it sounded like everything was underwater. I scanned the courtyard. The library tower was gone, reduced to a mass of rubble. Smoke billowed into the sky. Ash and debris floated down like freshly fallen snow. But no killer assassin.

Someday I would reflect on decimating the oldest collection of knowledge in Venterra. That explosion really was on a level well above anything I'd ever done before. The consequences for this would be extreme, but I couldn't focus on it. Not with a far more viscous threat looming somewhere in the smoke. Where in the Hells was she? The phantom woman had been knocked off of the stairs. I had seen that much, but she apparently couldn't die, and I wasn't foolish enough to think the blast had done her in.

And then, I spotted her, cutting through the smoke on the far side of the green. A layer of gray ash coated her leather suit, making her look even more ghostly.

I pulled Rei into the shadows of the doorway, hoping she hadn't spotted us. We should have made a run for it while we had the chance. My mind started reeling, trying to come up with some kind of escape. My racing thoughts screeched to a halt when she materialized before me. The distance she had covered in a single movement, and the speed at which she came at us, was wildly disorienting.

"You thought the shadows would protect you, little mouse? I am the shadows," she said, and reached into the darkness, grabbing hold of my throat.

The filtered moonlight disappeared behind a wall of enveloping darkness, blocking off my senses, and making me far too aware of my pounding heart.

I scrabbled my hand behind me, latching onto the hard, cold metal of the doorknob. I twisted it; the door pushed open. We tumbled backwards. I gripped the leather straps on the phantom's halter. Using my momentum, I tucked into a backward somersault and pulled her over me. Her nails scraped against my neck as I vaulted her body onto a table in the center of the room. It split apart, burying the woman under shards of broken wood.

Rei had fallen to the ground and was scrambling back onto her feet. Throwing her behind me, I took up a fighting stance with my remaining throwing knife poised to be released. Fire snaked around the knife blade and lit up the room.

The harsh light cast sharp shadows around the classroom we'd fallen into. The shadows seemed to shift and swell around the rows of tables.

A white silhouette formed against the slate wall at the back of the room. Blood streamed down the woman's perfect ethereal face, trailing through the ash and soot in bright red streaks. Her icy pale skin purpled into a sickening black around her throat. Splinters of wood punctured her leathers from the table that laid shattered on the ground. I smiled with grim satisfaction. The woman looked utterly wrecked, like a walking corpse. But she wasn't dead. Not yet.

"You put up a better fight than I thought, *little mouse*," she purred, and pushed the lectern beside her to the ground.

Despite appearing beaten, she sounded amused. How could someone be amused when they looked like that?

"Breaking you is going to be so sweet."

The assassin licked the edge of her knife in a long, slow drag. The blade sliced her tongue, and a stream of blood trickled out from the corners of her lips.

"What in the actual fuck are you?" I said, thoroughly shaken by how completely grotesque she was.

As if to prove every one of the horrifying thoughts running through my mind, she chuckled darkly, exposing a dark red maw filled with a sea of bloody teeth. Behind me, Rei took a panicked breath, sounding akin to a wounded puppy. I couldn't blame her. A very real part of me wanted to turn tail and run, but I knew we wouldn't make it to the end of the alley. No, this fight was happening right here and now. There was no escaping it.

Xoc's words of warning came back to me. This time, I wasn't going into a fight without some armor. Rows of golden scales, flecked with tiny shimmering bits of black, ran down my arms. There was a time when I cursed these scales. They damned me to a life apart from the masses, but tonight being draken would be my salvation. Tonight I was more than a showpiece. I let go of my fire and the flames rolled over me. Tonight I would avenge Duke's death. Tonight the dragon would roar more than pretty flames, and she would do more than shake and cower. This bitch would burn, even if I had to take down the entire damn world to do it.

"You want me so damn badly, then come and get me." I huffed. "I'm about to send you back to whichever pit you crawled out of."

Anticipation sparked in every cell of my body. Whatever move she made next, I was ready for it.

However, what I wasn't ready for was what happened next. A puff of air against my temple and an acrid smell were my only warning, before a second phantom manifested next to me.

I pulled The Sun Serpent from its sheath, and spun just in time to stop this new attacker's strike. They were nearly identical, with the same pale ghostly features and long, wispy white hair. Same spectral white eyes. Same demonic smile. They circled Rei and me like a pack of wolves cornering their prey. The woman, despite still having a broken knee, moved just as menacingly as her brother, but her limp gave her a grotesque quality that he was missing.

They edged closer to us, and Rei's back pressed into mine. She had her fists up. I admired the fight in her.

"What's the matter, *little mouse*? Seeing double?"

The voice sounded in tandem from both their mouths. It was the velvet voice of the boy in the pub, and of the rogue in the clearing. Hearing it multiplied was something straight from my nightmares. The kind that made you want to hide under your covers and pray for morning. Well, I wasn't going to cower now. If these two wanted to take me down, I'd be damn sure they tasted my fire first.

"No, just trying to decide which of you fuckers is going to die first."

I twisted and threw my last knife at the woman. She dematerialized into wisps of smoke, and it clattered harmlessly to the floor.

Fuck this, enough games. I pulled my hands together and shot a torrent of fire at the man.

"Rei, *hit the ground*."

Rei dropped flat to the ground at my feet. I exploded the fire out from us in a spiral of heat. It lashed into the air like a whip and pummeled against the walls. Smoke spun around us, but there were no ghostly corpses left in the fire's wake.

The man was gone. They were both gone.

I reached down and pulled Rei in tight to me. This wasn't over.

The woman reappeared first, directly in front of me, and I sliced low with my dagger. I knew she would come in close, to scare me or to toy with me. I was ready for her, and I felt my blade drive deep.

A faint scent of sour wine hit me, and I yanked the knife from the woman's gut and released it straight at where the man reappeared. The dagger embedded itself in the man's chest, piercing his heart. For a second, he smiled wickedly at me, then he went limp and crumpled to the ground.

That left just the woman. I needed to retrieve one of my blades. I was hardly defenseless, but I was clearly at a disadvantage without a weapon. The throwing knife laid discarded on the floor behind her. Much closer my dagger stuck straight up, driven down to the hilt in her brother's chest. She registered my plan and moved for the Sun Serpent. I loosed another torrent of flame with such force that it hurtled a table straight for her. She tumbled, hitting the ground in wisps of smoke.

I growled in frustration. "That's getting old."

I reached back to grab the dagger from the man on the ground. But my fingers wrapped around empty air. The blade was gone. I swiveled back around. My beautiful dagger, the one Duke had given to me, the symbol of everything I meant to him, was in this woman's filthy hands. She twisted the tip against her index finger. A stream of blood dripped to the ground in thick black drops. She flipped it deftly in the air before me.

With a sinking feeling, I knew exactly how this fight was going to end. I had dodged knives before, but those had always been trick throws. I knew where they were headed, and it was easy enough to pull a knife from the air if it was thrown correctly. Could I do the same here and predict her target? Could I move fast enough to stop my own blade from killing me?

We circled one another. Each step was purposeful, and my mind flashed over a dozen possibilities. Despite all my training, I couldn't shake the feeling that this was the end. My heart would be speared at the end of this dagger just as it had done countless times to the roses in my show. I might be able to appreciate how poetic it was, if the idea didn't make me so furious.

She cocked back her hand and released. The dagger flew straight for me with a speed I had never seen. I wasn't going to be able to dodge it. Images of everyone I loved flashed through my mind with each flashing revolution. Memories of times spent laughing around campfires, braiding Macie's hair, dancing with Duke in his caravan, kissing Cal beneath the spray of a waterfall. I braced for the searing impact.

It didn't come. When I opened my eyes, The Sun Serpent was frozen in midair an inch from my chest. I blinked at the floating dagger, then spun.

Cal stood in the doorway, furious. Relief washed over me.

"Cal." His name broke on my lips as almost a sob.

"You like that, Sunshine?" he snarled. "Then you're really going to like this one."

The dagger spun and flew back at the woman in a golden blur.

It sank deep into her throat, pinning her to the slate wall. Cracks splintered out from her body.

The world froze for a moment, silent except for the sound of blood dripping from her twitching fingertips. A river of red flowed from her neck and down over the crest stamped on her bracer.

Clarity clicked in my mind and suddenly I knew where I had seen that blood soaked symbol before.

I walked toward the phantom woman, reaching down to pick up my discarded throwing knife along the way. Cal came up behind me. I could feel him standing over me, felt the buzz that hummed in my veins whenever he was near. I reached forward, and pulled my dagger from the woman's throat. Her body slumped to the ground, lifeless. Chunks of slate clattered to the ground around her. I kicked the woman one extra time, just to be sure. "*Bitch.*"

Cal reached forward, brushing the hair from my cheek. "Are you o—"

I spun, slamming my leg into him and knocking him back against the wall. Before he could react, I moved in on him. The phantom woman's blood flew from the dagger, leaving a streak of red across Cal's white linen shirt. I pressed one blade to his throat, the other to his cock.

Cal lifted his hands into the air. "Whoa, Elle."

"You had better start talking right now. What the *fuck* is going on here?" I said to him, pushing the blade at his groin for emphasis.

Xoc moved into the doorway, and I could sense him assessing me. Cal lifted a single finger to him.

"You know a thank you for saving your life would have been enough," he said, trying to crack a smile.

"Don't joke with me, Callen Shadow. I want to know why two assassins bearing that crest—"

I threw my throwing knife at the hand of the woman. It pierced the bracer perfectly between the crossed swords at the center of the shield.

"—just tried to kill me."

"Wait, you actually think I would send people to kill you?" he said, disbelief in his voice.

"I don't know what to believe. You plied me with lies for weeks, and then they show up bearing the same sigil you wear on your wrist. The Innesvalen *Royal* Coat of Arms."

Cal groaned and went to move forward, but I tightened the blade at his throat. The edge bit into the tender skin beneath his jaw. Cal sucked air through his teeth in a low hiss.

"Okay, okay. I can see how that might seem incriminating. Except I did just kill one of them to save you. Which would be a bit counter-productive if I had hired them."

Cal took my wrist in his hand. I pushed against him, pressing a knee into his groin and digging the blade in deeper. But he didn't release me. He didn't even flinch.

"Elle," he said with a low, exhaling breath that caressed along my cheek. His amber eyes warmed. I could feel my confidence cracking, leaving space for doubt to creep in.

Cal slid his hand up my wrist and wrapped his fingers into mine. A shiver of energy tingled down my arm. Anger roiled in me for feeling this way about a man I knew was keeping the most dangerous of secrets from me.

I stepped away from him, pulling my hand from his lying, treacherous fingers.

"Unless you did it to win me back over, to assure I would trust you again," I said, wiping the back of the blade against my pant leg.

"You really think I would sacrifice two of my own people to do that?"

He almost sounded hurt. *Good.*

"I don't know who you are. I don't know how far you would go," I said, gesturing to all of him. The memory of his hands against my skin was still too fresh in my mind. My heart ached. "How do I know you didn't orchestrate everything from the moment I met you? How do I know it wasn't you who killed Duke, just so that I would trust you? So that I would leave with you?"

Angry tears fell from me. That suspicion which lingered at the back of my mind was finally voiced. If Cal had sent that spider after Duke, it would kill me, but not before I sank The Sun Serpent into his heart. A wave of pain rolled over me, radiating out from my core. The tether that connected us panged with sorrow.

Now Cal flinched. As if seeing me cry had sliced him open.

"I'm the same person I've been this entire time." Cal stepped forward. "And what's more, Elle, you know it."

"It's true," Xoc said. "He's still that same asshole."

"I would never, could never, hurt you. You have to know that."

His eyes looked pained as they roved over my face. I wanted to believe him—but there were too many loose threads. Too many unanswered questions.

"So, then..." I tapped the dagger against my hand. "Start explaining."

Looking between the two of them, I sat back against a table.

"And it better be good, or—"

"Or what?"

I shot a stony gaze at Cal, and drove my dagger into the table next to me.

"Or that violence you said I taste like will only be the beginning of what I do."

39

CALLEN

Heat rolled in angry waves off of Elyria as she stared me down expectantly. I looked over towards Rei. She was shaken, but seemed physically okay. She sat back against a wall with her arms wrapped around her legs, attentively watching everything unfold.

Xoc barred the doorway. He nodded at me. "It's time, tell her *everything*."

I took a deep breath, closed my eyes, and tilted my head back, trying to find the strength.

"I've known Malvat since we were kids."

"Lord Malvat?"

I nodded. "Any time there were official court events between kingdoms, we would skip out on the boring things and go get into trouble somewhere. Thanks to his draken abilities, he could shift the light to create illusions. He'd make it appear as though we were still there, or make it so that we disappeared and no one could see us at all."

I paused. Confusion twisted her beautiful features. I was sure she had no idea why I was telling her this.

"What does this have to do with anything?" she said, scowling at me. "I swear to the gods, Callen. If you are trying to deflect away from telling me the truth, I will drive this dagger into your heart and walk away from this room without ever looking back."

"You can try," growled Xoc.

"You're not helping." I threw up a hand to him, waving him off. Looking back to Elyria, I continued, "I'm getting to it. Just tuck away your need to stab something until I'm done. Then, if you still want to drive a dagger into my heart, I'll let you."

She shifted anxiously. "Fine. Get on with it."

"Somehow Malvat has twisted his draken abilities from manipulating light to manipulating darkness."

She leaned forward, not expecting what I had to tell her to take this turn.

"We call it The Shade. He infects people and can control them with it." I pointed to the body of Andros. "Those two are Innesvale's top spies. Andros and Andromeda Fasmaenia. They were loyal to the crown. I might even go as far as to say they were friends. Or, at least as much as those two were capable of friendship."

I looked down at the mangled body of Andromeda. Her twisted leg was grotesque, and the gash torn into her throat stained her white skin a dark crimson. She was beat to Hell. Elyria had given her a serious fight, a fight that I should have been there for.

I closed my eyes. "Before we left Innesvale, they were charged with trailing Malvat and reporting on his movements. The white and black eyes are the only signs of infection, and even those aren't always obvious at first."

"Infection?" Elyria looked over at Andromeda with a haunted expression and shivered.

What happened in that tower? What horrors had she been subjected to while I was down in the harbor feeling sorry for myself?

"The only conclusion I can draw is that the Fasmas were discovered, and somehow, Malvat managed to get his iron claws into them, turned them back on us. He's possessed hundreds of my people, making them kill my citizens and worse. The truly horrific things I've seen at the hands of Shade-infected people, it's nightmare inducing. Because I lo-"

I bit off the end of my confession. Swallowing down the words that almost spilled from me too easily.

"--I will spare you the trauma of knowing the details."

Despite the fingers running along the edge of her dagger I could see the icy wall around Elyria beginning to thaw with each tiny bit of information she processed. Whether she liked it or not, she could see where I was coming from.

"Once someone has been infected with The Shade, their mind is never their own again. It's not just my military forces, either. Malvat has attacked every part of my kingdom. I don't know why he changed, what his plan is, or why he's so fucking focused on destroying everything I care about."

My voice, which was just so heated with anger and hurt, dropped off. The image of that dagger flying at Elyria's heart was seared into me, something new to agonize over in my nightmares. Twice now, Malvat had tried to take her from me. Fire rumbled in my core over all that I had nearly lost.

Elyria's eyes tightened, marking the slip in my mask.

"He needs to be stopped," I said resolutely. "I need to free the minds of the people he has enslaved. Hundreds of innocent people."

She looked out the window at some distant place, taking the time to weigh that statement. Elyria had a good heart. She cared about people. She cared about the mistreatment of the innocent. No amount of vengeance and anger changed that.

"And... that's not all."

Her pained eyes slid back to me.

I swallowed. *Now or never, Callen.* My hands trembled. I clasped them together to hide it. This was going to fucking break her, break the last of whatever lingered between us and hadn't already been shattered by my lies. After this, she would never trust me again. I'd never feel her soft skin beneath my hands, never know what it was to feel her heart beat with mine.

She deserved the truth.

"He can use this new power to make physical manifestations too. He can make physical things noncorporeal, and he can manifest that darkness into solid matter."

"The way they could just vanish and reappear," she said, pointing down to Andros' limp body.

"Yes, that." I swallowed against the lump in my throat. "Or he could turn the shadow into a knife. Like the one that stabbed my heart and nearly killed me."

I raised my hand to my chest. Her lips parted with realization. The memory of her fingers tracing that scar was so fresh that I could swear I could still feel them lingering there.

"Or a spider," she whispered, realization dawning on her.

I held my breath, or maybe I just forgot how to breathe. The gold of her eyes shimmered, becoming glassy with unshed tears.

My soul was shredding apart.

"That night, those flowers were meant for you. That spider was meant for you. Malvat had planned to kill you because he knew that your strength combined with mine would be enough to stop him. That without you, I would have nothing. He planned to kill you, to punish me, to take away the only hope I had. *And that fucking note.* That note was never meant for you. I was supposed to read it after you had died. So that I would know it was him who took you from me."

I paused, a knot forming in my throat. Flames flared to life amid the gold of her irises.

"Say it," she whispered through gritted teeth.

I closed my eyes. I couldn't watch these next words crush her.

"Elyria, Malvat killed your father."

The heat in the room instantly increased, and concern had me looking back up at her.

Elyria leveled a glare at me I had never seen from her before. Although I knew it well, having seen it many times in my own reflection. I knew this pain. I knew this loathing. And I knew the utter rage she held within.

Her eyes shifted. The round pupils narrowed into slits, the fire in them ignited, and the gold of her irises became luminous. She tightened her hands into fists and fire rolled up her arms. Her lips narrowed, teeth bared with boiling rage.

I called out, "Xoc, take Rei and go."

From the corner of my vision, Xoc's dark mass grabbed Rei and made for the exit.

Elyria erupted. Fire rolled over the floor and crashed into the door as it closed behind them. I stood my ground, refusing to flinch from the intense heat that washed over me. The paint along the walls curled, and the delicate curtains that hung next to the window shriveled.

She started panting, deep seething breaths, and with each breath the flames grew, lashing around the room. Quickly, she had gone from cold concern to hot fury that spilled out of her in a torrent. It battered the walls and cracked the panes of glass in the windows.

Her hair flew around her, a black and golden whip that snapped with nearly the same ferocity that burned in her eyes. It was almost hard to look at her. She was the most beautiful and terrifying thing I'd ever seen.

I heard a crack and looked around us. The floor began to char, smoke drifting up beneath our feet. The lacquer in the tile bubbled. Fire ate away at the old and aged rafters. She was going to burn the entire building down. Fuck, she might take down the entire University.

I thought about it, calculated the risks. I was impervious to my own flames, but hers?

It didn't matter.

I moved through the wall of flame that she had erected around herself. Moved close enough to reach out and take her glowing white hands. I wrapped my fingers into their heat and let the flames that spilled from them envelop me. That charge of energy ran through my veins, forcing my eyes to shift. Their golden glow reflected in her own, but I held on and let the truth of them shine through. I knew she could feel the charge and hum of her power recognizing mine. For the first time since we'd met, I unleashed the tight restraint that I kept on it.

Elyria's eyes crinkled in confusion. She tried to pull her hands from me, but I held on tight.

"I hate you," she bit out.

"I'm not leaving, Elle."

The fire licked around us. It ran around my body, eating away at my linen shirt. Pieces of it floated on the updraft and turned to ash around us. I held her eyes with my own and let the gold in my hair grow. I wasn't holding back any longer. This was me, pure and raw before her. No more secrets. Never again would I hide myself from her.

"I know what you are feeling right now. I've felt it. Such burning anger and rage that it consumed me. That pyre of pent-up emotion that makes you want to burn, to exact how you feel on the world, to see the people responsible reduced to embers. I know exactly how this feels."

She shook her head and shouted at me, "You don't!"

"I do. He killed my father." The ache of that truth throbbed in my chest. "Malvat killed my father, after he made him drive a dagger into my heart."

I brought her hand up to my now bare exposed skin, and placed it over the deep, ridged scar that sat there. She flattened her hand against my chest and I rested mine atop it. My heart was pounding, and I knew she could feel every drum hit beneath her fingers. The surrounding flames pulsed with the beat. Her eyes softened with new understanding.

I moved in until the only thing between us were our joined hands.

"When I learned who was responsible, I boarded a ship. I was going to burn the entire kingdom. I was going to bring the Floating Lands down and would have seen my wrath exacted on every living soul there... And Malvat, I was going to incinerate his skeleton from within. I wouldn't stop until I saw his face crumple into ash and blow away on the wind."

The fire started over my heart, blue flames wrapping themselves around my arm and hers. I wove that rope of flame around our bodies, binding us together. Bright scales shifted over my shoulders and up my neck. I let myself go with a release that made the air around us vibrate. My power flowed over hers, caressing her fire with my own. I had been aching for this since the moment I first saw her descend on that ring. The euphoria of this connection was even more than I had expected. She gasped, and I knew the bliss I was feeling was coating her, too.

I lowered my forehead to hers, and against her lips I said, "I know, Elyria, because we are the same. I know, because we share more than scars."

The light surrounding us pulsed purple as her lips connected with mine. My fire mixed with hers. The roar of the flames drowned out everything but the moment. I felt the rage slipping away like sand between our fingers.

She traced a path up my arm, following the scales over my neck until she was cradling my cheek. I moved my large hand over her slender one, interlacing my fingers between hers. The mirror to the way I had touched her face that night on the cliff.

The fire dropped to a low ring, until eventually the last flames fizzled out and everything was wholly silent. The room around us was charred black, the curtains were nearly gone, and the furniture were mere skeletons of their original forms. Smoke swirled thick in the air. I raised a hand, and the cracked window blew out, pushing the smoke from the room. Fresh air and light poured in.

Her eyes blurred with tears, and she lowered her head to my chest. I draped my arms around her, feeling her muscles stiffen and tremble.

"You should have burned it down. You should have ended him." She pounded her fists against my sternum, and I let her. She looked up at me. The hot tears spilling from her eyes left white streaks as they ran down her soot-blackened cheeks. "You could have saved him."

I bent down, making her meet my eyes, using my thumbs to brush away the tear tracks. "You don't think I know that? I feel every innocent life that has been taken. I bear the weight of their deaths every day. And sometimes that guilt is so heavy I think it will crush me. If I had the strength, I would have given all of myself to end him. But it wouldn't have been enough. My thirst for revenge was so potent it blinded me to any kind of sanity. I stood on a ship, ready to sail for the Floating Lands. Going after Malvat alone was suicide. I would have killed myself, and he would still be standing with devastation trailing behind him, and leaving everything I cared about at his mercy. So I channeled my rage into finding a solution that was strong enough."

She tried to look away, but I turned her face to mine. "You are that solution, Elle. You are that strength that I need."

She closed her eyes, shaking her head.

"I'm not. I'm not strong," she whispered.

I pulled her into my arms, and this time she didn't fight me. She let herself sink into my embrace, and her resolve shattered as thoroughly as the blown out windows. I listened as the crackling of the cooling room mixed with the sounds of her crying. Her nails scraped against the scales that ran over my chest. She clung to me, riding the wave of emotion that seized her.

I stroked her back, running my hands up and down the length of her spine, anything to try and soothe her pain. I couldn't bear the ache that was welling up in me.

"Elle, I—"

Elyria sprung up, a moment of realization shocking her features. She gripped my shoulders, and spun me around.

I knew what she was doing. I knew what she'd see; the tail tucked under the leather band of my pants and a beast coiling up my spine. The twin to her tattoo. It would be glowing and golden against my tan skin. The truth of it bared fully. My dragon mark.

She began tracing the lines of the beast. I jumped with surprise under the light pressure of her fingertips. As she moved up my spine, the muscles reflexively shifted at the spark and charge of her touch.

"How?" she said.

I turned back around and ran my hands over her shoulders in a desperate attempt to maintain that connection between us.

"What do you know about Elyria Ascheshadow? What did Duke tell you of her legend?"

She stepped back and slipped from my fingers. The thrumming power stopped, a presence that I hadn't even realized I had become attuned to, and immediately mourned its vacancy.

She began pacing around the room, boots crunching against the broken tiling, nervously clasping and unclasping her hands. She stopped for a second and looked at me.

"The Gold Dragon fell in love with her. He took mortal form, and then she bore him a child."

She resumed pacing the room.

"No."

She stopped.

"No?"

"She bore him twins, a boy and a girl. Their birth split the line of draken into two, The Aschen Queens of Indemira and The Shadow Kings of Innesvale. I am Callen Shadow, and Elyria, your true name is Elyria Asche."

She stepped away from me, shock ricocheting around in her eyes. She reached back, leaning on a charred husk of a table for stability. Her eyes widened in realization, and then hurt crumpled her expression.

"*You knew*," she yelled, a great growling roar.

A ball of fire hurtled at me and I caught it in my hand. She screamed again in frustration and threw a second one. I caught that blast just as easily.

"*Gods! You backstabbing, gatekeeping bastard!*"

I extinguished the flames in my hands and she growled again.

"You knew this whole damn time. I wanted answers, and you fucking *had* them!" she screamed again, frustration bowing her back as she cried out to the ceiling. "You could have shown me weeks ago," she said, stomping her foot and sending sparks skittering out from under her feet.

"You. Fucking Duke. Joseph. Everyone feels the need to keep this from me. *Why?*"

Tears rolled down her cheeks. I felt hollowed out by them. I could go the rest of my life never seeing another tear fall from her beautiful golden eyes.

"Why didn't you show me?"

She started walking in circles again. Flames spraying out from each of her steps.

I couldn't stand the hurt in her eyes, or the waves of guilt that flooded me.

"I was going to," I mumbled. Then stronger, "Elle, *stop*. Just look at me."

She scuffed to a stop. Arms crossed in front of her.

"Go on, tell me all about how you wanted to tell me, but couldn't. Tell me you had responsibilities to your people, and I wasn't worth the risk to them. Tell me you just couldn't bring yourself to tell me the truth."

I swallowed, unable to refute any of those statements.

"Tell me that... *oh.*" She swallowed that next word and took a step back. "Oh. *Fuck me.* You *did* try to tell me." She laughed, clutching at her chest. "Demons below, you were going to tell me that morning... and... and I... fucking bottom ring of Kraav, Callen."

I flinched at my name and knew my confession was already plastered all over my face.

"You chose *that* moment to try and tell me?"

I swallowed. I'd never felt so low. I moved towards her. She threw her hands up, forming a wall of fire between us. She should just stab me with that dagger. I'd take the pain over this guilt.

"Well, obviously I realized it was a bad idea," I said and stepped through her wall of flame, "and then it never felt like the right moment. Elle, you have to realize. Next to no one knows what I am. Have you ever heard of the Shadow Draken? No. You knew who I was, but not what I was, right?"

She stubbornly guarded up her stance.

"That's because whenever one of our line is born marked, the crown hides it. They hide it because draken are targets. Do you know why?"

She shifted her weight to look away from me. I reached forward, grabbing her chin. Pushing my fingers into her flesh and forcing her to listen to me. She needed to hear this; she needed to understand the world she was actually living in, before that world lashed out and killed her.

"Because people don't like the idea of a chosen few being more powerful than them. Innesvale has a history of tolerance and love. Do you think they would still trust their monarch if they knew where he descended from? Because *look* what happens when one of our kind abuses their power. I hid my abilities for the same reason Duke had you pretend yours were just stage tricks."

I released her, pushing her back away from me and letting that sink in.

She curled her fingers into tight fists, and I studied her to see how much of a fight she was ready for. Then she shifted and opened her mouth to say something but thought better of it and closed it again. She looked at me, just looked at me with those tiny fierce fists bunched at her sides.

"I had always planned to tell you everything before we set sail, and ... and... Gods, Elle, stop looking at me like that."

"Like what, *exactly*?" she hissed the words through her teeth.

"Like I'm the enemy."

I ran my hands through my hair, and as it sifted through my fingers, I saw that it was still gold. I breathed my power back into submission in an attempt to regain some kind of control.

"I was wrong. It was wrong. And I can't justify it. It just is. You said whatever I was going to tell you that night wouldn't change anything, and you were right. It would change nothing that had happened, but I'm telling you now, and what we do from here will change *everything*."

I heaved a breath. "...Because it *has* to. Because I can't keep letting Malvat win."

Her hardened gaze softened some. The flames pulled back and her scales disappeared, revealing only her perfectly smooth skin. She closed her eyes and took a deep breath, nodding. She was resigning herself to something. I didn't dare to hope. The brittle remains of the sad muscle in my chest couldn't withstand any more blows.

"This doesn't mean I forgive you." She opened her eyes and walked up to me. "It just means I understand. Understanding isn't forgiveness."

"If your understanding is all there is, then I will take what I can get."

I felt like I was torn open, my burned heart exposed, and I waited for her to sink the killing blow.

"This conversation isn't over." Elyria tapped my chest, zapping me with that soul-piercing energy. "And put a shirt on."

She half-smiled, playfully flicking her eyes up to mine.

A whimper of relief came from me, and I forced a smile in return. I stepped back with a sweeping gesture. "And deny you all of this?"

She tilted her head to the side with a little "hmm," then made for the door.

I grabbed her arm as she passed, held it, felt her warmth pass into my hand for what I hoped wasn't the last time. I didn't have the words to say all the things I was feeling, but I did know that I couldn't let her leave either. So I held on and looked at her with absolute honesty in my eyes. I let every emotion paint my face and show plainly for her to see.

"I will never lie to you again, Elyria. No more secrets. I will spend every hour earning back your trust and every breath striving to be worthy of it."

She tightened her lips, and her eyes glistened with restrained emotion.

Elyria gave a single nod of her head, slipping silently from my hand and out the door.

And then it was just me, alone in a soot-blackened room.

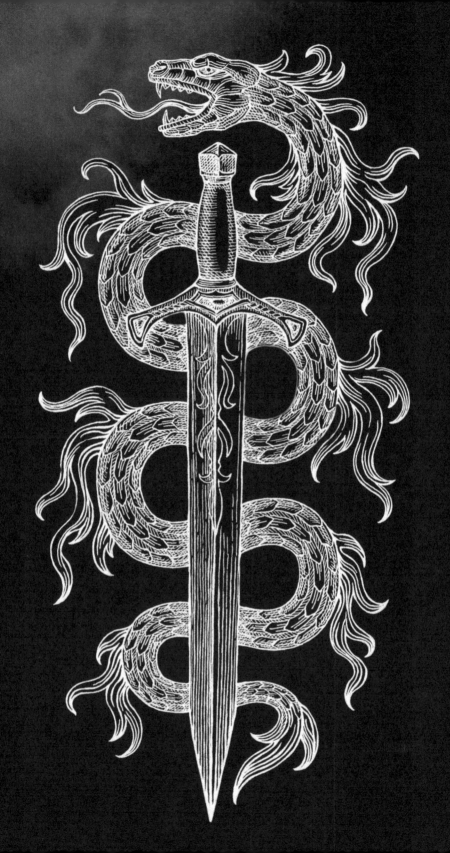

40

ELYRIA

The lingering warmth of his hand on my arm pulsed as I walked into the cold alley. Flickering light from the burning library filtered from the end of the street. I paused just outside the door, lifting my head to the stars and counting my heartbeats. Smoke drifted in thick, wafting clouds blocking out their light.

I heard a sound shift next to me and looked over.

Xoc was leaning back against a wall. He had pulled the book on herbs back out and was flipping lazily through the pages. To either side of him were several large bushes of lavender, and he was running his right hand through the blooms. Rei was curled up on the ground across from him, slicing a peach. She held up a slice on the knife point, waving it at me in a little hello. She smiled, gingerly biting it from the blade.

I paused for a moment, momentarily shocked. I couldn't tell which confused me more, the instant flower garden or the random peach. Somehow I was sure Xoc was responsible for both of them.

"Did you kill him?" Xoc said, peering at me from behind the book.

"No. But there's still time. I could go back if you want me to."

He raised an eyebrow in questioning.

I sighed, relenting. "It's fine. We're fine. I understand. But we need to leave this city tonight." Gesturing at the bushes, I added, "What's the deal with the lavender?"

"It makes me think of..." Xoc quirked up the side of his lips into almost a smile. "I just like it, and I thought it would be nice to smell something other than smoke."

"You are a much more complex man than you let on, Xoc."

I smirked at him before my attention was directed keenly to the end of the alley. The sounds of alarmed people trying to contain the fire on the other side of the clearing were growing louder. It wouldn't be long before they started evacuating the University, and I wanted to be long gone from this plateau before that happened. We didn't need anyone associating us with the damage I had wrought. My fight with Andromeda had destroyed the largest collection of knowledge in Venterra. There would be a reckoning, and it would be helpful to be safely in Innesvale when that happened.

Rei popped up from the ground, her skirts swishing. A broken chain jangled off of her hip. She chucked the peach pit over her shoulder into the alley behind her.

"With that, I can help. I... um, know someone with a ship."

"You do?" asked Xoc, surprised.

"I do. I know all kinds of people."

"And when you say you know someone, you mean ...?"

I made a twirly motion with my finger.

"She's a when in port kinda friend," she said with a smile and flipped her hair out of her eyes.

"And this friend happens to be leaving port soon?" I asked.

"I don't know. She doesn't exactly have a regular shipping schedule."

"So a pirate," Xoc said, a slight sneer on his lip.

"An opportunist is a more accurate description," replied Rei.

Cal came out of the building, a mostly singed curtain artfully draped around his shoulders.

I held in a snicker. Served him right, the arrogant ass.

"Ah, so he is alive," said Xoc with a roll of his eyes.

"Glad to see you were worried about me," Cal said as he waved his hand in an elegant bow.

The curtain slipped from his shoulder, revealing bronze skin and toned muscle that disappeared artfully beneath the waistband of his leather pants. Rei whistled. Cal winked at her, picking it back up and twisting it around himself again.

Rei leaned over to me, popping her hip out. "You ever get tired of playing that fiddle, you let me take a strum."

I gaped back at her. "I... that's not a thing that's happening. Not anymore. Not ever, " I said, waving my hands between me and Cal. "No fiddles, no strumming."

"You just keep telling yourself that," Rei said, laughing. She touched my arm and a warm glow slid over my body, healing each cut and bruise from my fight. She gave a loud exhale. "There, all better."

Xoc reached into his rucksack and pulled out a shirt, tossing it to Cal. "Here."

Cal snatched it from the air and quickly slipped it on. The shirt was about three sizes too big, making him look like a boy playing at being a man. It was actually adorable, and I hated it.

I deliberately turned away, but not before Cal marked my expression. Gods save me from that coy smile.

"So, does this when-in-port opportunist friend have a name?" I asked, trying to ignore the heat I still felt coming from him.

"Morgan Sangrior. Her ship is called Star Spear," Rei said, smirking at my too obvious attempts to avoid Cal's gaze. "She should be down at the docks now, or at the very least, in one of the taverns. If the money is right, she'd set sail for you during a hurricane."

"I think, given what happened here tonight, the sooner we get to Innesvale, the better. I don't want Elyria anywhere near Suman when they start questioning witnesses," said Cal, trying to tie Xoc's shirt tighter around his waist.

I looked back at him, ready to snap an insult. He saw my venom, and his entire form shifted. He looked beaten. And not just the purpling around his eye or the slice on his lip. It was his spirit. As if, with that single glare, I had broken some part of him. And he wasn't wrong. Someone surely saw the fit I threw on my way up the hill. It wouldn't take much to connect me to the fire, and how many golden-haired Fire Singers were there running around Venterra. I held my tongue, but refused to give him the empathy he so desperately was seeking.

"I agree," said Xoc. "Who knows how many people in the city Malvat controls? I would feel better if all of us were on a ship sailing east tonight." He looked over at Rei. Next to his enormous frame, she seemed so small. "Will you be coming with us, or staying here? Malvat will know about you now. I can't guarantee that you'd be safe if you stay."

"You can't guarantee I'll be safe if I go either." Rei looked at me and smiled. "Let's see where the road takes me. Meeting you all tonight feels like destiny, and fate's a surly bitch when you don't pay attention to her."

I was impressed by how quickly Rei had recovered from the trauma of being hunted through the tower. There wasn't an ounce of tension in her relaxed stance and free smile. It gave me the distinct impression that this wasn't the first close call she'd experienced.

"Good," said Cal. "Then maybe we can pick up my pack. It'd be nice to put on a shirt that actually fits. I left it at the docks when Andros showed up." He looked at me. "I was too concerned about you to even think of it."

"Yeah, well, I handled it just fine on my own," I snapped.

He wouldn't get to pretend like he came to my rescue after all of this.

"For sure, two seconds later, and that dagger you love so much would have made an exquisite ornament sticking out of your chest," he snapped. Cal pulled The Sun Serpent out of his back loop and extended it to me. "Which, by the way, I saved for you during your tantrum."

I growled, snatching the knife from him and slipping it into the sheath at my back.

I turned to Xoc. "I've changed my mind. I think I will kill him after all."

Rei walked between us, taking my arm and linking it with hers. She looked at Cal and said icily, "Yeah, your pack isn't there anymore. If you left it down by the docks, then those contents are already spread across half of the city. I hope you didn't come to Suman with something you loved, Cal, 'cause, I'm pretty sure you've lost it now."

I laughed, taking my victories where I could find them, and let Rei escort me down the hill. As I passed Cal, I made a point of flicking my hair at him. It whipped him across the face before swaying against my back. Cal groaned, and a devilish grin crested my lips. That man deserved a bit of torture.

The trip down from the University was much longer than I had expected. I had been so fueled by anger that I hadn't even realized how long of a walk it was during our trek up. Night had set in and the scent of supper cooking on stoves mingled with the smoke drifting down from the plateau. By the time we got to the harbor, the entire dock area was silent.

Rei led us over to a dark blue single masted sloop. White looping letters along the hull read Star Spear. The ship was vast. Iron plating curved gracefully along the bow. The lines of its form were silhouetted against the black night sky as it morphed into a massive dragon head at the tip. Its fangs were bared and scaled horns fanned terrifyingly behind a furrowed brow. The plating along the front were the armored breastplates of a dragon. The casting was so lifelike and detailed that I half expected the head to turn and look at me. The sides of the hull had been carved to resemble the dragon's wings. They extended back until, at the aft of the ship, an iron-spiked harpoon sat mounted to form the tail of the beast. I imagined the intimidating display this ship would make cutting across the ocean. Flying from the topmost mast was a flag bearing the sigil of a large blue dragon against a sea of black.

"That's it," Rei said, knocking me from my wonder.

Light spilled from rounded glass-paned windows at the aft of the ship. The captain's quarters were shielded by fanning wood panels, similar to the edges of dragon's wings, and the shadow of a figure moved about the cabin.

"Sangrior... Star Spear," Cal whispered, as if he was working something out. Rei eyed him wearily.

"Why don't I go on, and I'll bring her out?" she said, making for the gang-plank.

"This ship!" He pointed accusingly at the blue beast in the water. "This ship downed two of our merchant vessels last spring."

"And they were insured, unless the merchant was an idiot," she retorted. "Listen, you're going to have to get down with the morally gray if you plan on taking a ship like this into Innesvale. If you want no questions asked trans-portation, then don't ask any."

Rei clambered up the plank that extended from the outer deck. "You all just wait here."

I sat down on the edge of the dock and let my legs dangle. Moonlight gilded the black, moving water below my feet. Small blue water taxis were tied up to the post in various areas along the waterline, nearly choking the tiny harbor. They made gentle rattling sounds as they rolled with the lapping current, and it reminded me of the sound the trapeze bar would sometimes make at night when it banged against the rigging. A pang of homesickness clenched at my heart. Gods, I missed them. I missed Duke. I missed the simplicity of what life had been.

To distract myself, I threw a fireball onto the water. It hovered against the surface before disappearing in a puff of smoke. I cast a second, this one a bit larger than the first.

Cal silently sat down next to me.

"I used to do this when I was a kid. It was Duke's idea to try and cast a fireball over water, and then see how long I could maintain it before it fizzled out. It was a way to focus my power, so that I could learn how to control it."

"Smart."

I looked down. Our feet swung in tandem. "Now I do it when I need to focus my mind. It's not so much about control anymore."

Cal looked over his shoulder, then flicked his hand to cast a fireball alongside my own. They spun over the water in a small cyclone of flames, first fighting against one another, then merging and exploding in a shower of sparks. A piece of my soul wanted to smile at the display, but I couldn't make it reach my lips.

I looked sidelong at Cal. His right eye was now fully purple. I reached up, hesitated for a second, and then gently caressed it. "I'm sorry I hit you."

"No, you're not."

The split in his lip shined as he smiled at me.

"You're right, I'm not."

"And I deserved it."

"You did."

I nodded, and then I laughed. I wasn't exactly sure why I laughed, but something about us sitting here like this shifted the air between us. Things felt lighter, and suddenly this entire circumstance felt utterly ridiculous.

"You know, when we were in the Basilica, he recognized you, that teller. I was sure you'd come clean right then," I said, smirking and remembering the flustered way he had tried to cover up the man's slip.

"Joseph recognized me too," Cal said, and that caught me by surprise. "It's part of what he said to me before he left."

"And he didn't tell me?" I said, feeling a bit betrayed.

"There's safety in anonymity. I told him that the only reason I was keeping my identity a secret was to protect you. He made me swear on my life to do just that." His eyes softened. "I swore to put your life before my own, always."

I remembered what I heard him say. "*I give you my word.*" My heart twinged, and a sour feeling of guilt crept into me.

He hesitantly reached down towards the hand that rested on the dock between us. It ghosted over mine with heartbreaking gentleness. I stared at our hands, trying to decide what I wanted. I was still angry and hurt. But, godsdamn me, I couldn't deny the magnetic pull I felt towards him, no matter how full of burning rage I was.

"I'm angry at everything," I said, raising my eyes to meet his. "I'm angry at Duke for not telling me the truth of what I was, I'm angry at you for lying to me, I'm angry at Xoc for keeping your lies, but mostly I want to burn the world down because a man I've never known killed the only man who ever loved me."

The fire in my veins rose, and from the look on his face, I knew Cal could feel it too. His hand tightened against mine.

"He wasn't the only man to ever love you."

My heart hammered out of rhythm. Cal's golden eyes searched mine with a look of vulnerability I had never seen in him before.

Steps came from the deck of the ship behind us, followed by a playful whistle. Cal's hand slipped from my grasp and he stood up so quickly that part of me wondered if I had imagined the entire moment. I wiped the tears from the corners of my eyes before joining him.

Rei skipped down the plank, seemingly pleased with herself.

On the quarterdeck of the ship, looking out over the edge at us, stood a woman. Her petite frame was silhouetted, a black specter against the rising moon. Beside her stood an opposingly large shadow of cut muscle.

"Come on board," said Rei triumphantly.

"What did you tell her?" Cal asked.

"That you all need to get to Innesvale posthaste, and that you, Princey, have deep pockets. That's all she cares about," she said, and then, smiling devilishly, added, "Well, that, and I told her she could take your fee out on my ass if she wanted."

I choked down a laugh, watching her saunter back up the plank and hopping down onto the main deck. The laughter lasted about two seconds, until I locked eyes on Morgan. Suddenly, it didn't seem so funny anymore.

Morgan leaned forward, both hands braced on the railing. Rich blue eyes caught the moonlight. They were filled with the churning intensity of a typhoon. She was small, but the aura she exuded was that of menace and command. She wore a simple gray cotton shirt laced loosely over her chest, blue trousers, and sensible black boots. A silver rapier dangled loosely off her hip. But I had no doubt that she could brandish it in a single heartbeat.

Cal walked up to the base of the steps leading to the quarterdeck. He stood tall and proud. No playfulness or seduction. For the first time since we'd met, he looked like royalty, despite wearing an ill-fitting shirt and having a battered face.

"Captain Sangrior, I presume," he said formally.

Morgan tilted her head to the side, taking his measure.

When she didn't say anything in return, he continued, "I am Callen Shadow, Crown Prince of Innesvale. I seem to have found myself in need of emergency transport home for myself," he gestured to us, "and my retinue. If you can safely transport us back to Innesvale, the crown will pay whatever fee you demand, providing we leave at once."

"Your retinue?" I hissed at him under my breath.

That arrogant bastard. He ignored me, maintaining his pose of authority.

She looked from him, to me, and then finally to Xoc.

Morgan walked smoothly, in near silent steps, as she descended to the main deck. She walked right past Cal and up to me. I stood a good five inches taller than her, but in her presence, I felt small.

Her intense blue eyes studied me. The dark hue of her skin made them that much more striking. A dark black tattoo of intricately scrolling lines crested over her left brow before curling beneath her eye. It added to the mystery and allure of this tiny, powerful woman. Her lips were painted bright, matching her fiery curls. The mop of scarlet hair was braided up the sides of her temples in alternating rows, before piling atop her head in a thick comb that dipped in front of her brow to conceal the full extent of her glare.

"Rei tells me you all are in some kind of trouble. What kind?"

Morgan's tone was rough and clipped, like years of yelling commands and salt air had seasoned her voice to exude control.

"Don't you want to ask him?" I said, pointing to Cal, who had so obviously taken command.

"If I had wanted to ask him, then I would have," Morgan said, still not blinking.

From the corner of my vision I caught the mass of the large man move, and the desire to look at him hit me hard. But looking away from Morgan would be like looking away from a jungle cat. The second I did, I knew she would pounce.

I steeled myself and straightened my shoulders to make myself just a bit taller. She might be a jungle cat, but I was the Gold Dragon. I kept masses at the end of a leash until their hearts didn't beat unless I commanded it. She didn't want to do business with a prince, this water maven wanted to play with fire. If that's what she wanted, then I would give her sparks.

"Oh, you know—just the villain who wants to rule the world kind of trouble," I said coyly.

Her red lips curved up into a smile. "That's the best kind."

Morgan snapped her fingers and the water next to the ship began to rise. She turned her head to the side and the shadow man dropped into line next to her.

"Get 'em up. We're leaving."

End of Vol. 1

The fight against Malvat and the Shade continues in *Star Spear, Sun Serpent Saga Vol. 2*, available for pre-order now, coming August 2023

Need more Cal and Elyria? I have just the thing for that. Head over to www.genevamonroeauthor.com and subscribe to my newsletter for a bonus chapter, *That One Time at Joseph's*.

Demons below, that was a crazy ride. And it's just getting going. There's adventure on the high seas coming, intense duels, more firewhips, and a walk straight into Mt. Kraav's fires. I know we're all dying to find out what it will take to get Cal back on Elyria's good side. She clocked him good though, didn't she? Man, that was satisfying. It's going to take a lot more than just his charm to win her back.

Where was your favorite place in Venterra? Personally, I love Laluna. I'd give anything to be able to make that my next vacation destination, even the long sailing around the horn. Because there is no way I'm taking Elyria's shortcut. How'd you like my adorable, wittle beastie on the wall? Did you know he was based on a real worm? Google it, Velvet Worm. Even better, look at a Ribbon Worm. My poor friends and husband had to listen to me talk about nothing but worms for a week after I discovered those guys.

This book has been such a labor of love. Almost exactly two years before this book's release I was crafting a backstory for a new gaming campaign we were getting ready to start. I created this woman who was part dragon. She was bad ass and beautiful, and I kept telling everyone that I wanted to read her book so badly. After weeks of saying it and listening to me drone on and on about circus troupes and fire dances people started saying, "So write it already." At first, I was dumb founded. I couldn't write a book, could I? But, I couldn't get the idea out of my head. It consumed every single thought, owned me. And now we're here. If I'm being honest, it still occupies far too much real estate in my mind. I've got plans, big ones. Plans of behemoth velvet worm proportions. So, if you've made it this far, prepare yourself. The web only gets thicker, the night darker, and the fire hotter from here.

If I gave you the feels, please leave me a review. I want to hear about all the creeps, the eeps, and the jeeps. I don't know what a jeep is, but I'm thinking it's like when you had to fan yourself after Cal walked through that waterfall. Phew. Either way, I'm looking forward to reading all about it.

Make sure to join my reader group, *Geneva Monroe's Pretty Stabby Things*, if you want to get advanced access to all the upcoming details, plus the odd spoiler here and there. I'll be seeing you soon.

With love,

Gen

ACKNOWLEDGMENTS

I owe everything I am and have to the infallible love and support of my husband. Without him I would never have been able to bring Cal and Elyria's story into this world. He's the true hero of this book. My king, my inspiration, my sense of reason, my light at the end of the long night, and my strength.

To my father, from the second I heard the excitement and pride in your voice, I wanted nothing more than to put this book into your hands. Thank you for listening to hours of crazy plot ideas, and being my most ardent cheerleader during the entire process. This book is for you, as much as it was for me.

To my friends and family, thank you for letting me send you snippets at all hours of the night, and letting me talk of nothing but my book for the past two years. I wish I could say that it's out of my system and I've moved onto a new topic. But, let's be real, this became an obsession long ago. You are the best, and I love you. Did I just make it weird? I don't care. I love you guys.

Special thanks to my Beta Team, Lindsey Bliss Raab, Shio Mrost, C.D. Redman, Nova Lateulere, Poppy Jacobson, A. Mae. Cooper, Erica Karwoski, Elizabeth Muse, and Sophie B. for reading and providing invaluable feedback, especially those early drafts. There should be a medal for people who volunteer to read the early stuff.

Thank you to my editors, Robin Blanchard and Reanna Breaux, without whom this novel would not shine.

To Shelby Gunter I could not be more grateful for your help and friendship. Thank you for championing me into finishing my first draft, and then mentoring me through my first edits. For talking me out of several complete break downs, and convincing me that I had worth even when I felt completely worthless. I quite literally would not have finished this book without you.

And lastly, thanks to you, the reader. Thank you for taking a chance on this work of pure passion. I hope I did right by you, and made you feel something along the way.

9 781960 352019